The Blaize Amulet

M. W. Fulton

This book is dedicated to my husband, Tim, without whose constant encouragement I never would have finished. I love you.

Contents

Title Page	1
Dedication	3
Chapter One	7
Chapter Two	23
Chapter Three	37
Chapter Four	52
Chapter Five	67
Chapter Six	82
Chapter Seven	97
Chapter Eight	112
Chapter Nine	127
Chapter Ten	142
Chapter Eleven	157
Chapter Twelve	171
Chapter Thirteen	185
Chapter Fourteen	198
Chapter Fifteen	212
Chapter Sixteen	224
Chapter Seventeen	239
Chapter Eighteen	254

Chapter Nineteen	268
Chapter Twenty	282
About The Author	297

Chapter One

Farewells and Cat Burglars

"Seven, let's go! You are going to be late! Again!"

Seven moaned and turned over. Her long, dark hair covered her face, but it wasn't enough to keep the morning sun from poking at her eyes.

"Seven!" her mother yelled again.

"I'm up!" she yelled back.

Forcing herself from her bed, Seven dressed in her usual black jeans and a black shirt. In the bathroom, she splashed cold water on her face, pulled her hair into a ponytail, and studied her reflection. Even she could see how much she looked like her mom these days. Everything except the hair. Her mom had red, curly hair. Seven's was black and straight. It was the only thing she had gotten from her dad in the looks department though Seven would never know for sure. She had never met him. He and all the pictures of him were destroyed in a fire before she was born. But Seven didn't want to think of that today.

"Good morning, birthday girl," her mother sang as Seven sank into a kitchen chair.

"You know what a great birthday gift would be?"

"What?"

"A day off school," Seven said.

"Oh, I don't think so," her mom said. "I didn't make your favorite breakfast so you could crawl back into bed, but I thought that we could celebrate with a special dinner, maybe do some shopping or go to the movies tonight."

"Really?"

"Really. It's not every day a girl turns thirteen," her mom said. "Yes, we'll . . ." Suddenly, a loud noise like a million buzzing insects erupted from... everywhere. Her mom dashed out of the kitchen.

"What is that?" Seven yelled, covering her ears, but as quickly as it started, it stopped.

"Mom?"

"It's fine. Eat your breakfast," her mom called from the hall.

Seven didn't need to be told twice. She piled two pancakes on her plate, smeared them with butter, and drowned them in syrup. She finished them and two more as she thought about the night's plans.

Usually, birthdays were homemade cakes and sometimes a small gift. Money was always tight, so going to dinner *and* shopping was a real treat. Turning thirteen had its perks.

Downing the last of her milk and wiping away the mustache it left, Seven grabbed her backpack and headed to the front door. She passed the living room, caught sight of her mom, and stopped in her tracks. Her mom was holding a glowing pink crystal with a look of fear on her face.

"Mom, what's wrong? What is that?"

Her mom looked at the crystal and then at Seven. Quickly, she shoved the crystal behind her back.

"Oh, Seven, you weren't supposed to see that. You know, birthday present and all."

"If it makes that horrible noise, I don't want it," Seven quipped.

Her mom laughed, but it didn't reach her eyes.

"Hey, look at the time," her mom said, making a show of checking her watch. "We need to get going."

"*We?*" Seven asked, horrified.

"I am walking you to school this morning. Think of it as a birthday present."

"No offense, but it's mortifying to have your mom walk you to school when you are thirteen. Besides, you never walk me to school. Is something wrong? You're acting weird."

"Nothing is wrong. I'm allowed to act weird. My little girl is a teenager today," her mom said as the mantle clock chimed. "We better hurry." Seven didn't have time to argue.

On the way, Seven's mom was constantly looking around as though she was trying to see if someone was following them.

"What are you looking for?" Seven asked.

"Nothing," her mom said absently.

"Whatever," Seven mumbled.

Finally, they were in sight of the school. Seven's mom stopped.

"I'll watch from here. Will you be walking home with that friend of yours? Katie? If not, I can meet you back here after school."

"Kerry, and yes, I am," Seven corrected.

"Come directly home, okay?" her mom said as she continued to scout their surroundings.

Seven hurried away before her mom changed her mind and decided to walk Seven to class. When she reached the school's front steps, though, a chill ran down her spine. She suddenly felt watched. She looked around. Down the street, blocked from her mother's view, was someone. The person was dressed in a trenchcoat buttoned to the chin with the collar turned up, and even though the black hat was pulled down low, Seven could feel a hard stare. She ran into the building and up the steps to the windows that faced the street. However, when she looked out, the stranger was gone. She looked up and down the block, but she only saw a gray cat with white paws running across the street into a large rose bush. At that moment, the warning bell rang.

I can't be tardy again, she thought. She sprinted to class and jumped into her seat just as the final bell rang. She was sweating and breathless, but at least she wasn't tardy.

"Close call, birthday girl!" a familiar voice whispered

from behind.

"Yeah, I don't think Mr. Strickland would care that it's my birthday. He'd mark me tardy anyway."

"He would mark you tardy twice if he could get away with it," her friend agreed.

Seven turned to smile at Kerry Hollins, a short, plump girl with glasses, braces, and the beginning signs of teenage acne. She was dressed in her trademark smiley face shirt. Seven swore she must have one in every color. Today, the giant face was neon orange.

Kerry had moved to Rotherwood less than a week after Seven had moved there. Since they were both new in a school not very welcoming to outsiders, she and Kerry gravitated toward each other. Though they rarely saw or even talked to each other outside of school, Seven considered Kerry her closest friend.

Just then, the classroom door slammed, and Seven's least favorite teacher walked into the room. Mr. Strickland just stared at the class, almost daring someone to breathe too loudly. He was tall and beanpole skinny. His head seemed too large for his body. His nose was so pointy it could double for a sharpened pencil. Why he ever became a teacher was a mystery. He obviously didn't like children.

"Now that you have gotten all that useless chatter out of your systems, maybe we can squeeze some useful information into those pea-sized brains of yours. Open your book to page 136." He spun around on his highly polished shoes and began to write on the chalkboard. He was probably the only teacher in the world that still used a chalkboard. Though Seven couldn't imagine doing anything worse on her birthday, she grabbed a pencil, opened her notebook, and copied the notes.

"You and your mom doing anything special tonight?" Kerry asked as she and Seven walked home from school that day.

"She mentioned dinner and shopping," Seven said.

"Sounds like fun."

"Yeah. Would you like to-hey!" Seven stumbled as something jumped right out in front of her. "Watch out!" she shouted as a grey cat with piercing green eyes and white paws blocked their path. It hissed at her in response. Seven looked more closely. "That's the same cat I saw by the school this morning." She reached toward it but quickly pulled her hand back as the cat hissed ominously. "I wonder whose it is."

"I don't know," Kerry said, eyeing the feline. "Um, I gotta go. I forgot something." Without waiting for Seven to respond, Kerry darted down the street and turned the corner. Seven turned back to the cat, but it too had disappeared.

"What is the deal with everybody today?"

"Mom, I'm home," Seven called as she dropped her backpack on the table a few minutes later. No answer. Seven walked to the foot of the stairs and called again. No answer. She was about to go outside to see if her mom was in the yard when she saw a note on the table.

Seven,

Something very important came up at work. I know it's your birthday, and I promised we would celebrate, but it can't be helped. I left some money under this note so you could order a pizza. I will try to get home before you are asleep. Happy birthday.

Love,
Mom

Though the note was clear, Seven didn't understand. In all her life, she could not remember one time when her mom was gone when she arrived home from school. And now a work emergency? Her mom worked in a bookstore. What emergency could have possibly happened?

Seven flopped down on a kitchen chair. This birthday was supposed to be memorable. Now it just felt miserable. So far, she had spent it with Mr. Strickland, an angry cat, and an empty house. Furthermore, she had the feeling her mom was keeping something from her.

Since it was just the two of them, Seven and her mom

were very close. Though most kids Seven's age didn't want to admit they *had* parents, much less liked them, Seven considered her mom her best friend. Seven told her mom about things that happened at school, and her mom would share embarrassing stories about coworkers who had toilet paper stuck to their shoes. Even when it came to money, or lack of money more accurately, Seven's mom was always straightforward. Her mom never tried to hide anything until now.

"Thanks for the great birthday," Seven muttered. Then, she snatched her backpack from the table, grabbed some leftovers and a soda, and stomped off to her room. She plopped down at her desk, turned on some music, and grudgingly opened up her math book. Some birthday.

When Seven's alarm went off the next morning, she found herself still seated at her desk, her face lying in a small puddle of drool on her history book. She sat up and looked around groggily. Slowly, the events of yesterday emerged from the sleepy fog in her brain. The note. The missed birthday celebration. The anger.

Seven shoved her books into her backpack and headed toward the kitchen. She had a few choice words for her mom, but the kitchen was dark when she turned the corner. The coffee pot was cold. The note and money were still on the table. She checked her mom's bedroom. Empty. Bathroom. Empty. Laundry area. Empty.

Seven's anger dissolved into panic. Where was her mother? Her mom would never leave her alone overnight. Was she missing? Kidnapped? Hurt? Worry flooded Seven's mind. She dialed her mom's cell. No answer. Called again. No answer. What should she do? Should she call the police? A neighbor? No, she would call Kerry. Maybe her parents would know what to do. She had never met them, but she didn't have anyone else. However, just before she dialed, she heard a noise. A click. A creak. Behind her. She slowly turned around and, to her great relief, saw her mom walking through the kitchen door.

She threw herself into her mom's arms, feeling shaky with

relief.

"I was so scared. Where were you?" Seven said.

Her mom kissed the top of her head.

"Didn't you get my note?"

"Yes, but when you were still gone this morning, I was scared something had happened." When Seven finally pulled away, she was startled by what she saw.

Her mom was still wearing the same clothes from yesterday, only now they were very wrinkled, torn in places, and splattered with something resembling mud. Her curly, red hair looked dull and disheveled. Her deep blue eyes were bloodshot and encircled with dark patches.

"Mom, what happened?"

Her mom gave herself a once over.

"Oh, nothing, just a hectic night. I'm so sorry we missed your birthday dinner last night. I couldn't get away. Hey, the pizza money is still on the table. Didn't you eat?"

"Yes, I ate."

"What did you eat?" her mom asked as though everything was perfectly normal.

"You were gone all night, show up looking like you mud wrestled something, and you want to know what I ate? Seriously? What is going on?"

"Nothing, honey. Yesterday was just a weird day, that's all," her mom said as she melted into a chair.

"Yeah, I know—first you and then some weird person outside the school. Even Kerry and this stray cat were acting weird. But you are avoiding my question," Seven demanded.

"What person?" Seven's mom shot up from the chair as though shocked.

"Just some weirdo dressed in a trench coat. He was standing on the street corner when you walked me to school yesterday."

"Why didn't I see him?"

"He was down a side street," Seven said.

"Did he talk to you? Are you sure it was a man?" her mom

pressed.

"No, I couldn't tell. I guess it could have been a woman. He *or she* didn't stick around long. Besides, you are changing the subject!" Seven was shouting now.

"If anybody comes up to you..."

"Mom, I am not a baby. I know not to talk to strangers. What is your problem?"

"I know you are not a baby, Seven. That's the problem." Saying that seemed to drain her mom of any remaining energy. She sighed loudly. "We need to talk."

Four short words, but they hit Seven like a wrecking ball. This was not the first time she had heard them. And they always came right before her mother told her...

"We are moving? No way!" Seven yelled. "I don't want to move! I like it here. I even have a friend here."

"Seven, it's complicated."

"It's complicated? No, it isn't. It's simple. I like it here, and you don't care. You are ripping me away again after you promised we would stay. That is not complicated."

"I never said..."

"Yes, you did!" Seven screamed.

"Lower your voice this instant," she said in her stern mom's voice. "Things have changed. I didn't know-"

"I won't go." Seven shouted. Without another word, she spun on her heels, grabbed her backpack, and ran out of the house, ignoring her mom's pleas to come back.

Seven was so lost in her miserable thoughts that she didn't even hear Kerry walk up behind her. Today her friend was wearing a purple smiley face shirt. Purple was Kerry's favorite color.

"Well, someone looks happy today," Kerry said as they climbed the steps to school.

"Not a great morning," Seven snapped.

"Okay, so I'm guessing the birthday dinner didn't go well?" Kerry asked gently.

"It didn't go at all," Seven said.

"Oh," Kerry said uncertainly. "Is that why you are so . . ." Seven's glare stopped Kerry from finishing her sentence.

"No, that is not why. I am angry because we are moving."

"What?" Kerry's mouth dropped open, and her eyes nearly popped out of her head.

Seven answered by slamming her locker shut and heading to class.

"Why?" Kerry asked, running to keep up.

"I don't know."

"When?"

"I don't know."

"Where?"

"I don't know."

"For someone who is moving, you sure don't know a lot. What did your mom say?" Kerry asked.

"She said 'We need to talk.'"

"That's it?"

"That's all she needs to say," Seven said. "Every time she says that, I'm getting a new zip code."

"Well, maybe this time is different. Maybe your mom wants to talk about something else, like getting a new job, or maybe she has a new boyfriend."

"My mom does not have a boyfriend," Seven snapped.

"Maybe she does, and she is nervous about telling you," Kerry said.

Seven thought about the mysterious person she saw and her mom's overreaction. Could it have been her mom's boyfriend, and she didn't want Seven to meet him yet? Is that why her mom was acting so weird?

"That's ridiculous," Seven said weakly.

"Is it? Your mom isn't that old, and she is kind of pretty as far as moms go," Kerry pressed.

"That is the stupidest thing I have ever heard! And you're stupid for saying it!" Seven ran the rest of the way to class, leaving a stunned-looking Kerry behind.

At lunch, Seven was grateful when she didn't see Kerry.

She wasn't ready to face her yet. After getting her tray, she sat in a corner seat and sulked. Surely her mom didn't have a boyfriend. She was still in love with Seven's father. Her mom always wore her wedding ring, and the locket Seven's dad gave to her. It was a wooden, octagon-shaped locket strung on a leather cord. On the front was a green stone in the shape of a seven-pointed star and some beautifully ornate designs. The latch had been broken for as long as Seven could remember so that the locket wouldn't open, but her mom didn't even want to take it off long enough to have it repaired. It was too precious.

Over the years, Seven had tried to get her mom to talk about her dad. However, her mom would only say that he loved them both very much. Then, her mom would be depressed for a few days, so Seven stopped asking. Now, could some stranger be attempting to take her father's place? Just then, the end of lunch bell rang, pulling Seven's attention back to school. She carried her full tray of food to the trash and dumped it splashing corn juice on her shirt. Just great.

At the end of the day, Seven saw Kerry at the lockers. She needed to apologize. It wasn't Kerry's fault that her mom was keeping secrets.

"I'm sorry I yelled at you and called you stupid. I was just so mad at my mom," Seven gushed.

"Then you should yell at her and call her stupid," Kerry said without looking up.

Seven flinched at the words.

"You're right. I'm sorry. I am not sure what's worse, a move or a boyfriend," said Seven.

"I know what's worse. You're my best friend, Seven. If you move, I'll be in trouble." With that, Kerry slammed her locker and left.

Feeling miserable, Seven headed for home. As she walked, she thought about what Kerry had said. *If you move, I'll be in trouble.* That was a strange way to put it. They would miss each other, sure, but trouble? Seven was in such deep thought that she didn't notice the furry something on the sidewalk in front of her. She stumbled but got her balance before falling.

"Again? I could have broken my neck," Seven said to the gray cat from yesterday.

The cat, however, didn't seem to care. It didn't make a sound. It just looked at her. It seemed to be saying, *"I'll sit where I want to sit."* Then without warning, it jumped up and disappeared behind the little red brick house on the corner.

When she arrived home, Seven found her mom sitting at the kitchen table with a warm plate of chocolate chip cookies. She looked better than she had that morning. She had showered and combed her hair, but she still had dark circles under her eyes.

"How was your day?" Her mom asked as she sipped her coffee.

"Oh, it was just great," Seven said sarcastically. "I fought with my best friend because I was mad at you. I failed a pop quiz in history because I couldn't concentrate. And I smell like spoiled corn after splashing juice on my shirt at lunch. It was the best day of my life."

"Please sit. Have a cookie," her mom said, ignoring her complaints.

"No, thank you." Seven crossed her arms over her chest. Did her mom seriously think milk and cookies were going to make everything all right? What was she, five years old?

"Seven," Her mom said softly.

"Mom, let's just get this over with. I have homework."

"Seven, you know I love you." Seven tapped her foot impatiently, but her mom ignored it and kept on talking. "It has been the two of us for your whole life. It hasn't always been easy, but we've done all right. Sometimes, though, things change. Even when we don't want them to, they do. I have never lied to you, but I have something I should have told you a long time ago."

"Who is he?" Seven asked accusingly.

"What?"

"Who is he?" Seven repeated, her eyes narrowing.

"Who is who?" Her mom looked genuinely confused.

"Who is your new boyfriend? Was it that person on the street corner yesterday morning? Is that why you went all spastic when I told you about seeing him?"

"Seven, I don't have a boyfriend," her mom said, chuckling. "Whatever gave you that ridiculous idea?"

Thanks for nothing, Kerry, she thought. Now, Seven felt angry *and* stupid.

"If it isn't that, then I was right the first time. We're moving, aren't we?"

"Seven, I don't have a choice. I wish I did, but I don't. *We* don't."

"Yes, *we* do. *We* could stay here."

"It's complicated," her mom said evasively.

"You said that already," Seven retorted. "When?"

"Three weeks. I thought I would try to let you finish the school year."

"You're' so thoughtful," Seven said sarcastically. "Where?"

"A town called Briarwood."

"Why?" Seven demanded.

"Now is not the right time to explain that to you," her mom said, growing annoyed herself. "You are clearly very angry."

"You're damn right, I am!"

"Seven May Preston! Watch your mouth!"

"And you can just keep all of your stupid secrets, *Miranda Ann Preston*." Seven turned, ran out the door, and didn't stop until she reached the swings at a nearby park. She finally let the tears she had refused to shed in front of her mom flow freely down her cheeks.

How could this be happening? Less than 48 hours ago, things were going so well. She was planning a rare birthday outing, she had a real friend in Kerry, and now everything was messed up. She felt so lonely.

Something furry touched her leg, making Seven jump and nearly toppled out of the swing. She looked down to see the gray cat she nearly fell over earlier. It was staring at her with piercing, almost human-like green eyes.

"Are you following me?" she asked. The cat seemed to understand she was having a rough day. It rubbed its head on Seven's leg and purred but took several steps away when Seven tried to pet it.

"Still don't want me to pet you, huh? I guess I understand. I've had a horrible day myself. My mom just told me we are moving again. This makes the seventh time we moved. Seven times. Just like my name. I guess seven isn't a lucky number after all," she said, wiping her runny nose on her sleeve. "You know," she went on, "there is something familiar about you. Have we met? I mean before yesterday?" Seven laughed at herself. It wasn't as though the cat understood her. It was, after all, a cat.

Seven had met many cats in her life, and it seemed they always appeared when Seven needed them, even if she didn't realize she did. Once, when she was younger, a fat, orange tabby cat jumped in front of her just as Seven was about to step into the street. It hissed fiercely. Seven tried to shoo it away with her foot, but the cat wouldn't budge. Then, out of nowhere, a car zoomed by, passing directly over the spot where Seven was about to step. The orange cat looked at her as though to say, *I told you so*. Then it flicked its tail several times, raised its head into the air, and strutted away.

Now, this gray cat was staring at Seven in the same way, as though it knew something she didn't. After a while, it moved its head as though looking behind her. She turned around to see Kerry walking toward her. Seven quickly wiped the remaining tears as her friend plopped into the swing beside her.

"Hey, who are you talking to?"

"Oh, just the cat."

"What cat?" Kerry asked in confusion.

"This one." Seven jerked her head in the direction of the cat, but when she turned back around, the cat was gone.

"Okay," Kerry said skeptically but continued. "I figured

you'd be here."

"You did? Why?"

Well, um, you told me once you came here when you were angry or needed to think, " Kerry said.

"I don't remember ever saying that," Seven said and then shrugged. "But I guess you found me."

"Yeah, I guess I did." Kerry took a deep breath. "I am sorry I stomped off at school. I was angry."

"Yeah, I got that," Seven said.

They sat on the swings in silence, pushing the gravel around with the toes of their shoes.

"So, I guess your mom doesn't have a new boyfriend?" Kerry asked tentatively.

Seven shook her head.

"Moving?"

Seven nodded.

"When?" Kerry didn't try to hide her disappointment.

"End of the school year."

"Wow, that soon, huh? Well, I figured it wouldn't take long."

"Why would you think that?" Seven asked.

Kerry just shrugged and changed the subject.

"I got you something. It was supposed to be for your birthday yesterday, but I didn't have it yet. I guess now it can be a sorry-to-see-you-go present."

"Thanks, Kerry. You didn't have to do this."

"Yes, I did," Kerry said a bit forcefully. Then she reached into her pocket. She pulled out a long rectangular box. "I hope you like it. It is a bit unusual."

"I like unusual," Seven said.

Seven reached for the package but stopped when a hissing noise came from the other side of her. Both girls turned to see the gray cat. This time it wasn't alone. A larger white cat stood beside it with its blue eyes fixed on Kerry.

"See, I told you there was a cat," Seven said triumphantly. Kerry, however, did not look amused. She looked as though she had seen her worst nightmare. "Oh, come on, Kerry. Don't tell me you're scared of two little cats!"

"Of course, I am not scared of cats," Kerry said, although her gaze never left them. "I just, uh, well, I remembered I have a huge science test tomorrow, so I better go. Here." She tossed the box to Seven and ran from the park. Seven watched as the white cat slowly followed Kerry's shrinking form.

"I guess your friend scared her because I am in her science class, and we don't have a test tomorrow," Seven laughed.

Seven turned her attention to the box. It was covered in a shiny brown material like the color of liquid chocolate. There was no store name stamped anywhere on the box.

"I wonder where she got it?" Seven said as she opened the lid. It made an ominous creaking sound. Lying on the crimson, satin lining was a shiny, black charm bracelet, the most unique one Seven had ever seen. She lifted the bracelet from the box and was surprised at how warm it was. The gray cat gave a deep, guttural growl.

"Oh, be quiet," Seven said as she studied the three charms that hung from it. They were beautiful One was a golden tree with only bare branches. The second was a sphere filled with an iridescent liquid, but the last one was the most unusual. It was a black ring with four red spikes poking through it. In the center of the ring, the spikes twisted together to form a... what was that? A spider? A scorpion? The longer Seven held the bracelet, the warmer it seemed to grow. The cat growled again. Seven ignored it. Instead, she unhooked the clasp and attempted to put it on when a sharp pain pierced her ankles. In alarm, she dropped the bracelet and the box. She looked down and saw bloody scratch marks.

"Hey, you stupid cat! Why did you do that?" The gray cat crouched low to the ground and hissed in response.

"Knock it off! It's just a bracelet." Seven reached to pick up the bracelet, but just as her fingers touched it, the cat pounced on her hand and bit down. Seven snatched her hand away and saw blood pool between her thumb and forefinger.

Then the cat did something even more unexpected. It scooped up the bracelet *and* the box in its mouth and ran.

"Stop! Drop that!" Seven screamed as she chased it across the park. She yelled several more times, but the cat didn't stop or drop anything. Eventually, Seven gave up, put her hands on her knees, and gasped for air. She watched helplessly as the gray cat ran toward a small opening in some nearby bushes where the white cat who had been following Kerry was now waiting. There, the gray cat dropped the bracelet and the box. It shoved them closer to the white cat, like an offering. The white cat sniffed at the bracelet. Then, it picked up the bracelet in its mouth while the gray one grabbed the box. They gave Seven one more look and, with the speed of cheetahs, disappeared into the bushes taking her gift with them.

"This day just keeps getting better and better," Seven said to no one. "I find out I'm moving, my mom is keeping secrets, I was scratched and bitten, and I get to tell Kerry that a gang of cat burglars stole her gift. Yep, it sure has been a great day. And tomorrow doesn't look any better."

Chapter Two

A Disappearing Act

Seven slowly opened her eyes to see trees zoom by the car window. She had dozed on and off all day, so she wasn't exactly sure where they were. She didn't dare ask. She was giving her mom the silent treatment just like Kerry had to her after Seven told her about the bracelet.

Seven had sat down at lunch with Kerry the day after the cats stole the bracelet. She had watched with dread as Kerry's eyes had dropped to her empty wrist.

"I know what you are thinking," Seven had said. "Why isn't Seven wearing my bracelet?"

"The thought had crossed my mind," Kerry had answered.

Seven had explained about the cats, though she knew it sounded ridiculous and unbelievable. Apparently, Kerry had thought so, too.

"Seven, you have no idea what it cost me to get that bracelet. If you didn't like it, you could have just said so rather than make up such a stupid story. I guess my gifts aren't good enough for you. Maybe I'm not either," Then Kerry had run from the lunchroom, and Seven never saw her again.

Seven had tried to call Kerry, but she kept getting a message that the phone number had been disconnected. Seven had walked to the street where Kerry had said she lived, but Seven didn't know which house was hers. She knocked on a few doors, but none of the neighbors had ever heard of the Hollins family.

Seven had even worked up the courage to ask Mr. Strickland about Kerry, but he threatened to give her detention for making up lies. It was like Kerry never existed for anyone except Seven. She didn't know what else to do, so she finished her time at Rotherwood Middle School like she had begun it, alone and friendless.

Now she and her mom were on their way to their new home. The only real conversation they had had in the last weeks occurred when her mom had given Seven a belated birthday present. It was the locket her father had given her mother. Her mom had polished the wood and somehow fixed the locket's latch. The leather cord was long and hung low, but she didn't care. Seven treasured it because of what was inside. When she opened the locket, she found the only picture she had ever seen of her father. In it, her mom was kissing her dad on the cheek while he smiled widely at the camera. On the other side was a picture of Seven.

"This is from your father. He always meant for you to have it. I have been holding on to it all these years for a special occasion. Turning thirteen is pretty special. I am sure your father would want you to have it," her mom had said when Seven opened the gift. "Now, no matter where you go, you will have your family with you."

"I thought all of the pictures of dad were destroyed," Seven had said.

"Not that one," her mom had said.

From that moment, Seven immediately put it on and swore she would never take it off.

"You hungry?" her mom asked, breaking into her thoughts.

"No," Seven said.

"Seven, you haven't eaten all day."

"I'm not hungry," Seven said, refusing to give in to her growling stomach.

"Suit yourself," her mom said and drove past several restaurants.

After another hour or so, she saw a sign which read **Welcome to Briarwood** in big, bold letters. Underneath was written *Where There is More Than Meets the Eye.*

As they entered the town, Seven studied the houses. Some were brick, some were stone, some were big, some were small, some had enormous yards, while others barely had a patch of grass, but they had one thing in common. They were meticulously neat and tidy. The lawns were so perfectly manicured that it seemed as though someone had cut each blade of grass using scissors and a ruler.

At the first stoplight, Miranda turned left. The street widened so that two lanes were going in each direction. A few cars joined them. A large, square white building loomed straight ahead. It had concrete steps, four concrete columns on each side, and a tower that poked out the dome top with a clock face on all four sides.

"That courthouse has been featured in several magazines on small towns. It is semi-famous," her mom said. Seven rolled her eyes and quickly looked away as though she were not interested.

Miranda turned left again. Seven read the street sign – School Drive. Sure enough, up ahead was a rectangular brick building that filled up the entire block. It had three stories and a lighted sign out front that read *Briarwood Junior High School.*

My new school, Seven thought.

"That won't be your school," Miranda said as though reading her daughter's thoughts. "Seven, there is something I meant to tell you about Briarwood." Miranda cleared her throat before going on. "This is well, uh... this town is where your father was born. It's where we met and were married. The house we are moving into belonged to his parents, then to him, and now to us."

"What?" Seven said in exasperated confusion. All her life, she had longed to know about her father, but her mom gave little information. Now, out of nowhere, they were moving into his childhood home.

"I didn't know how to tell you. I wasn't sure how you'd react, whether you'd love the idea or hate it," her mom went on.

Seven wasn't sure yet, either. It was a lot to take in.

For the next few minutes, Seven looked at each passing house, wondering if it was the one. Finally, Miranda turned down a long, tree-lined driveway lined. The tall oaks looked like soldiers standing watch, waiting to see if they were friend or foe. As the leafy guards let them pass, Seven looked ahead and, despite her anger, opened her mouth in awe at what she saw.

It wasn't a mansion, but it was by far the largest home in which Seven and her mom had ever lived. She drank in the sight of the freshly painted, white two-story house. Green shutters flanked sparkling windows. On the wraparound porch, green wicker rockers and a wooden swing sat invitingly.

"Well, what do you think?" Miranda asked as she parked the car in the driveway.

"It's beautiful," Seven whispered, temporarily forgetting that she was giving her mom the silent treatment.

"Well, it has four bedrooms so we won't be cramped. It also has a well-stocked library. There is an enormous flower garden in the backyard, which I am sure Mrs. Brusk has in tip-top shape. There is also a small pond and small woods beyond."

"Who is Mrs. Brusk?" Seven asked.

"The caretaker. She isn't the friendliest person, but she does a wonderful job on the grounds and house. She has worked here for a very long time. She lives there." Miranda pointed at a small cottage way in the back near the edge of the woods.

Something was strange. In front of her was the most beautiful house she had ever known. A large yard. Even a caretaker.

"If this is ours, why haven't we lived here until now?" Seven asked.

"Because, up until now, I was hoping we wouldn't have to."

"Why not?" Seven asked, exasperated.

"For a lot of reasons," her mom said in a shaky voice, "but

mostly because it reminds me of your father. He grew up here. We were married near those woods. Seeing all of this just hurts." She took a steadying breath and then said, "Enough about that for now. Let's go inside. It's getting late, and even though you say you aren't hungry, your growling stomach says otherwise." Her mother tried to sound matter-of-fact, but her misty eyes betrayed her.

As Seven followed her mom inside, she prepared herself for the stale air of a house that no one had lived in for years and years, but the house smelled delicious - like freshly baked brownies. Sure enough, when they walked into the bright and cheery kitchen, two plates and a pan of brownies sat in the middle of the wooden kitchen table.

"Looks like Mrs. Brusk may have softened over time," Miranda said. On the refrigerator was a note. While Miranda walked over to read it, Seven headed for the brownies. She was hungry, and those brownies smelled like heaven.

"Mrs. Brusk says she did some light shopping and was able to get all of the rooms ready," Miranda read.

"She doesn't sound unfriendly to me," Seven said through a mouthful of brownies. "And her brownies are awesome and still warm."

"Well, maybe very businesslike is more accurate. She gets her work done and doesn't like to chit-chat. She keeps to herself so you won't see her much. Why don't you go upstairs and pick out a room while I get something a little more substantial than brownies for supper?"

Seven walked over to the refrigerator and opened it. Making sure her mom's back was turned, she opened a jug of milk, lifted it directly to her mouth, and guzzled. Quickly, she replaced the lid and put the jug back into the refrigerator.

"I'm going upstairs now," Seve said as she wiped her mouth.

"All right. And Seven," her mom added without turning around, "maybe next time you could use a glass."

At the top of the stairs, Seven found the first bedroom. It

was a little small, so she decided to keep looking. Across the hall was another bedroom. Maybe. She passed a linen closet and a large hall bathroom on her way to the next room. As soon as she opened the door, she knew she didn't need to look any farther.

The room screamed her name. It had a queen-sized bed and was entirely decorated in black and white. The carpet felt like marshmallows even through her shoes. There was a desk, a chair, and a bookshelf stuffed full of books. Next to the bookshelf was a white, very comfy looking chair with a small table next to it. On the table was a short stack of books and an unusual looking wooden box with golden markings. Seven picked it up and tried unsuccessfully to open it. It reminded her of one of those puzzle boxes that wouldn't open until it was solved. She put the box back down and continued to look around. She opened one door to find a walk-in closet and a second door, which led to a small bathroom. She pulled open the vanity drawers and found they were already stocked with the same ponytail holders, toothbrush, toothpaste, shampoo, and lotion that Seven used. Mrs. Brusk was good.

Already beginning to feel at home, Seven returned to the bookshelf and let her fingers run over the bindings as she read the titles. Some she had already read, and some seemed to be a little young for her. Titles like *Fairy Folk*, *This Spells for You*, and *Magic - The Hidden Truth Revealed* seemed more appropriate for bedtime stories for young children rather than a teenager. On the second shelf were books about Briarwood, *Briarwood: The Beginning*, *Briarwood: Past and Present*, and *Secret Small Towns in America*. She grabbed the one entitled *Briarwood: Past and Present*. She flipped through it, mainly just looking at pictures. There was the courthouse, some statues, a few ancient-looking people, and then something she recognized. Her father's house. This house. The chapter was called "Houses around the Town." She started to read:

No other house in the town is like the Preston House on Prim-

rose Drive. Dating back to before Briarwood was officially established, the Preston House has been passed down for generations. The family has always been very private; some would even say secretive. Therefore, very few people in Briarwood today have actually seen the house from the inside. It is rumored that the library in it would make any book collector green with envy.

She wanted to continue reading it, but her growling stomach overruled. She pushed the book back onto the shelf, intending to read it later. However, after supper and a short walk around the yard, she was so tired she forgot entirely about the book and collapsed into an exhausted sleep.

When Seven awoke the next morning, it took her a second to remember where she was. She was lying in her new bed in her new house in her new town. And she wasn't alone. Someone was in her closet.

"Good morning," Miranda said, peeking around her door. "I thought I would go ahead and hang some of your clothes in here."

"What time is it?" she moaned, pulling the covers over her head.

"Around ten. I have some errands to do in town today. I hope you will join me. It is a neat little town. I'm leaving in 30," Miranda said.

"It's not like I have anything better to do," Seven muttered.

Twenty-nine minutes later, Seven had dressed, eaten, and was getting into the car. The ride to town was a short one, and soon they parked in the part of town Miranda called The Square. In the center, standing alone, was the white courthouse Seven had seen yesterday. A one-way street encircled it. Many buildings faced the courthouse. Seven noticed law offices, City Hall, and various shops, including a pharmacy, a doctor's office, a shoe store, and even a small movie theater. Seven looked at some mannequins dressed in what she guessed were the latest fashion trends. Seven looked down at her black shirt and jeans.

Fashion was a foreign concept to Seven.

She followed her mom to a greenish brick building next to a jewelry store. On the door in red paint were the wood 'Harrington Realty.'

"Are we moving again already?" Seven asked.

"No," her mother answered, ignoring the sarcasm. "Mr. Harrington helped Mrs. Brusk manage the property all these years. I just need to settle a few things. Why don't you wait out here and look around? This won't take long." Miranda opened the door and disappeared inside.

Seven walked past a few shop windows until she stopped in front of a bookshop. History books, children's picture books, romance novels, and even a few cookbooks were all neatly displayed. A bright red sign alerted shoppers about a sale currently going on inside. Above the door was a large wooden sign with *Bigglesby's Books* carved in bright blue letters. On either side of the name were pictures of open books.

Peering through the window, Seven saw a grandmotherly looking woman helping a man select a book. He held a book in either hand and shifted his gaze from one to the other. She imagined he was buying it for his daughter. Maybe it was the recent move or the fact that their new house once belonged to her father, but a slight sadness tugged at Seven's heart. Her father would never buy a book for her. Without realizing it, she grabbed for her the locket held it in her hands, an action that had become an unconscious habit.

"What is this?" said a girl in a high-pitched voice.

Seven stayed facing the window. Surely she wasn't talking to Seven. She didn't even know anybody here.

"I'm talking to you," the voice said, saturated with irritation. Seven felt a jab on her shoulder and knew she wasn't going to be able to ignore it. She turned around to face the voice's owner. "I've never seen you before." The voice belonged to a very stylishly dressed girl who was wearing enough make up for an entire clown crew at the circus.

"I just moved here," Seven said, refraining from adding the

word *duh* at the end.

"That is obvious," the girl sniffed as she gave Seven a once over, "because you definitely don't belong here." The girl's two friends snickered behind her.

Seven knew this type. Her years of moving from school to school to school had taught her that there were bullies everywhere. And they never traveled alone. They always had a group of cronies to laugh at the right moments and shield adult eyes from the torment their leader inflicted. Seven had tried different methods of dealing with them. Most of the time, she just tried to blend in, to be invisible. She didn't linger at her locker and walked to class with her head down. She only used the school's bathrooms if it was an emergency. Unfortunately, she learned that some bullies wouldn't let their prey be invisible, and she was guessing that was the kind standing in front of her now.

"What's your name?" asked one of the girls in the back.

"Seven," she said.

"Seven? What kind of name stupid name is that? Are your parents math nerds or something?" asked the girl in front.

Seven's face burned red hot. She wished she could melt into the sidewalk.

"Is there a problem here, Miss Stevens?" Seven turned around to see the elderly woman from the bookshop. She nearly filled the doorway. A pencil tucked behind her ear was barely visible under her poofy gray hair.

"No, Mrs. Bigglesby. We were just introducing ourselves to Seven here. She just moved into town. We wanted to say hello and welcome." The Stevens girl's face looked sinfully sweet, but Mrs. Bigglesby didn't seem to buy it.

"Wonderful," the older woman replied, "but I think your mother is finished." Mrs. Bigglesby nodded toward the next block, where a woman was coming out of a store loaded down with overflowing shopping bags.

"I think she just bought me those new shoes everybody has been trying to get," squealed the Stevens girl. "We had to order them from New York. She had to pay double, but she says I'm worth it. Come on, girls, let's get out of here before we get infected with bad taste," the girl said, looking at Seven. The three of them left hooting with laughter.

"Don't mind them, honey. With all of their parents' money, you'd think they could afford some manners." Mrs. Bigglesby laughed at her own joke, but when she met Seven's eyes, she fell silent and put her hands on her cheeks. "Oh my goodness," she whispered, taking a step toward Seven. "You look just like . . . of course it isn't red, but you look just like . . ." The stranger didn't finish. She just stared at Seven as though Seven had four eyes.

"Mrs. Bigglesby!" a familiar voice shouted.

"Oh my goodness, Miranda Preston, as I live and breathe. I knew she..." the woman stopped as Seven's mother came around Seven and enveloped the stranger in a warm hug.

"It's been a long time," her mother said, breaking the embrace.

"Too long," the woman agreed. "You look beautiful, a bit thin, but beautiful."

"Oh," Miranda said, waving away the comment. "Mrs. Bigglesby, this is my daughter, Seven."

"Um, hello," Seven awkwardly said as she stuck out her hand, but the woman looked at it and just laughed. She pushed it aside and crushed Seven in a hug.

"I knew she was yours the second I saw her. She looks just like you, but I can see a bit of Jonathan in her, too. How old are you, dear?"

"Thirteen." Seven said, wishing the woman would let her go.

"Thirteen?" said Mrs. Bigglesby, thankfully releasing Seven from the hug. "It's been that long?" the woman asked Seven's mom.

"You knew my father?" Seven interrupted.

"Oh yes, dear, I knew your father quite well. I knew him from diapers. He and his family, well, I guess your family used to be my best customers. I was greatly saddened when I heard of his, well uh, that he was gone. I didn't like it when your mom left us before you were born, but sometimes we just have to start over," Mrs. Bigglesby said softly as her eyes misted. Quickly she waved her hand and continued, "Enough of that. We shouldn't focus on sad memories. You're back?"

Miranda nodded.

"Wonderful! Seven, do you like to read?"

Seven nodded. Since they had moved around so much, books had become a way of survival for her. She read voraciously, mostly to escape the real world when it became overwhelming, which had been often.

"Well, then you must come in and pick out any book in the store, my treat. I must have a few books in my shop that you don't have in that library of yours. Besides, I don't want those girls to leave a bad taste in your mouth about our little town."

"What girls?" her mom asked.

"Seven met Katherine Stevens' daughter," Mrs. Bigglesby said.

"She's still living here? I figured she would have moved to New York or Paris by now," Miranda said, rolling her eyes.

"Nah, she likes to be a big fish in a little pond, not the other way around," Mrs. Bigglesby said as she ushered them into her store.

"Seven, why don't you look around while I talk with Mrs. Bigglesby," her mom said. The two women exchanged a knowing look and headed to the back of the store. Mrs. Bigglesby pulled the curtains apart, let Miranda pass, and closed them tightly, but not before Seven caught her eye. What was that expression on the older woman's face? Sadness? Pity? Concern? Seven didn't know, but she had just about had her fill of secrets. She decided to get some answers.

Seven pretended to look at some oversized books stacked on the floor. She grabbed one whose cover seemed to be made of wood. She would act like she was reading it if her mom or Mrs. Bigglesby caught her eavesdropping.

Silently, Seven tiptoed toward the curtain, slowly pulled it apart, and peeked through the opening. Mrs. Bigglesby and her mom were standing next to a small table on which sat a solitary black wooden box. It was slightly larger than a shoebox. The antique hinges on it were quite large and matched the rusted metal latch on the front. Faded golden markings looped randomly about the box. It creaked as the shopkeeper opened it. Seven thought she heard the box hum, but she couldn't be sure. The two women just silently stared at it for a moment, and then her mom said something. Seven couldn't hear what she said, but she did hear Mrs. Bigglesby's reply.

"I was afraid of that when I saw you. You knew you couldn't run forever, dear. It's who you are. It's who he fell in love with. Jonathan knew the risks. You have to forgive yourself."

Who knew what risks? Why was her mom running? What did the book shop owner mean? *It's who you are?*

Miranda covered her face with her hands and shook her head. Mrs. Bigglesby reached across the table and gave her mom's shoulder a comforting squeeze.

"Are you sure you are ready for this? She's going to have a lot of questions."

"Is she talking about me?" Seven thought.

"I don't have a choice," Miranda answered loudly enough for Seven to hear.

Seven watched as her mom opened a large cloth bag and removed a faded yellow envelope. It was tied with a red ribbon and had a green wax seal melted across the back. Miranda also pulled several yellow scrolls from the bag. They had the same wax seal as the envelope but were tied with green ribbons. Attached to the green ribbons were tiny, purple, velvet-looking bags cinched with a thin golden string. Mrs. Bigglesby took the envelope and the scrolls from the table, placed them inside the box, and closed the lid. The store lights must have flickered then because Seven thought she saw the box's markings grow brighter and slither around it for a split second. When Mrs. Bigglesby opened the lid again, the envelope and the scrolls were gone.

Seven's gasped loudly. She covered her mouth with her hand, but it was too late. She had given herself away. She quickly closed the curtain and stepped back, knocking over a display of books about healthy cooking. She tried to catch the falling stack without success. It toppled to the floor with a loud crash.

"Seven, what's going on?" her mom asked as she appeared from behind the curtain.

"I, uh, knocked over some books, but I'll pick them up."

"You were looking at books on healthy cooking?" her mother asked suspiciously.

Seven shrugged and busied herself picking up the books. Just then, the front door jingled, and a customer walked in.

"Welcome to Bigglesby Books," the shopkeeper shouted from the back. "I'll be right there."

Seven could feel her mom's gaze on her. She took her time stacking the books as her mind raced with what she had just witnessed. Did she just see those things disappear? Did that little box *glow*? Surely not. It had to be a trick. Except, if that was true, why had her mom and Mrs. Bigglesby been so secretive? Why was her mom staring so hard at her right now?

"Can I help you find something?" Mrs. Bigglesby called as she passed by them, giving Miranda a nearly imperceptible nod. Then she floated away toward her customer.

When Seven finished restacking the pile, she grabbed the book with the wooden cover.

"Mrs. Bigglesby, I think I will take this one if that is all right," Seven said with exaggerated innocence.

Without looking away from the display she was showing the new customer, Mrs. Bigglesby nodded and waved her hand.

"Thank you for your help today, Mrs. Bigglesby," Miranda said.

This time, the older woman did turn around and looked at them. Her gaze went from Seven to Miranda and back again.

"Just doing my job," she said softly. "Anyway, it was so good to see you. Don't be a stranger. And," she said, looking directly at Seven, "good luck to you, my dear. I hope all goes well with your visitor."

"What visitor?" Seven asked her mom as they exited the shop.

"An old friend of mine," Miranda said without looking at her daughter.

"What friend?" Seven pressed.

"Someone who will change your life."

Chapter Three

A Visitor from the Woods

Crash! A scream! Seven woke with a start. Without thinking, she leaped from her bed. Fighting the covers, she freed herself and ran downstairs. There, at the kitchen door, she was stunned by what she saw.

"What the...?" The kitchen table and counters were full of pancakes, eggs, toast, bacon, sausage, and cinnamon rolls. Coffee perked happily in the pot. Her mother, already dressed and ready for the day, picked up a pan from the floor.

"I didn't realize the pan was still hot. I'm sorry if I woke you." Then her mom looked around at all of the food. "Too much?"

"Not unless the entire town is coming for breakfast."

"Nope, just one visitor," her mom answered as she ran cold water over her hand.

"Oh, yes, the mysterious visitor. Still no name, huh? Still keeping me in the dark?" Seven asked through a mouthful of cinnamon roll.

"In less than an hour, you will know more than I ever wanted you to," her mom said.

Seven rolled her eyes. Her mom had been even more secretive and cryptic since they left Bigglesby's Books a few days ago, not to mention jumpy and demanding. She made Seven clean the entire house even though Mrs. Brusk had already cleaned it, all the while refusing to answer any of Seven's questions.

"I am going to be late," Miranda said as she looked at the clock and tucked a stray curl behind her ear. "Please get dressed." Without another word, her mom walked out the back door, forgetting to close it.

Seven stomped over to the door, ready to slam it. However, as she looked out the door's window, she realized her mom had not gone to the car but into the woods. She was supposed to picking up their visitor. Why was she going to the woods?

Seven grabbed another cinnamon roll, stepped out onto the porch, and sat on the swing. She nibbled on the roll while never letting her gaze leave the path into the woods. After what felt like forever, a seething Seven rose from the swing and stomped toward the door. It was at that moment that she heard something.

Seven turned around and watched as her mom emerged from the woods, walking arm and arm with a shorter figure dressed in an unusual looking outfit. It looked sort of like a graduation gown with a hood. Seven slipped through the door and into the kitchen, shrinking away as they entered.

"Oh, this looks wonderful! I'm famished! I haven't been able to eat a thing since I received your letter. As you can imagine, it was quite a shock," the stranger said.

"Would you like some coffee?" her mom offered.

"Yes, please," the stranger said.

Her mom turned toward the coffee pot and noticed Seven.

"Oh, Seven, you're still in your pajamas," her mom said, glaring at her.

At this, the stranger turned around. Two milky white hands with short, chubby fingers reached for the hood and pulled it off. The woman underneath had a round face, curly caramel-colored hair that didn't quite reach her shoulders, and large brown eyes that glistened with tears. She stood just an inch or two taller than Seven.

"She looks just like you," the stranger whispered as she

studied Seven. "I can't believe...." Then without warning, the stranger grabbed Seven, and for the second time in just a few days, Seven found herself being hugged by a stranger. She looked pleadingly at her mom, but her mom just shrugged.

"You can't imagine my shock to find out my best friend was not only alive and well, but a mom," the visitor said, finally releasing Seven.

"Alive and well?" Seven repeated, confused.

"Just an expression," her mom said quickly. The stranger shot Miranda a quizzical look but remained silent.

"Oh, well, um, did I see you come out of our woods?" Seven asked.

"Of course," the stranger repeated as though it was the most logical thing in the world. "Under the circumstances, how else would I get here? Now, how about coffee?"

"Of course," Miranda said as she handed a steaming cup to the visitor. "And let's eat."

Seven was dumbstruck. She watched as her mom and the visitor sat down, filled their plates, and talked about places Seven had never heard of and people she had never met. She heard words like wielders, retrievers, guardians, Midia, Wyndamir. They had completely forgotten she was there. Finally, she interrupted.

"Excuse me, but who the heck are you, and where did you come from?" Seven said, not hiding her irritation. "Do you live in our woods or what?"

"Seven!" her mom scolded. "Don't be rude!"

However, the visitor just calmly put her fork down, swallowed more coffee, and dabbed her mouth.

"It's all right, Miranda. I can only imagine the questions she has. How much does she know?"

"Nothing," her mom whispered.

"Nothing? Nothing at all?" The woman asked in disbelief. "From your letter, I knew you didn't tell her much, but nothing? Really, Miranda," she scolded.

"I – I - I know...but I... I didn't... I mean... I wasn't..." Seven had never seen her mom so uncomfortable and unsure. It reminded Seven of a misbehaving student in the principal's office. "I was hoping that when we left there, she would be safe. I was hoping she would never have to know," Miranda went on.

"Miranda, it's who she is. It is who you are," the woman said quietly.

"Not anymore," Miranda said firmly. "Not ever again. I thought I made that clear in my letter."

Seven watched as their guest transformed from stern principal to comforting mother-figure.

"You did, but I was just hoping now that you had a daughter you would..."

"No," Miranda's voice held a finality to it.

"Um, hello, still here and still waiting for someone to tell me what's going on," Seven said.

An awkward silence fell. It seemed both women were waiting for the other one to start. Finally, the visitor spoke.

"Well, Seven, I can honestly say I don't quite know where to begin. I am not a Retriever, so I haven't been trained in this sort of thing."

"A what?" Seven asked, confused.

"A Retriever, a wielder trained to retrieve magical children born in the non-magical worlds and bring them to Midia to be instructed," the stranger said as though Seven should already know this.

"Um, what?" Seven asked.

"Oh, I am not doing this so well. Let me start over," the visitor said as she took a deep breath and looked directly into Seven's eyes. "My name is Phoebe Mcfee. I do not live in your woods. I am your mother's friend from a long time ago. For reasons she will explain later, your mom had kept something from you," Mcfee said, glaring at Miranda. "I am just going to say it. Seven, you are a wielder of magic."

Seven looked at Phoebe Mcfee like she just told her she had four arms.

"A what of magic?"

"A wielder. We have gone by many names - witches, wizards, magicians, conjurers, sorcerers. However, we prefer wielder." Mcfee said this like she just explained different names for something as common as a cover. *"You know, a blanket, a quilt, a bedspread."*

Seven looked from her mom to Mcfee. This had to be a joke. She watched the expression on both women's faces waiting for the laughter to start. It never did.

"Oh, come on! You don't expect me to believe that? I'm thirteen years old. I mean, this would make a great story and all, but tell me what is really going on."

The visitor looked around the kitchen and then at Seven's empty glass.

"All right. Let me show you." Seven watched as Mcfee raised her hand and flicked her fingers. A little purple spark flew from her hands, and then something happened that would change Seven's life forever.

Seven's glass floated off the table. It shot through the air toward the refrigerator. Before it smashed against the door, the glass slowed and *knocked* on the refrigerator door. *The glass knocked.* The door opened, and the milk jug popped out. The cap unscrewed and hovered in the air while the milk tipped over and filled the glass without spilling a drop. When the glass was full, the cap screwed itself back onto the top of the jug and returned to the refrigerator. The door closed, and the now full glass zoomed back to the table and landed directly in front of Seven.

"How about some pancakes?" Mcfee went on. With another flick of her hand, Mcfee sent two pancakes dancing through the air. They landed gracefully on Seven's plate. "Butter and syrup?"

A knife marched over to the stick of butter, scraped off a pat, and made its way to the pancakes where it dutifully spread the butter. The syrup bottle seemed to be waiting for the butter knife to fulfill its duties because as soon as it finished, the bottle scooted over to the plate, tipped, and covered the pancakes with syrup.

Mcfee said, "Well, have a bite."

Seven stared at her plate. She opened her mouth and closed it without saying anything. Did she just see that? She had to be dreaming. Magic wasn't real. It was from storybooks and children's imaginations. Maybe it was some kind of trick, some elaborate hoax set up by her mom and this woman. Maybe Mrs. Bigglesby was in on it, too. Seven looked around the room for any sign of wires or mirrors or anything that could explain this. She found nothing, nothing but the visitor's smiling face and her mother's downcast eyes.

"Well?" Mcfee asked.

"Did I really just see that?"

"Yes. Magic is as real as you and me and these wonderful pancakes," Mcfee said with a smile. "Of course, it is used for more than just getting breakfast, but I find it very convenient for that, too."

"And you think I'm . . . magical?" Seven could hardly say the word.

"No, I don't think so." Mcfee looked from Seven to Miranda and back to Seven. "I *know* so."

"But how do you know?" Seven persisted. "I mean if I was . . . I mean, if I am whatever you call it, wouldn't I know?"

"We know you are magical because I am," her mom's voice was softer than a feather. Without another word, Mirada waved her fingers. The coffee pot wiggled out from the coffee maker and flew toward the table. Halfway there, however, it fell out of the air and nearly crashed to the floor. At the last second, Mcfee cast a spell and sent it back to the coffeemaker.

"She's a bit out of practice, but your mother was once one of the most skilled wielders of our time. She could do things with magic that some of us could only dream about doing. When I thought she was, well, when she came here, I was devastated. I lost my best friend. These last years have been difficult without her," Mcfee's voiced trembled. "I understand why you did what you did though I don't agree with it," she said, turning toward Miranda. Miranda said nothing, just looked at her coffee mug as though she would rather be sitting in a den of vipers.

"W-w-why didn't you tell me?" Seven cried.

"Because I was hoping you would never have to know. I was hoping magic would never have to be a part of our lives, but I was wrong. Phoebe and Mrs. Bigglesby were right. It's who you are. I'm sorry, Seven," Miranda said. "So, so sorry."

"You're sorry? You have a friend mysteriously appear from the woods, sit at our table, make the milk pour itself, *you* make the coffee float, and all I get is sorry? I think I deserve more than that."

"You're right. You do. I'm so sorry," Miranda said.

"Quit saying you are sorry!" Seven yelled. "Just tell me why you would lie to me for my whole life?"

"To protect you," her mom answered.

"From what?" Seven asked.

"Not everyone uses magic to get their breakfasts. Some use it for horribly wicked things," Miranda said bitterly. "You see, with all of my wonderful gifts, I couldn't save him. He died because of me."

"Who?" Seven asked.

"Your father, Seven. Your father did not die in a fire. Magic is what killed your father. Evil, dark magic." Her mom's voice was tight and filled with emotion.

Seven felt as though someone had punched her in the stomach. There had never been a house fire? Her whole life had been a lie.

"I don't understand. Magic killed him?" Seven asked softly. "Does that mean that he was one, too? A wielder?"

"No, he wasn't, but he sure wanted to be." Miranda smiled weakly. "Oh, Seven, I never wanted you to know this story. It's so painful," her mom stifled a sob. Phoebe reached across the table, took Miranda's hand, and gave it a gentle squeeze. Miranda smiled weakly, took a breath, and continued.

"Seven, I am from Midia, a magical country. It is not on any map, and it is not a place you can get to by normal means.

There are enchanted gates that allow wielders to cross over between this world and that one. They are hidden or disguised to look like everyday objects like trees, stairwells, or even doors in old buildings.

"So, my dad found a gate and crossed into Midia?" Seven asked.

"No, no. Unwielders cannot see the gates, and even if they could, they couldn't cross on their own."

"So how did he..." Seven interrupted, unable to control herself.

Miranda put her hand up.

"Let me get this out, first. I am afraid if I stop, I won't be able to start again."

Seven leaned back in her chair wordlessly.

"I was a Guardian. My job was to cross the gates from Midia to make sure no magic had seeped between the barriers, either accidentally or not so accidentally. You can imagine that humans do not do well when they see magic. That's why Midian law states that wielders who cross the gates are not allowed to be seen by unwielders, like your father. The first time he saw me, I should have wiped his memory. But there was just something about him. I couldn't bring myself to do it," Miranda said, shaking her head.

"Was he scared when he saw you cross the gate?" Seven asked.

"No, he wasn't afraid at all. I think that is what made him so interesting. He was just sitting near the woods studying the stars. When I came through, he didn't gasp or jump or anything. He just smiled and said, 'Lovely night, isn't it?' Then he introduced himself and asked me if I would like a drink of his hot cocoa. He even had an extra cup. It was almost as though he was expecting me." Miranda smiled at the memory. "I was cloaked. He shouldn't have been able to see me, but he could. And from then on, he waited for me to cross every night. We would spend hours talking about this and that. He was so interested in Midia and magic. He wanted me to take him there so badly, but I always refused. By law, unwielders are not allowed to cross the gates. Any wielder caught bringing an unwielder into Midia without permission would have his or her powers stripped."

"Stripped?"

"Not important now," Miranda said.

"So, you broke the rules and took him across?" Seven deduced.

"I broke a lot of rules," Miranda admitted. "Letting him see me, not wiping his memory, talking to him about magic. I broke them all, but the biggest rule I broke was falling in love and marrying him." Tears formed in Miranda's eyes, but they didn't fall. "But I would do it all over again. Look what I got out of it," she smiled weakly at Seven.

Seven reached for the thin leather cord around her neck and held it between her fingers. She could feel the comforting weight of the locket under her shirt, but she didn't pull it out.

"After we married, we lived apart for a while. It was hard, but we would be together at night when I crossed. It gave me something to look forward to every day. Then, when we found out that you were coming along, we knew we couldn't keep living apart. He couldn't live in Midia, so the only choice was to live here. However, before I left for good, he made me promise him one thing."

"He wanted to see Midia," Seven concluded.

"He wanted to see what he was missing and what I was giving up," Miranda said, nodding. "At first, I refused, but he begged me. After all the other rules I had broken, I figured one more would not matter. Oh, how wrong I was.

"The night we crossed was the most nervous I had ever been. I showed him different towns, magical creatures, and Wyndamir Academy as quickly as he would let me. We were just heading back to the gate. Everything was going so smoothly that I guess I let my guard down. That is when it happened. The Shadow Raiders attacked."

"Shadow Raiders?" Seven asked.

"They are the most evil, vile, power-hungry, soulless

group of wielders in all of Midian history, and their leader is even worse," her mom spat the words. "Somehow, they had discovered I had a powerful relic, one their leader wanted. When they appeared, I tried to get your father out of there. I tried to fight back, but they outnumbered me. In the heat of the battle, your father sacrificed himself to save us. Even though I thought he was protected, I should never have taken him there. You see Seven. I am responsible for your father's death." Guilt dripped from these last words. Miranda got up and walked to the kitchen window.

"I didn't know. I'm so sorry," Mcfee said softly.

Seven barely breathed as she thought about her father's sacrifice. Questions chased each other around Seven's brain so fast she felt faint. This was too much. Magic. Midia. Wyndamir. Gates. Relics. Death.

Finally, Miranda walked back to the table and looked directly into Seven's eyes.

"Seven, when we found out you were coming, your father said it was the happiest day of his life. He couldn't stop smiling. He would make up these silly songs, and even though I told him you could hear yet, he would sing them to you. He loved you so much." She paused and took a deep breath before going on. "After the attack, I couldn't stay there anymore. I couldn't bear the fact that my magical world had taken what was most precious to me. I wouldn't let it have you, too."

"Did they get it from you? The relic, I mean?" Seven asked

"No," Miranda said.

"Where is it?'

"It is no longer in my possession."

"It's not?" Mcfee cut in with apparent surprise.

"It's not. I know where it is, and it is safe," Miranda said, looking hard at her friend. "It doesn't matter, though. The Shadow Raiders will continue to hunt me as they have always done," she said.

"What?" Seven asked.

"Seven, have you ever wondered why we moved so

often?"

Seven nodded.

"Well, that is why. Somehow, someone figured out the relic left Midia and sent a Tracker. I first realized it when you were about three. We were at a park, and I was pushing you on a swing. I noticed this man sitting on one of the benches. Something didn't feel right, so I picked you up out of the swing to leave. When I looked back at the bench, he was gone. In less than a second, he was gone. There is only one way for someone to disappear that quickly and that silently. Magic.

"After that, whenever I suspected a Tracker was on our trail, we moved. I wanted to keep running, but it's becoming too hard. They are finding us faster and faster. They have gotten too close. Remember that horrible noise on the morning of your birthday? I was holding this?" Out of her pocket, Miranda pulled the pink crystal Seven had seen the morning of her birthday. "These are dark aura crystals. They are a sort of magical alarm system. I have used them for years, but they had never been triggered until that morning. Someone tried to get into our house, a someone who shouldn't have been there.

"The reason I missed your birthday was that I was searching for whoever had tripped the alarm system. I didn't find anyone, but I knew our time had run out. I realized that we wouldn't be able to stay anywhere longer than a few weeks or months before long. That is not life, not for you. And what would happen to you if something happened to me? So, I decided to move here. When we went to Mrs. Bigglesby's shop, I sent a letter to Phoebe asking for her help. It is time that you learned how to protect yourself."

"It was quite a shock, you know," Mcfee said, shaking her head. "To find out after all these years that you were alive and that you had a daughter. I read that letter ten times before I believed it."

"You thought my mom was dead?" Seven asked in disbelief.

"Yes," Mcfee said. "Everyone does, well except for the

Tracker and whoever sent it."

"Seven, I broke a lot of laws in Midia," her mom explained. "If people thought I was alive, they would come searching for me or hurt the people they thought would know where I was hiding." Miranda looked at Mcfee. "I am sorry for what you went through, Phoebe."

"There is danger wherever you live," Mcfee pointed out. "The best way to handle it is to be trained."

"That is why Phoebe is here, Seven, to take you to Wyndamir Academy, where you will learn all about magic," Miranda explained.

"Wyndamir Academy?"

"Wyndamir Academy for the Magical Arts. Our old school," Mcfee answered, pointing to herself and Miranda, "and where I am Dean of Students. It is the best school there is. You will learn all the elements of magic, from the basics to the most advanced. History, Potion Making. Spell Casting. Transmorphology. Phytology," Mcfee ticked them off. "All of it."

"Oh," Seven said, not understanding a word Mcfee just said.

"I know this is a lot to take in, Seven. I'm still getting used to the idea that your mom is actually sitting across this table and not..." Mcfee left the word unspoken. "However, ultimately, the decision is yours. You have to decide if you want to stay here or go to Midia and attend Wyndamir."

"How will I get there? Do I ride a broomstick there every morning or a magic carpet or use a gate or something?"

Mcfee shook her head.

"No, Seven, we don't fly on broomsticks and magic carpets, at least not often. You will live there."

"Live there? For the whole school year?" Seven asked, incredulously.

"Other than a few breaks, yes."

"Whoa," Seven said. Then she asked, "Do I have to decide now?"

"Not this very second, but the school year starts on the

first Tuesday in September. I will need some time to make the arrangements, and it would be best to get your supplies early," Mcfee said. "Give you time to get used to them."

Seven sat there, numbly.

"Seven, I really am sorry. I wish...well, I wish a lot of things," Miranda said.

Seven nodded, got up from the chair, and headed for the stairs as though she were in a trance. She climbed the stairs to her room, where she sank into her bed.

In the last few hours, she learned everything she thought she knew was a lie. They never moved because of job transfers. They moved because they were being hunted. Seven thought of the person she saw on the street corner the norming of her birthday. Was that a Tracker? Was that why her mom acted the way she had?

And her father. He didn't die in a fire. He died protecting them. She pulled out her locket, opened it, and studied her dad's smiling face. He looked so happy as her mom kissed his cheek. She wished he would come out of that picture and tell her what to do.

And then there was magic. It was real. As irritated as she was at her mom for not telling her all these years, she had to admit it was pretty cool to watch the coffee pot float and the pancakes dance. And boxes that could make things disappear? Gates that led to a magical world? But her mom's warning rang in her ears. *Not everyone uses magic to get their breakfasts. Some use it for horribly wicked things.*

The Shadow Raiders had used magic for the most monstrous thing Seven could think of - to kill her father. And for what? A stupid relic that her mom doesn't even have anymore? Couldn't they tell them that, and the Shadow Raiders would quit hunting them?

Seven thought about the choice facing her - cross the gates or run? Could she pretend she never saw these things and forget about magic? On the other hand, was she brave enough to leave her mom and go to a strange place where she would know no one? To a place where magic was ordinary, and potions were probably bought in a grocery store? Did they even have grocery stores? She didn't know what to do. Finally, she fell into a fitful sleep.

When Seven awoke the next morning, she looked out her window. The day was sunny, and the sky was clear. So was her answer. She went to find her mom and Mcfee to tell them her decision. She found them in the garden behind the house. They had their backs to her, so she couldn't see what they were doing.

"Ms. Brusk is not going to appreciate your help," Miranda warned.

"What she doesn't know won't hurt her," Mcfee said.

"That woman knows everything. Besides, roses like that do not grow here. All she has to do is look, and she'll know."

"What are you two doing?" Seven asked.

"Oh, good morning," Mcfee answered brightly. "We..."

"Not *we*," Miranda interrupted.

"Okay, *I* am secretly giving Ms. Brusk a little help with the flowers. They looked like they needed a little pick me up."

Mcfee stepped aside and showed Seven her handiwork.

The rose bushes had flowers on them the size of dinner plates. Even from several feet away, Seven could smell the sweet aroma swirling in the air.

"Do you think she'll notice?" Mcfee asked innocently.

"Unless she is blind and has lost her sense of smell, I am pretty sure she will notice," Seven said.

Miranda gave Mcfee a satisfied smile, to which Mcfee just shrugged.

"We missed you last night," her mom said.

"I had a lot to think about," Seven said.

"And?" Mcfee prompted.

"Well, at first, I was ready to go. I mean, seeing what you did at breakfast was excellent. Then, I thought about the Shadow Raiders. I can't imagine going to Midia, where the people who killed my dad are walking around free. Everyone at that school probably knows everything about magic, so I decided there was no way I was going. This morning I was ready to come and tell you thanks, but no thanks.

"Was?" her mom asked.

"Then, I thought about my dad. He wanted to see Midia so badly that it cost him his life. I am sure my dad didn't die, protecting us so that I could run away scared. I think he'd want me to go, so I am going."

Seven watched the expressions of the two women's faces. They couldn't have been more different. Phoebe Mcfee clapped her hands as though Christmas had come early. On the other hand, her mother looked as though she just found out Christmas had been canceled.

"You don't want me to go?" Seven asked her mother.

"I just want you to be safe," her mom answered.

"Miranda, I will be there for her like she is my own daughter," Mcfee said, taking Miranda's hands. "I will make the arrangements, but we will get your supplies tomorrow."

"Tomorrow?" Seven asked with a mixture of shock and excitement.

"That soon? Really?" her mom interjected.

"The sooner, the better," Mcfee said and then added, "You could always join us. We could disguise you so no one would recognize you."

"It is not a part of my life anymore. I know that must be hard for you both to understand, but going back there..." Miranda didn't finish.

"Very well, Seven, tomorrow you and I will set off for Midia. We will leave early."

Seven's heart skipped a bit. Tomorrow? How would she get through the day?

Chapter Four

Through the Mist

The sun was barely up when Mcfee, Miranda, and Seven entered the woods the next morning. The walk would have been more enjoyable if Seven wasn't continually tripping over the cloak Mcfee made her wear.

"We're here," her mother said after a while.

Seven looked around, but all she saw were trees.

"Where is it?" Seven asked.

"Right here," her mom said, pointing to two trees. The trunks were about four feet apart and about five feet tall. They were completely white with bark as smooth as glass. The limbs were thin and reminded Seven of bony fingers. Purple leaves in the shape of a heart covered the branches.

"I don't see it. Does that mean I am an unwielder?" Seven asked, panicking.

"Relax, Seven. This is a special gate. I am the only one who can see it until it's opened," said her mom. "I will unlock it, so you and Phoebe can pass. Then I will close it again until it's time for you to return. Now, put this on." She handed Seven a silky rope on which hung a small medallion. It was silver with tiny emeralds around the edges that glittered in the sunlight. In the center, the letters MW were written in fancy gold letters.

"What is this?" Seven asked. "What does MW stand for?"

"This is a passkey. If anyone but me tries to pass through this gate without wearing this, that person will become trapped. Never mind about the letters."

"Do I have to take my other locket off?" Seven asked.

"No, no, don't ever take it off," her mom said, shooting a sidelong glance at Mcfee. Then, Miranda lowered her voice so only Seven could hear. "Keep it tucked in your shirt, so you don't lose it."

Seven nodded. Then, her mom placed one hand on each of the trees. She took a deep breath and spoke very clearly.

"*Junctus Ungradi*."

The trees grew immediately, creaking and moaning as they bent toward each other, forming an archway. At the top of the archway, the trunks twisted around each other becoming one spiral-shaped tree. A silvery mist slowly filled the space.

"Go," Miranda whispered.

As Mcfee and Seven went through, Seven expected to feel wet, but she didn't. As the mist engulfed them, she turned around to look at her mom, but all she saw was fog. Just as quickly as it formed, the mist dissolved, and Seven was shocked to see gray stone walls instead of trees. The air was no longer fresh but smelled like mildew and wet socks.

"Where are we?"

"Midia," Mcfee said simply

Seven tried to get a better look, but the only light source in the windowless room came from a dim candle in a sconce attached to the wall.

Mcfee led Seven up an old staircase that looked as though it would collapse if someone breathed too hard. Mcfee pushed open a door at the top, and light flooded in, revealing a dirty alley. Garbage cans overflowed, and the smell nearly knocked Seven over. She pulled her shirt up over her nose.

"Midia doesn't smell very good," Seven said, her voice muffled as she held her breath.

"Your passkey," Mcfee said, ignoring Seven's theatrics. Mcfee opened a purple velvet bag she pulled from her pocket.

"That looks just like one of the sacks my mom put in Mrs. Bigglesby's box," Seven said.

"Yes, your mother told me you were a bit nosy," Mcfee chided. "This is a nuper sack. Once closed, only the person who put in an object can retrieve it from the bag. If you opened it, all you would see would be an empty sack."

"Cool," Seven said.

"Handy," Mcfee corrected. "Now, let's go." She led Seven down the alley, carefully avoiding the questionable brown piles. They turned onto a much cleaner and better-smelling street. Seven looked at the street sign. Main Street.

"Main Street? I was expecting something like Leprechaun Lane or Spell Street or Potion Path," Seven said. "I mean, we have a Main Street in every town back home."

"Midia isn't unlike where you live, Seven. The sun still rises in the east and sets in the west, the sky is still blue, and the grass is still green. Children your age like the same things you do and probably worry about the same things, too. Our worlds are more similar than different."

Seven wasn't convinced but remained quiet.

"First stop, Swathmore's. This way."

Seven followed Mcfee down the cobblestone street. A beautiful fountain was in the center. Seven could see what looked like ordinary small silvery fish swimming in it. Then suddenly, one of them jumped out of the water. Immediately, she realized it was anything but ordinary. The fish's tail was bright red and nearly split in two resembling legs. Its head looked like a monkey, and it had fur.

"They are called monakara. They're really intelligent and near impossible to catch when they get to be adults, not that you'd want to," Mcfee pointed to its sharpened teeth.

As they walked, Seven drank in her surroundings. She felt as though she had stepped back in time. Uneven bricked sidewalks dotted with old-fashioned oil lamps flanked the cobblestone street. Steep, clay tile roofs topped tightly packed buildings made of stone, misshapen bricks, and greying wood. Some of the buildings looked so old that Seven was sure they had been there since the beginning of time.

Because of the early hour, the streets were nearly empty. A few window shoppers strolled lazily, but one man appeared to be on a mission. Seven watched as he marched very purposefully into one of the more run-down shops. Written in fading block letters, the sign above the door read: *Leaf Tarkem's: You need it, we have it, or something close.*

Seven heard a little bell jingle, but the man's tirade quickly drowned out the sound.

"You told me that table was indestructible! 'Merlin himself would want it,' you said. 'I performed the spell meself,' you said. 'Put extra oomf in it,' you said. Well, I don't know where you learned indestructible spells, Tarkem, but you need more lessons! You are the worst-." Seven couldn't hear what the shopkeeper was because the door slammed shut.

Mcfee just laughed.

"Anyone who believes anything old Leaf Tarkem says deserves what he gets. Leaf's been known to tell the truth every once in a while, but not often and usually not all of it at once. Ah, here we are," Miss Mcfee said, pointing to another shop.

Seven looked up to see a large, dark blue sign. In neat white letters was the store's name: *Swathmore Wands*. A swirling fog filled the store's front window. Seven watched as the fog changed from white to blue and snaked around to form the words *Swathmore Wands*. Then the words vanished, and the formless gray fog reappeared. It turned brilliant red, and the words *New Wands Low Prices* appeared. The letters grew bright green, then dimmed, and were swallowed up by the fog again.

"I need a wand?" Seven asked, confused. "You and mom didn't use a wand."

"Well, we don't now, but we did. Everyone starts with a wand, Seven, and unfortunately, some wielders never grow confident enough to do magic without it. Consider a wand like a, uh, well, like training wheels in your world. When you first learned to ride a bike, you needed them to help you balance, to focus until you felt comfortable enough to ride without them. Your ability to ride the bike didn't come from the training wheels but rather from lots of practice. Magic is the same. Magical ability doesn't come from a wand but rather from the wielder. The wand just helps you balance and focus your magic until you are comfortable and confident enough to do magic without it. Shall we?" Mcfee opened the door, and they entered the tiny shop.

A strong scent of wood and orange polish wafted out. Seven could see boxes unsteadily stacked and crammed into corners. Baskets overflowing with wands of all different sizes and colors lined shelf after shelf. Signs boasting discounts and two-for-one sales hovered in midair throughout the store.

"But, Daddy, you promised," a voice whined. Seven saw a girl who looked close to her age and a tall man with dark hair streaked with gray looking into a display case.

"I know, dear, but I am not convinced these are special enough for you," the man said as he wrinkled his nose.

"We've looked at four other places already. I do like the purple one. Can't we just get it, pleeeease?" The girl made *please* sound like a very long word.

"Honestly, Swathmore, surely you have better ones than these?" the man said to a shopkeeper Seven couldn't see. "Maybe some in the back?"

"Mr. Davidson, these are all the one-of-a-kind wands in the store. I am expecting another shipment from Blackpool in about three days. A willow wand made with an emerald scarab shell and a handle with gold inlaid runes is included in that order. It is extremely rare and quite beautiful, I am told," the shopkeeper said in a squeaky voice.

"Oh, Daddy, I don't want to wait," the girl whined again, flipping her long, honey-colored hair.

"Are you sure, Darcy? It sounds perfect for you and better than any of these," he said, gesturing toward the wands in the case.

"I want this one!" The girl stomped her foot.

"All right, but I wish to be informed when the other wand arrives." It wasn't a question.

"Very well, Mr. Davidson. Please wait while I box this for you," the shopkeeper squeaked again and disappeared before Seven could catch a glimpse of him.

"Well, Darcy, I think that is the last item on your list," the man said. He turned to look out the window and noticed Seven and Miss Mcfee standing by the door.

"Phoebe Mcfee, how nice to see you," he said, sounding as though he didn't think it was nice at all. "I didn't hear you come in."

"Good morning, Mr. Davidson," Mcfee answered politely, though not friendly.

"My Darcy will be starting at Wyndamir this year. Darcy, this is Miss Mcfee. She works at the school, but I don't know what she does," Mr. Davidson said in a condescending tone.

Darcy looked at Mcfee but remained silent. Then her gaze fell onto Seven. Her unblinking stare made Seven feel uncomfortable.

"Due to our full traveling schedule," the man droned on, "this was our only opportunity to get Darcy's supplies. I could have sent a servant to do it, of course, but it is the first time, and I wanted everything to be perfect. However, I am beginning to think that we should have purchased our wand elsewhere. The selection here seems to be limited and substandard."

Seven looked around the shop. There had to be hundreds, if not thousands, of wands.

"And who is this? I wasn't aware you had a daughter, and you know how I pride myself in knowing, well, not quite everything, I suppose," he said with an arrogant smile. "But close."

"She is not my daughter, Mr. Davidson," Mcfee replied politely. Seven noticed Mcfee took a small step to place herself in front of Seven as though hiding her.

"Niece? Cousin?" he probed, never taking his gaze from Seven. Something was going on here, but Seven didn't know what.

"Neither," Mcfee answered, refusing explanation. Though her tone was polite, Seven could feel the tension growing.

"Do I know your parents, young lady? You look familiar," he pressed, looking around Mcfee. However, Seven was saved from answering as the shopkeeper returned.

"Here you are, sir," Swathmore squeaked. "I've specially wrapped it for you."

Mr. Davidson snatched the package from the shopkeeper's trembling hand. "Come along, Darcy," he said as he glared at Mcfee. To her credit, Mcfee didn't shrink from the towering man. Instead, she watched him until the door closed behind him.

"Well, now, Mr. Swathmore, we believe you have a more than adequate selection of wands. Would you mind helping Miss Preston?" Mcfee said, turning to the shopkeeper, her tone losing its earlier coolness.

Seven finally got a good look at the shopkeeper. He was several inches shorter than she was. His thinning grey hair had a bluish tint and framed a wrinkled, pale face with watery yellow eyes that still lingered on the door as he nervously wrung his hands.

"Mr. Swathmore?" Miss Mcfee repeated more loudly as she put her hand on his. He jumped and looked at them as though just realizing their presence.

"Can I help you?" he squeaked. Then a look of relieved recognition crossed his face. "Ah, Miss Phoebe Mcfee, how nice to see you again. Surely you are not here for a wand? I am guessing it has been quite a while since you have needed one," he said with a strained laugh.

"True, but Miss Preston here does," she responded, gesturing toward Seven.

"Ah, of course. New student?"

"Yes," Mcfee said.

"Well, what kind of wand are you looking for, my dear?" Swathmore asked Seven.

"Uh, well, I don't, uh, um," Seven stammered. She didn't even know there were wands until about fifteen minutes ago, let alone different kinds. Immediately her stomach crawled into her throat.

"Oh, just a basic one. Nothing fancy," Mcfee said, rescuing a very thankful Seven.

Visibly relieved to have a more gracious customer, Swathmore pointed to wands around the store as he explained all the features each had to offer. Strength. Flexibility. Casting distance.

"Why don't you gather a few for Miss Preston to try out?" Mcfee suggested.

At once, he flew around his shop, gathering different wands chattering on about each one. His voice no longer squeaked, and he was no longer wringing his hands.

Though she was utterly lost, Seven nodded dumbly at all he was saying. When he had no less than twenty placed before her, Swathmore looked at her expectantly.

"So, which one do you like, dear?" he asked.

Seven looked at the collection of wands. Though all were wooden, they were different colors and lengths. Some were brown, while others were tinted red, purple, and gold. Some had markings on them, while others were plain. Mcfee told her the magic didn't come from the wand, so it didn't matter which one, right? She just wanted this uncomfortable moment to end.

"This one." Seven pointed to the first wand on the counter.

"Are you sure, dear? I have never seen someone pick out their first wand so quickly or without even picking it up. Maybe you should give them a flick or two," Swathmore suggested.

"Mr. Swathmore," Mcfee interjected, "I hear you have a Nigerian Nergul. I would love to see it while Seven makes her selection. She turned to Seven, "We will be back shortly. Take your time. Don't be afraid to pick them up and give them a good swish." Then, she put a comforting hand on Seven's shoulder. "You only get to buy the first wand once. Try to enjoy it," Mcfee whispered before she and Swathmore disappeared into a side room.

Feeling lost, intimidated, and completely out of place,

Seven looked at the wands. Enjoy it? Not possible. She was terrified. She wished her mom was here.

Reluctantly, Seven poked the first wand and jumped back. She expected an electric shock or lights to shoot from the end or an alarm to sound, saying, 'Intruder Alert!' However, nothing happened. Mustering all of her courage, she picked up the wand with a trembling hand. It felt heavy, and the large handle was difficult to hold. She was glad Mr. Swathmore encouraged her to examine them a little more closely.

The second wand was dark green. The handle felt warm and fit perfectly in her hand. She gave it a less than enthusiastic flick and was quite relieved when nothing shot from the end. Unfortunately, the wand felt a little too flexible and reminded her of an overcooked noodle.

Seven picked up more wands, and though some were more comfortable than others, none felt right. She was beginning to think that even the wands figured she shouldn't be there. Finally, she picked up the second to last one. Though the wand was highly polished, it was the plainest one in the group. It had no markings or fancy gems or emerald scarab shells. It was light brown, made from oak, and the handle a shade darker than the tip. She flicked it. Not too stiff, not too flimsy. Perfect. This was the one.

"Miss Mcfee? Mr. Swathmore? I found one." No answer. Seven repeated herself a little louder. No answer. She took a few steps toward the side room and heard hushed voices. As she peeked through the curtain, she saw Mr. Swathmore sitting in a high-backed chair, wringing his hands again. He stared at the floor while Mcfee, her back to Seven, gestured energetically.

"They are getting closer. You know what will happen if they get it. They will give it to him. That cannot happen, Swathmore. You need to fulfill your oath and trust me," Seven overheard Mcfee say.

"I know I promised, but I never thought I would actually have to fulfill it," Swathmore squeaked.

"Well, you do. The signed scroll, please." Mcfee held out

her hand. Swathmore handed Mcfee a yellow scroll tied with a green ribbon and a broken green wax seal without looking up. She untied the scroll, examined it, nodded in approval, and retied the ribbon before dropping it into her bag. Then, she handed him a purple bag with a golden string, cinching it closed. Were those the scrolls and bags her mom put in the disappearing box? What was Mcfee doing with them?

Sensing the conversation had ended, Seven soundlessly returned to the counter as though she had just selected her wand.

"You found one?" Mcfee asked.

Seven nodded, holding out her selection.

"Great. Mr. Swathmore will box it up after he puts his Nergul in its cage."

As if on cue, Swathmore appeared.

"Did you have any luck, then?" he squeaked.

Seven nodded and handed him the wand.

"I will box it up, and you can be on your way."

It didn't take long before Mr. Swathmore held out the package. A little color had returned to his face, but his voice was still squeaky.

"Here you are, Miss Preston. Good luck and study hard."

"Thank you," Seven replied.

Out on the sidewalk, Mcfee looked around and examined a list she kept in her pocket.

"Let's see. Next, you need potion materials."

"What is a Nergul?" Seven asked.

"Hmm?"

"A Nergul? You did see Mr. Swathmore's Nergul, right?" Seven pressed.

"Oh, yes, I did. It's an animal that looks like a giant puffball. It not very exciting. We better be off now. Lots to do," Mcfee said, obviously changing the subject.

Mcfee is up to something, Seven thought.

They walked the cobblestone street, passing store after store. Seven noticed a hair and nail salon. In big block letters, the shop window read Wicked Wanda's World-Famous Hair and Nails. Under it in smaller print read, *If your friends aren't amazed, get new ones*. They passed Leaf Tarkem's again and a few pubs and restaurants. When they passed a jewelry store, Seven paused to look at some of the necklaces in the window. The sign next to them read *Protection Amulets*.

"Protection amulets?" Seven asked in amazement. "What do they protect you from?"

"Nothing."

"So, they don't work?"

"I'm sure they protect the jeweler from going out of business but not against spells or enchantments. Supposedly only one amulet did, and it isn't in that glass case," Mcfee said.

"Which one?" Seven asked.

"Oh, it is more of a legend, you know. Most wielders don't even believe it exists."

"Do you believe it exists?" Seven asked.

"Seven, I really don't want to talk about it. It's rubbish."

"Tell me, please. I haven't heard any stories from," she leaned in closer and whispered, "this world."

"Oh, all right. Supposedly it would protect the wearer from any type of magic. Spells. Curses. Potions. But no matter how many wielders looked for it, and trust me, it was a load of them, not one ever found the Blaize Amulet."

"The Blaize Amulet," Seven repeated reverently. "You don't believe it exists?"

After a long pause, Mcfee shook her head, but her eyes didn't quite meet Seven's.

"Well, it doesn't matter. Even if it were real, I wouldn't give up my locket for the most powerful protection amulet in the world," Seven said, turning back to the display. "My mom gave it to me for my thirteenth birthday. She said it was really from my dad."

"Well, let's see this special locket," Mcfee said.

Seven pulled the locket out of her shirt and opened it.

"See, it even has a picture of my dad inside."

Mcfee scrutinized the locket.

"It's the only picture I have of my dad, so Mom made me promise never to take it off," Seven explained.

"I bet she did," Mcfee mumbled and then added, "Very nice. Better keep that tucked away. I am sure it is very special to you." Mcfee sounded annoyed, almost angry. Without another word, she stomped away, muttering to herself. Confused by this reaction, Seven struggled to keep up with a fast-moving Mcfee. She was glad when they stopped in front of a tidy shop called *Pepper's Potion Parts and Pieces.*

"Here we are. Pepper usually has fair prices, and she's a former Wyndamir student."

Seven walked into the store and inhaled deeply. The air swirled with lavender, mint, and a spicy scent Seven couldn't identify. This shop was busier than Swathmore's had been. One woman was carefully examining bags of neon green seeds muttering to herself.

"New students only need the starter pack," Mcfee announced to Seven. "That's a standard set of herbs and other ingredients you'll use during your first few years. The school provides cauldrons, stirring sticks, and vials, so you won't need those."

"May I help you?" asked a woman in a sing-song voice from behind them. Her sudden appearance made Seven jump. The shopkeeper was a thin woman with square-shaped glasses and a straight, pointy nose. Her bright orange hair was sticking out in all directions, as though she hadn't combed it in a few days. She wore an apron that read *Kiss the Potion Maker*. "Oh, Miss Mcfee, What a nice surprise!"

"Pepper, how are you?" The two women embraced.

"Wonderful. Just wonderful," Pepper sang. "I just received the last ingredients for a new potion I am developing to make hair self-styling. Wanda really will be wicked if I get it to work," she said as she ran her fingers through her hair, getting them stuck twice. "Of course, the potion will take another week to make, but you know how I love creating new potions."

The woman twirled in a circle.

"Oh, yes, I do. That corner in the library still has a faint odor of rotten fruit," Mcfee noted.

Pepper waved the comment away like an annoying fly.

"I am here with a new student," Mcfee continued gesturing toward Seven, "and we are looking for the starter pack. I thought they were by the bottles of brownie spittle."

"Oh yes, I had to move them," Pepper explained very dramatically. "Whenever a customer would remove the cork, the bottle would spew the spittle on them. Made them all slimy. Dreadful. Anyway, they are over by the bottles of newt nails now. How many would you like?" she asked Seven.

"One?" Seven answered.

"I suggest at least two for new students. We all tend to get a little overanxious our first year and add a little too much," Pepper stressed with a pointed finger. "Now, will that be it? Can I interest you in a new cauldron? Mine are so much better than those rusty pots the school provides."

"Just the starter pack, Pepper," Mcfee said firmly.

"Very well," Pepper huffed and headed toward the checkout counter.

"And I believe you have some paperwork for me?" Mcfee said.

Pepper stopped in her tracks. She didn't turn around but nodded, causing her bushy hair to bounce.

"Seven, why don't you wait for us outside? There is a nice eatery across the street. Be a dear and get us a table for lunch?" Mcfee gently shoved Seven toward the door and then followed Pepper to the register.

Seven pretended to leave the store, but she ducked behind a rack of various colored vials containing wiggly things just before reaching the door. She watched Pepper wrap the herbs packs and put them into a bag, but she slipped a scroll to the older woman when she handed the bag to Mcfee. In return, Mcfee inconspicuously gave Pepper a purple velvet bag.

"Thank you, Pepper. Come see us at Wyndamir," Mcfee

said a little too loudly as she headed toward the exit. However, she stopped when she saw Seven still in the store. "I thought I told you to wait outside," she accused.

"I was on my way, but have you ever seen these?" Seven held up the bottle of the wrigglers. "They go crazy when you put them directly in the light." She made a show of moving them from their shadowy corner into the sunlight. "See?" she asked innocently.

Mcfee's accusing expression softened as she replaced the vial and said, "I forget that all this is new to you. Let's go."

Seven followed, but a hundred questions swirled in her brain. *Were* those the same scrolls that her mom had given to Mrs. Bigglesby? What was written on them? Why did Swathmore and Pepper have one, and why did they give them to Mcfee? Did her mom know that Mcfee was collecting the scrolls? Seven had to find out.

The eatery was called Stella Sue's Soup and Sandwich Shop. Stella herself came out, handed them menus, and recited the daily special. Seven was relieved that the food sounded normal and decided on potato soup with a grilled cheese sandwich. Mcfee ordered a chicken club with a side of cottage cheese.

When they had finished, Mcfee ordered dessert and coffee. After Stella Sue placed Seven's sugar cookie cake and Mcfee's coffee on the table, she went to clean the table beside them. Seven watched in amazement as the dishes placed themselves in the tub while Stella Sue refilled the salt and pepper shakers with a lazy wave of her hand.

"Seven, I have some personal errands to run. You stay and finish your dessert. I will be back in a few minutes." Before Seven could protest, Mcfee grabbed her enormous purse and disappeared around the corner.

As she nibbled her cake, Seven thought about her day. What was Mcfee up to? Did Seven's mom know about it? Why did Mcfee seem to be upset about Seven's locket? She wished she could be sure that her mom's best friend was still her mom's best friend.

"Crickleberry beans," Mcfee said as she plopped back in her seat, interrupting Seven's thoughts. "Your mom loves this flavor, and you cannot get it anywhere but The Brew House. I thought I would pick some up while we were here." When Mcfee opened her bag to drop in the coffee package, Seven noticed the pile of scrolls had grown from just two. However, she couldn't tell how many because Mcfee shut it quickly.

"Are you finished?" Mcfee asked.

Seven nodded.

"Well, we best be off. We have a few more things to buy, and we cannot be late getting back," Mcfee said.

"What more do I need?" Seven asked.

"Uniforms, school books, writing supplies," Mcfee ticked off on her fingers. The list made Seven tired.

Before the day was out, Seven was sure they had visited nearly every store in Wyndamir Landing. They bought books, writing supplies, and her school uniform, including navy blue pants, white shirts, and robes. Seven wanted the blue robes, but Mcfee explained that the brown robes were for freshmen at Wyndamir. Seven noticed the matching pointy hats and was relieved when Mcfee said they weren't required anymore.

"They fell off at the most inconvenient times like during spell casting or into cauldrons while potions were brewing or, even worse, at breakfast. Soggy hats are not my idea of a great way to start the day," Mcfee explained.

After the last stop, they headed for the alley entrance. Seven was exhausted. When Mcfee cast a hovering charm making the overflowing bags weightless, Seven gratefully guided them down the dirty alley, through the creaky door, and down the rickety stairs. Despite all of the strange, secretive happenings of this day, Seven felt excited. She was going to study magic, and that thought made her smile.

Chapter Five

On the Way to Wyndamir

The rest of the summer passed in a whirlwind for Seven. She spent much time looking through her books and supplies. A few times, she had picked up her wand and tried a few spells from Spellcasting Basics: Level 1, but the only thing she managed to do was fling her wand across the room.

On several occasions, Seven tried to talk to her mom about Mcfee and the things she saw in Wyndamir Landing. However, it seemed as though every time she started, Mcfee would pop up suddenly and whisk her mom away for a private conversation. Seven was leaving in the morning. Tonight was her last chance.

Her mom seemed to be in a good mood. She had just given Seven a gift, a Bottomless Boulder Bag. It was a suitcase whose hard exterior protected all of her belongings. Seven found that it wasn't actually bottomless but was spelled to expand to hold all of her belongings while never appearing any bigger nor growing too heavy to carry.

"Here is the backpack version. It is softer and smaller but will still protect your school books and papers from rain or snow or even the occasional misfired spell."

"Thanks, mom," Seven said and then pressed on. "Can I tell you something?"

"Certainly," her mom said as she put more socks into Seven's suitcase.

"Please let me finish before you interrupt me, okay?"

"Okay," her mom said as she moved on to packing Seven's books.

So, Seven took a deep breath and spilled everything. How, on their shopping trip, Mcfee pulled shopkeepers aside all day, how Swathmore didn't actually have a Nergul, and how he and others, including Pepper, seemed to give Mcfee scrolls unwillingly. She told her about the purple bags Mcfee had, which looked just like the ones Miranda put in the box at Bigglesby's.

"By the end of the day, her bag was full of those scrolls. I think she was forcing those shopkeepers to do something against their wills." Seven took a breath and waited anxiously for her mom's reaction.

Miranda placed another book in Seven's backpack. Without looking up, she asked, "Anything else?"

"No, that's pretty much it."

"Let me see if I understand. First, you spied on Mrs. Bigglesby and me when we were attending to a private matter. Then you eavesdropped on a personal conversation between Mcfee and Swathmore. You did not leave Pepper's store when asked to, you looked through Phoebe's bag, and now you are accusing her of being up to something?"

Seven opened her mouth to argue, but her mom held up her hand.

"It's my turn to be uninterrupted. Despite what you may *think* you saw or heard, you are wrong. I trust Phoebe Mcfee with my life. I don't want to hear another word about it. Do you understand me?"

"But, Mom, you didn't ..."

"Not another word," Miranda growled. "Seven, this is your last night here. Let's not argue. Finish up here. Supper will be ready shortly." Miranda spun on her heels and left.

Supper was an awkward affair. Miranda was still visibly upset, and Seven wasn't very hungry. After being excused, Seven went up to bed. It seemed like it took hours before Seven finally fell asleep, and when she did, it was restless and filled with nightmares. She dreamed that she was in front of a class, and the teacher was yelling at her for not performing a spell correctly. She looked around the room and saw her mom and Mcfee shake their heads in obvious disappointment and walk out the door. She ran after them but could barely move. The teacher kept yelling at her.

Seven snapped awake. She sat up and looked around dazedly. The sun was just coming up. It was just a dream. Then, she heard it. Actual yelling. Not dream yelling. It was coming from outside. Slowly she crept over to her window and looked down at the yard. There she saw Mcfee and her mom. Talking. No, not talking. Arguing.

Determined to hear what they were arguing about, Seven very carefully opened her window just a little. Then she turned, so her ear was facing the screen to hear better.

"Miranda, please see reason. This is a bad idea. Use this one. Make something up, but get it back. It is too dangerous for reasons I should not have to explain to you."

"You don't have to explain. It was my task, not yours. I have decided. This is the best way," Miranda said.

"Let me guard it. I will keep it safe. I know the risks. Besides, she will have enough to deal with, don't you think?"

"You don't need to guard it. *It* will do the guarding. It stays where it is. I am not taking it back," her mother said.

"If you don't, I will," Mcfee threatened.

"No, if I don't, you can *try*, but we both know you will fail. Now, I am done having this conversation for the millionth time. I am grateful for all that you have done, but this matter is not up for discussion." Miranda stomped away. Seven looked back toward Mcfee, who had collapsed onto a bench, her face very red. She did not look happy, but Seven was. Though she didn't understand what they were talking about, it was apparent Mcfee wanted something, and Miranda wouldn't give it to her. Maybe her mom didn't trust Mcfee as much as she said she did.

Seven heard the kitchen door slam shut and the sounds of coffee being made. It was nearly time to get up anyway, so Seven walked into the bathroom. She brushed her hair into a ponytail, washed her face, put on her new school uniform, including brown robes, and headed downstairs.

"Good morning," her mom sang cheerfully from behind a cup of coffee with no sign of the recent argument. "We'll be leaving soon. Try to eat something."

Seven tried to eat, but she suddenly felt very nervous. Her mouth was so dry the bit of toast she chewed was like eating sandpaper. She tried some orange juice, but it turned sour as soon as it hit her stomach. Finally, she gave up and took her dishes to the sink. She heard the door open and looked over her shoulder to see a still red-faced Mcfee walk in the kitchen.

"We should go," Mcfee clipped. "We don't want to miss our gate time."

Seven followed the two women from the kitchen, grabbed her bags, which were at the bottom of the steps, and was a little surprised they weren't heading into the woods again.

"This time, you will use a public gate," her mom explained as she gestured toward the car.

After a short drive, Miranda pulled over along the side of an abandoned country road. Cornfields surrounded them. No houses. No buildings. No people. Just corn.

"Are we lost?" Seven asked.

"No, the gate is in the middle of this field," her mom explained as she pulled Seven's bags out of the car. When she placed them at Seven's feet, she put her arms on Seven's shoulders and looked directly into her eyes.

"I know this is scary for both of us, but I know you are going to be great. You are going to have so many friends and learn so much. You won't have time to be nervous or miss me."

"I will miss you a little," Seven said softly, willing herself not to cry.

"We best hurry," Mcfee said in a very business-like tone before whirling around and heading into the cornfield. Seven hugged her mom goodbye, took a deep breath, and dutifully followed Mcfee into the cornfield.

The field, as it turned out, was more of a maze. The path twisted and turned, dead-ended, and looped around. Finally, they reached the center. There, barely standing, was a tiny, dilapidated building. The red paint was chipped and faded. The door dangled on the hinges so that it didn't close properly, and the one dusty window Seven saw was broken. She peeked through it and saw cobwebs and dust at least two inches thick. Two mice scampered across the floor as a snake slithered after them.

"Uh, this is the gate?" Seven asked.

"Yes," Mcfee said distractedly as she dug in her cloak's pockets.

"Are you sure it won't fall on top of us?"

"Things aren't always what they seem, Seven. Trust me."

Sure, Seven thought sarcastically.

Somehow, the building's door did not fall off when Mcfee opened it. When Seven walked into the room, the sight left her speechless.

It was spotless, not a hint of dust or cobwebs. No mice. No snake. Nothing. Several dimly lit lanterns hovered in midair. As though sensing their arrival, the lanterns grew brighter and illuminated a solidly built red room in which at least ten more people and their luggage could fit comfortably. On the far side of the room, there were two sets of doors.

"Where is the door we came through?" Seven asked as she looked behind them.

"It disappears to let other wielders know it is occupied. Once we are through, it will reappear," Mcfee said as she continued to dig in her bag. "Here they are," she said triumphantly and pulled two pieces of paper out. One was a small brown ticket, and the other was a green piece of paper tied with a silver string.

"What are those?" Seven asked.

"Gate passes," Mcfee explained as she headed for the doors. She chose the one on the right, turned the knob, and opened it. With a final breath, Seven followed Mcfee through the gate and into her new life.

The room they entered was pitch black and smelled like rotten eggs.

"Not very welcoming," Seven observed.

"No, it isn't," Mcfee agreed. "This is the basement of the Gate House. This is where all the gates from non-magical countries open. Some wielders would like to see this part sealed permanently."

"Why?" Seven asked.

"Not everyone thinks Crossers should be allowed to study magic," Mcfee explained.

"Crossers?" Seven asked.

"Those who come here from non-magical places," Mcfee explained.

"You mean like me?" Seven gulped.

"Unfortunately, yes. It is better than it used to be, but there are still some who don't want Crossers here. I would suggest you keep your Crosser status a secret for as long as possible," Mcfee cautioned.

Seven swallowed the lump in her throat and fought the urge to turn and run.

"Where is that stupid door?" Mcfee said. "*Globus Lux!*" she shouted, and a ball of light appeared, illuminating the room and the lost door. "Ah, here we are," Mcfee said, grasping the handle. "*Extinguinum*," she said, and the ball of light shrank until it disappeared with a soft pop.

Seven followed the older woman into a musty hallway. Several doors lined the opposite wall. Seven assumed they were gates to other places. At the end of the hall was a rickety staircase like the one in Wydamir Landing. Those wielders Mcfee talked about earlier probably hoped the staircase would crumble, and the Crosses would have an unfortunate accident.

When she and Mcfee reached the top, they walked through yet another door. The cavernous room they entered was very much different than the one they just left. It had white marble floors and walls, which made everything seem bright and cheery. And it wasn't empty. It was packed with wielders. Nearly all of them were carrying bags and bustling toward the front of the building where Seven saw a sign that read, *Thank you for using the Bridgeway Gate House.*

"It's always this busy when school starts," Mcfee said. Suddenly, a deep voice came from behind them.

"Gate pass?" It was phrased as a question but felt more like an order.

Seven turned to see a very tall, beefy man looming over them. His black eyes fixed on her with an unblinking stare. Unconsciously, she took a step back.

"Right here," Mcfee said as she handed him the green piece of paper. The man took it, but his gaze lingered on Seven before he examined the paper.

"And you?" he asked, pointing to Mcfee.

"I am the Dean of Students at Wyndamir Academy for the Magical Arts," Mcfee said as she puffed her chest out. "I don't need one."

"Then you have a badge?" the man said, not sounding impressed at all.

"Yes," Mcfee said. She pulled on the lanyard that she had tucked under her robes and removed the golden badge that she had clipped to it.

"I need to verify this." He murmured something, and a jet of red flame shot from his fingers and wrapped around the card. Seven expected the card to disintegrate into ashes. However, the flame only lasted a few seconds before it winked out, leaving the badge unmarked.

"Verified," he said, sounding very disappointed. "Proceed." He pointed toward the large archway on the far side of the room.

"Gate Security. They take their jobs very seriously," Mcfee whispered as they exited the Gate House onto an equally crowded street. People dressed in robes were everywhere. Students and their families looked into shop windows or perusing elaborate carts where vendors were selling their products.

"The bus station is this way," Mcfee said, pulling Seven's sleeve. Suddenly, something flew past Seven's ear.

"What the . . ?" she said, swatting at it.

"Postal pixie. Probably express. And given how low and close it flew, one in training," Mcfee explained.

"Postal pixie?" Seven asked in wonderment.

"That's how we send our mail here. They are quite small but strong and fast. There is the post office over there." Mcfee pointed across the street.

Seven saw the sign, Bridgeway Postal Pixie Office. On the roof were various sized tubes. Creatures that resembled over-sized butterflies flew in and out of them carrying packages and envelopes.

"Madam Sure's All-In-One Cure-All! Colds, boils, jinxes, and hexes - all gone with one swallow! Get it while it lasts!" yelled a peddler who was waving around a small yellow vial. Judging from the lack of people gathered around his cart, Seven figured his supply would last a while.

Mcfee pulled Seven across the street, where it was a little less crowded. Soon they reached the bus station. When she first heard they would travel by bus, Seven was a little surprised and disappointed. She expected flying brooms or magical portals, but no such luck. The bus station stood in front of them. It was a small stone building with sidewalks running every which way to different parking areas for the busses. Most of the parking areas were empty, but over at the far end was a group of bright golden buses lined up end to end. The words *Wyndamir Academy for the Magical Arts* were written in large looping letters on the sides of the buses. They wriggled and twisted into other words. Expressions like "Welcome Students" and "Another Wonderful Year Ahead" formed and reformed. A list of names followed each phrase. Seven was surprised when her name flashed on the side of one of them.

Just then, a familiar whiny voice assaulted her ears.

"My dad just bought it for me. Isn't it beautiful?" Seven

looked ahead, and sure enough, there was the girl from Swathmore's Wand Shop. Even from a distance, her voice grated on Seven like nails on a chalkboard. What was her name? Danielle? Dicey? Darby?

"My mom gave me this pin before I left. She said it's a family heirloom," said another girl Seven couldn't see.

"Heirloom is another word for 'old.' It's what parents say when they cannot afford to buy a new one," Whiny Girl said.

"You will be riding bus number one since this is your first year," Mcfee explained, drawing Seven's attention away from Whiny Girl's cruel comment. Mcfee handed the brown ticket to Seven. "All right, then, I will see you at school."

"You aren't riding the bus?"

"Busses are for students. Besides, I have some personal errands to do before heading to Wyndamir. Now, off you go and remember, Seven, the students here are more like you than you think. Just be yourself." Mcfee gave her an awkward smile and disappeared into the crowd.

Mustering all the courage she had, Seven walked toward buses. She tried not to notice mothers and fathers hugging their children and wishing them luck. A feeling of loneliness washed over Seven, nearly drowning her. Why couldn't her own mother see her off? Immediately, her hand went to the locket tucked safely under her robes. Right now, it offered her little comfort.

Seven's wallowing was interrupted by a commotion. Passing right in front of her, she saw a truck-sized suitcase hit a short, sandy-haired boy sending him sprawling to the sidewalk. The bag he carried burst open, and clothes, books, and potion bottles crashed to the ground.

"Look what you did! You spilled goo all over my new cloak!" shrieked Whiny Girl. "Oh, and it stinks! It's horrible!" She frantically tried to wipe it off. What *was* her name? Darcy. That was her name. Darcy Davidson.

"Do you know how much this cost?" Darcy spat.

"I'm s-s-sorry," the boy stammered as he gingerly held his right wrist.

"You should be! You are going to pay for this, you clumsy freak!"

"It was your fault," said a voice behind Seven. She turned to see a girl whose hazel eyes showed no fear of Darcy. She marched right past Seven and up to Darcy. "The way I saw it, you were the one who knocked into him."

"Then he needs to get his clumsy butt out of my way, and so should you, Collins," Darcy growled, her words low and threatening.

"You may scare a lot of people, Darcy, but not me," the girl named Collins said, her voice strong.

"That can be easily fixed." Darcy took a step back, opened her robe, and pulled out her wand. Several students took a few steps back.

"Go ahead, Davidson," Collins said without missing a beat. "You'll get thrown out of Wyndamir before you even start. Not even your daddy's money could buy you a spot."

This made Darcy pause. Then, she lowered her wand and put it away before any of the adults standing by saw.

"This isn't over, Collins. You better watch your back. A year is a long time for payback." Darcy turned to leave, and her cold eyes fixed on Seven. "What are you...hey, don't I know you?" she asked, her tone softening somewhat.

"Sort of," Seven said shyly. "I think we briefly met in the wand shop this summer."

"Oh yeah. You were with that ghastly Mcfee. My father found you very interesting. He's been talking about you all summer. Not by name, of course, because Mcfee was too rude to introduce you. I'm Darcy Davidson."

"Oh, uh, I'm Seven Preston."

"Seven? Your name is Seven? Do your parents not like you or something?" Darcy said, laughing.

Seven could feel her face flush.

"Well, I have to get to my seat and see if I can do something about this disgusting mess," Darcy said, gesturing to her robles. "I'll save you a seat." Then, without waiting for Seven to answer, she marched onto the bus.

"She is a real piece of work. I mean, she insults your name and then expects you to sit with her." Seven turned to see the girl who just bravely stood up to Darcy. "I am not looking forward to a year with her around."

Seven didn't know what to say, so she just nodded.

"My name is Cully Collins, by the way."

"Seven Preston," Seven said.

"You are a freshman, too," she said, pointing to Seven's brown robes. "Do you want to sit together on the bus? I mean unless you are sitting with Darcy?"

Seven didn't even have to think.

"I think I will sit with you," she said.

The two girls deposited their bags on the pile, handed their tickets to the driver, and hopped on board.

Seven was surprised to see how big the inside of the bus was. The ceiling was so high that Seven figured she could stand on her tiptoes on a seat with Cully standing on her shoulders, and they still wouldn't be able to reach the top. There were about forty rows of seats with three seats on each side. The bus didn't look that large from the outside.

Seven followed Cully down the aisle. They passed the boy Darcy had knocked over, sitting alone looking out the window. He was still holding his wrist, and his face was still flushed red. As they walked on, Seven noticed that many students had turned some of the seats around to form groups of six with three seats facing forward and three facing backward.

"Cully?" asked a tentative voice to their right.

Seven watched as Cully hugged a plump girl with brown hair held in place by a sparkling headband.

"I didn't know you were going to Wyndamir!" Cully said. "It has been ages since I've seen you."

"I know."

The two girls chatted for a moment. Seven felt awkward staring at them, so she looked around the bus. Her gaze made it to the back where Darcy was sitting. She was still fussing over her cloak, apparently retelling the story of what happened. She paused when she noticed Seven. Darcy gestured to an open seat next to her and smiled. Seven froze. Something told her this was a crucial decision she was about to make, one that would affect the rest of her time at Wyndamir. She looked from Darcy to Cully and back to Darcy. Then, Seven shook her head and signaled she was going to sit with Cully. The look on Darcy's face was cold and full of hate. Seven knew that she had just made her first enemy in Midia.

"Let's sit here," Cully said as she turned two of the seats around to face the other girls. "This is Sophie Martin and Adria Anderson. I lived by Adria, and my older brother is in the same class at Wyndamir as Sophie's sister. We just had a run-in with Darcy Davidson," Cully said, recounting the story to the new girls.

"What I wouldn't have given to see that!" laughed Sophie. "Darcy and I live on the same street. She is a spoiled brat."

"You better be careful of her. You know who her parents are," warned Adria.

"I met her dad once," Seven said. "He wasn't the friendliest of people."

"You must have made an impression if he's been talking about you all summer like Darcy said," Cully noted. Seven just shrugged.

"I haven't met either one of them, but from what I have heard, unfriendly is putting it kindly," Adria said.

Just then, a crackly voice came over the speaker.

"The buses to Wyndamir Academy of the Magical Arts are now departing. Thank you." After a few bounces and jolts, the golden busses left the station.

"Does your sister like Wyndamir?" Adria asked Sophie.

"Mostly. She complains about the exams. This is her last year, as long as she can keep her mind on her work and not on Austin Greenwell," Sophie twisted her face into a dreamy smile and spoke in a high-pitched voice, "I miss Austin. I wonder what Austin is doing. I'll die if I don't get back there soon to see Austin." Then in her normal voice, she added, "It got rather old rather quickly."

Suddenly, two boys collapsed in the open seats next to Seven and Cully shaking with laughter. One's face was so red it reminded Seven of an overgrown strawberry.

"Samuel Walker!" Cully shouted. "What kind of trouble are you getting into now?"

"Oh, hey, Collins, how's it going?" the tall boy finally said, gasping for breath. "Oh, that was funny. Devlin Mulzer was his usual egotistical, obnoxious self when he saw Charlie and me chewing some gum. He asked for a piece, or rather demanded a piece, and of course, I told him no way. Well, he was too quick for me. He snatched it from my hand and shoved two pieces into his mouth before I could stop him."

The two boys erupted into laughter again.

"I don't get it. Why is that so funny?" Sophie asked.

"Because it was glue gum!" Samuel explained in between his fits of laughter.

"He'll be trying to get his lips apart all the way to Wyndamir!" Charlie said.

"Could you offer a piece to Darcy, too?" Cully asked. "By the way, this is Seven Preston."

"Sam Walker at your service," Sam said, bowing to Seven. "And this is Charlie Cooper."

"Hello," Charlie said.

"Is that Anna Watts?" Adria said, looking across the aisle and back several rows. "She went on vacation with her family this summer to see the Lost City of Garidon. I'll be back," she said, getting up.

"I want to hear, " Sophie said, trailing after.

Sam and Charlie moved into the empty seats. Sam leaned in close and gestured for the others to do the same.

"Hey, do you see that kid four rows up? The one with the curly brown hair, reading?" Sam asked. Cully and Seven leaned into the aisle and nodded. "He's a Crosser," Sam whispered.

"Really?" Cully asked.

"Yeah. Charlie and I were at the Gate House today, wasting time, and we *accidentally* wandered into the basement."

"Sam!" Cully said. "You aren't supposed to be down there!"

Basement. Gate House. Suddenly, Seven felt very nervous. Mcfee's warning came to her mind. *I would keep your Crosser status a secret for as long as possible.*

"It was just an honest mistake. We took a wrong turn. Right, Charlie?"

"Yep, wrong turn," Charlie said with a mischievous sparkle in his eye.

"Anyway, we saw him come through," Sam continued. "He was all alone. No parent. No Retriever. Nobody. Not too many Crossers anymore, eh?"

"My mom would like it to be none. She doesn't think Crossers should be taught. She says their families made a choice a long time ago when they left the magical world, and they shouldn't be allowed back in," Cully said.

At Cully's words, Seven felt sick. She swallowed hard and willed away the heat from her face. Maybe she should have sat next to Darcy.

"Well, I have to disagree with your mom. And so does my dad. It wasn't his fault his family chickened out," Sam said, pointing to the brown-haired boy. "Why should he miss out on being taught magic for something his great, great, great, and a few more greats, grandparents did? My dad says all magical people should learn at schools like Wyndamir. Otherwise, they may turn to the darker schools to learn it," Sam whispered the last part.

"I wonder if he is the only Crosser starting this year?" Charlie asked.

Seven tried to keep her expression blank though she wanted to throw up. She was grateful when Adria and Sophie returned.

"Hey, guys, look! Sophie said as she excitedly pointed out the window.

"It's Wyndamir Landing. Something big happened. Look at all the MSO's," Adria said excitedly.

Seven didn't know what MSO meant, but as she looked out the window, she saw a mass of people. Many of them wore shiny, crimson cloaks. They positioned themselves in front of the gathered crowd with their hands opened in front of them as though they were prepared to cast a spell. Off to one side were two men also dressed in crimson cloaks, but theirs had golden hoods. They were talking with someone whose bushy red hair bounced wildly as she spoke. Pepper.

"Whoa! Those are Guardians First Class," Sam said, pointing to the wielders talking to Pepper. "They are only called in on the big stuff."

Seven watched the crowd part. Two people dressed in white robes appeared flanking a thin, floating bed. On top, partially covered, was a tiny, still, form.

"That looks like it could be a child," Adria gasped.

"No, look, the hair is gray," Cully pointed out.

Just as a building blocked the view from the bus, Seven noticed a wielder backing away from the crowd. The wielder pulled the hood of a cloak low as though trying not to be recognized. It was only a glance, but Seven swore the face she saw belonged to Phoebe Mcfee.

Just then, a soft bell rang, and the driver's voice crackled again. "We will be arriving at Wyndamir Academy for the Magical Arts momentarily. Please return to your seats." At the realization that Seven was about to get the first glimpse of her new school, excitement replaced any thoughts about Wyndamir Landing and anyone she may or may have seen there.

Chapter Six

Doubts Awakened

The busses parked around a flagstone circle in front of a white, crescent-shaped stone building. It had windows as tall as Seven's house, some clear, some stained glass. Round marble columns and enormous stone statues guarded the porch. The words Wyndamir Academy for the Magical Arts were carved into the front of the building in large, block letters.

The sprawling lawn was perfectly manicured with colorful flowers and bushes sculpted into the shape of all kinds of animals, both real and mythical. Smaller buildings dotted the grounds. Some looked so old that Seven was sure a slight breeze would knock them over. One was glowing. Another looked as though it was fading in and out of existence.

As Seven and Cully disembarked from the bus, they were greeted by a bubbling fountain in the middle of the flagstone circle. Streams of water chased each other around the fountain. They gracefully twisted and curled around themselves like airborne worms. Soon, they all shot to the middle, where they collided in midair, changing into a variety of colors. Then, it all started over again.

"Welcome to your first year at Wyndamir Academy for the Magical Arts!" shouted a familiar voice. Seven looked up to see Mcfee standing on the white marble steps.

Maybe it wasn't her in Wyndamir Landing, Seven thought.

"Freshman, please gather quickly," Mcfee instructed as

students made their way to the steps of the building. "My name is Miss Mcfee, and I am the Dean of Students here at Wyndamir Academy. This is Miss Poxley," Mcfee explained, pointing to a tall, spindly woman who wore velvety green robes and a forced smile. "She is the matron of Terramin Tower, where all first-year students reside. Both of us are here to help you settle into life here at Wyndamir Academy.

"Your belongings will be taken to your assigned rooms in Terramin Tower. We will proceed to the dining room where you will meet Headmistress Bellatora and your teachers, receive your class schedules and room assignments, eat, and of course, be Awakened. Please follow me to Wyndamir Hall."

Be Awakened? Seven thought. What did that mean? She wanted to ask, but she feared it would reveal her Crosser status. Instead, she followed Cully.

As they passed through the enormous oak doors, they entered a vast foyer with a dome ceiling. Several large chandeliers hovered at various places around the room. Two grand staircases covered in crimson carpet led to upper floors. Display cases, framed articles, pictures, and large portraits of intimidating-looking men and women decorated the walls.

They continued walking straight through the foyer to the dining room. Round tables covered with brown, red, blue, and yellow colored table cloths sat around the room. Candles, cutlery, and cups lay on each. Off to the right and left were four serving lines. As soon as Seven walked through the door, tantalizing smells greeted her nose. She had not eaten anything substantial since the night before, and she was suddenly ravenous.

"You may choose any of the lines, but please sit only at any tables with brown table cloths. Our upperclassmen will be joining us momentarily, and they are a bit possessive of their tables. After you are seated, our student liaisons will mingle and introduce themselves. They are students entering their final year, so they know quite a bit about our school and are a wonderful source of tips and advice. Now, let's eat."

Mcfee and Miss Poxley each walked to a separate serving

line. After a slight hesitation, the students filtered into one of the four lines. Seven followed Cully to the first one. She couldn't believe all of the food. There was salad, fresh vegetables and fruits, roast, turkeys, hams, several kinds of potatoes, corn, loaves of bread, soups, and even seafood.

Seven grabbed her plate and reached for a serving spoon. She was quite surprised when she couldn't find one. How was she supposed to get the food? Then, she heard Cully.

"Salad, please."

Seven watched as a small mound of salad disappeared from the salad bowl and reappeared on Cully's plate. Magically served food. Brilliant! Seven imitated her new friend. Just as it did for Cully, the salad magically disappeared from the serving bowl and appeared on the plate. Trying to hide her astonishment, Seven continued down the line asking for different foods and intently watching as they appeared on her plate. When their plates were full, she and Cully joined Adria, Sophie, Sam, and Charlie at a table.

Seven noticed several matching glass pitchers filled with different colored liquids in the center of the table. Sophie explained.

"Strawberry juice, pomegranate punch, apple juice, tea, and water," she said, pointing to each one. Seven tried the strawberry juice.

"I wonder what happened at the Landing," Adria said as she buttered a roll.

Sam and Charlie just shrugged and continued to stuff their mouths.

"There were too many Guardians First Class for it to be something minor," Cully said. "It looked like an attack of some sort."

"An attack this close to the school," Adria said with a shudder. "We are safe, right?"

"We are perfectly safe," Sam said. "Bellatora has this place so well protected that the Shadow Raiders wouldn't dare try to come onto school grounds," Sam said.

"I hope. If they send us home, all I will hear from my sister is how her life is over if she can't see Austin every day," Sophie said as she faked a gag.

"Are there even Shadow Raiders anymore? Adria asked skeptically. "With their leader gone, a lot of wielders think maybe…"

"Oh, they are most definitely around," Sam insisted. "My dad says they are buying their time until their leader returns."

"Where do you, uh, um, where do you think he is?" Seven asked, trying to sound casual.

"That's the million-dollar question, isn't it?" Charlie said. "I heard he went underground because he lost his powers."

"My mom thinks he's dead," Sophie said.

"He's not dead. There have been sightings. Maybe," Sam lowered his voice and paused for dramatic effect before continuing, "maybe he is in Wyndamir Landing. That's what all the commotion was."

"None of those sightings were confirmed," Cully countered. "Besides, what would he be doing in the Landing?"

"Looking for a way to exact revenge on those who stole his powers," Sam said ominously.

"Knock it off, Sam. You are giving me the creeps," Adria said. "Besides, I have been waiting forever to come to Wyndamir. Best school, wands down."

"My dad had to convince my mom to let me come here. My mom thinks Bellatora is brilliant, but she disagrees with her about educating Crossers," Cully said.

At the mention of the words, Seven could feel her face flush. She nibbled on a piece of bread, trying not to look guilty.

"The Doyle School only educates Midian-born students. Even if you were born in one of the other magical countries, you couldn't get in," Cully went on.

"You could go there, but then after you graduate, changing a pin into a toothpick would be the only thing you could do. My dad works with several of their graduates, and he says they are dumber than a box of beetle eyes," Sam said.

As the debate on the merits of the Doyle school continued, Seven tried to distract herself from the feeling of dread caused by the mention of Crossers and Shadow Raiders. She noticed the tables covered by blue, red, and yellow cloths were filling up with returning students. Near the front of the room was a long table filled with teachers. Most of the staff looked friendly as they chatted amongst themselves, though a few looked as though they wanted to be anywhere else. Mcfee and Poxley seemed to be involved in an intense conversation judging from the glares they were shooting each other.

"I can't eat another bite," Sophie said, putting her chocolate cake covered fork down and drawing Seven's attention back to the table. On the other hand, the boys made their way back to the food line for seconds, thirds, and fourths.

"May I sit here?" asked a deep, velvety voice. An older boy with stylish blonde hair that framed a tanned, handsome face pulled an empty chair from a nearby table, turned it around backward, and plopped down between Sophie and Adria before anyone could answer. "My name is Nicholas Sanders. I am one of the student liaisons. I am a Level II Senior, which means all advanced courses for me," he said proudly. "I am also the face of WANN. Isn't it wonderful that you get to start every morning and end every evening with me?" He flashed everyone at the table with a brilliant smile. Undaunted by their lack of enthusiasm for him, Nicholas continued, "As you know, all freshman stay in Terramin Tower, well, I should say it is mostly freshman."

"Mostly?" Seven asked.

"The ones who were deemed Unplaceable the year before stay there, too. They never want to tell you that right off, but I think you deserve to know," Nicholas said righteously.

"Unplaceable?" Seven asked.

"After your first year, you are placed into one of the other three dormitories. Some students need another year before they are placed. I feel terrible for them. It is quite embarrassing being labeled Unplaceable. Some of them don't come back.

Anyway," he said, flashing his brilliant smile again, "it rarely happens."

The word echoed in Seven's head. Unplaceable. She could see the teachers now. They would probably all shake their heads as her name came up.

Big mistake letting that one in, one of them would surely say.

Her lack of magical talent is an embarrassment to Wyndamir and all of Midia, another would agree. Then they would stamp her placement papers in large, flashing red letters: UNPLACEABLE! Seven shuddered at the thought.

"The other dormitories are named Pontus Hall, Bortally Hall, and Vesterly Hall," Nicholas continued. "Vesterly is mine," he said proudly, noting his red robes. "Pontus is blue, and Bortally is yellow."

"About this Unplaceable business," Sam said, totally ignoring Nicholas's speech. "Anyone from last year?"

"No, and I would know since I am the senior reporter for WANN." There was that blinding smile again. "Wyndamir Academy News Network. That's what those are." He pointed to some cracked wooden boxes with grayish screens. "I come on several times a day to report the news. I will be on a little later."

"So, do you know what happened in Wyndamir Landing?" Cully asked.

"Not yet," he said and then leaned in conspiratorially, "but I am going down there later. I'll get to the bottom of what's going on."

Just then, Mcfee stood and walked up to an elevated podium. She struck a tiny gong that was so small that it would fit in the middle of Seven's palm. The sound it made, though, was anything but tiny. Its loud crash echoed around the hall and made Seven's bones shake. It didn't take long for the students to quiet.

"Freshman, I hope you all enjoyed your first of many meals here at Wyndamir. The rest of you, welcome back. Unfortunately, Headmistress Bellatora has been delayed. Older students, you already have your class schedules from the summer mailing. While we are waiting for the headmistress, Miss Poxley and I will pass out the schedules and room assignments for the first years."

"I wonder why she is late?" Nicholas mumbled to himself. "She has never missed the Welcome Dinner or an Awakening."

"I guess our ace reporter doesn't know everything that happens at Wyndamir," Cully whispered to Seven, who coughed to hide her laugh.

"I must prepare for the evening newscast," Nicholas said with a glance at his watch. "Remember, if there is something you need to know, be sure that I know it, or if I don't, which is highly unlikely, I can find out," Nicholas said, flashing them one last blinding smile.

"What a windbag," Sam said. Then he proceeded to flash them his not-so-blinding brilliant smile. "I must prepare for the evening newscast," he mimicked.

Miss Poxley returned with a tray full of brown envelopes stacked so high Seven was sure they would fall. Mcfee raised her hands, said something, and a blue light shot from her hand and swirled around the tray. The stack of envelopes rose lazily into the air, and then as if they were shocked into life, they zipped and zoomed around the room in all directions. Some bumped into each other as they changed paths midair, searching for the right students.

"Just great," mumbled a boy sitting at the table next to them. Seven turned to see the boy Darcy had nearly mauled earlier with her suitcase. His envelope landed in his unfinished bowl of soup.

Seven sat back as her envelope arrived and landed neatly in front of her. She unsealed it and pulled out a small card that revealed her class schedule and dorm room assignment. She was glad to see her roommates were Cully, Sophie, and Adria. As she studied her schedule, she discovered she and Cully were in all the same classes, and Charlie, Sam, Sophie, and Adria were in some of them. After another few minutes, the gong sounded again. Silence fell, and the students looked toward the teacher's table.

"Students, Headmistress Bellatora has arrived," Mcfee said with noticeable reverence in her tone.

A wielder dressed in brilliant blue robes with silver trim entered the stage from a side door to polite applause. Her long, rusty red hair, streaked with gray, was pulled into a braid that reached past her waist. She walked gracefully to the center of the stage, smiling all the while. She nodded at Poxley, who quickly returned to her seat where she sat so stiffly, it was as if someone had spilled a bottle of starch on her.

As Bellatora stood at the podium waiting for the applause to stop, Seven noticed a thin, slightly raised silvery scar that ran from the corner of the older woman's mouth toward the outer edge of her right eye. There, it turned and disappeared into her hairline. Her voice was soft and melodic when she spoke but carried a sense of authority that held everyone's attention.

"Welcome freshmen to Wyndamir Academy and to our returning students, a pleasure to see you all again. I apologize for missing this year's Welcome Dinner, but alas, I was summoned on important business. However, I am here now and will only bore you for a moment before we begin the Awakening.

"I have a few rules that first years need to know. Please be advised that leaving school grounds is strictly prohibited by any student unless accompanied by a Wyndamir teacher.

"As far as the school grounds, please consider this your home away from home. You are free to go anywhere except into another student's dormitory. The Whispering Woods is not off-limits during daytime hours. You must stay on the paths along the outer edge for your safety, keeping the school grounds in sight at all times and exit the Woods before dark.

"Also, students are not allowed to use magic on each other unless under the supervision of a Wyndamir teacher. You all look like a wonderful group of young wielders. I am sure we will not have any trouble."

"I am pretty sure 'wonderful' does not describe them," Cully whispered as she pointed at Darcy and friends.

"Now, it is time for the Awakening. This ceremony has been a cherished part of Wydnamir Academy since the school was founded. It is a time where new wielders like yourselves will call up the magical talents that have been gifted to them. When Miss Mcfee calls your name, you will join me in this small chamber," Bellatora instructed as she pointed to a room off to the right, "place your hands on the Awakening Stone, and exit over there. When all are finished, Miss Poxley will lead you to Terramin Tower. Miss Mcfee, if you please," Bellatora said before disappearing into the chamber.

Mcfee held up a thick book with a faded green cover and wrinkled, yellow pages. She must have said a spell because the book rose from her hands and opened. Its pages flipped frantically for a few seconds. When they stopped, the book settled back into Mcfee's hands, and she read the first name in a loud voice.

"Cody Simmons." A tall, lanky boy behind Sam gasped slightly. His eyes grew wide, but he walked up to the steps and disappeared into the chamber without hesitation. Within a few seconds, he reappeared at the second door, looking relieved.

"Emma Miller." A short, determined-looking girl marched up the stairs as though she did this every day.

"Stanley Nogginhollow." Seven watched as the boy whose schedule wound up in his soup ascended the stairs. He was trembling so badly that he missed the top step and sprawled to the floor. A few students snickered, but none louder than Darcy. Clumsily, he picked himself up and disappeared into the room.

"Darcy Davidson," Mcfee went on. Seven was glad to see that Darcy's face turned a few shades of green after her name was read.

"I hope she falls," Cully whispered. Unfortunately, Darcy didn't even stumble a little bit.

"Cully Collins."

"Good luck," Seven whispered.

Mcfee continued to read off the names in no particular order.

"Brigit Murdock."

"Adria Anderson."

"Jennifer Hollinder."

"Devlin Mulzer."

"Eric Marsden."

"Ignatius Everett."

Seven noticed Charlie elbow Sam. He mouthed the word *Crosser* as he nodded toward the boy Mcfee just called. She tried to move around them to catch a better look, but the boy had already disappeared into the chamber.

"Charlie Cooper."

"Sophie Martin."

"Samuel Walker."

Students took their turns, disappearing into the room and reappearing at the second door, visibly relieved. Finally, there were just two students left.

"Anna Watts."

The girl named Anna gave Seven a sympathetic look before ascending the stairs.

Finally, Mcfee called her name. She gathered her courage, climbed the stairs, and entered the chamber.

It was so dim that Seven could only barely make out Bellatora, who stood quietly in a corner. The only light came from a large, egg-shaped crystal that sat upon a cushion on top of a wooden pedestal. Inside the crystal, iridescent lights danced and twirled. It gave off a soft hum. Seven stared utterly entranced.

"It is quite a sight," Bellatora said softly.

"It is," Seven agreed, not taking her eyes from it.

"However, we can't keep the others waiting so . . ." Bellatora gestured for Seven to touch the stone.

Seven reached her trembling hands forward but stopped just before they reached the stone. Was it going to hurt? What if she broke it? What if alarms sounded because the stone figured out that she wasn't supposed to be there?

As though reading her thoughts, Bellatora encouraged her.

"Miss Preston, I assure you. You are meant to be here."

Still unsure, Seven forced her hands forward and laid them on the stone. She waited for a feeling of electricity to shoot through her. Heat. Cold. Tremors. Anything. Instead, she felt, well, she felt nothing. She squeezed harder and spread her fingers around the Awakening Stone, hoping for something. Nothing. Not even a spark of static electricity.

"Miss Preston," Bellatora said gently, "it is done. You may release the stone."

"But I didn't..."

"You did fine." Bellatora gently placed her hand on Seven's shoulder, and their eyes met. "You did just what you were supposed to do. And the stone did exactly what it was supposed to do. Now, please release the stone. The others are waiting."

Giving it one final, desperate squeeze, Seven reluctantly returned it to the cushion and left the chamber.

"What took you so long?" Cully asked as soon as Seven joined the rest of the students. "The Anna girl came out ages ago."

Seven just shrugged.

"Wasn't the stone beautiful? I could have stared at it for hours," Cully gushed.

"So, what did you feel?" Sophie asked in a hushed voice.

"Feel?" Seven asked.

"When you touched the stone, what did you feel? The second I touched it, I felt alive. Like energy was exploding inside," Sophie whispered. "I still feel jittery." She shook all over to emphasize her point.

"I didn't feel so much alive, but more as though I sank into a warm bath," Adria shared.

Seven looked at Cully, who nodded in agreement. Not

wanting to feel left out, she nodded, too.

"Now that the Awakening is over, we will dismiss to Terramin Tower where you will unpack," Poxley instructed. "Afterward, you should find your classrooms so that you will be on time in the morning. Classes will commence after breakfast tomorrow. Now, follow me." Poxley turned with a flourish and headed down a corridor.

The students followed her through corridors, arched doorways, and up several flights of stairs. Seven tried to memorize their path, but she was distracted by all of the other students' whispers. They were sharing their Awakening experiences. Some said they felt hot, some felt cold, some felt prickly, but it seemed that everyone felt something, everyone except her. Doubts about her decision to come to Midia, to Wyndamir, again exploded inside her brain.

Miss Poxley stopped in front of a large stone arch that protruded slightly from a stone wall. About halfway from the floor, Seven noticed an old rusted handle. It looked very out of place, given that there did not appear to be a door.

"This is the door to Terramin Tower," Miss Poxley announced. "As Headmistress Bellatora already stated, this will be the only dormitory you will be allowed to enter during your first year."

"Uh, that looks like a wall," said the lanky boy named Cody, who was first at the Awakening.

"That is precisely the point, Mr. Simmons," Poxley said somewhat sarcastically, shooting him a disgusted look. The doors to each dormitory will only allow the students of that dormitory to pass. Could I have a volunteer?"

No one raised their hand. Suddenly, Stanley Nogginhollow stepped, or rather nearly fell, forward. Darcy and a dark-haired boy beside her must have pushed him.

"What a jerk," Cully whispered. "She's too chicken to volunteer, so she does that. Typical."

Poxley looked down at the fallen boy.

"Well, are you going to get up, Mr. Nogginhollow? We

don't have all night."

"S-s-s-sorry," Stanley stammered as he rose from the floor, keeping his eyes low.

"Now, would you please walk through the stone archway?"

Stanley stared at the stone wall. His face was glowing brighter than the torches. He looked uncertainly at Poxley, who looked like she had swallowed something sour.

"Go on," she said impatiently. Seemingly not wanting to look afraid, Stanley marched forward and collided with the wall. He fell onto his backside again to the amusement of Darcy.

"As you can see, it will not allow Mr. Nogginhollow to pass because it does not recognize him. If you should try to enter another dormitory, you will not be permitted either. Be aware that some of the doors will try to trick you. They will let you partially pass and then trap you before you make it through. It is not fatal should this happen, but be advised it is a quite long and painful process to remove you." Miss Poxley turned toward the door, laid her hands on the stones, and said, "*Amicus Penetro.*" The wall seemed to swell as though taking a breath and then returned to normal. "Now, Mr. Nogginhollow, would you mind going through the door again," Miss Poxley asked.

Stanley looked at her uncertainly, but apparently looking for some redemption, he bravely marched through the stone and disappeared.

"The door recognized him and will allow passage to him for the rest of the school year. The rest of you will follow Mr. Nogginhollow one at a time and be recognized." Miss Poxley instructed. Seeing Stanley's success, everyone quickly lined up and went through.

The room they entered reminded Seven of a mix between a large den and a classroom. There were several small chalkboards on the walls, tables and chairs, four dusty half-full bookshelves, mismatched couches, overstuffed chairs, and several enormous fireplaces. They crackled with welcoming fires, which magically gave off no heat, a good thing since it was already warm in the room. In a corner was a tiny rectangular box like the ones in the dining hall.

Miss Poxley explained, "This is the recreation room. The television will only get the school news channel and WNN, which shouldn't be an issue because you will be too busy to watch it anyway," she said with a snide grin.

"Sleeping areas for girls are on floors one, two, and three that way," Poxley explained as she pointed to a set of spiral staircases to the right and then one to the left, adding, "and boys sleep on four, five, and six that way. Your rooms will act similar to the door to the dormitory. Once the four assigned occupants pass, the door will not let anyone else enter without the permission of one of the occupants." She paused and looked at her watch. "Curfew for freshmen is in one hour. Any freshmen not in Terramin by then will not be granted passage by the doors. They will not reopen until morning, and the halls do not make for a comfortable sleep." She sounded ominous. "I am off to bed. Don't make me have to come back here tonight." Poxley swept from the room.

"I wonder where she sleeps," Cully asked.

"A coffin?" Sam said.

"For someone who works at a school, she doesn't seem to like students much," Sophie said.

"Let's find our room," Cully said. Seven followed Cully up the stairs to their room.

"This room isn't much to look at," Sophie said. "No wonder my sister takes so much stuff with her. She is trying to make these rooms livable." She gestured toward the dull gray, stone walls that were empty of any decorations. Along with the bed, each girl had a desk and a chair, and a small armoire.

"We will have to dress this room up a little bit," Adria said. "It is so drab."

Seven's bag was on the bed next to a small window. It had a cushioned seat on the sill, so she sat on it and looked out. She could see the woods and a small stream, but it was too dark to see much else, so she began to unpack.

"Let's unpack later and go exploring," Cully suggested.

"Yes!" Adria and Sophie said in unison.

They all looked at Seven.

"Um, you know, I am exhausted. I think I am just going to stay here. Unpack. Get to bed early," Seven said.

"Come on, Seven," Cully pleaded.

"Yes, come with us," Adria chimed in.

"We can unpack when we get back," Sophie added.

A part of Seven did want to go, but she couldn't get the Awakening out of her mind. Why didn't she feel anything when she touched the stone? Did this mean that she wasn't magical? Did her mom and Mcfee make a colossal mistake? And Mcfee? Was that who Seven saw at the scene of a possible attack on the way to school? Was Mcfee trustworthy or dangerous?

Seven looked at the girls, who were obviously anxious to leave.

"Okay," Seven agreed. She decided she needed a distraction. "Let's go exploring."

Chapter Seven

A Krisp First Day

The next morning, Seven woke and felt as though someone had used her head for a soccer ball. After they returned from exploring last night, she had trouble falling asleep. Doubts about her place here, frustration at her mom for abandoning her to face Midia alone, distrust of Mcfee, and most of all, anxiety for today's classes kept her up until late. With it being the second night in a row that she hadn't slept well, the last thing she wanted to do was go to class. With great effort, she sat up and blinked hard against the bright sun.

"Well, it's about time," Cully said. She was already dressed and tying her shoes. "I was just about to leave you."

"I think I slept all of five minutes," Seven complained.

"Well, too bad, so sad. Get up anyway. Adria and Sophie have already gone to breakfast, and I am starving," Cully said. "Besides, I do not want to be late for the first day of class."

Seven replied with another groan. Then she felt something hit her head. Lying on the floor was Cully's pillow.

"Really?" Seven said.

"It will be my spellbook next," Cully said determinedly.

Begrudgingly, Seven heaved herself out of bed and dressed for the day. After brushing her teeth and hair and splashing water on her face, she started to feel halfway human again.

When they reached the dining hall, they filled their plates and sat down with the rest of the group. Returning students filtered in, chatting noisily. Stanley Nogginhollow sat a few tables over frantically writing in a book. Several other freshmen students had replaced their breakfast plates with what looked to be schoolbooks.

"What are these people thinking?" Sam asked. "Don't they know classes haven't started yet? What could they possibly be studying?

"I like to wait and see what the professor wants. No use in doing extra work," Charlie said through a mouthful of food.

"Exactly," Sam agreed.

"Has anyone heard any more about what happened at the Landing?" Sophie asked.

"Sam and I ran into wonder boy last night after he had returned from there. He was so excited I thought he was going to make a puddle on the floor," Charlie said as he swallowed a bite of bacon.

"After he gave a tour of the WANN office and pointed out the award he won for some stupid article, he finally told us there was for sure an attack on a shopkeeper in Wyndamir Landing," Sam said.

"Attacked?" Seven asked. "By who?"

"No one knows. A few witnesses said the attackers were dressed in black and kept their hoods up to hide their faces."

"Black cloaked wielders," Sam commented. "Sounds like Shadow Raiders to me."

Any appetite Seven had immediately vanished at the name of the group responsible for her father's death.

"I've heard Shadow Raiders are a nasty group," said an unfamiliar voice. Everyone turned to see a mop of curly brown hair. It was the boy Sam and Charlie said was the Crosser. "Can I sit here?"

"Yeah!" the boys said in unison as Sam scooted over and gestured to the newly vacated seat between Charlie and him.

"Thanks. The only empty seat was that one," he jerked his head in the direction of Darcy's table, where one seat remained open. "And, well, I didn't want to sit there."

"Can't blame you," Cully said. "I'm Cully Collins."

"My name's Iggy Everett."

"I'm Sam Walker, and this is Charlie Cooper," Sam said. "We haven't seen you much since yesterday, and Charlie and I have been everywhere," Sam said.

"Even the library?" Iggy asked.

"Why would we go there?" Charlie asked, genuinely dumbfounded.

Iggy just smiled.

"What can I say? I like to read. Anyway, we don't have any libraries like that back home."

"And where is home?" Sam asked.

"Well, my family is spread out all over," Iggy said, not exactly answering the question.

"Like where?" Sam pressed.

"Oh, a few here and a few there. Scattered everywhere, really," Iggy said as he shoved a piece of sausage into his mouth. Seven noticed how he dodged the question. Did he know what Sam and Charlie were really asking?

"Well, what city do you live in?" Charlie tried.

"It's tiny. Most people have never even heard of it," Iggy said, taking another bite.

"My family has traveled a lot. Maybe I've heard of it?" Charlie said with frustration in his voice.

"I doubt it," Iggy said, swallowing his sausage. "Anyone else nervous about classes? My grandfather said not to be, that everyone starts on page one, but I am still nervous."

"Did your grandfather go here?" Adria asked.

"Not exactly," Iggy said.

"That is about as clear as a mud puddle," Sam said to Iggy.

"He never attended, but he is very familiar with the school. I am the only one out of my family to go here," Iggy said, ignoring Sam's comment.

"Don't tell me they went to the Doyle School," Charlie said with a disgusted look, but a musical jingle signaling the beginning of the WANN newscast saved Iggy from having to answer. All the television screens lit up, and the letters WANN flashed across them. They faded away, and the giant, smiling face of Nicholas Sanders filled the screen.

"I am Nicholas Sanders, and this is the morning edition of WANN, your only network for what's happening at Wyndamir." He fiddled with some papers on a desk. "As you know, classes begin this morning. First-year students are encouraged to give themselves extra time to get to classes. Don't want to start your first day by being late," he admonished with a smile. "Upperclassmen are encouraged to be helpful and polite and not send our younger schoolmates in the wrong direction. As Bellatora says, as soon as we walk through those big oak doors, we are all a part of the Wyndamir family."

A groan broke out around the room. Several groups of older students rolled their eyes at the screen and went back to their conversations. They didn't find Nicholas as fascinating as he found himself. He continued with information on last-minute room changes for classes, a second-floor hallway closed due to an infestation of acid-spitting beetles, and other school information.

"Please tune in at lunchtime for a special report from Wyndamir Landing. Good morning and good luck to you all." Another round of groans and eye rolls. "I am Nicholas Sanders, and as always, I will keep you posted."

"That was thrilling," Sam said sarcastically. "He is an ace reporter." Before the hall could go back to its noisy din, Bellatora stood and asked for attention.

"Good morning," Bellatora said. "It sounds as though all of you are enjoying your breakfast and are ready to get this school year started. The beginning of a new school term is always exciting. New students are eager to begin their magical training. Second-year students return more capable after conquering their first year, and of course, our older students are ready to master the more challenging aspects of the craft," she said. "Remember, it does not matter from where we came, but only where we are going. With those final words, classes are ready to commence. Good luck to all." At that moment, the grandfather clock that towered over them from the corner gonged loudly, signaling the end of breakfast and the beginning of the school day.

"Thank you for letting me sit with you," Iggy said as he stood. Then he bent low and looked directly at Sam and Charlie. "And to answer your unasked question, yes, I am a Crosser." Sam and Charlie gaped at him with wide eyes. "I wasn't supposed to tell, but I know you figured that out already since you saw me in the basement of the Gate House yesterday. You know, spying is so much better if the people you are spying on don't see you." With a wave and a wink, Iggy departed.

Sam and Charlie looked at each other for a split second before chasing after Iggy.

"We better go," Cully agreed.

The first class of the morning was History of Midia with Professor Brimbal. He was a bubbly man who thought everything was exciting. He nearly jumped up and down when he greeted students as they entered the classroom.

"Welcome to the History of Midia," he said enthusiastically. "Though we don't learn how to make things move or change pins into pencils in this class, learning the history of our land is important. We don't want to repeat the mistakes of the past. Instead, we want to build on the progress we've made.

"In this class, we will relieve victorious battles and mourn terrible losses. We will explore the decisions of the Grey Elders and the aftermath of their choices. We will learn about the devastation of families torn apart and the joyous meetings of those reunited. We will explore the laws and rules of magic and how they affect you.

"Now, let's see me see. Who can tell me when Midia was founded?" Seven looked around the room as several students eager to impress the teacher frantically raised their hands. She was surprised that Iggy was one of them.

"Midia was founded nearly a thousand years ago. No one can agree on the exact year, but it is considered the youngest of all the magical countries," a boy from the front row answered.

"Excellent!" exclaimed Brimbal.

"Who can name the other magical countries?" Brimbal bubbled.

A girl a few seats away from Seven raised her hand. Seven thought her name was Emma, but she wasn't sure.

"Nadwana, Binter, Viridia, Algora, Mondavia, Tova, and of course, Midia," the girl answered, smiling proudly.

"Wonderful!" Brimbal said excitedly as a small ball of spit went flying from his mouth. He didn't seem to notice. Instead, he went on with his lesson as though it would change the world.

"Now, why were these magical countries founded?" Brimbal pointed at someone behind Seven. When the girl spoke, Seven didn't even have to turn around to know who it was.

"They were formed to protect the weak and unimportant people who were not magical. We call them Expendables because that is exactly what they were. Anyway, Expendables tried to learn magic and made bad choices that got them into trouble. They couldn't accept that they were unimportant and unnecessary in a magical world, in any world. A few generous and thoughtful wielders tried to show the expendables that magic wasn't their gift by performing some harmless demonstrations so that expendables would learn their place. However, they complained to some traitorous wielders who persuaded the Grey Elders to help. The Grey Elders overreacted and separated the magically gifted from *them*. That is why Midia and the other magical countries were formed." Darcy sat down, a satisfied smile on her face.

The class fell silent. Students were looking at each other, at Darcy, and then at Brimbal. The professor stared at Darcy for a long moment. His face was expressionless. Finally, he spoke.

"Well, Miss Davidson, thank you for that, uh, explanation. Unfortunately, aside from your misguided opinions and poor choice of words, your answer is mostly correct. Let me clarify a few things, though.

"Wielders and - " he turned toward Darcy, "I prefer the

term unwielders to be used in my class not 'expendables' - lived in relative harmony for many, many years. However, over time, more and more wielders grew frustrated and angry toward their nonmagical neighbors feeling like the country's leaders gave unwielders special treatment and protections due to their inability to perform magic. Some wielders formed hate groups that took the growing anger toward unwielders, twisted it, and helped it spread. They persuaded many that unwielders were nothing more than a plague that needed to be enslaved or annihilated. Slowly, wielders who were initially on the side of the unwielders began to fall under the spell of the hate groups, either by choice or forced coercion. Even if they didn't actively torture their nonmagical neighbors, they wouldn't stop it or report it. Unfortunately, the demonstrations to which Miss Davidson referred resulted in the torture and death of many unwielders.

"Unwielders were not able to protect themselves against the cruel, dark magic-wielding tyrants," Brimbal said heatedly. "Magical law enforcement officers could not keep up despite harsh punishment for those who were caught hurting others. It was a dark, scary time for everyone. Wielders were afraid of being unjustly accused of torturing unwielders by jealous, nonmagical neighbors. Unwielders were terrified of actually being tortured. In exchange for protection, many unwielders agreed to serve wielding families. This usually did not turn out well.

"After many failed attempts at peace in addition to the growing number of unwielders' deaths, a decision was made to separate the magical from the nonmagical. The Grey Elders decided for everyone's safety to form several purely magical countries throughout the world where unwielders would not be permitted to live.

"Professor?" Iggy interrupted. "What happened to the families who had both magical and nonmagical members when the Grey Elders separated the worlds?"

"That was one of the saddest consequences," Brimbal said, shaking his head. "When the worlds were separated, families were torn apart. Magical family members could stay, but those members not gifted had to leave. Some families split bitterly over the decision, with some staying and some going. Other families chose to leave the magical world to stay together. The magical members agreed to have their powers bound or even stripped before they crossed the veil. Imagine having to choose either your magic or your family."

Murmurs erupted around the room.

"I'm glad my family didn't have to decide," said one boy.

"I would go with my magic," said another.

"You would keep your magic and never see your parents again?" asked yet another.

Magic or family? That was precisely the decision Seven's mom faced all those years ago. Her mom chose to give up everything - her family, friends, job, and home - all for Seven's dad. All for Seven.

"To make sure wielders didn't cross into nonmagical worlds and wreak havoc, a gate system was created. Even today, passing through the gates without permission is a crime punishable by a life sentence in prison or worse."

"Sir, what happens if unwielders who live across the gate have magical children?" asked a bespectacled girl in the back of the room.

Seven noticed Iggy squirming a bit in his chair.

"Well, it doesn't often happen anymore, but there are specially trained Guardians called Retrievers who handle that very thing."

"They should just seal the gates and forget about them," Seven heard Darcy say to Brigit, who nodded in agreement.

"What do the Retrievers do?" asked Charlie.

"Well, when a child who lives across the gates is born with magical gifts, a Retriever is alerted. The Retriever monitors the child as he or she grows. Sometimes, a child's magical gift is weak and fades away over time. Then, the Retriever usually does nothing but checks in occasionally," Brimbal explained.

"You mean our magic can disappear?" Stanley Nogginhollow blurted out.

"No, Mr. Nogginhollow, you can't completely lose your magic, but it can become, well, fragile," Brimbal explained. "Think of magic like a muscle. If you don't exercise it, it becomes weak. Those who don't practice their magic find that spells they could once cast with barely a thought become difficult or impossible for them to perform at all." Seven remembered her mom's failed attempt at making the coffee pot fly.

"What about those children whose magical abilities don't go away?" pressed another boy. Brimbal grinned at him and clapped his hands excitedly.

"My, oh my, this group surely does like to jump right in. I usually don't cover all of this for weeks." His eyes gleamed like a child who had no limits in a toy store. "Yes, that does happen. In that case, Retrievers are sent to the family's home to discuss the matter. Those children are given a choice. They can either have their powers bound and memories wiped or come to a magical school like Wyndamir and learn how to use their magical powers. These children are called Crossers."

"My mother says any wielding families who chose a non-magical world are a bunch of dirty, rotten traitors," Darcy whispered loudly to those around her. "Their children should not be allowed to study magic. She thinks their powers should be sucked out in the most painful way possible."

Seven saw Iggy's face go white and hoped hers didn't as well.

"Unfortunately, Miss Davidson, others share your view, which is why many Crossers try to keep their status a secret," Brimbal continued. "Boys and girls, I am afraid that this lesson has turned in a direction that I wasn't prepared to teach today. Let us backtrack to where we should be and leave this more complicated topic for later." For the rest of the class, he talked about the characteristics of the different magical countries.

"Your homework is to read chapters one and two and write a two-page paper on the Council of Bergen," he said as the bell signaled class was over.

Seven gathered her things as someone knocked into her sending her books and papers scattering to the floor.

"So sorry," said Darcy in a tone that didn't sound sorry at all. She appeared next to Seven's desk along with Brigit Murdock. "This class just has me all out of sorts. Every time I hear about traitors who left Midia, I just get all worked up."

Brigit smiled snidely and nodded in agreement.

"Whatever. Just leave, Darcy. Class is over," Cully said.

"I wasn't talking to you," Darcy sneered. "and don't tell me what to do, Collins." The two glared at each other before Brigit spoke.

"Here is your book, Seven." She held it out, but as soon as Seven reached for it, she dropped it on the floor. It made a loud *thwack* that echoed in the empty classroom. She and Darcy turned to leave, laughing all the while.

Cully reached down to help Seven gather her things.

"She never quits," Cully sighed.

"She is such a jerk."

"Always has been. You met her dad. She's just like him. Anyway, forget her. We have to get to Morphology," Cully said, stuffing the last paper into Seven's bag. "And my brother says never be late for Morphology."

They had fifteen minutes to get to class, but with having to gather Seven's things and the crowded corridors, they arrived in the classroom just as the bell sounded. Seven sat in her chair and did her best to ignore Darcy and Brigit, who whispered conspiratorially as they kept glancing at her.

"Get your books out and turn to chapter one," said a deep voice from a darkened corner of the room. When the professor emerged, Seven wished he would have stayed in the shadows.

She didn't remember seeing Professor Krisp at dinner the night before nor at breakfast this morning. He was not a welcoming sight. His eyes were cold and flat. His face was skeletal with sunken cheeks and a protruding chin. He wore no smile or any hint that his face had smiled, ever. Seven swore he could have been related to Mr. Strickland from her last school.

Seven reached in her bag for *Morphological Magic: Book 1*. She pulled it out, opened it to the first chapter, and immediately felt sick. Staring back were not diagrams and instructions on how to change a coffee mug into a water goblet, but rather pictures of jewels and talismans. She had the wrong book.

"Is there a problem, Miss Preston?" Seven looked up to see Professor Krisp staring down his long, narrow nose at her. From her seated position, she swore he was twelve feet tall.

"My book," Seven said. "It's not in my bag. I just had it."

"You did not just have it, or the book would be in your bag, would it not?

Seven's face went scarlet.

"You are to come to my class prepared, Miss Preston. I am your professor, not your parent," he growled.

Darcy's hand shot into the air.

"Professor Krisp?" she said sweetly.

"Yes, Miss Davidson? Can you not see I am talking with your fellow student about class preparedness?" Krisp said without looking away from Seven.

Darcy's smile slipped slightly, but she continued.

"Well, I found Sev, I mean Miss Preston's book in the hall. I tried to get it to her before class, but she came into the room so close to the bell that *I* didn't want to be marked tardy if I got up from my seat to give it to her. If she had only been a bit earlier," Darcy allowed the sentence to trail off. A sickeningly sweet smile on her face.

Seven's face went hot but not with embarrassment. Darcy didn't just "accidentally" knock into her at the end of Brimbal's class. She did it on purpose so she and Brigit could switch Seven's books.

"Please return the book to Miss Preston," Krisp instructed. "And Miss Preston, that will be one demerit for coming to my class unprepared. Not a good way to start your year."

With a triumphant smile, Darcy walked over and politely set the book on Seven's desk. Cully put her hand on Seven's arm when Seven tried to stand up and gave a quick shake of her head.

"Not now," Cully warned.

"Let's finally begin," Krisp said as he whirled around to face the class. His chilly gaze lingered on Seven. "We've wasted precious class time with sophomoric concerns." Seven wasn't sure what that meant, but it didn't sound like a compliment.

"As you know, morphology is the field of magic where we learn to change one thing into another. Unless I can fill your small brains with some useful and critical information, the only thing you will learn how to change is schools." Here, he paused and looked around the room, letting his gaze land directly on Seven. "And we don't want that, do we?" His voice dropped to a whisper, but his words were not soft. "Do you think you are here on vacation?" Students looked at each other in confusion. "Well, do you?" he barked. Three brave students shook their heads. "Then I suggest you write this down lest your puny brains forget," he growled. Not even a second passed before every student, Darcy included, bent their heads low and took notes furiously.

For the rest of the class, Seven wrote and wrote. Her hand cramped painfully, but she didn't stop until the bell sounded. Relieved sighs echoed around the room as students dropped their pencils and massaged their aching hands. Seven, too, rubbed her hand and stiff fingers. Then, she put her book in her bag.

"What are you doing, Miss Preston?" Krisp said coolly.

Seven looked around to see that students were putting books and notes in bags just as she was. Some were already on their way to the door though they froze at the sound of his voice. She forced herself to meet his eyes and tried not to melt under the intensity of his stare.

"Uh, that was the bell, sir. Class is over," she said, wishing her voice was steadier.

"My hearing, Miss Preston, is impeccable. I am perfectly aware the bell sounded. Though you may be an exception, this is not a class of werewolves. We do not jump at the sound of the bell. *It* does not dismiss you." He bent over so that his face was close to hers. "I do. Do you understand, Miss Preston?"

Seven hated the way he said her name, as though his mouth would rather chew on pointy nails than speak it. Nonetheless, she nodded.

"Very well. And the next time you come to my class unprepared, I will skip the demerits and go straight for detention. You are dismissed," he said, turning from her as though she were nothing.

Resisting the urge to throw her book at the back of his head, Seven stuffed everything into her bag and marched from the room. Cully and Iggy were waiting for her just outside the door. They didn't speak but fell into step with her. Cully looked sideways at Seven, opened her mouth to say something, but closed it without speaking. Twice more, she did this.

"What?" Seven snapped as she marched straight ahead.

"Forget him. Krisp is a jerk," Cully managed.

"And he is not the only one." Seven quickened her pace as she locked on her target – a long, honey-colored braid. When she reached it, Seven grabbed it, forcing Darcy's head to snap painfully back.

"What is your problem?" Seven's voice quivered with rage.

"My problem?" Darcy shot back as she pulled her braid from Seven's grip. "I don't have a problem, but you will if you ever touch me again."

"And *you* will if you don't leave my things alone. I didn't drop that book. You and your pathetic friend stole it when you knocked my bag over in history. I'm warning you, Darcy. Just back off."

"Or what? Tell all of us what you will do." Darcy gestured to the students who had gathered to watch them. Then she leaned close to Seven and whispered, "I tried to be nice to you, but you chose your side when you dissed me on the bus. I would rather have my fingernails ripped out one by one than be friends with you as my father wanted."

"I will gladly help rip out your fingernails," Seven shot

back.

"Get out of my face, Seven," Darcy said.

"And as for what your father wants, I would rather eat your nails than be your friend. Now, *you* get out of *my* face."

"What is going on here?" asked a soft angelic voice. A few students parted to make way for Professor Willowisp. "Surely we don't have trouble on the first day of class," she said.

Cully tried to pull Seven away.

"Oh, n-no, Professor, there is no problem. We were just heading back to the dormitory, weren't we Seven?" Cully gave another tug, but Seven didn't move.

Professor Willowisp looked appraisingly at Seven and then at Darcy.

"Miss Davidson, do you have a problem?" Professor Willowisp said in a not-so-friendly tone.

"No problems here, Professor. I think Preston is just upset because she earned a demerit. She accused me of stealing her book, but I was only trying to be helpful," Darcy said innocently.

"I see. Well, maybe you should try to be a little less helpful in the future. I would hate to give out detention on the first day of school." Willowisp's tone was cool. She was not buying Darcy's sweet and innocent act.

Darcy seemed surprised at her inability to charm the teacher. She shot one more nasty look at Seven before storming away with Brigit in tow. Since the show was over, the rest of the students quickly dispersed as well.

"All right then, Miss Preston?" Willowisp asked Seven. All coolness had left her voice, and she wore a bright smile.

Seven nodded.

"Wonderful. Have a good rest of the day then." She turned with a flourish and floated down the corridor, humming a lively tune.

"What did you do to make Darcy so angry?" Iggy asked.

"I declined her seat invitation on the bus," Seven said. "Apparently, her father wants us to be friends."

"Why would he care if you are friends with her?" Iggy asked.

"I don't know and don't care," Seven said.

"Well, we've got some time before lunch," Cully said. "Let's go outside...unless you've changed your mind?"

"About what?" Seven asked, genuinely confused.

"About eating Darcy's fingernails."

Chapter Eight

Stares and Glares

It looked as though everyone else at Wyndamir had the same idea. Students and some teachers were scattered about the vast lawns. Some were talking, some were studying, and others were throwing a flat disc back and forth using their wands to make it do tricks in the air.

"Let's walk in there," Cully said, pointing to the gardens.

Several paths led into the garden, each one guarded by a different set of statues. The way they picked had a flowering bush that formed an enormous archway. Two cow-sized dog statues sat on their haunches on either side as though ready to spring. As they passed, Iggy looked closely at the face of the one on the right.

"It looks so real," he said. "like at any second, it will lick my face."

"Or eat your head," Cully said.

Iggy took an involuntary step backward.

Inside the gardens was a unique collection of plants, flowers, bushes, and trees. Many of the bushes took the shape of mythical creatures like unicorns and centaurs. The flowers were colorful and fragrant.

"I like these." Seven pointed to a deep crimson plant whose large wrinkly flowers felt like velvet. "They look like furry brains. Maybe I will pick one for Darcy."

A rustling sound nearby made them jump. A white cat

shot from a low bush, sat in the middle of the path, and stared at them. When Cully bent to pet it, it hissed.

"Okay, no petting," Cully said, yanking her hand back. She stood up and noticed Seven, who was transfixed by the cat. "Seven, this is a cat," she joked.

"I know it's a cat," Seven said without taking her eyes off the creature. "But, I think I have seen *this* cat before at a park near my house."

"There have to be a million white cats," Cully said dismissively.

"I know, but its eyes. There is something familiar about them." She took a step closer to it, but a loud bark erupted from another bush, and the cat bolted away just before its pursuer stumbled into the path. A tiny brown beagle with oversized ears and a tail with chunks of hair missing sniffed at the ground. It stopped, looked at them, and made a noise that sounded like *harrumph* before it plopped down in the middle of the path, looking very disappointed.

"Max! Get back here! Leave that cat alone! Are you trying to get me fired?" shouted a deep voice. Instantly, the dog took off again.

A large man appeared from behind a tree. He stopped shouting when he saw the three of them.

"Sorry, I didn't know anyone was in here," the stranger said. He had broad shoulders, enormous hands and wore a red plaid shirt splattered with mud. He stroked his neatly trimmed salt and pepper beard as he asked, "Um, have you seen my dog?"

"He found us. He was chasing a cat. He went that way." Iggy pointed.

The four of them stood there in awkward silence, looking at each other. The man looked from Seven to Cully to Iggy, but his gaze seemed to linger longer on Seven.

"No matter," he said, finally looking away from Seven. "He'll turn up sooner or later and empty-handed, I am sure. Where are my manners?" He looked at his shirt, apparently searching for a clean spot. He wiped his hand, gave a friendly grin, and said, "Durward Skelly is the name, but most people just call me Skelly."

"I'm Cully Collins. This is Iggy Everett, and that's Seven Preston." All three gave a small wave.

"Preston, you say?" He seemed confused.

Seven nodded.

"Preston?" He repeated.

"Yes, sir. Preston. Seven Preston," Seven repeated.

"Well, welcome to Wyndamir, Miss Collins, Mr. Everett, and Miss Preston." He kept stealing glances at Seven.

"Are you a teacher?" Cully asked.

"Oh, no, not me. That would be a disaster. I just take care of the lawns, gardens, grounds, a little bit of everything, I guess."

"Like beetle infestations?" Iggy asked, remembering the announcement earlier.

"Acid spitting beetles are a pain," Skelly said, holding up his other hand, which had several angry red burns on it. After a pause, he said, "Well, I best find that dog before he, uh, well, I'd better find him." Skelly gave Seven one more hard look and then turned down another path.

"Did I imagine that, or was he staring at me?" Seven whispered.

"Definitely staring," Cully said.

"And he acted as though I gave him the wrong name," Seven went on. "Like I don't know my name."

"He was strange," Iggy agreed.

They discussed the stranger's odd behavior as they continued along the garden's winding paths. They passed statues, fountains, smaller courtyards, and stone archways. None of them seem to notice how deeply they had traveled into the garden or how dark and secluded the area in which they found themselves was.

"This part is creepy," Cully said.

Seven looked around. Everything was overgrown. The meticulously kept plants had given way to wild foliage, which partially hid crumbling statues and broken stone benches. Tall, ivy-covered stone walls blocked out the sun, making it seem nearly dusk when it was not even noon. They could no longer see Wyndamir Hall or any other school building, nor could they hear students they knew were on the lawns next to the garden.

"It's almost as though this part of the garden has been forgotten," Seven said.

"Not forgotten," said a voice. "Just avoided."

The three jumped. An older man sat on one of the benches, partially hidden by some dead vines. He was dressed in shiny black robes. His hair was stark white, his face a bit wrinkled, but his blue eyes wide and alert.

"I'm sorry. I didn't mean to frighten you."

"We were just startled, that's all," Cully said.

"Well, you better get that out of your system," the old man said with a laugh. "This part of the garden especially is not for those who startle easily, but it is the only place in the garden where you can find these." He held up a bright yellow teacup flower covered in green, orange, and red spots. "I never learned their true name, but once I heard them called Heaven on a Stem." He inhaled the flower, a faraway look in his eyes. "Anyway," he said, seemingly coming back, "the butterflies love them, but for some reason, the bees don't, which is good for me because I don't particularly like bees."

"Why is this part avoided?" Iggy asked.

"Tragedy happened here," the man said softly as he twirled the flower.

"Tragedy?" Seven asked.

"Someone was killed in this very courtyard. Being surrounded by death leaves some uneasy."

Cully, Iggy, and Seven looked at each other and then around the courtyard.

"Killed? What happened?" Cully asked.

"Who wants to talk about a tragedy on such a lovely day?" the man said, inhaling the flower's scent again. "They smell like peppermint mixed with lavender and vanilla. Here." He held the flower out to Seven. Not wanting to be rude, she smelled it.

"Now, you must be freshmen, yes?" he asked, looking directly at Seven.

She nodded, feeling uncomfortable under his piercing gaze.

"I thought so," he smiled. "Most upperclassmen don't take the time to enjoy the gardens, and if they do, they avoid this area."

"Who are you?" Cully asked.

"Just an old man who enjoys the gardens. No other gardens like Wydnamir's gardens," he said evasively. Without looking at them, he asked, "Classes began this morning?"

"Yes," they answered in unison.

"Which ones?"

"History of Midia and Morphology," Iggy said.

"That would be Professors Brimbal and Krisp?"

"Yes, sir," Iggy replied.

"Good ones. Dedicated."

"If you say so," Seven said before she could stop herself.

The older man laughed.

"I know that Professor Krisp can be a bit stiff, but he knows his subject and is committed to this school," he said as his gaze again fell upon Seven.

"Uh, we better go. Our friends are waiting for us," Cully said, seemingly feeling Seven's discomfort.

"Oh, yes, yes, certainly. One cannot have too many friends. You never know when you might need them."

They waved awkwardly and headed out of the courtyard. Before they turned the corner, Seven looked back to see if he was still staring at her. However, when she turned around, the bench was empty except for a single flower that lay upon it.

"Is there something wrong with me? Is my hair sticking up, or do I have something hanging out of my nose?" Seven asked as she turned back around.

Cully made a show of studying Seven. "Nope. No hair is sticking up. Nothing is hanging out of your nose. Your face, on the other hand," Cully said, shaking her head.

"Shut up," Seven said, playfully pushing Cully. "Okay, surely you two noticed that old man stared at me, too, just like Skelly. What is going on?"

Iggy shrugged.

"I wouldn't worry about it. Come on. Let's get out of here. It has to be getting close to lunch, and I want to see Sanders' news report on Wyndamir Landing."

As they walked, Seven retreated to her thoughts. She was sure that Skelly was surprised when she told him her name was Preston, as though he expected to hear a different name. And that cat. It looked just like one of the cats that stole the bracelet Kerry had given to her in the park before she moved. Then, that old man kept staring at her. What was going on?

As students settled into their seats for lunch, conversations about morning classes and homework complaints on the first day were everywhere. Only a few professors were at the teacher table, including Mcfee and Poxley, who seemed to be doing more arguing than eating. Whatever Mcfee said did not seem to please Poxley, judging by the glare on her face as she stomped away. Mcfee shook her head and left, too. Bellatora, who was talking with Durward Skelly, watched them both go.

Just then, the televisions came on, and Nicholas's dazzling smile came into focus. "Good afternoon, Wyndamir students, and congratulation on surviving the morning classes. I have been asked to report that a section of the sophomore year potions class had a minor incident this morning. If you are in any of the lower hallways and notice green fog, you are to avoid it and report to the infirmary immediately." A few second-year students jumped from their tables and ran from the hall.

"Now for an update on Wyndamir Landing." At the word Wyndamir Landing, the room grew quiet. "As we saw on the way to school yesterday, a major tragedy occurred in our neighboring town. Our generous headmistress allowed me to venture out last evening to get the scoop." He paused, arranged his papers, and continued in his best news anchor voice. "After some creative investigative maneuvers on my part, I was able to ascertain that Mr. J. Swathmore sustained life-threatening injuries when two unidentified assailants dressed in black entered his store, Swathmore Wands, yesterday afternoon." A still picture of the mob scene appeared on the screen with security officers and medics surrounding the gurney on which Swathmore lay. Seven scanned the image to see if Mcfee was in it, but the screen flashed back to Nicholas before she could get a good look. "A passerby heard a commotion and entered the shop to investigate. I was able to gain an interview with said passerby. Please be aware that I air this segment at great personal risk, but I feel that you, my fellow students, have a right to know."

The picture broke away to a previously recorded interview. Nicholas was standing next to a wide-eyed man with a broad smile. He was excited to be interviewed, even if it was by a lowly school news reporter.

"I am standing here with Wally Fargles, the brave civilian who discovered the injured Swathmore earlier today. Sir, can you tell us what happened when you entered the shop?"

The man leaned close to the microphone.

"Yes, I can," he said and then stood back up, grinning even bigger if that were possible.
For a minute, Nicholas stood there waiting for the man to continue, but the man just smiled and stared into the camera.

"Uh, Mr. Fargles?"

Fargles turned and looked at Nicholas.

"Huh?"

"Can you please tell us what you found?"

"Oh, you mean, right now?" the man asked.

"Yes, sir. Right now," Nicholas said, trying not to sound annoyed.

"Well, the front of the store looked normal, just dark. Then I heard someone scream. I made my way to the back room and yelled for Jup, I mean Mr. Swathmore. He and I are real good friends, you know. We met about eighteen years back when we both lived in Leotte. That's a small town just north of..."

"Sir, I'm sure that is very interesting, but could you please tell us what you found when you entered the store?"

"Oh, yeah, sure. Well, as I said, I heard someone scream, so I went into the back of the shop and called out. It didn't take a genius to know something was wrong."

"Good thing it didn't take a genius," Iggy murmured.

"Boxes were ripped and torn and tossed all over. Broken wands were scattered all over the floor."

"And the shopkeeper," Nicholas prodded, "what was his condition?"

"Well," the man said, his smile finally faltering, "that's bad business right there. It looked like he had been hit repeatedly with spells, dark spells. His face was cut and bruised, and there were scorch marks on his clothes and the walls. The back door was blown off the hinges. Jup – I mean Mr. Swathmore, wasn't, you know, with it. He kept mumbling. It was tough to understand him because his lips were so swollen, but it sounded like, 'Can't trust her. She will give it to him.' I am not sure what the *it* is or who the *him* and the *her* are. He never said."

At that moment, a crimson gloved hand covered the camera lens. A gruff voice said, "This interview is over." When the hand was removed, Nicholas stood there looking a bit shaken. Wally Fargles was gone.

"Well, it seems Mr. Fargles won't be able to continue the interview." He looked around and then lowered his voice. "There is something big happening here, and you can bet that I will get to the bottom of the story. This is Nicholas Sanders, WANN News, reporting from Wyndamir Landing. As always, I will keep you posted."

The screen broke to Nicholas, who was currently in the school's news studio.

"Only with quick thought and journalistic cunning was I able to get out of the Landing with this clip. Upon returning to school late last evening, I tried to reach the Midian Security Office to discuss the matter. They would only say the investigation is ongoing and wouldn't comment further.

"I was also able to uncover that this was not the first time in recent weeks a shop in Wyndamir Landing was attacked. The first incident happened earlier this month at a pastry shop. The shop was closed at the time, so no one was injured." Nicholas almost sounded disappointed. "The MSO claims the two incidents are not related. Spokeswielder Officer Brody Stoutman of the MSO has this to say."

The screen broke to a photo of a tall, burly man wearing crimson robes. The voice that accompanied the picture sounded similar to the one that stopped the interview with Mr. Fargles.

"The pastry shop was not attacked. It was damaged when the owner was experimenting with imported yeast. Now, you need to get out of here, little boy, before ..." the voice stopped abruptly.

A red-faced Nicholas came back to the screen.

"Sorry, folks, technical difficulties. Unfortunately, the pastry shop's owner, Regina Kettlekamp, was not available for comment. No one has identified the assailants of this latest attack against Mr. J. Swathmore, though murmurs of black cloaks with a certain white and red symbol on the back are growing louder. With the presence of Guardians First Class in Wyndamir Landing, this reporter wonders is wondering if this attack is only the beginning. This is Nicholas Sanders for WANN News. As always, I'll keep you posted." Nicholas flashed his signature smile as the screen faded to gray.

"Black cloaks. Freaky white and red symbol. Like I said, Shadow Raiders," Sam said confidently.

"We don't know that for sure," Cully countered, but she didn't sound very convincing.

"That's where I bought my wand this past summer," Seven said.

"Yeah, me too, but I didn't see anything unusual in the shop," Cully commented.

Seven thought about the conversation she overheard between Mcfee and Swathmore during the summer. What was it Mcfee had said? *"They are getting closer. You know what will happen if they get it. They will give it to him. That cannot happen. You need to fulfill your promise and trust me.*" Now, he gets attacked and tells his friend, *Can't trust her.* Could Swathmore have been talking about Mcfee? She decided to keep this to herself for now.

Afternoon classes were thankfully less eventful than the morning, but the homework amount was a bit overwhelming. Iggy headed off to the library. Seven joined Cully, who wanted to see if she had received any mail.

The mailroom was located on the lowermost floor of Wyndamir Hall, tucked away in a back corridor. Hundreds of circular openings covered the walls, each labeled with a student's name. They were grouped by color to identify the different dormitories. As Cully and Seven headed to the brown ones, something zipped over their heads. Seven looked around but only saw a blur of pale yellow. It zoomed one way and then the other. Finally, it landed in front of a red opening long enough to shove a package into a Vesterly student's box. It was a pixie that was slightly larger than a hummingbird. It had two small arms, two pencil-thin legs, and enormous translucent wings that shimmered in the torchlight. Seven couldn't believe that something so tiny could carry a package that large. When it finished, it zipped back behind the counter, reappearing a second later with three envelopes and one small box.

"I think that school pixies are a bit smaller than the regular ones. What do you think?" Cully asked.

I think it is really bizarre to have a huge butterfly thingy deliver your mail, Seven thought, but, not wanting to give away her Crosser status, she opted for nodding her head.

"Have you ever tried to take a package from one of them?" Cully asked mischievously.

"No," Seven said.

"Well, let's just say they may look small and fragile, but try taking their package away, and they are vicious. I snatched my brother's package once, and look." Cully showed Seven a small scar on the palm of her hand. "Here it is," Cully said as she reached into the opening below her name. A smile blossomed on her face as she pulled out a small box with an envelope tied to it.

"Thank you, Dad!" she said excitedly. "What about you?" she asked, pointing down to where Seven's box would be.

Seven shrugged but went to investigate. She walked by a few slots noting some familiar names. Darcy's mail slot was empty. Seven thought about a few nasty things she'd like to shove into it but decided against it. She saw Stanley Nogginhollow's mailbox. She was glad to see that it was not empty. Finally, she found hers and was quite surprised to see something inside. She pulled out an envelope addressed in her mother's neat handwriting. Inside was a note:

> *Dear Seven,*
>
> *I hope you are settling in at Wyndamir Academy. I know it is big, and many of the halls look the same, but it won't be long until you can walk around the campus with your eyes closed. Be aware of the west corridor on the third floor of Wyndamir Hall. Sometimes the brownies put an extra coat of wax on the floors and have surfing parties after hours. I found that out the hard way. I still have the bruises to prove it.*
>
> *I received a note this afternoon informing me of your demerit. Seven, you must not get on Krisp's bad side. He does not forget things easily.*
>
> *Also, stay away from Darcy Davidson. She and her family are dangerous. They are very wealthy and very powerful. She can make your years at Wyndamir miserable.*
>
> *I love you, Seven, and miss you so much already. Study hard and stay out of trouble.*
>
>   *Love,*
>   *Mom*

"What did you get?" Cully asked.

"A letter from my mom," Seven said. "She told me to stay away from Darcy and be nice to Krisp."

"Too late," Cully said. "I wonder how she knows about the

demerit anyway? My brother has gotten a ton of those over the years, and my parents never found out about them. Bellatora only writes to parents for serious infractions," Cully said.

"Yeah, I don't think Bellatora had anything to do with this," Seven said, knowing full well Mcfee had to be behind it. She changed the subject. "What was in your package?"

"Homemade sweets," Cully beamed as she opened the box. It was filled with all sorts of candies and chocolates. "Chocolate bombs are my favorites. Try one."

Seven cautiously put one in her mouth. She was surprised to taste only chocolate, delicious chocolate, but just chocolate. That's when the bomb part happened. It gently exploded, showering her mouth with sweet, cherry syrup while making her cheeks puff out slightly.

"Good, huh?" Cully said as she popped one into her mouth. "My dad makes these with his special recipe. Sometimes he gets a little crazy with the puff powder, and they explode a little painfully, but for his chocolate bombs, I'll risk it."

They ate a few more on their way back to the library. Suddenly, they heard raised voices, so they ducked behind a glass cabinet filled with trophies and awards. Just then, Mcfee and Nicholas Sanders appeared.

"I told you not to air that report," Mcfee hissed.

"Well, Professors Willowisp and Brimbal disagreed with you. Besides, I worked all night on that report!" Nicholas shot back.

"Lower your voice, Mr. Sanders. I am the Dean of Students at this school, and you will keep respect in your tone."

"What about journalistic freedom? The students' right to know?" he continued with only a little more respect.

"The students don't need to be distracted by events that likely have been blown out of proportion. You have no idea what your meddling could do."

"Blown out of proportion? They didn't summon Professor Bellatora to Wyndamir Landing for a few fireballs. A man almost died. Besides, I have the right…"

"No, Mr. Sanders, that is where you are wrong," Mcfee interrupted. "You do not have the right. You are a student who works at Wyndamir Academy News Network. Your rights are what I tell you they are. And if you ever disobey me again, the only thing you will be reporting on is how fast a student can get expelled from here. Do I make myself clear?"

"But, Professor, I only..."

"Am I clear?"

Nicholas gave a curt nod and stomped away, muttering what Seven guessed were a few choice words aimed at Mcfee.

Mcfee watched him go. She shook her head and was beginning to walk toward the mailroom when a voice stopped her. The owner was around the corner, so the girls could not see who it was.

"He is just doing what he thinks is right," the voice said softly.

"Well, his right is wrong. He overstepped his bounds and put the plan at risk, even if he doesn't realize that."

"He is not the only one overstepping his bounds, is he Phoebe? You were in Wyndamir Landing yesterday, at Swathmore's? You could have been seen. No one can know what you are doing, what we are doing," the voice reprimanded.

"I was checking on things," Mcfee said.

"It was a bad decision." The voice sounded vaguely familiar to Seven, but she couldn't place it.

"A bad decision?" Mcfee huffed. "I am not the one who made a bad decision. If anyone else was going to get it, it should have been me. I know how powerful it is. I can..."

"But it wasn't your choice. Not then. Not now. Your job is to take care of things here," the voice interrupted.

"I know what my job is," Mcfee said, sounding more sad than angry. "I just feel so betrayed."

"I understand."

"I guess you do," Mcfee conceded.

"I better go before someone sees us, but before I do, remember you need to leave Wyndamir Landing to the others.

Your job is here. You know what you have to do."

Seven heard the footsteps fading into the distance. Mcfee and the visitor must have gone down the opposite corridor.

"What the heck was that about?" Cully said as they came out from their hiding place.

"And who was she talking to? That voice sounded familiar, but I can't quite place it," Seven said.

"I don't know, but let's get out of here in case they come back," Cully said. They headed to the library and found Iggy tucked away in a corner.

"Why would they summon Bellatora to Wyndamir Landing?" Iggy asked after they told him what they just heard.

"Because she single-handedly stopped the Shadow Raiders on more than one occasion when they were at the height of their power," Cully said. "Where do you think she got that scar? She used to be a Guardian First Class. My dad says she turned down an offer to become Head Guardian in Charge to come here."

"Why didn't Mcfee want Sanders to air that news report?" Iggy mused. "It isn't like she attacked the shopkeeper."

"Maybe she did," Seven said.

Both Iggy and Cully whirled on Seven.

"What?" they said in unison.

"Well, at least maybe she had something to do with it," Seven said. "Remember when you asked me if I saw something weird at Swathmore's when I was there over the summer?"

Cully and Iggy nodded.

"Well, I did. I just don't know what it means." Seven recounted her shopping trip with Mcfee and how the Dean of Students seemed to threaten Swathmore. "By the time we left, she had a ton of scrolls from others, too," Seven concluded.

"It does sound strange," Iggy agreed, "but I am just not ready to believe Mcfee attacked someone. I want to know what she thinks she should have gotten and who she thinks betrayed her."

"I'm confused about something else," Cully said, turning

to Seven. "Why did Mcfee take you shopping and not your mom?"

"Oh, uh, Mcfee is an old friend of my mom's, and she wasn't able to take me, so I went with Mcfee."

"Was your mom sick or something?" Cully prodded.

"Or something," Seven muttered.

"Well, if your mom and Mcfee are old friends, maybe you could ask your mom about it?" Iggy suggested.

"Been there, done that," Seven said. "My mom essentially told me to mind my own business."

"Well, maybe you should, unless..." Iggy trailed off.

"Unless what?" Seven said.

"Unless your mom is the person who Mcfee thinks betrayed her," Iggy said gently.

"That's ridiculous. My mom wouldn't betray anyone," Seven said, but then she thought about the conversation she overheard the morning she left for Wyndamir. Mcfee wanted *it*. Her mom would not give *it* to her. Had her mom betrayed Mcfee by not giving her something? Is this the same *it* that Swathmore was talking about to Wally Fargles? No, her mom wouldn't betray anyone.

Of course, hadn't she betrayed Seven by not telling her about being a wielder? By lying about her father's death? By keeping Midia a secret? Maybe her mom wasn't the person Seven thought she was. And Seven didn't even know the biggest secret her mom was still keeping.

Chapter Nine

The Drama Teacher

Finally, it was Friday, and they only had one class left. Though the other lessons had been less frightening than Krisp's, they were more boring as well. Initially, Seven had been excited to go to potions. She had ideas about bubbling cauldrons and brewing truth tinctures. Unfortunately, she couldn't have been more wrong.

Professor Mulciber was so tiny that Cully swore he had dwarf blood. He was dull, straightforward, and spoke in a monotone voice the entire time. Then, they spent two classes learning how to make an all stain remover.

"Stain remover? My mom has a whole laundry room full of stain removers, and she's not even magical," Iggy had said.

That morning's Phytology class was more exciting. Professor Snodgrass demonstrated how to milk a pulsating purple plant called Violetus Squidmatum. She gently coaxed the octopus-like plant into filling three vials with its valuable nectar.

"Remember," Snodgrass advised, "Violetus does not like loud noises. Talk softly, walk lightly, work quietly."

The students tried to heed those instructions, but it wasn't long before chaos erupted. When the students milked the plant, it didn't flow out quite as smoothly as it had for Snodgrass. Instead, it spewed out with a loud belch. Then, Darcy's plant hurled some ooze into her hair, causing her to scream in disgust. This riled up Stanley's plant, which soon resembled a sprinkler as it squirted juice in all directions saturating Sam and Charlie's plant, Sophie and Adria's table, and the plant Iggy and his partner, a girl named Jenny, were successfully milking. Apparently, along with loud noises, Violetus Squidmatum also did not like other plants' nectar to touch it. The more upset the plants became, the thicker and darker their nectar turned. Before long, the room looked as though several giants had shoved grapes up their noses and sneezed simultaneously.

Snodgrass walked around the room with a sigh of annoyance and sprinkled calming powder on the plants, which promptly ended the lesson. After class, Cully, Iggy, and Seven used their stain removing potion to clean their clothes and themselves. It worked amazingly well.

"Maybe Mulciber knew what he was doing after all," Cully noted.

Now they were on their way to Spell Casting. Professor Willowisp was by far the favorite teacher of nearly every student at Wyndamir. She was funny and kind and didn't overload them with homework.

"Good afternoon! Good afternoon! One more class to go, and then you can celebrate surviving your first week at Wyndamir," Willowisp said. "So, let's end the week with some fun. For today, we'll skip the boring theory stuff and get right to it, shall we?"

The class all nodded in anxious agreement.

"Now, because you are all beginners, I, too, shall use a wand to demonstrate. As we all know, the wand is just a tool to help us focus and concentrate. Before long, you will be able to do this!" Instantly, the room fell into complete darkness. Then, a small ball of light became visible directly in front of Willowisp. It hovered there while it slowly grew. When it reached the size of a tennis ball, it danced around the room, zooming close to students and zipping away before they could touch it. When it was the size of a giant pumpkin, the light floated to the ceiling and exploded into several smaller spheres of various colors. They danced and spun, growing bigger and smaller before they suddenly crashed into one another and showered the room with all sorts of sparkly flowers. Willowisp brightened the room as the students erupted in cheers.

"Simple yet entertaining. The kinetic spell you will learn today is a bit more practical. Kinetic spells move objects. There are spells to move objects toward you and away from you. You might use them to turn in a paper or to call a book that is out of reach. Even Guardians use them in their defense against black magic. I am afraid you cannot use these spells to move money from a bank to you for those of you with a more creative mind. That would be illegal." Sam and Charlie looked at each other and shrugged disappointedly. "Beginners usually need to be near the object you wish to move. With experience, the distance can increase. To call something toward you, simply point your wand at the object, wave it in an arc-like motion, and say *Motus Ipseum*." She pointed her wand at Iggy's spell book and said, "*Motus Ipseum*." The book immediately jumped off his desk and landed gently on Willowisp's open hand. "To send it away, just reverse the movement of your wand and say *Abirum*." The book gently slipped from her hand and returned to its place in front of Iggy. Willowisp waved her wand again. A stack of sponges rose from her desk and made its way around the room, depositing one sponge between two students.

"I have learned that small, soft objects are best for beginners. I recall a terrible day with rocks. I was hoping the possibility of harm would promote concentration. Not my brightest idea, to be sure. Nurse Medwell was quite unhappy with me. So, for the remainder of the class, I would like you and a partner to stand on opposite sides of the table and practice moving the sponge between you. You may begin."

"You want to go first?" Cully asked.

"No, you can." This was the moment Seven had been dreading since the Awakening. All week in classes, she had mixed potions, milked magical plants, and taken copious notes on various magical topics, but now she had to use her own magic. She tried to push the memory of the quiet awakening stone away.

Around the room, her classmates were achieving all levels of success. Sam managed to move his sponge a few inches. Stanley's moved, too, though Seven couldn't be sure if it was the spell or the tip of his wand that was the cause. Iggy's sponge traveled all the way across the table once, but then it ended up knocking Charlie on the back of the head because he couldn't stop it.

"Excellent! What a talented bunch I have! Now switch," Willowisp said after a bit.

"I never thought moving a sponge would be so tiring," Cully said, collapsing onto her stool after mixed results. "Your turn."

Seven picked up her wand with trembling hands. She looked at the sponge and tried desperately to push the fear of failure from her mind. She screwed her face up in concentration, closed and eyes, and flicked her wand.

"*Motus Abirum*," she said very clearly and very loudly.

She took a breath and peeked at her sponge. Her heart sank. The sponge was precisely in the same spot. She tried to keep her disappointment in check by reminding herself that many of the other students failed at their first attempts. It didn't mean that she wasn't magical, right?

"The spell is *Motus Ipseum*, not *Motus Abrium*, you idiot," Darcy said from the next table.

"Shut up, Davidson," Cully shot back. "or you'll get a mouth full of sponge."

Darcy made a rude gesture.

"Forget her. Try again," Cully encouraged.

Mustering her courage, Seven tried again, this time with a correct spell. Warmth grew in Seven's chest until a spark shot from her wand tip and hit the sponge. It jumped off the table, twisted in the air, and landed directly in front of Cully.

"I did it!" Seven said a little louder than she had intended.

"It's a sponge, Preston. Chill out," Sam said from a few tables away.

"Sorry, I guess I got a little excited," Seven said. Relief poured through her. She had performed her first magical spell. Despite not feeling anything at the Awakening, magic was alive inside her.

"Wonderful!" Willowisp said, walking up behind her. "Your wand waving is perfect. First attempt?"

"Sort of. I didn't say the spell right the first time," Seven admitted.

"You are a natural, Miss Preston. Excellent!" Willowisp said as she moved onto another student who was waving her wand incorrectly.

By the end of class, Seven moved her sponge a few more times, and Cully's sponge did more than just shiver. Charlie's sponge hit Devlin Mulzer in the face several times, but despite Charlie's apologies, Seven got the feeling it was not an accident.

"Students," Willowisp called as she clapped her hands together, "class is nearly over. Wonderful wand work! Some of you are quite talented," she said, looking directly at Seven. "The key is not to get frustrated. Frustration can block magic from working properly. For homework, I would like for you to take your sponges and practice, practice, practice. I will ask that you refrain from trying to move anything other than the sponges for now. Nurse Medwell has only just forgiven me for the rocks. Enjoy the weekend."

Iggy needed to talk with Willowisp, so Cully and Seven went on ahead. They were discussing the class and failed to notice that Darcy and Brigit walked up behind them.

"Oh, Brigit," Darcy said, obviously mocking Seven, "did you see it move? I made my sponge move!" Then she looked at Seven with a sour expression. "Idiot didn't even know the right spell."

"Stuff it, Darcy," Seven said without stopping. She was too excited to allow Darcy to ruin it.

"What's the matter, Preston? Afraid you can't do any real magic?" Brigit added, seemingly in an attempt to impress Darcy.

"No, Brigit, didn't you hear Willowisp? Preston's a natural. Ah, if only we all could be so gifted." The sarcasm dripped from Darcy's words like a leaky faucet. Then she turned on Cully. "Of course, if *your* magic fails, Cully, you could just look at the sponge. Your face would scare it into moving."

"Well, she certainly wouldn't ask you for any beauty secrets," said Iggy as he walked up behind all of them.

Darcy whirled on him.

"Stay out of this, Ig-na-tius," Darcy emphasized each syllable of his name. "Or is Cully here, your girlfriend, Crosser?"

Iggy's face looked surprised.

"That's right. Your secret is out, Crosser." Darcy's voice was low and full of hatred. "You can't keep a secret like that for long, especially when you and Cooper and Walker are dumb enough to talk about it in the halls." Charlie and Sam had asked Iggy many questions about life across the gate without magic, but Iggy had always taken care to make sure no one was around. Obviously, he had not been careful enough. "Others may be impressed, but I am not. You shouldn't even be allowed in Midia. You and your family are no friends to magic."

"Friendship, Darcy, is something you shouldn't talk about," Cully said. "The only people who are your friends are the ones too chicken to tell you what they really think of you."

Ignoring Cully, Darcy took a step toward Iggy.

"You better watch yourself. You never know when a spell might fly off wildly. I would hate for something to happen to you," Darcy said before turning to Brigit. "Let's go. This hallway is starting to stink like dragon dung."

"Oh, that?" Iggy said, regaining his composure. "That is just your breath blowing back in your face." Darcy looked as though she were going to blow fire. Quick as lightning, she whipped out her wand and pointed it at Iggy's chest.

"Shut up, Crosser," Darcy hissed dangerously.

Without even thinking, Seven pulled out her own wand and pointed it at Darcy.

"Put your wand away," Seven ordered. She had no idea

what she would do if Darcy didn't, but she refused to stand there while Iggy was threatened.

Darcy turned her wand on Seven.

"Come on, Preston, use it. I dare you."

"Seven, don't do it," Cully said. "She is just trying to get you into trouble."

Suddenly another wand was aimed at Seven's face. She glanced to her right and saw Brigit's shaking hand holding a wand.

"Put your wands away," Cully said as her own wand made its appearance.

"It is two versus three, Darcy. Are you sure you want to do this?" Seven said.

Seven watched Darcy's face falter before she slowly lowered her wand. Brigit followed suit, looking relieved the standoff was over.

"You had better watch your step, Crosser. There won't always be someone around to rescue you," Darcy warned as she and Brigit walked away.

"Well, that was fun," Iggy said sarcastically as he replaced his wand in his robes. "Let's do that again real soon."

"That girl brings out the worst in me," Seven answered.

"She brings out the worst in everybody," Cully said. Then she turned to Iggy. "I guess your secret is out."

Iggy just shrugged.

"I guess it was bound to get out sooner or later. In a school with this many people, secrets don't stay secrets for long."

Yeah, that is what I'm afraid of, Seven thought to herself.

At dinner, Cully told the rest of them about their encounter with Darcy.

"With her big mouth, I am sure by this time tomorrow, everyone in the school will know about Iggy," Sophie said.

"She's a real piece of work," Adria said. "How can someone so horrible be accepted into Wyndamir?"

"Magic isn't just for the good ones," Sophie said.

"Yeah, just look at Nikris," Sam said. "He's as bad as they

come, and he went to school here. He was Midian born and more evil than any Crosser could ever be."

"Who's Nikris?" Seven asked as she buttered a roll. As soon as she did, she knew it was the wrong thing to say. Except for Iggy, they all looked at her as though she were the dumbest person in the world.

"*Who's Nikris?*" Sam looked at her in shock. "Have you been living under a rock? The leader of the Shadow Raiders, of course. Maybe Iggy isn't the only Crosser at the table."

Seven had to say something. Despite Iggy's revelation, she wasn't ready to share that yet. She opened her mouth to make some excuse about her brain being fried from homework when Adria saved her.

"Well, Iggy isn't the only one at the school, that's for sure," Adria said. "There is a junior girl who was in the bathroom talking about some trouble she had with her gate pass. Another second-year boy talked about all the chores he could get done if only his mom would let him use magic at home. I heard a few mean comments, but nobody attacked them or anything. I think most people don't care so much anymore."

"Darcy and her friends care," Iggy said.

"Yeah, but Darcy is nothing but an overgrown pompous frog who likes to blow smoke. She may talk big, but she is nothing but a coward," Cully said.

"Unfortunately, she can convince a lot of people to think the way she does," Sophie said ominously.

"Or threaten them," Adria said.

"That's true," Sam said, "but she doesn't scare me."

"That's right, Iggy. If Darcy gives you any more trouble, you let us know. We got your back," Charlie added.

At that moment, the televisions came to life. Nicholas Sanders appeared on screen, his smile as bright as ever.

"Hello, students of Wyndamir Academy, and congratulations on surviving your first week of classes. Headmistress Bellatora told me that everyone is off to a good start this year with the fewest number of demerits and detentions on record."

"No thanks to you, huh, Seven?" Sam teased.

Seven shot him a dirty look.

"Now, many of my faithful viewers have been asking for more information on the attack at the Landing," Nicholas continued. "Unfortunately, due to circumstances beyond my control, I have not been able to make another trip to our neighboring town, but our very own Dean of Students has been in contact with the security officers still stationed there. They informed her there have been no new developments, and things are back to normal." Nicholas's voice lost some of its enthusiasm.

Cully, Iggy, and Seven shared a look. Seven thought it was very convenient that Mcfee was the one who said all was well. Seven replayed the conversation she and Cully overheard in the hallway.

Leave Wyndamir Landing to the others. Your job is here. You know what you have to do.

"I was able to contact the hospital where Mr. Swathmore was taken," Nicholas continued. "Though they would not comment specifically on his condition, they did say that it was still touch and go. Since no new information is available, I thought I would show you some of the highlights of my interview with Wally Fargles."

Sam and Charlie groaned.

"I don't think I can watch that again," Charlie said.

"Yeah, let's get out of here," Sam agreed.

"I guess I am going to the library," Adria said without much enthusiasm. It was surprising how much homework was already starting to pile up, and it had only been a week. "If I don't start now, I will be way behind."

"I'll join you," Sophie said, sounding even more unenthused than Adria.

"Are you crazy? It is the weekend. Are you going to spend Friday night in the library?" Sam asked.

Sophie and Adria nodded and left.

"Well, we're not, are we, Charlie? Besides, I work better under pressure," Sam said, nudging Charlie. "Don't you?"

"Oh, yes. We like to think about our homework thoroughly before we begin," Charlie agreed. "Tonight, we are going into the forbidden part of the woods."

"Maybe we will run into a werewolf or a unicorn or a squonk. Bet you've never seen one of those across the gates," Sam whispered to Iggy before leaving.

"Those two are going to get into real trouble one day," Iggy said.

After the excitement of the first week, things at Wyndamir settled into a comfortable routine. There had been no more attacks, and Nicholas Sanders had reported a few weeks after the attack on Swathmore was much better and would be released from the hospital soon. The Midian Security Office had declared the case closed. The only person who seemed upset by this was Nicholas. His big story was over, and his newscasts were back to general school information.

After her secret meeting in the hallway, nothing new had happened with Mcfee, though the Dean of Students did seem to bit preoccupied. More than once, Seven noticed her running into students in the corridors or looking thoughtful during meal times. She and Poxley still didn't seem to care for each other too much. Seven couldn't help but observe that Mcfee had been more visible around the school in the last weeks. Was that why the attacks had stopped? Mcfee couldn't get away from Wyndamir? Cully and Iggy felt like she was reaching.

Darcy did her best to make life miserable for Iggy. Devlin Mulzer joined her and Brigit in giving Iggy a hard time every chance they could. They made a show of moving to the other side of the corridors so they wouldn't catch 'Crosser-itis' or pretended to get a whiff of something and announce it was the putrid smell of rotten Crossers. When Iggy outperformed Darcy in classes, which was almost daily, the comments became even nastier. Each time, Seven felt even worse about not sharing her Crosser status, but she just wasn't ready.

"Let's study outside," Cully suggested one day after a particularly odoriferous potions class. They made their way to the largest oak tree near the smallest pond, a spot that had become their favorite. The October air was crisp and cool. Fall had arrived.

"It sure does smell better out here than whatever Mulciber was cooking today," Seven said.

"It smelled worse than rotten socks and two-week-old fish. What do you think it was?" Iggy asked.

"His dinner," Cully joked as she opened her book to review the parts of the bugloss plant for an upcoming exam.

"Now, this is the one where you can use the roots only if they are red?" Seven asked.

"Only if you want your potion to blow up," Iggy said. "Only use them after they have turned yellow."

"Ugh! I am never going to get this," Seven said as she slammed her book closed. "Hey, what are they doing?" she asked, pointing in the direction of Wydnamir Hall.

Darcy, Brigit, Devlin, and two other students were poking and prodding something in the middle. Or rather someone. Seven caught a glimpse of a very red-faced Stanley Nogginhollow. Then, Seven watched as Devlin put his arm around Stanley's shoulders and not so gently led him around the building and out of sight while Stanley frantically shook his head no.

"Devlin and Darcy got Stanley. Come one!" Seven jumped up and sprinted across the lawns, not waiting for Cully and Iggy to catch up.

When Seven reached the corner of the building, the group was nowhere to be seen. She looked around frantically and noticed a door closing on a building Seven had never been in before. Without missing a beat, she sprinted toward it, tore open the door, and ran inside. Whatever they had planned for Stanley, Seven was sure it wasn't good.

The building was dark, and it took Seven's eyes a moment to adjust. A dimly lit hallway stretched up ahead and to her left was a set of steps that led to another door.

"Please, don't!"

Stanley's voice came from the other side of the door.

Seven sprinted up the steps and flew through the door. Something soft and flimsy was in front of her and on both sides. Up ahead, she saw a faint light as though she were in a tunnel. She crept toward the light and finally realized the soft, flimsy thing was a black curtain. When she reached the end, she saw a stage. In the center of it, Darcy's group surrounded Stanley. She looked back, hoping Cully and Iggy were right behind her. They weren't, but she couldn't wait.

"What are you doing?" Seven said, stepping out from the curtains hating that her voice did not sound strong as she had hoped it would.

The group turned and looked at her.

"Get out of here, Preston," Darcy ordered.

"Well, well, well," said Devlin Mulzer, who stood in front of a cowering Stanley. "The loser's girlfriend is coming to the rescue. It's Preston, right? You sure you want her to leave, Darcy? I mean, we have enough for two." He took a menacing step toward Seven.

"Leave Stanley alone," Seven said, trying to calm herself. "He's never done anything to you."

"Or what?" asked Darcy as she stepped next to Devlin. "In case you haven't noticed, this time, you're outnumbered."

Seven turned, hoping to see that Cully and Iggy had finally caught up with her. They hadn't. She had to buy some time.

"Why is it, Darcy, that whenever you decide to cause trouble, you are never alone? Are you too much of a coward to take on someone without a group of goons to back you up?"

"You think I am afraid of you?" Darcy laughed coldly. "Let's go right now!"

"Fine," Seven said, pulling out her wand, "but let Stanley go."

"Oh, he's free to go anytime," Devlin said as he turned to the side, revealing Stanley. Lying next to him on the floor was an empty potion bottle. Seven watched in horror as Stanley's skin changed color. He went from yellow to green to multi-color. Then Stanley groaned and fell to his knees.

"Exactly what is going on here?" boomed a voice with a thick English accent. All of them turned to see a rather large woman marching down the center aisle carrying a suitcase. Her brilliant purple robes billowed out behind her. "Students are not allowed to be in this building unless specifically invited by me. Explain yourselves." The two students Seven didn't know started to run, but they froze in their tracks. "I wouldn't do that if I were you," the woman warned. She had hit them with some kind of immobilizing spell.

Not surprising to Seven, Darcy spoke up.

"Well, you see, Professor…"

"Madame Flouriche," the woman corrected. "Drama Teacher, extraordinaire."

"Oh, well, Madame Flouriche, we saw Preston and Nogginhollow entering the building without permission. We didn't want them to get into trouble, so we followed them to warn them," Darcy said silkily with a practiced look of innocence.

"Is that so?" Flouriche said.

"Yes, mam. Then we saw Preston pouring some kind of dye onto his skin," Darcy said, pointing to Stanley. "We tried to stop her, but we were too late." Her friends confirmed the story with enthusiastic nods. "She is so mean."

"You are such a liar!" Seven yelled." I followed…"

"Enough!" Flouriche boomed. She peered down at Stanley, who looked like a neon sign. Her nose wrinkled as the pungent smell of the potion hit her. "I don't care why you are in this building," her voice was low and dangerous. "It seems the only one who did not come here willingly is you," she said, pointing at Stanley. "Go to Nurse Medwell immediately before the color permanently stains your skin." Not needing to be asked twice, Stanley bolted.

"As for the rest of you, whatever your intentions may have been, you are still in *my* theater without *my* permission. This building is my treasure, my home, my castle." She gestured to the empty seats in the audience. "And you have defiled it. Disrespect of this theater is disrespect of me. Each of you has earned one demerit." She pointed to the floor where some of the potion spilled. It was flashing all sorts of colors. "I suggest you find a way to clean this immediately," she said, releasing the two frozen students who fell to the floor before scampering up in search of cleaning supplies.

"Now, since you love my theater so much that you cannot stand to stay away from it, I will expect to see all of you at auditions in two weeks. I am always looking for stagehands to do the grunt work. A demerit can easily become an expulsion should you *forget*. Do I make myself clear?"

Seven wanted to argue, but the look in Flouriche's eye told her it would be dangerous to do so.

"Now, get out," Flouriche hissed. Darcy and her friends ran from the stage as quickly as they could. Seven followed far enough behind to avoid another confrontation, but she was still fuming. She tried to save Stanley, but the only thing she earned for her good deed was another demerit and an unwanted job. And what had happened to Cully and Iggy, her *friends*?

"Seven!" shouted a relieved Cully crossing the lawns holding Seven's backpack.

"There you are!" shouted Iggy, who was holding his wrist.

"Nice of you two to finally show up," Seven snapped.

"Where did you go? We looked..." Cully

"Really? Well, you certainly didn't look too hard," Seven spat. "I was in the theater waiting on my *friends* to help me?"

"We tried. The doors..." Iggy explained.

"Worked just fine for me," Seven said, crossing her arms. She knew she was being unfair, but she was just so angry.

"What's the matter with you? You're acting like a jerk," Cully said sharply.

"You abandoned me, and I am the one being a jerk?" Seven couldn't stop herself.

"Abandoned? I think you are being a little unfair, Seven," Iggy said.

"And dramatic," Cully added.

"Dramatic? Unfair?" Seven yelled. "I got another demerit, nearly got expelled, and I didn't do anything wrong. How is that for dramatic and unfair!"

"Expelled? What happened?" Cully asked, genuinely.

"Well, if you hadn't abandoned, you would know. Thanks for nothing." Seven snatched her bag from Cully and stomped off, leaving Iggy and Cully standing there open-mouthed.

Chapter Ten

Another Wyndamir

The next two weeks were lonely ones. At no other school did Seven ever feel as alone as she did during those days when she wasn't talking to Iggy and Cully. Maybe she should have just kept to herself from the start. If she kept people at a distance, she couldn't get hurt by them. That was how she had survived at her other schools, that was until Kerry, and look how that turned out. But still, the last two months with them had been, well, nice.

She had tried talking with Stanley. She thought he would be grateful, but she was wrong.

"Look, Seven, I know that you thought you were helping, but you have only made things worse," he had said. "Darcy and Mulzer remind me every chance they get that I can't fight my own battles. They ask me where my girlfriend is. It's humiliating. School's hard enough for me without their constant ribbing. I got to go. Please leave me alone." Then, he had headed off to class.

Now Seven was on her way to the theater for -how had Flouriche put it - "grunt work." When she reached the theater building, she found it was packed. Students from all grade levels were spread out all over the theater quietly, reading a script or loudly practicing lines with each other. Darcy, Brigit, and Devlin were all sitting together in the back row, so Seven headed to the front. As soon as she plopped into a seat, two people flanked her. Each one grabbed an arm to hold her down.

"Hey! What are..." She stopped as a hand clasped over her mouth.

"No, you will listen to what we have to say," hissed a very stern voice. "You have been a stubborn mule. Now you will shut up and listen, and if you fight us or try to run, Iggy is prepared to perform an immobility spell that he has been working on for this very occasion. I will warn you, though, he doesn't have it perfected yet. Got it?" Cully words were forceful.

Seven glared from one to the other, trying to decide what to do. One thought kept her seated. What would Flouriche do if Seven caused a scene in her theater? Reluctantly, she nodded but refused to look at either one of them.

"Now, when you ran off like a crazed maniac the other day..." Cully began.

"I was not crazed," Seven objected.

"Like a crazed maniac," Cully repeated. "Iggy and I *did* follow you, but I tripped over *your* potion book and sprained my wrist." Cully held up her bandaged wrist. "By the time we caught up, Madame Flouriche was already walking through the doors. We tried every door, but they were locked. We even tried a few spells, but we couldn't get the stupid things to budge. Iggy tugged so hard that he wore a blister on his hand." Iggy held up his hand to show Seven his healing blister.

"Then, you didn't even give us a chance to explain. Not for the last two weeks. You are the most pig-headed person I have ever met, and I have six brothers and two sisters!" Iggy finished breathlessly.

"So, to show you that we are your friends and we forgive you for being a butthead, we signed up to help with the play," Cully said.

Seven was speechless. She had assumed the worst, and she didn't allow them to explain. She chose to believe the worst about the two people who had been nothing but kind to her. She hadn't even noticed Cully's injured wrist. She finally came up with a weak, "Oh."

"Oh? That's it?" Cully asked in exasperation.

"What do you want me to say?" Seven said defensively. "That I was a jerk to both of you?"

"I believe the word Cully used was butthead," Iggy said.

"Fine, I was a *jerk*," Seven said, refusing to use Cully's word. Iggy and Cully both nodded.

"You don't have to agree so easily," Seven muttered.

"Well, when you are right, you are right," Iggy said, smiling.

"I'm sorry," Seven said seriously. "I haven't had a lot of friends. I am not very good at it."

"Yeah, you do kind of stink at it," Cully said, smiling.

"I'm sorry about your wrist," Seven said softly.

"What about my blister?" Iggy said, holding up his finger.

"That, too," Seven said.

"Great, then let's just pretend the last two weeks haven't been awkward and uncomfortable, and move on, agreed?" Iggy suggested.

"Agreed," Cully and Seven said simultaneously.

Though Seven felt relieved that the fight was over, she still felt a little awkward. After all, it had been all her fault. She was thankful that Flouriche chose that moment to appear on stage.

"Welcome to Wyndamir Theater. This year's production will be the acclaimed story, *Stolen Powers*, written by Nubilia, a tortured soul who kept many secrets. It is the only piece she ever wrote, likely because the emotion and passion she poured into the telling left her empty." Flouriche's voice dropped in volume but not intensity. "We will be diving into the dark world of black magic, betrayal, and murder. We will portray characters whose moral fibers are so twisted and horrid that you will feel it necessary to scrub the foulness from your skin when you leave this theater. We will create magic without casting a single spell." Seven had to admit that the woman knew how to grab an audience.

"For those of you new to my theater," Flouriche hissed,

"be warned. I do not call it a play because we do not play here. We will work until you bleed because it is that blood that will transform you into the characters. It is that blood that will bring the crowd to the edge of their seats. It is that blood that will bring about the intoxicating and addicting sound of thunderous applause." She paused, closed her eyes, and took a deep breath. When she opened her eyes, her face was stern. "Tardiness is not acceptable. Misbehavior will be tolerated." She scanned the crowd allowing her glare to land on Darcy, Brigit, Devlin, and Seven. "Whatever I ask, you will give. If you are wondering, 'Can I do this?' the answer is no. There is no room for doubt. The theater is like a dragon. It will burn you alive if you are not on guard at all times, but wielders from all around will come to pay you homage if you conquer it. So, for those of you unwilling to make the sacrifice, I suggest you leave now."

Some students looked at each other questioningly. A few looked as though they were going to be sick, but no one left.

"Wonderful," Flouriche said, clapping her hands cheerfully. Her moods changed faster than a pixie's wings. "When I call your name, you will read the lines I have marked on the script, and then you will leave the stage. My assistant Malcolm will direct those of you who have volunteered to help behind the scenes. Meet him backstage."

Seven, Cully, and Iggy joined a group of students who made their way behind the curtains. A tall boy with oily hair that hung like wet noodles met them.

"Name?" he said in a condescending tone.

"Seven Preston."

"Oh, yes, the trespasser. Where are the other delinquents?" he asked, looking over his clipboard. "Dicey Davidson."

"It's *Darcy* Davidson," Darcy spat.

Malcolm ignored her and continued down his list assigning jobs as he went.

"Preston, Collins, Everett, you will be in the prop room," he said in his condescending tone. "Davidson, Murdock, and

Mulzer, you are the cleaning crew."

"I do not pick up trash," Darcy objected.

"You will do whatever is assigned to you," Malcolm said, not even looking up from his clipboard.

"Then, you will have to assign me a different job," she said defiantly.

"Miss Davidson, you have a choice. You may either pick up the trash or be expelled. I do not care which one," he said dismissively.

With a huff, Darcy stomped off to where the cleaning crew was assembling, mumbling words under her breath that Seven was sure were not complimentary toward Malcolm or Flouriche.

"Prop room is up the stairs, stage right, first door on the left. There are several boxes that
need unpacking, with the contents organized by scene. You'll need this." Malcolm tossed Cully the script. "The rest of you, this way, and be silent. Madame Flouriche is beginning auditions." When Malcolm said the drama teacher's name, a sort of faraway, dreamy look crossed his face.
It made Seven do a full-body shudder.

"This is several?" Seven said as they entered the prop room. Malcolm's *several* were actually hundreds of boxes stacked in no discernible order. "This will take until next year."

"Or the year after that," Cully agreed.

"Well, we don't have that long, and to be honest, that Flouriche woman terrifies me, so let's get going," Iggy said as he popped open the first box.

Inside the first box were a crown, a scepter, and a very real looking dagger.

"Whoa, these look real," Iggy said, and he touched the blade. "Ouch!" He quickly put his finger in his mouth. "They feel real, too," he mumbled with his finger in his mouth.

After several hours of unpacking and organizing, they barely made a dent.

"I'm pooped," Cully said.

"Me, too," Seven agreed as she collapsed next to a partially unpacked box. "Let's call it a night. I still have my history report to finish."

"Me, too," Cully said.

"I told you two to get it done days ago," Iggy chastised.

"Shut up, Iggy," both girls said in unison.

Over the next several weeks, the three of them quickly fell into a routine of classes, homework, and prop room duties. Seven couldn't believe the calendar when it said it was Halloween.

They were on their way to History of Midia. Seven had been pleasantly surprised how must she enjoyed it despite her usual dislike for history. Brimbal used spells and charms to create holographic reproductions of historical events. On occasion, he would even temporarily morph himself into various historical figures. Once, he turned himself into Groggin the Great, a tiny gremlin with a high voice who was wrongly accused of starting the Gremlin Games Uprising of 1374.

For today's class, Brimbal instructed them to meet in the foyer of Wyndamir Hall. To celebrate the holiday, Brimbal dressed as the great Epacris Critch, a famous botanist known to wear pots for hats. The pot Brimbal was wearing had a flower that kept reaching around and tugging at his nose and ears. Then it would stand back up and shake as though laughing.

"I know you have all walked through this foyer a thousand times," Brimbal began. "However, most students never take the time to examine the items in it. We will use this class to do just those things.

"First, let me draw your attention to the Wall of Headmasters and Headmistresses. These
wielders have faithfully led this academy from its beginning. Most taught at this or other magical institutions before becoming headmaster or headmistress. Of course," he pointed to a picture of a familiar female wielder with red hair streaked with gray, "there is Professor Bellatora, our current headmistress.

"Walking over this way, you will see smaller portraits of

all current Wyndamir professors with a short biography of each one. This professor, in my opinion, is the most handsome of the bunch." He pointed to a portrait of himself. The flower on top of his head pretended to get sick. "Somewhere in here ..." his gaze finally settled on a space to the left, "Or maybe not. That space is supposed to house a portrait of our current Board of Advisors. I suppose the brownies are cleaning it, again. Very curious." Then he waved his hand. "Since the school was established, a Wyndamir has served as ChairWielder on the Board of Advisors. Unfortunately, that may soon change."

"Why is that, professor?" Iggy asked.

"Though Mr. Harrison Wyndamir is still officially on the Board, he hasn't taken an active role in many years. He no longer attends the beginning of the year banquet, and he hasn't dropped in on a class in ages. With his daughter gone, once he retires, there will not be a Wyndamir serving on the Board."

"What happened to his daughter, Professor?" asked Anna Watts.

"Well, that is one of the biggest mysteries in Wyndamir history now, isn't it?" he said. "The only heir to the Wyndamir family disappeared without a trace over thirteen years ago. Some suspect that the Shadow Raiders killed her. I don't believe that because she was mighty powerful, and I would know. I taught her," he smiled sadly.

"Why do people think the Shadow Raiders killed her?" Iggy asked.

"Well, around the time of her disappearance, a man was found murdered. He had no identification on him, but he did have one thing - the mark of the Shadow Raiders." A few of the students gasped. Brimbal continued. "And allegedly beside him was a ring, a gold ring with one emerald, one amethyst, and one ruby. Mr. Wyndamir's daughter was known to have an identical ring. When several years passed and an extensive search turned up nothing, some used this as evidence of her death. However, others used the fact that her body was never found as evidence that she betrayed the magical community."

"Was that man ever identified?" someone called from behind Seven.

"He was not," Brimbal said.

"Where did the murder happen?' asked Charlie.

"Here," Brimbal said grimly, "on school grounds."

"The Shadow Raiders came onto school grounds?" Emma Watts asked in disbelief.

A few students began panic murmuring about the attacks in Wyndamir Landing and whether the school was safe. Brimbal's flower used the leaves on its stem to cover itself as if in fear.

"Calm down!" Brimbal shouted. "We must not panic nor start rumors!" After a few more gasps and shrieks, the class calmed down. "When studying history, it is vital to pay attention to facts. Wild speculation turns people into unthinking, panicky mobs who cause more harm than the event itself did. Now, it is a fact that a man was murdered. It is also true that Wyndamir's daughter disappeared at that same time. What is not known is whether the Shadow Raiders were behind either one. We don't even know if Harrison Wyndamir's daughter is dead."

"Come on, Professor, she hasn't been seen in how long? What other explanation could there be?" Sam argued.

"I am not saying it isn't possible. I am saying it hasn't been proven," Brimbal countered. "As far as the safety of the school, security is Bellatora's number one priority. She has added many hidden safety measures over the years."

"Like what?" Charlie asked.

"Well, I am not supposed to ..." Brimbal's voice trailed off, and he made a show of looking around the room conspiratorially. The flower atop his head did the same. "Have you ever noticed all the statues that line the corridors on the fourth and fifth floors? Well, let's just say that you cannot wiver directly into the school any longer," he said in a near whisper.

Several students gasped. Seven didn't know what wivering was, so it made no sense to her.

"You said the Wyndamir woman betrayed the magical

community. How?" a student near the middle of the group asked.

"No, *I* didn't say she did. I said some wielders thought she did. If you want to know more," Brimbal gestured around the foyer, "find it for yourself. Later in the term, you will write a report on someone in this foyer. Maybe some of you will choose her. For now, just roam and read."

The class dispersed throughout the room, pointing and talking and laughing at some of the old portraits. There were pictures of famous wielders who were graduates from the school, along with framed newspaper articles about wielders who had done a great service either to the school or to the wielding community in general.

"This woman is the inventor of the sunfield potion," Adria said. "When my baby cousin was deathly sick, this potion cured her. I didn't realize she was a Wyndamir student."

"This Oisin fellow battled Rourkus Durn. He won, but he lost his right pinky finger and his left leg in the battle," Stanley Nogginhollow read aloud.

"Stellanina Noom looks friendly," Sophie said sarcastically, pointing to a painting of a grey-haired woman sitting stiffly in a high backed chair. Her pinched face appeared as though she smelled something rotten.

"This one looks like he couldn't blast his way out of a paper bag," Cully said, pointing to a skinny man with wide eyes that made him look perpetually surprised. She read the plaque below his name. "Darvis Humperdinkus, Master Phytologist. The only known wielder to successfully harvest the corpse flower. Graduate of Wyndamir."

"Corpse flower?" Seven repeated. "Gross. I am not sure I could swallow any potion made from a corpse flower."

"Hey, Seven, check this out. The woman in this picture looks just like you," Sam called from across the room.

"Too bad you aren't related to her. You'd be filthy stinking rich!" Charlie added.

"Oh yeah? Seven asked as she and Cully made their way

over to Sam and Charlie. "I hope her name isn't Humperdinkus."

"It's that Wyndamir woman," Sam said. "Listen to this." He read:

> *The whereabouts of the daughter of Harrison William Wyndamir, ChairWielder of the Board of Advisors for Wyndamir Academy for the Magical Arts, are still a mystery. However, Three years after her disappearance, the most widespread wielder hunt in Midian history continues. Though reported sightings have come in from Torva and Viridia, further investigations have yielded no useful information. Many are questioning the continuing effort saying that after three years, it is time to mourn the loss and allow the search teams to attend to other critical matters. Harrison Wyndamir, however, has vowed never to stop looking for his only daughter.*
> *"It is no secret that my daughter and I have had disagreements in the past, but she still was – no, she still is, my daughter. I will use every resource I have to find her."*
>
> *When asked why the search continues after three years, one source close to the investigation speaking on terms of complete anonymity had this to say. "Ms. Wyndamir had been given a top-secret assignment before her disappearance. The Midian government is quite anxious to retrieve an item entrusted to her care. Some of us believe, however, that their efforts are in vain. we are certain that she stole this item she was supposed to be guarding and disappeared of her own volition."*
>
> *When asked about the possibility that his daughter is not the victim but the mastermind behind her own disappearance, Harrison Wyndamir had no publishable comment.*
>
> *Speculation also continues as to whether there is a connection between Ms. Wyndamir's disappearance and the un-*

identified man found murdered that same evening on the grounds of Wyndamir Academy.

"There is no evidence that Ms. Wyndamir suffered the same fate," Guardian First Class Myra Huggins stated but would not comment on the alleged ring found near the body.

The citizens of Midia are wondering how much longer the investigation will remain open and whether the question of if Ms. Wyndamir is a thief or an unfortunate victim will ever be answered.

"Intense," Sam commented. "Maybe you don't want to be related to her. She may be a thief." When Sam stepped out of the way, Seven couldn't believe her eyes. There had to be a mistake. This had to be a joke. A cruel, cruel joke.

"Well? Don't you think she could be your mom or something?" Sam said.

"He's right, Seven. If your hair was red and curly and you were a little older, you could claim to be Miranda Wyndamir. Then you would be loaded," Adria agreed.

"Or in jail, if you proved to be a thief," Charlie added.

Miranda Wyndamir. The picture was Miranda Wyndamir. Her mother. Miranda Wyndamir Preston.

Seven's heart was beating so hard that it felt like a bass drum, keeping the beat as questions exploded in her mind. Was her mother the missing Miranda Wyndamir? Harrison Wyndamir's daughter? That would make Harrison Wyndamir her grandfather, a man her mother told her was dead. That unidentified man? Was that her dad?

"Seven?" Cully asked. "What's wrong?"

Seven thought back to the summer. The passkey her mother had given her had the letters MW. It stood for Miranda Wyndamir, the missing thought dead Miranda Wyndamir.

"Hello?" Iggy said, waving his hand in front of Seven's

face. "Are you all right?"

"I'm…" Seven began.

"She's probably wondering how she can use her resemblance to the family to get at the fortune," Sam joked.

"I don't see it. You don't look anything like a Wyndamir. You look more like a Humperdinkus," Darcy said as she strolled over to the group.

"Yep, definitely a Humperdinkus. She smells just like the corpse flower," Devlin said as he pretended to sniff Seven.

Stifled snorts of laughter sounded from around the room.

"Even so," Darcy said, "I would much rather be a Humperdinkus than a Wyndamir. My father says she's nothing but a dirty thief who stole what she was supposed to be protecting and killed that man they found. He says she is holed up in some dark corner of the magical world living off the fortune she made by selling whatever it was she was *protecting*."

"That's ridiculous," said Iggy. "Why would she do that when her family was already rich?"

"Everyone knows you can never have enough money. Besides, my father went to school with her. He said she wasn't half as talented as everyone believed. The teachers gave her high marks because they were afraid they would get fired. My dad says she was a spoiled brat," Darcy said.

"I guess he would know since he raised one," Cully said.

"Shut it, Collins," Darcy warned.

"I suggest you shut it before I shut it for you," Seven growled, finally joining the conversation.

"Is that a threat?"

"A promise," Seven said, taking a step closer to Darcy.

"What is going on here?" Brimbal asked, breaking through the crowded foyer.

"Nothing, Professor. We were just, uh, we were just discussing the corpse flower. It is so interesting," Iggy said innocently

"I'm sure," Brimbal said unconvinced, looking from

Darcy to Seven. "That is enough for today. Class dismissed." Neither Darcy nor Seven moved. "I said class dismissed," Brimbal repeated firmly.

"Whatever," Seven said as she stormed across the foyer and out the front doors. Though she didn't have her cloak, she needed some fresh air and some space.

"Seven!" Cully shouted. "Wait!"

But Seven didn't wait. She was so angry. She was nearly running now. She didn't know where she was going. She was near one of the entrances to the gardens when Cully and Iggy finally caught up with her.

What was that all about?" Cully asked breathlessly.

Seven whirled on them

"Darcy Davidson is the most horrible person I have ever met," Seven said.

"True, but not newsworthy. What is this really about?" Iggy said. "And why do you care what she says about that Wyndamir woman?"

"I don't," Seven said a little too quickly. "Look, I just need to be alone. I will meet you later."

"No," Cully said simply. "You are not running off half-cocked again."

"I just need to be alone," Seven insisted.

"Look, Seven, if you don't want to tell us, fine. But we aren't leaving you alone," Cully said. "Right, Iggy?"

"Right," Iggy agreed.

"But," Seven tried to argue.

"Look, you said it yourself. You aren't very good at friendships. Letting people help is part of friendship, so spill it," Cully said.

Seven looked from Cully to Iggy. She wasn't sure what to say. *My mom is Miranda Wyndamir, and she isn't really dead.* She collapsed on a nearby bench and took a few deep breaths to buy some time.

"That picture," Seven began as tears stung her eyes. "The one Sam showed us. It's-" Just then, something jumped onto the bench.

All three of them jumped up. A white cat with blue eyes stared at them.

"You nearly gave us a heart attack," Cully said, visibly relieved as the cat sat back on its haunches and stared at them. "Are you the cat from the garden the dog was chasing?" It looked as though the cat gave a nearly imperceptible nod.

"What's all this?" asked a voice from inside the garden. The three turned to see Durward Skelly pop into view.

"Oh, nothing," Seven said as she frantically wiped at her eyes.

"This doesn't look like nothing to me," Skelly said, noticing Seven's wet eyes.

"Honest. We just needed some fresh air," Seven said, sniffing.

"Hmm, fresh air, huh? Well, I have something better than fresh air," Skelly said with a smile. "Muffins."

"Really?" Iggy said, wide-eyed as his mouth watered.

"Hot chocolate and warm muffins. I just pulled them out of the oven when I saw Willie sitting on my window sill. He was mewing like a, a, well, like a cat. Anyway, I followed him, and here you are."

"Willie?" Iggy asked.

"Yes, Willie," Skelly said, gesturing to the white cat. "Now, let's go to my house, and you three can tell me all about nothing."

Seven wasn't sure she wanted to go, but Iggy and Cully were already following the big man.

Skelly's house was small but very inviting, and it smelled delicious. He gestured for them to sit at the table while he put the muffins on a plate and poured hot chocolate. As they sat, Seven looked around the cottage.

It was very tidy. The kitchen was spotless. A vase of wildflowers sat in the middle of the round wooden table covered by a yellow tablecloth. Two overstuffed chairs sat in front of a large, stone fireplace where a crackling fire gave off a warm light.

Skelly placed a mug of hot chocolate in front of each of them and a large plate of muffins in the middle. Willie snagged one, jumped off the table, and sat next to the door to eat it.

"Now, those are apple cinnamon, and those are chocolate chip and pumpkin in the spirit of Halloween," he said, pointing to various muffins. "And this," he raised his own mug, "is the best recipe in all of Midia for hot chocolate. It has been in my family for generations. Try it."

They all took a cautious sip.

"This is very good," Iggy said, reaching for a pumpkin muffin. Cully snagged a chocolate one while Seven picked at an apple cinnamon muffin.

"So, how are classes going?" Skelly said, sitting down and grabbing a pumpkin muffin.

"Interesting," Iggy said.

"Good," Cully said, "but I wish they didn't assign so much homework. My hand is going to fall off from writing so much."

"Yeah, they work you hard for sure," Skelly said. "I have seen more than a few students run out of the school buildings over the years. Sometimes, you just need a break."

"That's true," Cully said.

"What class was it tonight that made you need a break?" Skelly asked.

"Brimbal's," Seven said. "But it was really more Darcy Davidson than Brimbal's class. She's horrible."

"Ah, yes, the Davidson's. Nasty family, for sure. Lorcan Davidson is her father, I believe. He is a powerful man in Midia, powerful and cruel. He rubbed more than a few students the wrong way during his time here. As a matter of fact," Skelly said, looking at Seven, "you remind me of one of them. Lorcan couldn't stand her. She was smart, friendly, and outperformed him in about every class."

"What was her name?" Seven asked.

"Miranda Wyndamir."

Chapter Eleven

Taking a Chance

Seven sat there, stunned.

"I…I…I.. don't know who that is," Seven lied.

"That is who the article was about that Sam was reading," Cully said, taking another bite of her muffin.

"The resemblance is uncanny. I mean, if your hair was red and curly, you could almost be her twin," Skelly said.

Seven didn't say anything hoping the subject would change. However, Iggy already put it together.

"You know her, don't you?" Iggy whispered.

Seven wasn't sure what to say. Should she deny it? Should she run? Should she take a chance?

"Seven, she's your mom, isn't she?" Iggy repeated. "That's why you reacted like that. Darcy wasn't insulting some stranger. She was insulting your mom."

"That's ridiculous," Cully said. "She's not Seven's mom."

Speechless, all Seven could do was stare at her muffin and fight against the tears. The awkward silence grew uncomfortable. Finally, Seven nodded.

"I thought so," Skelly said, nodding. "The first time I saw you in the garden, I thought so. Why do you think I kept asking you to repeat your name, Seven?"

She shrugged and continued to pick at her muffin, which was now a pile of crumbs.

"Thought I was mad, didn't you?" he asked, his eyes

twinkling with mirth.

This made Seven smile despite her tears.

"Maybe a little," she whispered.

"I was a bit surprised when you said Preston. Then later, I thought that, of course, your last name wouldn't be Wyndamir. It would be your dad's last name."

"Wait a minute!" Cully interjected. "Are you all crazy? Your mom cannot be Miranda Wyndmir. That's...that's... just..not..possible."

In answer, Seven pulled the locket from her robes. She opened it and showed them the pictures. Cully sat back, too stunned to speak.

"Is that your dad?" Skelly asked.

"Yes. Did you ever meet him?" Seven asked hopefully.

"No, I never had the pleasure," Skelly said. "But your mom. I sure knew her. Lovely lady. Always nice and kind. Never threw her name around. Quite talented, too. At the top of her class, if I remember."

"I wouldn't know," Seven said dryly. "She didn't tell me anything."

"I knew she wasn't dead, knew it as much as I know my name is Durward Skelly!" Skelly whooped as he smacked the table, causing Willie to jump. "She was too talented to let those goons get her. How did she do it? Why did she do it? I mean, she must have had a good reason," Skelly said as much to himself as to her.

"She just said it was to protect me."

"Protect you?" Skelly asked, but Seven just shrugged.

"I just learned about magic this summer. I didn't know my mom was a member of a well-known family in Midia until I just saw her picture in the foyer."

"Well-known? That's putting it mildly. The Wyndamir name dates to the formation of this world. This academy has served as a model for many schools in other magical countries. It is not unusual for staff and students from other schools to visit to learn how we do things around here."

"She's not even the one who told me about this school. Mcfee was."

"That's why Mcfee is the one that took you shopping. Your mom couldn't risk someone seeing her," Iggy observed.

Seven nodded.

"So, Phoebe Mcfee *did* know your mom was alive all this time. She sure put on a good show all these years, crying and mourning. It was a performance worthy of Madame Flouriche.

"Actually, Mcfee didn't know. When she came to my house this past summer, she was
surprised. She kept staring at my mom as though she were a ghost," Seven said.

"Well, I guess that makes sense," Skelly nodded thoughtfully. "If your mom were going to go through the trouble to disappear, she wouldn't tell Mcfee anything because she knew Mcfee would be questioned. And questioned she was. That was bad business." He paused here, shook his head, but didn't explain. Then he continued, "Even truth spells and potions can't make you say something that you don't know. Your mom was right not to tell her anything," Skelly said. "And brave to leave on her own. Where did she end up?"

"Wait a minute!" Cully said, finding her voice at last. "You didn't know about magic until this summer. That means you're a ...."

"Crosser," Seven finished for her, looking sideways at Iggy. "I'm sorry I didn't say anything earlier, Iggy. All those hateful things Darcy said about Crossers, well, I should have stood up for you or at least said something sooner."

Iggy just shrugged.

"Hold on a minute!" Cully shouted. "You're a Wyndamir and a Crosser?"

"Welcome to the party," Iggy said sarcastically.

Cully shot him a nasty look.

"I mean, I heard it, but I just can't believe I heard it," Cully said, sitting back again.

"So, does anyone else know about your mom?"

"Only Mcfee, and now you guys."

"Well, it isn't my secret to tell, so I won't, but don't be surprised if someone else puts it together. Many of the current staff were here when your mom was a student, and you do look an awful lot like her."

"So, I've heard," she said dryly.

"And when this secret comes out..." Skelly just whistled. "And your grandfather-" Skelly stopped abruptly. "I guess you didn't know about him, either?"

"Nope. Not a thing. The article said his name is Harrison and that he and my mom had some problems. What is he like?"

"That is a tough question to answer," Skelly said as he rubbed his hairy chin. He looked over at the fire and Willie, who was curled up on the rug. "He is not the same man he was before your mom left. Her disappearance changed him."

"Changed him?"

"He used to be a very, well, uh focused man, not the warm and fuzzy type, but always respectful. He wanted this school to be perfect, to be a shining star among all magical schools, and it was. It still is. He worked very hard and demanded hard work from everyone, especially your mom, but like I said, it changed him after she disappeared. When the search turned up nothing, it was like something inside him broke. He made very few public appearances and became somewhat of a recluse."

"That's what Brimbal said, too. I guess he doesn't come to the school much, either, huh?"

"Oh, he's around," Skelly said with a sly smile, "but keeps it quiet when he is here.

"You know, all this time, I thought he was dead."

"Your mom told you that?" Cully asked in surprise.

"Yep," Seven said, nodding.

"Wow," was all Cully could say.

"We probably should be going," Iggy said. "It is getting late. Thanks for the muffins and hot chocolate."

"Yeah, thanks," Cully said, quickly finishing the last of her drink.

Skelly walked them over to the door.

"Thanks for everything, Mr. Skelly," Seven said.

"It's just Skelly," he said. "My door is always open anytime you all need a break," he said, smiling. "Take care of yourselves and Seven, don't let Darcy Davidson get to you. That gives her too much power."

Seven nodded, but she had no idea how she was going to do that.

The night air had turned very chilly, indeed, and their thin robes did not provide much warmth. They walked in silence until Cully sighed loudly.

"I cannot believe you are Miranda Wyndamir's daughter."

"Yep," Seven said.

"I mean, everyone wants to know where she is, and I know, well sort of know, I guess. Where do you live across the gate?"

"Cully, you can't tell anyone. Not anyone. Not Charlie or Adria. Not even your brother or your parents. No one can know," Seven said.

"Yeah, I know, it's just, do you think I could go home with you sometime? I would love to meet her."

"I don't know, maybe," Seven said. "But seriously, not a soul?" She looked from Cully to Iggy. "I am trusting you, and that's huge for me."

"Seven, we won't tell anyone. We promise," Iggy said.

"Besides, without that locket's picture, no one would believe us anyway," Cully said.

"Well, if Skelly figured it out, it probably won't be long until others do, too," Seven said. "But we will NOT talk about this at school. No use in helping everyone figure it out."

"We won't talk about it unless we are at Skelly's, and I intend to visit him frequently if he continues to make those muffins," Cully said.

"Still, I wonder why my mom didn't tell me?" Seven wondered. "I mean, I am sure her picture is in other places, too, like yearbooks and stuff. It isn't like I wasn't going to find out, eventually."

"We could check the library. We still have time before curfew," Iggy suggested.

They bound up the stone steps and made their way to the library. They were nearly there when they heard loud voices from behind a classroom door. It stopped them in their tracks.

"I can't believe this happened," hissed a voice. "I thought I could trust you to keep your word." This was not the same voice she and Cully heard earlier, but it too sounded familiar.

"You knew the risks. You are not a young, naive student anymore. You are a full wielder who knew what she was getting herself into," another voice shot back, but this one they all recognized.

"Mcfee," Cully whispered. Iggy gestured for them to stand behind a statue of a large mermaid and merman in case someone opened the door.

"I didn't sign up for this," the visitor argued. "You made a promise to me that if I cooperated, my shop would be safe."

"I thought it could be spared, but I was wrong. I am not going to apologize," Mcfee said. "Now, did they find it?"

"Yes, just like they were supposed to, but I'm sure they will figure out soon enough that it isn't the one they want," the visitor answered.

"It will buy me some time. By the time they figure it out, I am sure I will have the real one in my possession."

"Just like you were sure my shop would be safe?" the voice asked sarcastically. "I am beginning to think you don't know what you are doing." Seven knew this voice. Who was it?

"What is that supposed to mean?"

"People are getting hurt, Phoebe. Swathmore..."

"Swathmore is going to make a full recovery," Mcfee interrupted. "That wasn't supposed to happen, but dangerous times are upon us. He knew that just like you do."

"And what about the Preston girl?" the visitor asked. "Does she know yet?"

At the name Preston, Cully and Iggy both looked at Seven

wide-eyed.

"Not that I can tell, but you let me worry about that. I'll take care of her," Mcfee said. "Now, you better leave. Go the way I told you so that any prying eyes won't see you. And Pepper, don't come back here. It isn't smart."

Pepper! That's is why the voice sounded familiar. Just then, Seven heard what sounded like a chair scoot. Mcfee and Pepper were finished. The statue wouldn't hide them if Mcfee walked past them. They had to get out of there before the door opened.

Seven gestured for the others to follow. She led them down the corridor, turned the corner, and slammed right into something. Or rather someone. She stumbled backward and fell. Cully and Iggy nearly tripped over her.

"Miss Preston, no running in the halls!" shouted the shrill voice of Miss Pamona Poxley. She was rubbing her boney shoulder. "I have been all over this building looking for you. Come with me right now."

Seven got up, and they followed the quickly moving Poxley. Seven glanced over her shoulder a few times to see if Mcfee or Pepper had seen them. She nearly knocked into Poxley again when the woman abruptly stopped right outside Terramin Tower and whirled around.

"Well, where were you?" she demanded.

"Outside," Seven said.

"Library," Cully said at the same time.

Poxley looked at them suspiciously.

"We were outside, but then we remembered we needed to look something up in the library for Professor Willowisp's class," Iggy lied smoothly.

"Didn't you hear the announcement that all students were to return to their dormitories
immediately?"

"Why? What happened?" Cully asked.

Poxley, however, seemed not to hear Cully's words. Instead, she was focused on something else.

"What a lovely locket," she said, pointing around Seven's neck. Seven felt around her neck and discovered her locket had fallen from inside her robes when she fell backward.

"Thanks," Seven mumbled as she tucked it away.

"Where did you get it?"

"From my parents."

"Is it one of those that opens and holds pictures?"

"Yes, but it's broken, and there isn't a picture inside," Seven lied.

"We are exhausted, Miss Poxley," Iggy said. "We probably better get to bed."

"You know, Miss Preston, my brother, is a jeweler," Poxley said, ignoring Iggy. "He is very talented. If you want, I would be glad to take your locket and have him fix it free of charge."

"That is very nice of you. I'll think about it."

"Well, think quickly because he does get pretty busy around the Christmas holiday. I'm sure he would put a rush on it if I asked him."

"I'll let you know. Thank you."

"If you give it to me now, I could have it back in a few days, well before you leave for break," Poxley said, holding out her hand.

Seven was saved from refusing a third time because Sam and Charlie picked that moment to round the corner, laughing and whispering. When they saw Poxley, they stopped. They began to stammer an explanation of why they weren't in the dormitory.

"Miss Poxley, we were just looking for..." Sam began, then had a brain freeze.

"Seven," Charlie finished quickly. "We were just looking for Seven. We noticed she wasn't in the Tower, so we wanted to find her before anything happened. It looks like you beat us to it." Charlie smiled innocently.

Poxley glared at the two boys.

"I should give all five of you a demerit. Get in the dormitory right now," Poxley spat and stormed off, muttering about how children should be strung up or something like that.

"Whew," Sam said. "Good thinking, Charlie. Thanks, Seven."

"For what?" Seven asked.

"For whatever you did to Poxley. She has never turned down a chance to give us a demerit, has she, Sam?" Charlie explained.

"Not one time," Sam agreed.

"Well, let's get inside before she changes her mind," Iggy said.

They all walked into a very crowded rec room. Everyone was vying for a good view of the only television in the room. On it, a young, very pretty reporter was talking in front of a charred building. It took Seven a minute to recognize the mess. They were all that remained of a shop she had visited once over the summer and whose owner had just been in this very building. Pepper's Potion Parts and Pieces lay in a smoking pile.

"What happened?" Charlie asked no one in particular.

"There's been another attack. Someone destroyed Pepper's Potion Parts and Pieces. She wasn't there, thank goodness, or she would have been turned to ash like the rest of her store," Adra said.

For the next few days, the destruction of Pepper's store was all over the news. The shop had been destroyed, but Pepper was unhurt in the incident. Whispers of Shadow Raiders were growing louder, but the Midian Security Office refused to comment as usual.

"Looks like we can forget those weekend passes," Sam said. "I was looking forward to getting away from here for a few hours." It was a Wyndamir tradition to allow students a weekend trip to Wyndamir Landing once a month. As freshmen, they would have to have a staff chaperone, but any opportunity to get off campus was treasured.

Unfortunately, Sam was right. Later that day, Miss Poxley put an announcement on the bulletin board in the main rec room of Terramin Tower. The upcoming weekend trip was canceled.

"If we go in a group, we should be safe," a brown-haired girl said. "I need to get out of here, or I'm going to go crazy!"

"They should let us go. We aren't babies," Sam said.

"Yeah, we aren't babies. We can handle it," Charlie agreed.

"Bellatora doesn't want to take any chances," Poxley said firmly and looked around the room until she caught Seven's gaze. Then, Poxley managed a small smile that didn't look painful or scary. Seven smiled back if, for no other reason, then she was so impressed with the effort. Then, without a word, Poxley left the freshmen to their complaining.

Seven wasn't complaining. She was grateful. The usual chaperones for the freshmen were Poxley and Mcfee, and Iggy and Cully thought that Seven should keep as far away from Mcfee as possible until they figured out what was going on. Seven kept replaying the conversation she had heard between Mcfee and Pepper.

"And what about the Preston girl? Does she know yet?"

"Not that I can tell, but you let me worry about that. I'll take care of her."

Yes, staying away from Mcfee was a good idea. However, it wasn't as easy as they had hoped.

Mcfee had sent a few campus pixies with requests for Seven to come to her office, but Seven just stuffed the envelopes into her bag.

"Mcfee?" Iggy asked.

Seven nodded.

"How long do you think you can keep avoiding her?" Cully asked.

"Until I graduate?" Seven said hopefully.

Once, they were on their way to Terramin Tower. When they turned the corner, Mcfee was waiting outside the entrance. Iggy saw her just in time, and the three of them ducked back around the corner, passing Poxley for the second time.

"Forgot something," Seven had said.

Poxley just shrugged and muttered something under her

breath. However, a second later, they heard Poxley and Mcfee talking.

"I am waiting for Miss Preston," Mcfee had said, annoyance in her voice. "I have been
trying to see her for a while now, and I always seem to miss her."

"Oh, well, I just saw her in the library," Poxley had answered, which completely took all of them by surprise because the library was in the complete opposite direction of where they had just passed Poxley.

"The library, huh? I was just there," Mcfee said in disbelief.

"It is a large library," Poxley said. "Maybe you missed her."

"I guess," Mcfee said doubtfully but headed in the opposite direction anyway.

"Why would she lie?" Cully whispered.

"I think it has more to do with her dislike of Mcfee than love for me," Seven said.

"Who cares? Thank you, Poxley!" Cully said.

The attack on Pepper's and Mcfee's threat weighed heavily on Seven. She was grateful she had Iggy and Cully, but the reality was the threat was made against her, not them. They could only help so much.

"Seven, your potion!" Cully hissed one day in Potion Making.

"Oh no!" she gasped as the potion bubbled over. Orange colored liquid leaked onto the table, where it solidified right away. "My potion! Iggy, what do I do?"

Iggy calmly reached over and turned down her fire.

"You had it too hot." Then he leaned closer to her and whispered, "Maybe if you would concentrate in class, your potion would still be in your cauldron."

"Having trouble Miss Preston?" Mulciber asked as he looked from her cauldron to the spilled potion. "I have it right there to cook it over a low flame, or your liquid will become solid." He flicked his hands, and the instructions on the board that read, **Turn flame on low for thirteen minutes before adding hollyhock seeds**, began to glow, so they stood out. "Obviously, you forgot that part. Mr. Everett, on the other hand, has produced an exemplary potion." He inhaled deeply. "Oranges with the crisp scent of grass. Perfect." He looked back at the mess Seven had made and walked away, shaking his head.

"What is it like to be perfect in everything you do?" Seven asked Iggy.

"Oh, it is something you never get tired of hearing. You know, you wouldn't need my help if you weren't so distracted all the time," he said as he helped her salvage her potion. "Quit worrying about Mcfee."

"It doesn't take a genius to see that your mind has been anywhere but here the last few weeks," Cully said. "Let's go to Skelly's tonight. You could use a distraction."

"Yeah, right. I think you just want some more sweets," Seven said, to which Cully just shrugged.

After their last class and a few hours in the prop room, the three of them headed to Skelly's. He greeted them warmly, but more importantly, with treats. This time, it was chocolate cake.

"Thanks for this, Skelly," Seven said, gesturing to her near-empty plate.

"Yeah, Seven needed a distraction from Mcfee's threat," Cully said distractedly.

"Mcfee's threat?" Skelly said, stopping the spoon halfway to his mouth.

Seven shot Cully a dirty look.

"Oops," Cully said.

"What is this about?" Skelly pressed, so Seven recounted the conversation between Mcfee and Pepper. When she finished, he was shaking his head.

"I think you got that all wrong," Skelly said. "Your mom and Phoebe Mcfee were inseparable when they were in school. They were best friends. There is no way that she would hurt Miranda Wyndamir's daughter."

"You didn't see them argue this summer, Skelly." Seven protested. "Mcfee wanted my mom to give her something, but my mom refused. That made Mcfee really angry...like really, really angry. And she was forcing those shopkeepers into helping her with something. Swathmore was about ready to cry when he handed Mcfee that scroll. Now Pepper's shop was destroyed, and Mcfee didn't even apologize for it. I just wish I could figure out what Mcfee meant when she said she would have the real one in her possession soon. I bet that is the same *it* she and my mom were arguing about this summer."

"The newspaper said your mom was protecting something when she disappeared. Any idea what it was? Maybe that's the *it*," Iggy said.

"Not a clue. I plan on asking her when I go home for Christmas. I just hope I can stay clear of Mcfee until then. Even Poxley doesn't seem to like Mcfee too much."

"Poxley?" Skelly said. "Why doesn't she like Mcfee?"

Cully, Iggy, and Seven all shrugged.

"I don't know. She and Mcfee have been shooting each other dirty looks all year, from the first day."

"Yeah, even I can tell there is no love lost there," Cully agreed.

"Was Poxley ever a student here?" Iggy asked. "Maybe they have a history."

Skelly wrinkled his face in thought before he shook it.

"I don't think so, at least not that I can remember."

"Whatever the reason, she has helped me a few times avoid Mcfee, and for that, I am grateful," Seven said.

"Maybe she helped you because she hates Mcfee. Sort of like the enemy of my enemy is my friend," Iggy said.

Cully and Seven just looked at him.

"What?" he asked innocently. "You never heard that before?"

They both shook their heads.

"I think you are barking up the wrong tree. Phoebe Mcfee loves your mom. She was devastated when your mom died, well, when everyone thought she did."

"That was a long time ago, Skelly. And Mcfee said it herself. She feels betrayed. Maybe she isn't' the person my mom thinks," Seven said.

"I think you're wrong," Skelly insisted. "Very, very wrong."

Chapter Twelve

Mistaken Identity

It was hard to believe December was upon them, and so were final exams. Seven almost welcomed the distraction. She had so far been successfully able to avoid Mcfee. A feat made easier since it seemed Mcfee was off school grounds more and more. Seven wasn't sure why, but she had a bad feeling about it.

Seven had already taken her History of Midia and Spell Casting exams. She felt confident she did well on those. Potions had been next, and Seven thought her shriveling potion was passable at least. Mulciber was a pretty easy scorer. Krisp, on the other hand, was not. That was the exam that they were all preparing for now. Seven closed her eyes as she mentally reviewed the 10 Principals of Inorganic Change.

"You're doing it again," Seven said without opening her eyes.

"Doing what?" Cully asked.

"Staring at me."

"Your eyes are closed. How can you tell?"

"How would you know my eyes are closed unless you are staring at me?" Seven said, finally looking at her friend. Since the big reveal of who Seven's mom was, Seven caught her friend staring at her more than once.

"I'm sorry. Sometimes, I still can't believe who you are that your mom is…"

"Would you hush?" Seven hissed, looking around to make sure no one was listening.

"Do you know what my mom would say if she knew I was friends with…" Cully began, but Seven cut her off.

"It doesn't matter what she would say because you are sworn to secrecy."

"I know. It's just that wielders have been trying to figure out what happened forever, and I know the answer to the puzzle."

"Well, I hope you have the answer to the morphology exam questions because we have to go. Krisp will fail us if we're late," Iggy snapped. He was almost as tired of the topic of Seven's mom as Seven was.

Seven was incredibly nervous about this final. She had been so distracted that her performance in the last several morphology classes had not been stellar. They were supposed to be working on transforming a pig's ear into either a purse or a wallet. Seven was able to produce a nice-looking purse, but she realized that she skipped a step when she tried to open it.

"It doesn't do much good to have a purse that you can't open, does it, Miss Preston?" Krisp had said loudly to embarrass her, which it did even though hers was not the only failure.

Sam's wallet looked okay but smelled so strongly of swine that Krisp ordered him to immediately remove it from the classroom. Given the sly smile on Sam's face, Seven was pretty sure he had done it on purpose.

Iggy's wallet had turned out perfectly, of course. He even added a type of alarm system so that if anyone other than Iggy opened it, the wallet squealed. Seven thought it was clever, but Krisp said it was showy and deducted several points.

Today, as expected, Krisp greeted them for their examination with a scowl.

"Well, I guess we will finally see if you have absorbed anything this term. I have a feeling some of you have brains of concrete that cannot even absorb water," he said. "When I pass the exams out, you will not speak. If you do, I will collect your exam, and you will get a failing grade. When you have finished the written part, you will complete the practical piece. You have a total of one hour. You may begin."

Seven looked at the exam. It was six pages long. She would have to work fast if she wanted to finish. Fifty-eight minutes later, Seven dropped her pencil and massaged her aching hand. She guessed at more than a few, but at least she finished. As she looked around the room, the only person left was Stanley, whose face dripped with nervous sweat. She walked up to Krisp's desk and handed in her paper. He motioned for her to follow him into the next room where the practical exam took place.

"Now, change this sow's ear into a purse," Krisp said with a cruel smile. "And it had better open if you want to pass. You have two minutes. No, make that one and a half minutes."

When Krisp told her this, she was secretly excited, a fact she dared not show. She figured this would be the one Krisp would give her since she failed it so miserably during the term, so she had enlisted Iggy's help. Feeling confident, she pulled out her wand and mimicked the movements she had practiced over and over. Blue and red sparks flew from her wand tip and wrapped around the pig's ear. It stretched and twisted, shook and rolled. She watched in triumph as Krisp's smile evaporated when it fell back to the desk shaped like a proper coin purse.

"Don't get too excited. I haven't tried to open it yet," he hissed. Seven wished she had a camera to snap a picture of Krisp's face when the purse opened.

"You are excused," he said with a scowl. Seven nearly skipped out of the room.

"What teacher gives an exam like that? I thought teachers were supposed to want their students to succeed," Cully said a while later as she flopped down in one of the chairs by the fire in the rec room. "Did you see poor Matilda Mately?"

Seven and Iggy nodded solemnly.

Matilda was a very quiet, shy freshman girl. She dropped her pencil during the test. When another student handed it back, she whispered a thank you. Krisp snatched her test up so fast that he was a blur. She tried to explain what had happened, but Krisp didn't care. He just stood and pointed toward the door. Matilda left the classroom in tears.

"I saw Willowisp in the hall with her. Maybe she can talk reason into Krisp," Cully offered. "She is so nice. No wonder she is everyone's favorite."

"I wouldn't hold my breath. I think I saw the first genuine smile of Krisp's life after he snatched that exam. He enjoyed it."

"You know what I would enjoy?" Seven asked. "A night when we didn't have to go to that stupid prop room. I guess we better go, or Krisp won't be the only one who tortures students today."

"These are the last boxes," Seven said a while later in the prop room. "Finally. I mean, how many props does one play need?"

"It's not a play. It's a production," Cully said, mimicking Flouriche. "And if I hear you call it that again, I will boil you in a vat of pudding."

Seven looked at her and started laughing.

"What are you wearing?" she asked Cully.

"Oh, this old thing?" Cully said as she twirled around in a circle and dramatically flipped the wig of long, black hair that she had put on. "This is for our leading lady, Liriel." Liriel Rathbone had been cast as the lead female character, and she acted every bit the part of a diva actress. "If she had hair like yours, she wouldn't need it. With this on, I look just like you from the back." She turned around to demonstrate. "Don't you agree, Iggy?"

"Yeah, I guess so."

"What you look is ridiculous," Seven said.

"Ridiculous?" Cully said dramatically. "How dare you say that about Eildh! I am the star of this production. Don't you know that?" she said in her most Liriel - like imitation sending both of them into a fit of giggles.

"When you two are quite finished," Iggy said to them, "I'd

like to get out of here.
All we have to do is shine these." He pointed to some amulets that were lying on the table. "Malcolm told us they better shine like an exploding star in the sky. He gave us this to use." Iggy pointed to a little black bottle with a label that read, Sloupy Scott's Shining Salve -If you
find it dimmer, we'll make it shimmer. "It only takes a few drops. I just finished this blade, and I could use it for a mirror." He held up a sword. "I am going to put this on the shelf in the other room with the scene four items," he explained. "You two finish the amulets.

"Yes, sir," Cully said with a mock salute, but she did as he said. Watching Cully shine the amulets made Seven think of her own locket. She pulled it out and looked at it. It was very dull and dirty.

"Do you think that would work on my locket?"

"Probably, but you should take it off. This shining salve might ruin your robes."

Immediately, the words her mom spoke echoed in Seven's head.

"Don't ever take this off. No matter what, ever."

She had promised. But it was only for a few minutes, and it would never leave her sight. What could it hurt? Besides, she wanted it to shine when she went home for Christmas. She wanted her mom to know that she took good care of it. Feeling like she was doing something wrong, she took the locket off anyway.

"Where should I put it?"

Cully looked around at the messy table and then at her own dirty hands.

"Just put it around my neck," she said, leaning slightly forward. "Can you take these prop amulets and lock them away? Then I'll get a new cloth for your locket and shine it up."

Seven put the locket around Cully's neck and took the finished amulets. Just then, a loud clatter echoed throughout the theater, followed by a bloodcurdling scream. Iggy's scream.

Seven looked at Cully with wide eyes before racing to the other prop room.

She saw Iggy in the corner on his knees, rocking back and forth as blood gushed from his arm. The sword he was supposed to be putting away lay beside him. Blood dripped down the blade. Seven dashed over to him.

"It slipped," Iggy groaned.

"Cully, grab that towel," Seven said, pointing to a table. She took the towel from Cully and wrapped it tightly over the cut. It didn't take long before a bloodstain blossomed on the towel.

"I need to get him to the infirmary," Seven said to Cully.

"Do you need help?"

"Iggy, can you walk?" Seven asked. He nodded.

"You sure?" Cully pressed.

"Yes, besides, if we don't get those props locked away properly, this cut will be nothing compared to what Flouriche will do to us," Iggy tried to joke though his face looked ashen.

"All right, I will lock everything up and meet you there," Cully said as she and Seven helped Iggy to his feet.

Seven half dragged, half carried Iggy across the lawns. The air was cold, and a few flakes floated in the slight breeze. Seven took deep breaths of the fresh air but also caught a whiff of the coppery scent of blood. It made her stomach curdle, but she swallowed it down. She had to be strong for Iggy, who was looking paler by the second.

"We're nearly there, Iggy. Just a few more steps," Seven encouraged when they finally reached the infirmary wing.

Iggy groaned in response.

"What is this?" asked a stern voice. "What happened?"

Seven saw Nurse Medwell coming toward them with her hands on hips. She looked from Iggy's face to the now dripping towel.

"Accident with one of the play props," Seven explained.

"I have told that woman a hundred times that there is no need to use such realistic props in her productions," Medwell

said as she shook her head. "Never mind that now. Let's have a look." Seven watched as she pulled the towel from Iggy's arm. It made a wet sucking sound that
pulled at Seven's stomach again. She looked away and swallowed hard.

"Yep, you sure did this up right. Cut a few blood vessels you did. Now, don't you worry. I'll have you fixed up in no time," she said to Iggy, a comforting Irish lilt in her voice.

The nurse guided Iggy to an empty room and helped him lie down on the bed. She dipped some clean towels in a bowl filled with a solution she poured from a tall, blue bottle. She gently wiped at Iggy's arm. As she worked, she hummed a soft tune.

"There is a pitcher of water on a table in the hall. Fill two cups bring them here," Medwell instructed. When she returned, Medwell was just finishing the wrappings. Seven offered her the cups, and the nurse smiled. "I only need one. The other one is for you. You look like you could use some water." Medwell took one of the cups from Seven, added several drops from a small potion bottle that she pulled from her apron pocket, and handed it to Iggy. He took it gratefully and sipped it. Seven was relieved to see a little color return to his face.

"This should ease the pain and help you sleep. How's that, young man?" Medwell asked after Iggy swallowed the rest of the concoction.

"Better," Iggy whispered as he sank back into the pillows.

"I think I will keep you here overnight to make sure that cut heals properly," she said and then turned to Seven. "You best say good night, and then go get yourself cleaned up."

"Cleaned up?" Seven asked. Then she looked down at her hands and robes. She was
covered in Iggy's blood. Though it made her feel a bit disgusted, she tried to keep her face neutral so that Iggy wouldn't feel bad.

"Thanks, Seven, you know, for half carrying me over here. I wouldn't have been able to
make it without you." He slurred his words as the potion took

effect.

"Feel better, Iggy," Seven said. Iggy nodded as his eyes drooped. "I'll go and-."

"Medwell! Medwell, come quick!" That sounded like Skelly.

"What has that man done to himself now?" Medwell groaned as she calmly walked past Seven. "Oh my! What happened?" the nurse said, all calmness gone.

"I don't know," Skelly said. "She was like this when I found her. She was lying on the ground at the bottom of the theater steps."

Seven froze. Theater steps. Cully.

"Bring her in here. Gently, now, very gently," Medwell instructed.

Seven crept to the room Medwell and Skelly entered, but her view was blocked.

"Is she going to be all right?" Skelly asked.

"I need some water," Medwell said. "In the hall. Go."

Skelly backed out of the room, nearly knocking Seven over.

"What are you doing here? You hurt, too?" Skelly asked, giving her a once over presumably to look for injuries.

"Not me. Iggy. He cut himself," Seven said so softly she could barely hear her own voice. "Skelly, please tell me it isn't Cully."

He didn't answer. He didn't have to. The look in his eyes was answer enough.

Seven peeked around the corner and saw Nurse Medwell examining her patient. She was mumbling under her breath. When she turned to get some clean towels off a side table, Seven finally saw her friend clearly, and it made her gasp. Cully, who was still wearing the black wig, was bleeding and bruised. A large gash on her forehead was pouring blood down the side of her face. More cuts were on her neck, arms, and hands. Her robes were dirty and torn. In several places, burn holes were still smoking as though spells had hit her. On the floor next to the bed was Seven's backpack. Cully must have grabbed it from the prop room on her way out the door.

"You shouldn't be here, child. This is not for your eyes," Medwell said, blocking Seven's view.

"But . . . she's... she's my friend," Seven said. "What happened to her?"

"I won't know until I examine her fully, and I can't do that with you here. Mr. Skelly found her at the bottom of the steps. It looks like she fell. All I know for certain is that she took a bump to the head that knocked her out."

Seven looked back at Cully, and, even from the doorway, she could see an enormous knot protruding from the side of Cully's head. "I need you to go so I can tend to her. Mr. Skelly?" Medwell looked up at the caretaker.

"Come on, Seven. You can't help her now." Seven reluctantly allowed herself to be pulled away. He led her over to some chairs that were sitting in a large waiting area. She did not believe for one minute that Cully just fell. That would explain the cuts and bruises for sure, but not the burn holes in her robes.

"Try not to worry yourself, Seven," Skelly said as he rubbed his beard. "Nurse Medwell is the best healer there is. You'll see."

But at that very moment, a very worried looking Medwell rushed passed them. She stopped at the front desk and rang a small bell. Then she scribbled something on a piece of paper. A few seconds later, a school postal pixie flew into the room.

"Take this to Bellatora immediately," she instructed the pixie. It took the paper, saluted Medwell, and flew off in a flash.

"What's wrong?" Seven said, standing up.

Medwell looked at her very hard.

"You were in the theater with Miss Collins?"

Seven nodded.

"Who else was there?"

"Nobody. I mean, nobody except Cully and Iggy and me. Practice let out early, and everyone left. Cully stayed to lock up when I brought Iggy here. She was supposed to be right behind us," Seven said.

"So, she was there alone?"

"Yes, I think so. Why?" Seven asked.

"Mr. Skelly, please escort Miss Preston back to the dorm," Medwell ordered. As though anticipating Seven's impending protests, she looked at Seven and said, "You cannot help them tonight. Mr. Everett is sleeping, and I need to be able to attend to Miss Collins without distraction. The best thing you can do for your friends is to go and get some rest. You can check on them in the morning after you eat breakfast."

Seven wanted to argue, but Skelly put a strong arm around her and herded her to the exit.
As he opened the door, Seven turned back to Nurse Medwell. "She's going to be all right, isn't she?"

"She'll be fine, dear." The healer said, but Seven wasn't sure she believed her from the look on Medwell's face.

Neither Seven nor Skelly spoke all the way back to Wyndamir Hall. When they reached the stairwell that led to Terramin Tower, Seven turned to him.

"I can make it from here. Thanks," she said.

"But Medwell wanted me to walk you all the way," he said.

"No offense, Skelly, but you can't follow me into the bathroom," she said as she held out her dirty robes. "I have to shower."

"Of course," he said, a bit embarrassed. "But then straight to bed. No detours. No sneaking back to see Cully or Iggy. Promise me."

Seven rolled her eyes. "Skelly, I really don't . . ."

"Promise?" he pressed.

"Fine, I promise."

"Seven, try not to worry. Medwell is the best. Remember that."

Seven nodded and walked up the steps feeling as though her legs weighed a thousand pounds. When she reached the top of the first flight of stairs, she turned to see if Skelly was watching her. He wasn't. He was gone. She turned to climb up the second flight when she heard footsteps below. She looked over the railing and saw Bellatora rushing toward the front doors.

"Headmistress!" shouted a voice coming down another hall. Seven went back down the stairs and ducked behind a column. She watched as Poxley came running, trying to catch Bellatora. "Headmistress, I received the message about the Collins girl. What happened?" Poxley asked, gasping for breath.

"I'm heading down to the infirmary to find out myself. Did you notify Miss Mcfee?
Since this is a student matter, she should be involved."

"I sent a school postal pixie with a note to inform her, and it returned to me mad as a hornet because it couldn't deliver the message. You know what that means." Poxley spoke as though she had just caught Mcfee taking the last cookie in the cookie jar before supper.

"She's not on school grounds," Bellatora said. "Well, no matter. I know she has had some personal family matters lately. She may have been called away again. Send a regular postal pixie to inform her of what has happened. They will find her wherever she is. I also would like for Professors Brimbal, Willowisp, Snodgrass, and Mulciber to meet me in the infirmary."

"Yes, Headmistress," Poxley said and inclined her head in a small bow. After Bellatora left the building, Poxley turned around with a triumphant smile on her face.

Seven stood up. Medwell would never have summoned Bellatora over a fall. And where was Mcfee? Seven was not buying that Mcfee had a family emergency. Every part of her wanted to run back to the infirmary, but she knew that she would only get herself and possibly Skelly into trouble. Besides, the feel of Iggy's dried blood on her robes and hands was beginning to get to her.

She went to the shower, stripped off her dirty clothes, and put them in the laundry shoot. So many times, she had wondered how the clothes always seemed to make it back to the right person, fresh and new no matter how dirty they were.

Tonight, though, she only had thoughts for Cully. She bathed, dressed in a clean pair of pajamas, but knew she wasn't going to sleep anytime soon. Instead of climbing into bed, she tiptoed to the rec room and curled up in one of the overstuffed chairs. There was still a small fire burning in the fireplace. As she watched the flames dance, she replayed the night.

Iggy's bloody arm. Cully - wearing the wig and covered with bruises and cuts. The worried expression on Medwell's face. The late-night gathering of teachers in the infirmary. The absence of Mcfee. She felt like she was missing something. As the night wore on, Seven finally fell into a fitful sleep, but disturbing dreams haunted her. She saw Cully laughing, flipping the long, black hair of the wig. *I look like you.* Iggy's scream and bloody arm. Medwell's worry. Cully's cuts and bruises. The dark wig. She was missing something.

Seven awoke with a start. The sky was beginning to lighten as pinks and oranges streaked the horizon. Though it was early, she knew she wasn't going back to sleep, so she quietly crept up to her room and changed into her school uniform. Then, she silently left Wyndamir Hall and made her way to the infirmary, where she slipped through the door. The front desk was empty. It was eerily quiet. She tiptoed to Cully's room only to realize that she was not Cully's first visitor despite the early hour.

Iggy sat in a chair next to Cully's bed. A candle next to the bed flickered, sending light dancing over his face. Seven stepped into the room and closed the door. She walked over to Cully, who was still unconscious. Medwell must have taken the black wig off Cully because now her short, blonde hair framed her bruised, swollen face. The bump on her head had gone down some, but not much. Seven's gaze trailed down Cully's chin, which was covered with a large bandage. She noticed a thin red line that was somewhere between a cut and a bruise that completely encircled Cully's neck. Then, she saw the leather cord.

"My locket," Seven whispered. "I completely forgot about it with everything that happened last night." Seven looked closer at Cully's neck. "She must have caught it on something when she fell."

Iggy just stared at Seven.

"Why are you looking at me like that?" Seven asked.

"Seven, Cully didn't fall down the stairs. She was pushed. Someone attacked her."

"Attacked?" Seven whispered as she slumped into a chair across from Iggy. "I mean, I knew there was more to it than just a fall. Medwell wouldn't have summoned Bellatora over a fall but attacked? How do you know that?"

"With all the commotion, I woke up. I got out of bed to close the door to my room when I saw all of the teachers and Headmistress Bellatora. They were talking about an attack. At first, when I heard them, I thought there had been another attack in Wyndamir Landing. I figured I would hear about it later. I was still so tired, and my arm hurt, so I was just going to close the door and go back to sleep. That's when I heard someone say Cully's name. Poxley asked Medwell if Cully was going to be able to remember who attacked her or if her memory was going to be fuzzy."

"What did Medwell say?"

"She said she didn't know what Cully would remember," Iggy said.

"Did they say why they thought she was attacked?" Seven asked.

Iggy shook his head and stared at Cully's face. His eyes began to water. He wiped furiously at his tears with the back of his hand.

"If I hadn't cut myself, she wouldn't have been alone. Whoever attacked her probably wouldn't have tried if we had been with her."

"Oh, Iggy, it isn't your fault," Seven said, but she could tell that he either didn't hear her or didn't believe her. Silence fell as they both watched Cully sleep. Seven kept looking at the bump on Cully's head. The bruises on her face. Her swollen lip and the burns around her neck.

Her gaze fell on the black wig, which was in a crumpled heap in the corner next to Seven's backpack. Then, Cully's words rushed into Seven's memory like a freight train.

"With this on, I look just like you from the back."

The wig. The locket. The backpack.

Mcfee's threatening words. *I'll take care of her.*

The attack. Mcfee was gone.

Suddenly Seven shot out of the chair as the pieces fell into place.

"Seven, what's wrong?" Iggy asked.

Seven couldn't breathe. It felt as though a hand was squeezing her lungs.

"With this on, I look just like you from the back."

"Seven, what's wrong? You look like you are going to faint." Iggy's voice sounded muffled and far away.

"Oh, Iggy, it wasn't your fault that Cully was attacked. It was mine. They thought she was me," Seven whispered before the blackness took her.

Chapter Thirteen

Up in Smoke

Seven awoke in a strange bed. Sunlight poured through a window along one wall, forcing her to squint. She propped herself up on her elbows and immediately wished she hadn't. Dizziness and nausea washed over her. When it passed, she looked around. She was in a tiny room with grey stone walls identical to the one in which Cully lay. She was in the infirmary.

"Oh, awake, are you?" said Medwell from the doorway. Her dark-rimmed glasses hung around her neck on a chain. "I expect you got one banger of a headache, eh?"

"Yes," Seven said quietly.

"Well, that is not surprising one bit. Do you feel like you could stand?"

"I'll try," Seven said, anxious to check on Cully. However, as she rose to her feet, her head exploded, and her legs wobbled. She sank back on the bed, put her head in her hands, and wished the room would stay still.

"Still a little shaky, I see. Well, it is not a wonder," the nurse said kindly. "You hit your head full-on. Trying to outdo your friends in there, I guess."

"What happened?" Seven asked, her voice gravelly.

"Well, you fainted, didn't you? I'm guessing you didn't eat anything before you rushed down here, exactly what I told you not to do if you remember," Medwell chastised as she poured the contents of a brown bottle into a cup. "I mean, it isn't like I know what I'm talking about, right? I'm just a healer," the nurse said sarcastically as she handed Seven the cup. "Likely, the stress of your friends' injuries, the late night, the pressure of final examinations, and your empty stomach caught up with you. Mr. Everett said you dropped like a sack of potatoes."

"Nurse Medwell, Cully is going to be fine, isn't she? I mean, she's going to wake up, right?" Seven asked.

"Eventually. Now enough about your friend. You'll be no good to her in this state. Drink up."

Seven drank a few sips. It tasted like cinnamon but felt like fire sliding down her throat.
She gasped and coughed and sank back against the pillows.

"Got a bit of a bite, doesn't it?" Medwell asked with a smile. "Well, no matter. It will have you up and going in a jiffy. Mr. Everett has been anxiously waiting to see you. I told him he could talk to you for a few minutes, but then, I want you to rest. You should be able to leave by dinner time." Nurse Medwell passed Iggy on her way out the door.

"You okay?" Iggy asked as he shut the door and took the seat next to her bed. Seven nodded.

"Medwell says you fainted because you didn't eat breakfast. Do you agree?"

Seven just looked at him

"I was afraid you didn't. So when you said, '*They thought she was me,*' you meant ..."

"Cully," Seven finished. "She had that wig on, she was wearing my locket, and she was carrying my backpack. From the back, I would think she was me. I was the target, not Cully."

"You don't think..." Iggy began.

"Mcfee," Seven finished.

"You know, I've been thinking about that. If Mcfee wanted to attack you, she had plenty of opportunities when you were alone with her, like when she took you shopping over the summer and when she brought you to school. Why would she wait until you were at school? That doesn't make any sense."

"Who else then?" Seven asked. "I mean, Darcy hates my guts, but this seems extreme, even for her. With all the whispering, disappearing acts, threats, who else but Mcfee? She did tell Pepper that she would take care of me. Maybe she finally tried," Seven said.

"If we believe that, we've got to tell Bellatora," Iggy said. "She's got to know that one of her staff members might be a deranged lunatic."

"But we don't have any proof. I mean other than guesses and overheard conversations. Besides, Mcfee's gone," Seven said.

"Gone?" Iggy said.

She told Iggy about Mcfee's sudden disappearance last night and how Bellatora said she'd been having family problems all semester.

"Then, Poxley turned around and whispered something about how she had Mcfee," Seven concluded. "Maybe Poxley suspects Mcfee's been using her "family problems" as a cover story so she could go to Wydnamir Landing and look for whatever she's been trying to get her hands on. Remember what she said to Pepper. It sounded like she planted fake ones to buy her time until she can find the real one. I bet that is what those scrolls were about this summer. Maybe they were some sort of contract she made the shopkeepers sign to force them to help her get her hands on *it*. I just wish I knew what *it* was," Seven said, exasperated.

"Yes, but didn't you say she got those scrolls from your mom?" Iggy asked. "So, if it was a contract, it was your mom making them sign it, not Mcfee."

Seven threw herself back on the pillows in exasperation, which made her wish she hadn't as fresh pain erupted in her head. What was she missing?

"Maybe it has to do with whatever my mom was guarding. My mom told me that she was supposed to be guarding a relic, something the Shadow Raiders wanted. It must have been extremely powerful because they were willing to kill for it," Seven paused to steady her voice. "Anyway, my mom never told me

what it was, but she did say she didn't have it anymore.
Maybe that's the *it*. Mcfee has figured out what *it* is, and she's going after it for herself."

"But that would mean..." Iggy began before they were interrupted.

"All right, Mr. Everett, you need to let Miss Preston eat and rest. I also want to clean that cut one more time. Then, you are free to leave."

"Just a few more minutes?" Iggy begged.

"No, not just a few more minutes. Miss Preston will be out by later today. Then you can
have all the time you want. For now, move it. Go sit in your room, and I will be right with you." Iggy looked from the healer to Seven and reluctantly left the room.

"As for you," Medwell said as she set a tray in front of Seven, "I want you to eat this soup and sandwich, slowly. If you can keep it down and your headache is gone, you are free to leave. Remember, s-l-o-w-l-y," she repeated stretching the word.

Seven wasn't the least bit hungry, but she knew Medwell would never let her leave until the tray was empty. She took a few small bites as she thought about the last twenty-four hours. Assuming it was Mcfee who had attacked her, the woman must be getting desperate to risk doing it at school. That meant time was running out.

A few hours later, Medwell released her. She went straight to the rec room, where she found Iggy. They talked and brainstormed. Finally, they decided Seven would go back to Skelly's to pick his brain and then meet Iggy in the library that evening. However, it had only been an hour when Seven slumped in the seat next to him in the library. She looked around to make sure no one was close enough to hear them.

"Don't worry. I cast a stillness spell," Iggy said. "I could blow this book up, and unless you are sitting at this table, you wouldn't hear a thing. Now, judging by your expression and your early arrival, I'm guessing it didn't go well with Skelly."

"Not well at all," Seven said, discouraged. "He insisted he had no idea about my mom's assignment, only that it was highly classified. Not even my grandfather. .." she paused. It sounded weird to speak of her grandfather in the present when all this time she had been told he was dead. She quickly pushed that thought away. They didn't have time to tackle that one now. "Skelly said that my grandfather didn't even know, and he was one of the Midian President's friends. Then, as soon as I told him that I thought Mcfee attacked Cully because she thought it was me, he put his hand up. He told me that he didn't want to hear another word against Mcfee. He said I had it all wrong and that if I didn't quit, I was no longer welcome at his cottage. Then, he kicked me out."

"He kicked you out?" Iggy said. "Rude."

"That's what I thought. Anyway, have you found anything?"

"Not a lot, he said, shaking his head. "Most of the books that reference your mom are missing. I found these," he gestured to a few books and magazines, "completely by accident. None of them were in the proper place. Mr. Page would explode if he knew." The school librarian was a little overprotective of his library, to put it lightly. Once, when he found a book on the wrong shelf, he tried to close the library for the whole week. Bellatora had to step in because it was the week of final exams. "Anyway, from the little I was able to find, your mom was amazing." He slid a book around to Seven and pointed. "Read this."

Miranda Ann Wyndamir, the only daughter of Harry and the late Maeburn Wyndamir, is currently a senior at Wyndamir Academy for the Magical Arts. She has more than lived up to her family's reputation for producing great wielders. Miss Wyndamir has developed new potions that are being used in hospitals around the magical world to treat such afflictions as boils, reeker rash, and the excruciating Fethergill disease. Her affinity for potions rivals that of established healers. If Miss Wyndamir can concoct such potent and effective tinctures before she even graduates, what will this amazing wielder have in store for Midia as she gains further experience and knowledge?

Seven flipped to the cover. The book was titled *Healing Today: Amazing Breakthroughs in Magical Medicine.*

"Then, there are these." Iggy pointed to a stack of magazines, all titled *Wielders at Wyndamir.* "Nearly every issue mentions your mom, but nothing helpful to us. Then there's this." He handed her a small, worn book called *Midian Mysteries.* "Chapter 13 is all about your mom, but again not helpful."

Seven turned to the correct page. The entire chapter was indeed about her mom. It followed her mom's academic career, graduation from Wyndamir, her father's sadness, and uncensored disappointment that she chose not to stay on at Wyndamir and his continued hope that she would return. It mentioned her prominent post with the Midian government and subsequent promotions, including her latest assignment, which was not detailed, her disappearance, and the wielder hunt that went on for years, all without success. Finally, the last paragraph all but declared her dead and a possible traitor.

"Did you find anything from when Mcfee was here as a student that shows her with my mom?"

"There are some pictures of them together in this yearbook. Skelly was right when he said they were inseparable," Iggy said.

Seven looked at the pictures Iggy found. There was one of Mcfee and her mom in front of the fountain at Wyndamir Hall. They were sticking their hands in the water and trying to splash each other. There was a class photo where everyone looked serious except those two. Finally, there was one in the potions lab where Miranda was adding some ingredients to a cauldron that Mcfee was stirring. Someone must have said or done something funny right before the picture was taken because Miranda looked like she was laughing, and Mcfee was covering her mouth.

"They look like good friends," Iggy commented.

"Yes, but that was then," Seven said firmly. "No information on what my mom's assignment was? That has to be the key to all of this."

Iggy shook his head. "It was classified, remember?"

Seven reached for her locket, which had become a habit when she was nervous or in deep thought. She did that a lot in Krisp's classes.

"My locket! It's still around Cully's neck. I've got to get it back before we leave for Christmas Break. If I don't, Mcfee won't be the only one trying to kill me. My mom forbade me to take it off."

"Good luck with that. I tried to see Cully after Medwell finished rewrapping my arm. She was unmovable, insisting that Cully needed rest and that I could see her when she wakes up. The only person allowed in was Cully's brother, Chris. He was sitting beside her when I left." Iggy and Seven had met Chris earlier in the year, but their paths rarely crossed since he was an upperclassman. " I guess her parents are on the way."

"But I have to get it back before we leave for break," Seven insisted. "Will you help me?"

"I don't know," Iggy said. "Medwell looks all gentle, but when you cross her, well, honestly, she's a bit scary."

"Please?" Seven begged. "Christmas break is already going to be hard enough when I tell my mom her best friend is attacking students. If I also have to tell her I don't have that locket, I may not be back at Wyndamir, ever."

"Oh, all right, but we'll need a plan." Iggy conceded.

The next morning, the two stood outside the infirmary door, reviewing their plan. It wasn't the greatest one, but hopefully, Iggy would be able to buy Seven the few minutes she needed to retrieve her locket.

"Remember, wait until I sneeze. That is your cue," Iggy said. "You have to hurry. If Medwell catches you, she'll know I was in on it, and we'll both get detention or worse." Iggy took a deep breath and pulled open the infirmary door. "Nurse Medwell!"

"Well, Mr. Everett. What brings you back here today? I thought I cleared you yesterday? No new injuries or illness, I hope?"

"Not new, exactly. My arm was hurting a lot last night, and when I woke up this morning, I saw this." Seven waited for the reaction. Iggy had taken gargle root, mashed it up, and smeared it on his arm. It looked like a green fungus was growing over his cut.

"Oh, my lands! Come in here. Have you been using the..." Her voice faded. She must have taken him into a room. Seven crept in and crouched by the front desk.

"Come on, Iggy, sneeze," Seven whispered to no one. And then, as though he heard her, Iggy gave off a loud ah choo. Seven counted to five and then crept as quiet as a shadow past the room where she heard Iggy saying, "I thought I used it correctly." She slid into Cully's room and gently closed the door behind her.

Seven was relieved to see the locket still around her neck. She looked down at her friend's closed eyes.

"Cully, I am so sorry this happened to you and for taking this when you are, well, you know. I hope you will understand." Then Seven reached for the leather cord and tried to pull it over Cully's head as gently as possible. She was not expecting what happened next.

A searing hot pain shot through her hands, and the leather cord seemed to catch fire. She snatched her hand away. It throbbed in pain as she cradled it to her side. Even in the dim light, she could see angry, red blisters popping up in a straight line across her palm. What had happened? Desperate to finish the job and get out before Medwell caught her, she reached for the leather cord again with her other hand. This time, though, she was prepared for the heat. As soon as it got warm, she dropped it. It was as though the cord was made of fire. What was going on? How was she supposed to get the locket if it kept burning her? How was it not burning Cully's neck?

Just then, Iggy sneezed again. The signal that Medwell

was almost finished with him. Seven was running out of time. She frantically looked around the room and saw a few towels on the table next to the bed. She grabbed one and wrapped it around her non-throbbing hand. She scooped up the locket cord. She could feel the heat through it, but the towel provided some protection. She pulled gently on the cord, trying not to catch Cully's hair. That's when the second strange thing happened.

The cord turned to smoke and fell through her hand. When it fell back around Cully's neck, it was solid again. Seven looked at the necklace in disbelief. Did that *really* just happen? However, upon hearing footsteps in the hallway, she knew she didn't have time to figure it out. She just had to try again. The heat seemed more intense this time, but she didn't let go. She didn't have to because, for the second time, the cord turned to smoke and slipped through her hand - literally *through* her hand.

"What is going on?" Seven said out loud.

"My thoughts exactly." Seven turned to see a very unhappy Nurse Medwell standing in the doorway. "Care to explain yourself, Miss Preston?"

"Well, I was, I mean, I well, I wanted to see my friend."

"And the towel?" Medwell pressed.

"Oh, she looked like she was sweating, so I was going to wipe her face," Seven said, not sure where the words came from but thankful nonetheless.

"I see. I suppose next, you are going to tell me that Mr. Everett wasn't distracting me? Don't think I don't know a gargle root rash when I see one." Seven flushed bright red. This woman didn't miss a thing. "What were you doing in here?" the nurse demanded.

"Nothing," Seven said softly. "I just wanted to see her."

Medwell looked hard at Seven. Her gaze dropped from Seven's face to the towel and then the hand that Seven was cradling against herself.

"What did you do to your hand?"

"My hand? Oh, it is nothing," Seven said and hid her

burned hand behind her back.

"Let me see your hand," Medwell demanded. Reluctantly, Seven held out her hand. "My goodness, child! I think you alone could keep me busy." Once she had Seven seated in another room, she asked, "How did you burn your hand?"

"Potions," Seven said, not making eye contact. "I burned it on the edge of my cauldron."

"Potions, huh? " Medwell said, her tone screaming liar. However, she didn't press the issue. Instead, she brought over a bowl already filled with a clear liquid. "It's a burn bath. Put your hand it," she instructed Seven. The cold concoction provided Seven immediate relief. It wasn't long before the clear liquid turned pink as though it was sucking the burn right off. Medwell pulled Seven's hand from the bowl, dried it, and wrapped it carefully. "That should do it. Now, I think you and your co-conspirator best be off. You have to pack your things. The buses will be here later today."

"But what about Cully? I mean, she can't ride the bus. Will she have to spend the holidays alone?"

"Her parents are on their way here."

As if on cue, the infirmary doors opened, and two people rushed into the waiting room. Seven could immediately tell that these were Cully's parents. Like her daughter, Mrs. Collins had short, blonde hair with a few streaks of gray. Her eyes were red and swollen. Mr. Collins was tall and thin with a bald spot just visible on the top of his head. Behind a pair of glasses, dark circles rimmed his eyes. They briefly looked at Seven and Nurse Medwell, who pointed to Cully's room. Without a word, they barreled into their daughter's room. Seven's stomach dropped when she heard Mrs. Collins cry out.

"I must go to them," Medwell said. "You best be off."

"When will she wake up?" Seven asked, needing reassurances.

"These things take time. Everything will be okay. Your friend will be fine." Seven wished that Medwell was a better liar.

Seven turned to leave the infirmary only to see Bellatora

standing in front of the doors.

"Here to check on your friend this morning, Miss Preston?" Bellatora's tone was full of concern and comfort.

Seven nodded numbly.

"What happened to your hand?" Bellatora said, pointing to the wrappings.

"Potions," Seven said.

"Potions? I thought that final was days ago," Bellatora said knowingly.

Seven thought it best to remain silent. Luckily, Bellatora excused herself. She needed to speak with Cully's parents. Seven exited the infirmary and found Iggy waiting outside.

"Don't ever ask me to do that again. It's like Medwell has eyes all over the place. She knew exactly what I was doing. Anyway, did you get it?" Iggy asked.

Seven held up her bandaged hand in answer.

"What happened?"

"My locket burned me."

"What?" he exclaimed. Seven recounted what had happened in Cully's room.

"It has never done that before," Seven said dumbfounded. "It was like it went up in smoke for a second, and then it was solid again. It didn't burn Cully either. I looked at her neck, and there were no burn marks. It was like the locket didn't want to come off."

"Interesting," Iggy mused as he pulled open the front door of Wyndamir Hall. Inside, they found that preparations to leave were in high gear. Students were hustling every which way straining under the weight of suitcases, trunks, and bags. Sounds of runaway luggage echoed down the stairways. Teachers were stationed throughout the foyer and nearby corridors with clipboards trying to keep some sort of order.

Seven and Iggy made their way through the pandemonium and up the stairs until they reached a second-floor corridor.

"Where have you two been?" Poxley demanded. "The buses are going to be here soon, and I know you haven't packed anything."

"We were in the infirmary checking on Cully," Seven said.

"I see," Poxley said, her tone not softening at all. "Well, you need to pack. I will expect the both of you back in the main foyer in 15 minutes." As Poxley stomped away, Seven noticed her hands were wrapped, too.

"Guess she's been to potions, too," Iggy said.

Seven found herself packing very slowly. She did not want to go home and face her mother, especially without the locket she had promised on several occasions not to remove. On top of that, she had to figure out a way to convince her mom that Mcfee was not the friend she remembered. She wasn't sure how she would do that, but she had the whole way home to figure it out.

Seven stuffed the last of her clothes into her bottomless boulder bag. She checked under her bed and found her favorite pajamas, which she must have thrown under there earlier in her hurry to get dressed, and a book. She grabbed them both. She was just latching her suitcase when she noticed an envelope on her desk. She recognized the writing on the front. With shaking hands, she opened it up.

> *Dear Miss Preston,*
> *I am very sorry that I have not been able to meet with you these last few weeks. You haven't been avoiding me, have you?*
> *Your mother will be waiting for you once you cross the gate. I have enclosed your gate passes in this envelope. I will see you over Christmas break. We all have some things to discuss.*
> *Sincerely,*
> *Miss Phoebe Mcfee*
> *Dean of Students*
> *Wyndamir Academy for the Magical Arts*

Seven's stomach flip-flopped. Seriously? Mcfee was going to be coming to her house over break? She had to get her mom to believe her about Mcfee. Both of their lives could depend on it.

She shoved the note into the book and headed to the bus. Once they were on their way, she showed the letter to Iggy.

"Aren't you lucky? You get to spend the holiday with Mcfee?"

"Yeah, lucky," Seven groaned.

"What's that?" he said, pointing to the book.

"I don't know. I found it under my bed when I was packing. I stuffed Mcfee's letter in it."

Iggy looked at the title, *Amulets, Charms, and Talismans: Wishful Thinking or Real Treasure*.

"Looks interesting. Where did you get it?"

Seven shrugged.

"Do you care if I read it?"

"Knock yourself out. I am just going to sit here and feel sorry for myself. I get to look forward to confronting my mom, hiding the fact I don't have my locket, and spending the holidays with the woman who is trying to kill me. This is going to be wonderful," Seven said sarcastically, but Iggy was already lost in the book.

Chapter Fourteen

Forgotten Friend

Christmas Break did not go like Seven thought it would. She thought she would have time to find the right moment to speak to her mom, one where Miranda was in a good mood and her defenses were down. However, Mcfee ruined that idea.

Seven had only been home two days when her break took a very 'unrelaxing' turn. She was on her way to the kitchen to get some breakfast. Her mom was already there, drinking coffee. The second that Seven rounded the corner, her mom set her cup down with a loud clang.

"Sit down," her mom commanded without even a good morning.

Seven sat across from her mom, dreading what was coming.

"Why didn't you tell me about your friend Cully's accident?"

Seven wanted to say *Because it wasn't an accident. Your friend attacked her,* but instead, she asked, "How did you find out about that?"

"Phoebe wrote. She sent the letter by pixie late last night, so I knew it was an emergency. I just didn't know how much of one."

"Did she say whether or not Cully was awake?"

"Yes, and Nurse Medwell sent her home with her parents."

"She's okay," Seven said with relief.

"She is, but you are not. Phoebe wrote that when she went to see your friend in the infirmary before Cully went home, she saw something very disturbing. Your locket around Cully's neck. When she said this, I thought she must be mistaken. My daughter wouldn't do that. She promised never to take it off."

"Mom, I can explain."

"No, you can't. Whatever reason you think justifies lying to me and breaking your promise doesn't."

"I lied?" Seven said in disbelief. "I didn't lie."

"You kept it from me on purpose, which is the same thing. You have no idea what you have done."

Seven sat there, stunned. She could not believe the hypocritical words that were coming from her mom. Finally, her disbelief turned to anger.

"Are you kidding me? You have the nerve to accuse me of lying and keeping secrets when you have been keeping the biggest one of all, Miranda Wyndamir!"

Her mom's head jerked back as though Seven had slapped her. Seven watched as various emotions crossed her mom's face. Finally, Miranda closed her eyes and took a deep breath.

"Phoebe said you might have figured that out. She said she tried to meet with you, but it didn't work out before she had to, well before she was called away from the school. Who told you?"

"Obviously not you," Seven shouted. "You accuse me of lying, and you are Miranda Wyndamir, the long-lost daughter of Harry Wyndamir, my grandfather, who is NOT dead, by the way!"

"How long have you known?" her mom asked, ignoring Seven's tantrum.

"A few months," Seven said harshly.

"And did you tell anyone?" her mom said, feigning calm.

"Cully and Iggy, but they promised not to tell," Seven admitted.

"How did you find out?"

Seven explained about the newspaper article.

"I asked Phoebe to remove any evidence of my identity from the school until I found the right time to tell you. I guess she missed one."

"I felt so stupid when my classmates kept going on and on about how I could pretend to be Miranda Wyndamir's long-lost daughter and get my hands on the Wyndamir fortune. They didn't realize how right they were, at least about the daughter part."

"The fortune part, too," Miranda added with a tired smile. "I guess I should have told you. Phoebe thought I should. That's one of the things we argued about this summer. I just figured finding out about magic and the Shadow Raiders and Midia and going away to a magic school was enough for you to handle at one time without the Wyndamir part. I didn't want to put more pressure on you."

"Pressure?" Seven asked. "Why would that put more pressure on me?"

"Because I know how hard it is to go to that school as a Wyndamir. I was expected to get perfect grades, to perform perfect spells, to be perfect. If I messed up even a little bit, I could expect a visit from my father. He would show up, embarrass me in front of my friends, and remind me who I was." She lowered her voice to imitate her father. "'You are a Wyndamir, Miranda, and with that comes great responsibility. You don't have time for childish antics or anything less than your best. I will not have you tarnish our name by failing to perform up to your potential. You are a Wyndamir, and you need to act like one.' I heard that speech a thousand times. I felt so much pressure I could barely breathe."

"I never thought of it like that," Seven admitted. "But it would have been different because I would have been the only one who knew. Well, Skelly and me. He figured it out the first time he saw me."

"Durward Skelly! He baked the most wonderful treats."

"Still does," Seven said.

"Phoebe and I would spend hours together in his cottage eating those treats and drinking his amazing hot chocolate. They didn't care that I was a Wyndamir." Her mom was smiling at the memory, but then worry settled in. "If he figured it out that fast, it won't be long before others put it together," her mom said more to herself than to Seven.

"That's what Skelly said," Seven said. Then, she said a little more hesitantly, "Mom, some people in Midia are saying horrible things about you. Darcy was going on about how her dad said that you were a thief. Did you steal that relic you told me about?"

"Was this Darcy Davidson?"

Seven nodded.

"That sounds like the Davidson family. Her father doesn't like me for many reasons. He is dangerous, Seven. That entire family is dangerous. That's why I told you to keep your distance from her."

"She doesn't exactly make that easy," Seven muttered.

"Well, to be clear, I did not steal that relic. It was entrusted to my care to protect at all costs, and it cost me everything." Miranda paused and then added. "Seven, when the fact I am alive gets out, it will be big and messy. A thief will be one of the nicer names some people say. You will need to lean on your friends, Skelly, and Phoebe and before you argue," Miranda said, holding up a hand, noticing that Seven opened her mouth at Mcfee's name, "I know that you aren't as sure about Phoebe as I am Seven, but you are wrong. When we were in school, and other students found out who I was, they wanted to be my friend because they thought it would give them an advantage. Phoebe didn't, not one time. To this day, she is willing to take enormous risks to help me. Despite what you may think, she is the most trustworthy person I know."

I don't think she is, Seven thought, but instead asked, "Why did you tell me my grandfather was dead?"

"If you thought he was dead, you wouldn't press me to

meet him," her mom answered simply. "He is a complicated man. We disagreed about almost everything. He believed I should have become a teacher and supported the school, but that wasn't what I wanted. I wanted to use my skills to improve relations with our non-magical neighbors and maybe, eventually, remove the veils. He believed that not only should the veils be kept, but they should be fortified.

"After I graduated and applied to work as a Guardian for the Midian government, he was furious. He tried to use his influence to prevent me from getting hired. When I confronted him, he told me I was making the worst mistake of my life. He knew how I felt about unwielders, how curious I was about them. 'It is too big of a temptation for you, Miranda. You have too much of a soft spot for them,'" she said, imitating her father's tone again. "I guess he was right about that," Miranda conceded.

"Are you saying my grandfather would hate me because my dad was an unwielder?" Seven asked in disbelief.

"I don't know, Seven. I wish I could say that he wouldn't, but I just don't know," Miranda said quietly.

"So, you won't tell me what the relic was that you were supposed to guard?" Seven asked quickly, changing subjects.

"I can't tell you," her mom said.

"Why not? You told Mcfee, I bet," Seven spat.

"It isn't because I don't *want* to tell you. It is because I *can't*. When I took the assignment, I made a vow of secrecy. If I try to talk about it or write it down, I will die before I can even get the first word out."

"Whoa," Seven said.

"Yeah, whoa," her mom repeated. "As far as Phoebe goes, whatever she knows, she figured out on her own."

"Mom, Mcfee is not who you think she is. A lot happened this semester. I think Mcfee is trying to steal the relic for herself, and for whatever reason, I think she thinks I have. I believe she attacked Cully thinking Cully was me," Seven said quickly.

"Why would say such a terrible thing?" her mom asked incredulously.

Seven blurted out everything she had been holding in. The attack on Swathmore. The conversation she overheard between Mcfee and the unknown person and the one between Pepper and Mcfee. The threat. The fact that Cully didn't accidentally fall. Mcfee's timely disappearance with *family matters*.

"And you have proof of these horrible allegations?" her mom asked with quiet fury when Seven finished.

"Well, I...."

Her mom stood and held up her hand for silence.

"I have had it. Phoebe has taken risks for this family without understanding why or even agreeing with my actions. She has done all of this because she is my friend, my trusted, loyal friend. There are things in motion in which you have no business getting involved. Your job, *your only job,* is to go to school, study hard, and stay out of things that are not your business. Am I clear?"

"But mom, I..." Seven protested.

"Am I clear?" her mom repeated.

Seven gave a quick nod but remained quiet

"And don't forget the first thing you will do when you return to school is to get your locket back," her mom scolded.

"I did try to get it back, you know," Seven said, trying to defend herself. "I tried to take it off Cully's neck while she was still... out." She hated admitting that she attempted to take back her locket while Cully was still unconscious.

Her mom closed her eyes and took a long, slow deep breath.

"Of course, Cully couldn't tell you to take the locket because she was unconscious. You couldn't get it off her neck. It burned you before it turned to smoke and slipped through your fingers."

"How did you know that?" Seven asked, her eyes as wide as a frog's mouth.

"Because the locket is enchanted. I put a spell on it before you left that makes it impossible to remove without the permission of the one who is wearing it."

"Why would you do that?"

"Well, I uh, didn't want to take a chance of anyone getting their hands on it and finding my picture," her mom said. "When you took it off and freely gave it to her, the enchantment partially transferred to your friend. Even though it is your locket, because she was not able to give you permission to take it, you couldn't."

Her mom knelt in front of Seven. She looked directly into her eyes.

"The minute you get back to school, you get it back. Put it on and never take it off again. Understand?"

Seven nodded.

"Christmas is in two days. Mr. and Mrs. Bigglesby *and* Phoebe are coming for dinner. For me, please do not say anything to her about your outrageous suspicions. Let's just find a way to enjoy it," Without waiting for a response, Miranda left the room.

"That really would be a Christmas miracle," Seven muttered when she was sure her mom was out of earshot.

The next day Seven went out to the mailbox. Inside, a letter was waiting for her. There was no return address, and she didn't recognize the handwriting. She opened it and read:

Dear Seven,

I am not even sure if this is the right address, so I may be writing this to no one. I didn't like the way we left things, and it has taken me forever to work up the courage to apologize. I started this letter a thousand times, but they all sounded stupid. I'm not sure this one is any better, but I figured I would send it anyway.

I was such a jerk the way I acted when I didn't see you wearing the bracelet I gave you. I was going to apologize, but then my aunt got sick, and we had to take care of her. When I got back, you were already gone.

The new school year is about the same as last year. Mr. Strickland is still mean as ever. I haven't made any new friends since you left. It doesn't matter, though, because we are moving after the holidays. Maybe my new school will be better. I hope your new school is good and that you made some new friends, but if you did, don't forget about me.

    Hopefully, still your friend,
    Kerry Hollins

Guilt flooded Seven. She hadn't thought about Kerry at all in months. After going off to Wyndamir Academy, she hadn't given her old best friend a second thought. She had met Iggy and Cully and forgotten all about Kerry, who was still miserable and lonely.

I need to write her back, Seven thought. *I don't want her to think I did forget about her, even though I sort of did.* She ran to the library, pulled out paper and a pen, and wrote *Dear Kerry.* Then she wrote...nothing. That was it. She was stuck. She stared at the empty lines screaming for words, but she didn't know what to write. She picked up the pen and set it down several times. After a while, out of frustration, she wrote:

Dear Kerry,

My mom and I left because some dark wielders were after us. They think my mom has a powerful magical relic, which she did but doesn't anymore. On top of that, I found out I can do magic. Now we live in a house where there is an enchanted gate in our woods that leads to a magical country called Midia. I attend a school named after my rich and powerful family, and I have made two great friends named Cully and Iggy. They are so fun that I haven't missed you at all. Oh yeah, about the bracelet, it really was stolen by a band of thieving cats.
Merry Christmas,
Seven

Seven crumbled the paper and threw it into the fireplace. She couldn't tell Kerry anything about her new life, but she had to write something. After several more failed attempts, Seven gave up and went to her room. Christmas was the next day, and she was going to need her strength to face Mcfee. Maybe inspiration would come to her while she slept.

Unfortunately, inspiration didn't come. Fortunately, neither did Mcfee.

Seven woke up early and found her mom sitting by the Christmas tree drinking coffee. She had two extra cups next to her, a coffee for Mcfee and hot chocolate for Seven. Miranda decided that she and Seven would open gifts while they waited.

"I am sure Phoebe will be here shortly," Miranda said. "Besides, I am excited to watch you open them."

The first package Seven opened was a set of EverWarm socks. They were enchanted to continually feel as though they had just been pulled from a warm dryer.

"Phoebe picked those up for me. You will appreciate those when the snow piles up in January and February," her mom said. "I also had her pick up an EverWarm blanket, too." There was also something called ghost paper. It was a way to pass secret messages. You wrote the message, ended it with the word *celare*, and the message disappeared. When the person was ready to read it, they wrote *revelare*, and the message would appear.

"Don't try to use it to cheat on homework or tests, though. The teachers are on to that," her mom cautioned.

Seven's gift to her mom had been a big hit, too. During the fall, Seven had Cully take a photograph of Seven next to the fountain in front of Wyndamir Hall. She put it in a simple framed and wrapped it. When her mom opened the gift, she stared at it, speechless.

"I know you haven't been back there for a long time, and I thought you'd like to see it. I don't know if it looks the same or not."

"Thank you," her mom whispered in a wavering voice. "I love it." Then, as though the picture was as delicate as a snowflake, Miranda put it on the mantle over the fireplace.

"I best get in the kitchen. Dinner isn't going to cook itself," Miranda said.

"It could with a little magical help," Seven said.

"You're funny," her mom said as she checked her watch. "I thought Phoebe would be here already.

"Maybe she is still attending to those *family matters*," Seven said sarcastically, but Mirada ignored her and headed to the kitchen.

Seven tried to help her mom make dinner, but her mom was so distracted, the meal didn't turn out as well as it could have. They nearly burned the pies and undercooked the dressing. Miranda almost forgot to bake the ham, but the mashed potatoes and gravy turned out well. This was mostly because both of them came right out of a box.

Even when the Bigglesbys came for Christmas dinner later that day, Miranda couldn't stay focused on the conversation.

"Are you all right, dear?" Mrs. Bigglesby asked as Miranda served dessert. "Your mind seems to be somewhere else."

"I'm sorry, Mrs. Bigglesby. I thought Phoebe would be joining us."

"I am sure she is fine, probably something at the school."

"Yeah, that's probably it."

"Anyway, we must be going. We need to check on the store for our after Christmas sale tomorrow morning. Thank you for everything. Dinner was…nice. Merry Christmas." Then, she and her husband left.

For the remainder of the break, Miranda barely spoke to Seven. Her mom looked as though she was hardly sleeping as the circles around her eyes darkened by the day.

She would jump up at the slightest noise and run to see if Phoebe had arrived at last. Phoebe never did.

When it was finally time to head back to school, Seven was relieved. When she saw the rickety old barn that led to Midia, it took all of her restraint not to take off and run to it just to get away from her mom.

"You mail those letters I wrote, and if you see Phoebe, you write to me immediately, okay?" her mom said for the thousandth time. "And your locket. The second you see Cully, you get it back, put it on, and never take it off again. You understand?"

"Yes, mom," Seven said, annoyed. "I got it. I better hurry or I will miss the bus. Love you," Seven waved and entered the barn door.

When she collapsed next to Iggy on the bus to Wyndamir a while later, relief washed over her. She was not only away from her mom, but she had run into Chris, Cully's brother. He said that Cully would meet them at the school. Their parents insisted on talking with Medwell before allowing Cully to return for classes. Apparently, she was having some memory issues but was okay other than that.

"You look more stressed than before the break," Iggy commented. "Did you talk to Cully's brother?"

"Yeah, I saw him. As for break, despite what that song says, it was not the most wonderful time of the year this year," Seven said. "I never thought I would say this. I am glad to be going back to school,"

"That bad?" Iggy asked.

"That bad," Seven answered.

"Tell me everything," Iggy said. Luckily, the bus was loud with students sharing Christmas break stories, and no one sat in the seats next to them, so they did have some privacy as Seven told Iggy everything.

"So, Mcfee never showed up?"

"Not once. I am glad, but my mom is worried. She

thinks something happened to Mcfee."

"Well, I guess we will see when we get back to Wynadamir," Iggy said. "I am still confused about something you said, though. Cats stole the bracelet that your friend gave to you?"

Seven nodded.

"Sadly, I don't find that stranger," Iggy said before a sudden invasion by Adria, Sam, Charlie, and Sophie halted their talk.

The rest of the trip to Wyndamir was lighter in conversation, something for which Seven was grateful. Soon, they were pulling around the snow-covered flagstone circle. Even the fountain had given in to the colder temperatures as the water stood frozen in place. Iggy and Seven hopped off the bus as soon as it stopped. They headed straight for Terramin Tower to find Cully.

When they walked through the wall, however, a raucous rec room greeted them. Somehow, Sam and Charlie were already unpacked and showing off some of their new Christmas presents to other first-year students. On the table was a miniature figure of a woman. She was singing and playing a little guitar. Sam poked her, and she stopped and gave him a dirty look.

"Do you mind, young man? I am trying to sing here," she scolded.

"Not that one, Bizzy. Sing '"Spells Around the World'."

"Again? I have sung that one twenty times today. I have recorded other songs, you know."

"Come on, Bizzy. You know it's my favorite," Sam said with a huge smile on his face. Then he added, "No one sings it like you." The figure's face went from annoyed to flattered in the blink of an eye. The statue started singing a song as the students near it danced and sang along. Unfortunately, Cully wasn't one of them.

"Where is she?" Iggy asked.

"Maybe she's up in our room. Let me..." Suddenly something collided with them. Then, it shrieked and grabbed them in a hug so hard it was hard to breathe.

"What took you so long?" Cully scolded as she spun Seven around to face her.

"We just pulled in like five minutes ago," Seven said, shrugging free to look at her friend. The bump on Cully's head wasn't visible anymore. She still had a few bruises on her face, but they were fading.

"Yeah, well, that's five minutes too long," Cully said. Then she leaned in close and whispered, "Let's get out of here and find somewhere quiet to talk."

The three turned around and nearly knocked right into Miss Poxley, who seemed to be forcing her lips to form a smile. Seven thought it looked rather painful.

"How was your break, Miss Preston?"

"Okay," Seven said, noticing that Poxley's hands were no longer bandaged.

"Mr. Everett?"

"Fine."

"And you, Miss Collins? How are you feeling?" Poxley asked.

"Good," Cully said.

"What about your memory? I heard you cannot remember anything. Is that true?" Poxley stared at Cully.

Cully just nodded.

"Well, I'm sure it is just a matter of ..." Poxley stopped mid-sentence. A loud bang and a chorus of cheers erupted from the group surrounding Charlie and Sam. Poxley's pained smile immediately vanished, and her more comfortable, natural-looking scowl took its place. Faster than an express pixie, she stormed over to the group and quashed the fun.

Before Poxley or anyone else could stop them again, Cully pulled Iggy and Seven through the wall. She led them down the darkening corridor until they came to an empty classroom. After they were inside, Cully closed the door. Then, to Seven's astonishment, Cully pulled out a wand and whispered something. A light shot from the end of her wand. It snaked around the edge of the door and seemed to seal the room.

"Cully, what are you doing?" Seven asked.

"Stillness spell. I don't want to take any chances of being overheard." When she finished, she pointed to the far corner of the room. "Let's sit there." Her voice was so serious, Seven and Iggy didn't protest.

"Uh, what's going on, Cully? Why are you so secretive?" Seven asked when they were sitting in a circle knee to knee.

"Because, if my parents knew what I am about to tell you, they would yank me out of here and back home so fast that it would make time go backward."

"Why?" Iggy and Seven said in unison.

"I lied to my parents," Cully began. "and to Medwell, Poxley, Mcfee, and even Bellatora. Everyone."

"About what?" Iggy asked.

"I told them that I couldn't remember anything from the night I was hurt. Every time they asked me, I would close my eyes and pretend as though I was trying hard to remember, but then I would just shake my head."

"Why?" Seven asked.

"Because if they knew, not only would my parents take me out of school, but Wyndamir
Academy would probably close."

"Why?" Seven asked.

"Because I didn't fall down those steps by accident. I was pushed."

Chapter Fifteen

Cully's Story

Apparently, Seven and Iggy didn't give her the reaction she was looking for because she asked, "Did you hear what I said? Someone attacked me."

"Yeah, we know," Iggy admitted and explained what he had overheard when he was in the infirmary.

Cully looked from Seven to Iggy, disappointment blooming on her face.

"Well, that's rather a bummer," she said.

"But we haven't heard your side of the story. I'm sure we don't know everything," Iggy suggested.

"Yeah, Cully, we don't know what happened before you were pushed down the steps. Tell us," Seven added. Not needing much encouragement, Cully told her tale.

"Well, after you two left the theater to get Iggy's arm looked at," Cully began, "I hurried to put the rest of the polished amulets away. I was nearly out the door when I realized I was still wearing the wig. I knew if Flouriche came in and saw it was missing, I would probably be joining Iggy in the infirmary."

"I guess you did that anyway, huh?" Iggy quipped.

Cully made a face at him but continued her story.

"Anyway, I went back to the prop room to put the wig away. That's when I heard a door squeak. I thought maybe it was you guys back for another rag or something to put over Iggy's arm, but no one answered when I called out. I thought maybe

I was hearing things, so I stood still and listened. That's when I heard footsteps, so I called out again."

"Who was it?" Iggy interrupted, apparently not able to stand the suspense.

"Shhh, I'm getting to that, Iggy. Don't rush me," she said, glaring at him. Seven got the feeling Cully was relishing this moment of having their rapt attention. Iggy made a motion like he was zipping his lips closed and locking them.

"Anyway, I called out again, but no one answered. I was getting a little nervous being in that dark theater by myself, especially with the Landing's recent attacks. So, I stepped back into the prop room and closed the door leaving it open just enough so that I could see if someone was coming. Someone did. She stopped right in front of the door."

"She? Was it Mcfee?" Seven asked, hopeful that they finally had evidence of Mcfee's dark intentions.

"Would you two quit interrupting me?" Cully said, annoyed. "I'll get to that. Where was I? Oh yeah, I pulled my head behind the door so she couldn't see me. I was hoping she wouldn't come to the prop room, but she did. I nearly screamed when the door started to open. I flattened myself behind it and tried not to breathe when she came inside. I peeked around the side of the door to see who it was, but she was wearing a dark cloak and had the hood pulled low so that I couldn't see her face."

"Then how did you know it was a she?" Iggy said, interrupting again.

"*She* walked right over to the box that held all of the amulets," Cully continued ignoring Iggy's interruption. "She tried to open it, even cast a few spells, but Flouriche designed that box so that when it is closed, she is the only one who can open it. The intruder picked up the box and threw it. She cast several more spells and was getting angrier and angrier because it wouldn't open. That's when I decided to sneak out.

"I tiptoed around the door and was nearly through it when I heard her call out to me. The voice was soft and high.

That's how I knew it was a woman," she said, looking straight at Iggy. "She hissed, 'Open it and give it to me.' I didn't turn around. I explained that only Flouriche could open it, but she just repeated for me to open it. I told her that I would get Flouriche, but when I started to walk away, she shot a spell right past me, so I stopped. Then she," Cully paused and swallowed. Her face paled, and a cold sweat was breaking out on her forehead. She wasn't enjoying this anymore.

"Cully, we can stop if you want to," Seven said, but Cully shook her head.

"No, I want to finish." She took a deep breath and continued. "She said, 'It is you. You have it. Give it to me.' I told her I didn't know what she was talking about, and then I just ran. She shot some kind of energy ball at my feet. Luckily, it missed. She yelled, 'Give me the blaze, and I will let you live.' At least it was something like that."

"The blaze?" Iggy said. "What's that?"

"I don't know," Cully said. "I was too busy running for my life to stop and ask."

"The blaze," Iggy repeated.

"Anyway, she chased me and kept shooting all kinds of spells. Luckily, most of them missed hitting the walls and the sets. Then, she hit me with one, and something really strange happened."

"What?" Iggy and Seven asked in unison.

"I absorbed the spell."

"Absorbed the spell?" Iggy asked. "I've never heard of that."

"Me, neither," Cully said, "but that is the best way I know how to describe it. I know it hit me because I could feel it. I tripped and nearly fell. I caught myself on one of the tree props and watched as blue flame snaked up my leg. I could feel the warmth of it like a fire was starting in my nerves, but then it just disappeared like it never hit me in the first place."

"Is that possible?" Seven asked.

"I don't know. I have been hit by spells before. My brother shot a cackle curse at me once. Hit me square in the back. It knocked me down before I went into uncontrollable cackles, and that was just a minor spell. These were not minor spells. She was trying to do some damage," Cully said.

"And you are sure it hit you?" Iggy asked.

"Positive. I saw it on my legs. Plus, my robes were smoking."

"There were burn holes in your robes when you were in the infirmary," Seven said.

"Well, I wasn't going to stand around and try to figure it out, so I kept running. She started throwing spells even faster. How the entire theater didn't blow up, I will never know. Finally, I made it to the doors and then the concrete patio. I was at the top of the steps when a second person stepped out of the shadows."

"There were two people?" Seven asked.

Cully nodded.

"Man or woman?" Iggy asked.

"I don't know. I couldn't tell. Anyway, the woman running out of the theater yelled for the other person to stop me. The second one hit me with a spell, too, but the same thing happened. It hit me and then disappeared. I made it down two or three steps, and then one of them pushed me. When I hit the bottom step, it felt like someone had taken a hammer to my head. Everything went fuzzy. I tried to get up, but I couldn't," Cully said, her voice shaking. "Before I knew it, they were standing over me. They were talking, but it sounded like we were in a tunnel. I could understand what they were saying. All I remember is I felt someone pulling at me, then someone screamed, and that's it. The next thing I knew, I woke up in the infirmary a few days later."

The three sat in silence, turning over in their minds the story Cully just recounted. Guilt formed like rocks in the pit of Seven's stomach as she realized she had been right. Someone had attacked her friend, thinking it was Seven.

"This is all my fault," Seven finally said.

"Your fault? How is it your fault?" Cully said. "You didn't

shoot those spells or push me down the stairs."

"I know I didn't attack you, but ..." Seven couldn't finish. Instead, she looked at Iggy silently, begging him to explain.

"Seven has a theory," Iggy said. "She thinks that you were attacked because whoever it was thought she was you or rather that you were her," he said quickly.

"What? That's ridiculous," Cully said.

"Think about it, Cully. You were wearing the wig with the long black hair that even you said made you look like me from the back. You had my backpack," Seven said.

"And you were wearing her locket," Iggy added.

"True, but why would someone attack Seven?" Cully asked, not convinced.

"Not someone. Mcfee," Seven said without hesitation. "You said it was a woman. I'm sure it was Mcfee. This blaze must be the 'it' Mcfee's been after. But, before I forget, can I have my locket back?"

"I'm glad to be getting rid of this." Cully pulled it over her head and handed it to Seven.

"You don't like it?" Seven asked, feeling a bit of relief at its familiar weight around her neck.

"No, it isn't that. It's actually the opposite. *Everyone* likes it."

"Huh?"

"Everyone who came to see me in the infirmary commented on it. Medwell thought it was unusual. Willowisp kept saying how beautiful it was and how she wished she had one just like it. My parents wanted to know where I got it. Poxley even noticed it, and she doesn't like anything."

"Yeah, she saw it on me, too, one night," Seven said. "She wanted me to open it, but I couldn't let her see the picture of my mom inside, so I lied and told her it was broken. She said her brother or someone could fix it for me."

"She made me the same offer when I told her it was yours, but of course, I said no. She seemed annoyed, but no one got angry like Mcfee did when she saw it. I thought she was going to erupt. She accused me of stealing it from you. I tried to tell her that I was only going to clean it and then give it back, but she wouldn't listen. I bet she tried a hundred times to get me to give it to her. She kept saying that she would see you over the holidays and that your mom would be furious that you didn't have it."

"Well, that was true. My mom was pretty angry when she found out I didn't have it," Seven said as she looked at the locket. "How did Mcfee take it when you wouldn't give it to her?"

"Not well. She kept mumbling about responsibility and better choices," Cully said.

"Maybe it's your locket," Iggy suggested. "Does it have a fire symbol on it or something that has to do with a blaze?"

Seven studied the locket. The stone in it was a green emerald. If it were a ruby, that would make more sense – red like fire – but it wasn't. None of the markings resembled a fire, either. She opened the locket. Nothing engraved on the inside. Nothing special, except the picture, of course.

"It's just a locket," Seven said.

"Maybe, maybe not," Iggy said. "There has to be something about it. For now, don't take it off, not even to clean it."

"No need to worry about that," Seven said.

"I think you need to keep up the memory loss act," Iggy said, turning to Cully. "If the attackers think you can identify them, they might try again. Just keep pretending you don't remember until we have proof Mcfee is involved."

They all agreed.

"We better get going," Iggy said. "I do not want to get locked out of the dorm and spend the night in the hallways." He involuntarily shuddered.

They entered the corridor and were almost to Terramin Tower's entrance when Cully said, "Hey, we spent the whole time talking about my break. How was yours?"

"It was about as fun as polishing Krisp's shoes with my toothbrush," Seven said as she gave Cully the highlights of her miserable break.

The next morning at breakfast, Iggy announced the need to return to the library.

"Really?" Cully whined.

"We have to look in every book that has anything to do with talismans, charms, amulets, fires, blazes," Iggy said, ticking them off on his fingers.

"I guess we just booked season tickets to the library. Woo hoo," Cully said with no enthusiasm at all.

The next several weeks went by in a blur. Between their regular class load, their time in
the library, and the extra time they had to spend in the theater because of the mess caused by
Cully's attackers, they barely slept. And with their lack of progress, they were starting to lose hope.

"I wish my mom could just tell me," Seven said one afternoon in the library as she slammed shut another book on charmed jewelry.

"Not if she took a vow of secrecy. My brother tried one of those on me when he broke my mom's favorite cauldron. Luckily, he didn't know what he was doing. I don't think I have
ever seen my dad that angry," Cully said.

"How did he break a cauldron?" Iggy asked.

"Don't ask," Cully said.

Just then, a school postal pixie arrived and landed on Seven's shoulder. They hardly ever did that, and Seven was bracing herself for a bite or pinch or something. However, it only landed long enough to catch its breath and hand the envelope to Seven.

"Thanks," she said. Then the pixie took a deep breath, jumped into the air, and flew down the hallway weaving as it went.

"Must have had to work a double shift," Cully guessed.

Seven opened the letter and scanned it.

"Skelly wants to know why we haven't been to see him since we got back. If we don't come for a visit this instant, he will be forced to eat the double chocolate fudge brownies he is making all by himself and will hold us responsible for any indigestion he may suffer," Seven read.

"He doesn't have to ask me twice," Cully said.

"What about your report for Brimbal's class?" Iggy asked. "I *know* you two aren't finished." Iggy, on the other hand, had finished a week ago.

"Iggy, it's double chocolate fudge brownies. Brimbal can wait," Cully said as she shoved her books into her bag.

A little while later, they were outside Skelly's house, waiting for him to open the door. They had already knocked twice, but the door did not open until they knocked a third time.

"Can I help you?" Skelly said as he wiped his hands on a cloth.

"Uh, yes, you can let us in," Cully said, trying to slip past him. "I smell heaven." Skelly, however, blocked her path.

"I'm sorry. Do I know you?" he asked. "You sort of resemble three bratty kids who used to come to visit me, but they seem to have forgotten all about me. So, you can't be them."

"Sorry, Skelly, we've been busy. Now, let us in. It's freezing!" Seven said as she danced in place to keep warm.

"Oh, come in. I'm just making a point, is all," Skelly said as he stepped to the side to let them in. "What could you possibly have going on that takes so much time? Surely the homework level hasn't kicked in already. It's the beginning of the term."

"Well, we are here to learn," Iggy pointed out.

"And we've been spending a lot of time in the prop room," Cully said. "You know how Flouriche is. If one stone is an inch off from where she wants it, we have to start over."

"And we've been researching my mom," Seven said.

"What in the world about?" Skelly asked.

Over brownies and milk, Seven talked about her mom's final days in Midia before she left.

"You mean that man that died in Wyndamir gardens was your dad? That's terrible." Skelly said sympathetically.

"The Shadow Raiders attacked my mom because she was guarding something. We are trying to find out what it was. Any ideas?"

Skelly shook his head. "I heard that was a top-secret assignment, that was."

"It amazes me how many people know that she was given a secret assignment. Doesn't seem very, well secretive, does it?" Iggy said.

"Didn't you ask her?" Skelly said.

Seven explained about the vow of secrecy.

"I think Mcfee knows what the relic is," Seven said, "and we are pretty sure it has something to do with my locket."

"You're not still on about her, are you?" Skelly said, rolling his eyes.

"Well, I just think there are a lot of unexplained things. I remember that it was a woman that attacked me, and it could have been Mcfee," Cully said conversationally, but as soon as the words were out of her mouth, she slapped her hands over it.

"Cully! You weren't supposed to tell!" Iggy shouted.

"So, you do remember that night," Skelly said, looking at Cully.

"A little," Cully lied.

"And you think it was Mcfee?" Skelly asked doubtfully.

"You were the one who found me. Did you see something?" Cully asked.

Skelly shook his head.

"I only saw you lying on the ground."

"Well, we think Mcfee was actually trying to attack me," Seven said.

"Would you stop saying that?" Skelly said, irritated. "She'd never attack any student, much less her best friend's daughter."

"Mcfee wants my locket. I know it," Seven said. "Maybe she thinks it will lead her to whatever my mom was guarding when she left Midia. We haven't figured it all out yet. We know it has something to do with fire or blazes or something. We are …"

"Stop and listen to me, you three," Skelly said, holding up his hand. "Phoebe Mcfee would never do anything to hurt you. It is a shame that the woman is not even here to defend herself against these ridiculous accusations."

"She still hasn't returned from break, has she?" Iggy asked.

"I wonder what would be so important to keep her away from her school duties," Seven said sarcastically.

"Family business," Skelly said. "She wrote to Bellatora saying that she had a family matter and needed a leave of absence. She's probably taking care of a sick aunt or something, and here you are accusing her of terrible things." He shook his head and stood. "Look, I enjoy your visits, and I am very thankful that you are all right, Cully, but I told you three no more of that kind of talk about Mcfee. You should probably head back."

"But, Skelly," Seven tried.

"I'm serious. I don't want to hear another word against Phoebe Mcfee. No, go on back." He was holding out their cloaks. The conversation was over.

"I can't believe he threw us out," Seven said.

"Yeah, I didn't even get a second brownie," Cully said.

They were climbing the steps to Wyndamir Hall when Iggy groaned.

"I left my bag at Skelly's," he said. "I have to get my it tonight. It has my report on Sherlock Lumpenfield for Brimbal's class tomorrow."

" Really, Iggy? It's freezing out here!" Cully whined.

"I'm sorry," Iggy said. "I'll go by myself."

"No. We will all go," Seven said, thinking about the attack on Cully and not wanting to take any chances. They turned around and headed head back to Skelly's. As his cottage came into view, what they saw stopped them in their tracks.

Skelly was standing in the open doorway, talking to Phoebe Mcfee. They jumped behind a unicorn-shaped bush.

"So much for being gone," Iggy said.

"Well, that traitorous jerk," Cully spat.

"I would give anything to hear that conversation," Seven

said bitterly as they watched Skelly hand something to Mcfee. She stuffed it inside her cloak and shook his hand. Then, she pulled the hood of her cloak over her head, walked down the stairs, and disappeared around the corner of Skelly's cottage in the direction of Whispering Woods.

"I can't believe he betrayed us. I'm going to give him a piece of my mind," Seven said, furious.

"Seven, don't," Iggy said as he grabbed her cloak. "We don't want him to know we saw this." But it was too late. Seven stepped out from behind the bush just as Skelly was closing the door. He froze when he saw them. Even in the dark, Seven could see the color drain from his face. He had been caught with the enemy.

"I can't believe it," Seven said for the tenth time as they sat in the empty rec room. It was very late, and everyone else had gone to bed. "Everyone my mom thinks is her friend is betraying her."

"I bet he told her everything we told him," Iggy said. "She knows we know there is something about your locket. We have got to figure it out."

"We've been looking for weeks," Cully said, exasperated.

"Let's look at the locket again," Iggy said.

"We've looked at this thing fifteen times. It is just a locket," Seven said just as exasperated as Cully.

"Then let's make it sixteen," Iggy said firmly.

Feeling desperate, Seven took off her locket and handed it to Iggy. He held it up to the firelight and turned it over in his hands. He studied the markings, the stone, the clasp, and the pictures of her parents and her.

"See, I told you," Seven said, holding her hand out for him to give it back to her. He didn't.

"These pictures have been cut, so they fit in the locket," he said.

"That's how it usually works. Not too many people get tiny pictures developed," Seven said, still holding her hand out.

"The picture of your parents doesn't fit as well as the one

of you. It's pushed out in the middle as though there is something behind it," Iggy said.

Seven took the locket and examined the pictures. Iggy was right. She carefully pulled the photo of her parents out, hoping not to tear it. As it pulled free, a tiny piece of yellowed paper fell out.

"What's that?" Cully said.

"I don't know. Maybe a tiny map that leads to the relic?" Seven said, picking up the tiny paper. She carefully unfolded it. When she flattened it out on the table, the paper was about half the size of a baseball card. Tiny letters and symbols covered it, front and back.

"What language is that?" Cully asked.

"I have no idea," Iggy said as he carefully held it up to the firelight. "A few markings that look like Latin and ancient Greek or something like that, but I don't know for sure." He gently set it back down on the table. They just stared at it as though it might do something on its own. It didn't.

"And the rest of it?" Cully asked.

"Not a clue," Iggy said. "I guess I can check the runes and symbology section tomorrow. For now, fold it back up and put your locket back together. I'm going to bed. Have fun," Iggy said, stifling a yawn.

"Have fun?" Cully asked absently as she watched Seven carefully refold the fragile paper.

"You two still have to finish your reports for Brimbal's class," Iggy reminded them as he headed for the stairs to his room. "See you in the morning."

Seven and Cully looked at each other.

"I really hate him sometimes," Cully said.

Chapter Sixteen

Unexpected Help

"I will never procrastinate again," Cully said, her voice muffled because she had her head down on her desk. She and Seven had stayed up very late to finish their reports.

"Yes, you will," Iggy said.

"Yeah, you're probably right," Cully agreed, sitting up. "By the way, what did Skelly say when you went back for your bag?"

"I didn't have to go to Skelly's. My bag was waiting for me in the rec room this morning. I guess he used school mail."

"I hope I never see that traitor again," Seven said just as Brimbal entered the room.

"Good morning, class," Brimbal shouted as he rubbed his hands together and smiled widely. "Today, we will begin giving our oral reports on the wielders you have been researching. I am excited to hear what you have learned. Mr. Everett, you are up first." Brimbal took a seat in the back of the room as Iggy walked to the front.

"Sherlock Obert Lumpenfield was born in 1694. From an early age, his parents knew he was special," Iggy began, his voice strong and sure. "His mom recalled the time when a crying and hungry Sherlock summoned a bottle from the kitchen table to his crib in the next room where he grabbed it in midair and began drinking hungrily." And on Iggy went. He recited Lumpenfield's life accomplishments and magical contributions. When he finished, the class applauded politely.

"Wonderful, Mr. Everett, very thorough," Brimbal said, beaming. "Does anyone have any questions for Mr. Everett?" The teacher asked as Iggy collected his notes, which he barely used. "Miss Davidson. A question?"

"Iggy, did you choose this wielder for your report because you could relate to him?"

"Relate to him?" Iggy asked.

"I mean, since you are both Crossers," Darcy asked snidely.

"Oh, well, I..." Iggy stammered. Seven watched as Iggy's face went scarlet, his neck blotchy.

"Professor Brimbal, Darcy has a point," Seven interjected as she shot to her feet. "I'm sure Iggy can relate to him. Just like Iggy, Sherlock Lumpenfield proved that being a Midian-born wielder isn't everything. After all, you are from Midia, right, Darcy? And as far as I can tell, Iggy outperforms you in every class."

Darcy shot Seven a look that was full of venom, but before she could respond, the bell rang.

"Well, that does it for today. We will finish next time," Brimbal said, obviously relieved.

Seven, Cully, and Iggy were headed back to Terramin Tower. Suddenly Darcy appeared right in front of them. Devlin and Brigit were right behind her.

"That thing," Darcy said, gesturing to Iggy, "is not even close to the wielder I am."

"I know," Seven agreed. "He's way ahead of you."

"Say that again," Darcy challenged as she drew her wand.

"Way, way ahead of you," Seven repeated and drew her own wand.

"Careful, Preston, you don't want to curse yourself accidentally," Darcy said, and then without warning, shouted, "Baca silencia!" Seven turned and ducked, bracing for the impact of Darcy's spell. However, Seven didn't feel a thing. She turned back around and faced Darcy, whose eyes were saucers.

"What's the matter, Darcy? Shocked you could miss me

from such a close distance?" Then before reason could catch up with her, Seven shouted, "Puermos!" A blue ball of light shot from Seven's wand. Darcy stood there, staring wide-eyed and opened mouth at Seven, making no move to try to avoid the spell, but when it was about six inches from its target, the ball of light froze in midair, quivered, and then vanished with a tiny, harmless pop.

"Well, well, well, I shouldn't be surprised," said a familiar voice. Krisp strode up to the group with his wand outstretched. "I knew it was only a matter of time. Miss Preston," Krisp spat, "what do you have to say for yourself? How can you possibly defend attacking an unarmed student?"

"Unarmed?" Seven began, but the words died in her mouth. Darcy's wand was gone. The only thing she saw was Brigit tugging hastily on her robes, apparently covering the wands she had hidden away.

"What was this? An ambush?" He turned to Darcy, Brigit, and Devlin.

"Yes," Devlin lied smoothly.

"You three return to Terramin Tower immediately," Krisp ordered, pointing at Darcy, Devlin, and Brigit. Without hesitation, Brigit and Devlin dragged a still shocked Darcy down the corridor. Then, he whirled on Seven. "Turn around," Krisp commanded.

"What?" Seven asked in confusion.

"Turn around," he repeated louder. Seven, still not understanding, turned a complete circle. "Just as I thought. There are no scorch marks, burn holes, or any evidence of a spell hitting you anywhere. The only spell I saw was the one you cast that would have hit Miss Davidson directly in the face if I hadn't stopped it."

"But, she st..." Cully tried.

"Silence," he hissed. "Not another word, Miss Collins. Since neither of you cast a spell, I am only giving you and Mr. Everitt a demerit for this atrocious attack. I won't be so generous next time." Then, he turned back to Seven. "To my office,

Miss Preston. Now!" Seven reluctantly followed as she stole one last look at Cully and Iggy. They were looking at her with a mix of pity and shock.

Seven had never been to Krisps office, but from the number of turns and stairs they descended, it was underground. Like a bat in a cave.

When they finally reached it, Krisp opened the door and entered without looking back at Seven. He marched to his desk, turned with a flourish, and sat down, placing his fingertips together.

"Sit," he commanded like he was talking to a dog.

Seven walked in, purposely leaving the door open. As she sat in the most uncomfortable chair ever invented, she couldn't help but think that his office was as inviting as Krisp was. It was dark, damp, and smelled of rotting things. She wouldn't have been surprised to find a coffin hidden in the dark corners.

For a long minute, Krisp just stared at her. Finally, he spoke.

"From the first day of classes, l knew you were going to be trouble. You always have an excuse. Well, there are no excuses that can get you out of this," he said, smiling with satisfaction.

Seven opened her mouth to argue, but he raised his hand for silence.

"Save whatever pathetic lies you are concocting in that puny brain of yours. They will not change what I saw with my own eyes. You attacked another student. That is indefensible. If it were in my power, you would be packed and on a bus before nightfall. However, be that I am not Headmaster yet, I cannot expel you. I can, however, give you a fitting detention." A cruel smile curved his lips. Two of his long, bony fingers stroked his pointy chin. "This matter will require some thought. You will be notified as to the nature of your punishment within twenty-four hours by campus pixie post. Until then, you are dismissed." She got up and walked toward the door. She was nearly through it when he said, "And Miss Preston, watch your step. I've got my eye on you."

Anger flared in her as Seven walked out of his office. Krisp was only doing this to intimidate her. For the next twenty-four hours, she would be left to wonder what terrible task awaited her. She was so deep in thought, wondering what horrors Krisp would give her, that she didn't realize she had company.

"How did you do that?" Cully said as she and Iggy dragged Seven into an empty classroom.

"Make Krisp act like a jerk? It isn't that hard," Seven said sarcastically. "His office is like a breath of fresh air. He isn't going to give me my detention for a whole day. He needs time to think of something good and nasty." Seven collapsed on top of an empty desk. "I'll probably have to wash Darcy's feet."

"Are you serious?" Cully asked. "I'm not talking about your stupid detention. I am talking about what you did to Darcy's spell," Cully said, exasperated.

"I didn't do anything. Darcy is just the world's worst shot," Seven said, sitting up.

"She hit you dead on! We both saw it," Cully said, gesturing to Iggy, who was nodding furiously.

"You guys are wrong. I would have felt something. Now, what do you think Krisp will give me for ..."

Before she could finish, Iggy took his wand from his robes' pocket, aimed it directly at Seven's chest, and cast the exact spell Darcy did earlier. Seven had no chance to react. She could only watch as a jet of light shot from Iggy's wand and hit her square in the stomach.

"What the hell was that for?' she yelled. "Are you nuts?"

"Did it hurt?" he asked.

"No, it didn't, but..."

"You shouldn't be able to talk, either," Iggy said, cutting her off. "That spell is supposed to make you mute. And you are obviously not mute, potty mouth."

"Are you sure you did it right?" Seven asked.

Iggy just looked at her.

"Nevermind. Stupid question," Seven conceded.

"That's what happened when Darcy shot you. It was like

the spell couldn't reach you," Cully said.

"Does that happen a lot?" Seven asked.

"Oh, yeah, sure. It happens all the time," Cully said nonchalantly. Then she yelled, "Of course it doesn't! Wielders can't absorb spells without the spell affecting them."

"Isn't that how you described what happened in the theater?" Iggy asked Cully.

"Yeah, it was kind of like that, but I could feel those spells. They stung and singed my robes," Cully said. "Seven's robes did nothing."

They sat in silence and stared at each other.

"Seven, you are wearing your locket, aren't you?" Iggy asked after a while.

"Of course," Seven said, pulling it from her robes.

"That has got to be it," Iggy said, snapping his fingers.

"What has?" Seven asked.

"Your locket! Cully was also wearing it when she was attacked. It must be some sort of protection amulet."

"Why wouldn't it protect me like it protected Seven?" Cully asked. "I mean, those spells hurt and burned my robes. You didn't even flinch."

"I don't know," Iggy admitted, "but it would explain why everyone was so interested in it when they saw it around Cully's neck in the infirmary." Suddenly, he shot up. "We need to get to the…"

"Library," Seven and Cully finished in unison.

After several hours, Seven added *Magical Fire: The Hot and Cold of It* to an already tottering stack of books.

"Another dud," she said. "You guys having any luck?"

"Not really," Iggy said, pouring over a book called *Forgotten Languages of the Ancient World*. "Pretty fascinating stuff, though. Did you know that if you switch this letter with that one, instead of mending a broken bone, you will disintegrate it? Scary."

"Well, I'm exhausted. I'm going to bed," Cully said as she looked at the large clock in the corner. They checked out a few books, much to Mr. Page's great annoyance, and headed to Terramin Tower.

The next morning, Seven was on edge. She had hoped Krisp's detention notice would greet her at breakfast so she could get it out of the way, but the only note she got was from Skelly. She opened it and read:

> *Dear Seven,*
> *Please let me explain. It isn't what you think. Come to my cottage after your classes today. Bring Cully and Iggy with you.*
> *Your friend, Skelly*

"Maybe we should go see him," Iggy said. "Maybe there is something we don't understand."

"No way. He probably has Mcfee there lying in wait. I wouldn't have even opened it except I thought it was my detention notice from Krisp," Seven said.

"He is just trying to scare you," Cully said.

"It's working," Seven answered.

"Look on the bright side, Seven," Iggy said, "at least Darcy hasn't bothered you at all since yesterday's *incident*. Maybe she won't bother you at all for the rest of the year."

"The only bright side would be if Krisp forgot about my detention," Seven groaned.

"Maybe he did," Cully offered half-heartedly.

"There is a greater chance of Darcy and me becoming best friends than of Krisp forgetting my detention. Anyway, let's get to the theater. I would hate to be late for this emergency meeting. Flouriche scares me almost as much as Krisp."

It was now the middle of February, and opening night was only about six weeks away. Though the two lead characters knew their lines, they were the only two. Furthermore, the sets had to be redone several times because they weren't Flouriche-approved.

"I don't think you all understand the gravity of the situation," Flouriche said after she called the meeting to order. "I will not put on a production that is less than perfection. Except for Liriel and Avram, the rest of you are stinking up my theater. The sets look like a toddler colored them, the props are still disorganized, and..." Flouriche was on such a rampage that she overlooked the campus postal pixie that had entered the theater.

For some reason, the pixie was having trouble finding the letter's intended recipient in the darkened theater. It soon became so annoyed at its inability to complete its task that it went crazy. It picked up several rocks and threw them at Flouriche.

"What the ..." Flouriche said, as she turned around and got a face full of pixie spittle. The theater teacher cast a freezing spell, but the pixie dodged it easily. Instead, the spell hit one of the sets and burned a massive hole in it. Liriel and Avram tried to help, but that only made matters worse. The pixie took a swipe at Liriel, who, in an effort to dodge the spittle, tripped over Avram, pushing him *through* the castle door. She screamed as the pixie ripped the wig painfully from her head. Then the creature broke into a series of aerial acrobats before dropping the wig into a bucket of water. With a final twirl and flip, the pixie threw the letter at Flouriche's feet and zoomed out of the theater. An irate Flouriche picked up the envelope.

"Seven Preston!" Flouriche screamed.

Seven wanted to run but knew that would only be worse. Feeling the weight of everyone's gaze, Seven walked onto the stage.

"Don't you realize that when a campus postal pixie is ignored and cannot deliver its mail,
it becomes quite agitated and often destructive? Look at what you've done! What do you have to say for yourself?" Flouriche spoke through gritted teeth.

Seven was pretty sure any attempt to defend herself would make the situation worse, so she remained quiet.

"If I didn't know that kicking you out of my theater would be a reward, I would ban you for life. You will report here first thing tomorrow morning, during your lunch break, and any other free time you may have so that you can fix this mess. You will do this without help. Understood?" Flouriche didn't even wait for an answer before you stormed off the stage, muttering some very unteacherlike words.

The next morning Seven was running as fast as she could. She had already been to the theater where Flouriche met her and yelled some more. Now she was behind, and of course, she had Krisp's class. She could not be late. She slid into her seat only a few seconds before the bell rang. Cully and Iggy gave her a sympathetic look. They had tried to get Seven to let them help her, but she had refused, fearing Flouriche's wrath.

After Morphology, she ran back to the theater. She worked through lunch and barely made it to class on time for the second time that day. She tried to pay attention to Willowisp, but her stomach was not cooperating. She had barely eaten breakfast and missed lunch, so it was rumbling so loudly that Willowisp kept pausing the lesson to look at her. When the bell rang, hungry and irritated, Seven went back to the theater.

However, when she emerged onto the stage, Seven was startled to see she wasn't alone. Willowisp was there, surveying the remaining damage from last night's pixie attack.

"Bellatora really needs to talk with the head of the campus postal pixies. This is ridiculous," the professor said.

"It's a mess," Seven agreed.

"This is not the first instance of pixies gone wild. Last year, I was in the middle of a very complicated Spell Casting lesson when one came to deliver a message to me. I didn't see it until I nearly shot it with a spell. What it did to my classroom makes this stage look neat and tidy. Anyway, I was curious why you hadn't eaten. Since my class is right after lunch, I don't often hear stomachs growl so loudly and persistently. Now, I know why."

Seven's face reddened, and then as if on cue, her stomach growled again.

"I have to get this all fixed before the next rehearsal."

"Without help?"

Seven shook her head.

"I know in the world of drama that woman is brilliant, but she drives me crazy. She could have fixed all of this in no time if she wasn't so stubborn about making a point." Then, before Seven could protest, Willowisp waved a hand, and all the dents in the rocks popped right out, the hole in the castle door repaired itself, and the tangled mess that was Liriel's wig straightened into a shiny mane of black hair.

"Not that I am not grateful," Seven began, "but Madam Flouriche said..."

"Let me handle Flouriche," Willowisp interrupted. "I know it may come as a shock to her, but this is first and foremost a school to learn magic. I can't have my students running around half-crazed and starved. It affects learning. Now," Willowisp said, and, with a flick of her hand, an enormous plate piled high with finger sandwiches appeared on a nearby table. Next to it were two glasses of juice. "Care to join me?" Willowisp's eyebrows danced up and down.

Seven didn't need to be asked twice. She was so hungry that she had to remind herself to chew.

"Thanks, Professor," Seven said through a mouth full sandwich.

"So, how are classes going since coming back from the holiday break? You seem very distracted in class lately. Is there anything I can help with?"

"Classes are okay," Seven said. "Morphology is a bit tricky, but it's fine."

"Oh, yes, Professor Krisp can be, well, somewhat trying," Willowisp said.

"Well, I am not exactly his favorite student," Seven said.

"Well, I am not his favorite colleague. Neither he nor Miss Mcfee finds me very appealing, I'm afraid."

"Mcfee doesn't like you either?" Seven asked, then flushed at the rudeness of her question, but Willowisp only smiled.

"Let's just say that Miss Mcfee and I don't see eye to eye

on many things," Willowisp said. "But it seems there is more on your mind than just classes and Flouriche."

As Seven chewed, she wondered. Should she ask Willowisp about her locket? She had always been so kind and helpful. She was no friend of Mcfee's, so Seven felt like she could trust her, right?

"Professor, do you know anything about protection amulets?" Seven asked as casually as she could.

"Protection amulets?" Willowisp asked curiously.

"Well, our production has to do with a protection amulet, and I was wondering if they were real and how they worked." Seven didn't know where she pulled that from, but she hoped it sounded believable.

"The production, huh?" Willowisp asked, disbelief in her voice. "Protection amulets do exist, but none of them provide complete protection. Some will offer protection against certain potions or spells, but they all eventually lose their power. Well, except for one, but it's more of a legend," Willowisp said dismissively. "Many have searched for it, but you can't find what doesn't exist."

Something about this story sounded familiar, but before Seven could ask anything more, they were interrupted.

"What is this?" boomed a voice, nearly causing Seven to choke on her sandwich. Flouriche came bounding onto the stage. "Having a picnic, are we? You are here to fix your mistake, not have tea and sandwiches, Miss Preston."

"Actually, it is juice," Willowisp said. "Miss Preston and I were just having a nice chat since she finished her work."

Flouriche looked around at the pristine sets. Then she glared at Willowisp.

"I think Miss Preston had nothing to do with this," Flouriche gestured.

"Oh, pish posh. It's done. That's all that matters," Willowisp said.

"Miss Preston," Madam Flouriche hissed, "You may go. Professor Willowisp and I have to discuss sticking one's nose where it doesn't belong."

Seven didn't need to be told twice. She ran from the theater, leaving Professor Willowisp and Madame Flouriche to work out their very loud difference of opinion. Unfortunately, she escaped one uncomfortable situation only to walk into another. When she entered Wyndamir Hall, Krisp greeted her.

"Ah, Miss Preston, aren't you heading in the wrong direction? As I recall, you have another matter to attend to this evening, don't you? Professor Mulciber is waiting for you," Krisp said.

"I still have ten minutes, and I haven't eaten dinner yet," Seven protested. She only had one sandwich before Flouriche interrupted.

"That is probably for the best. Now, hurry along." He smiled cruelly, which made her want to kick his bony shin.

When she reached the main potions building, a note was pinned to the door covered in brown smudges of what she hoped was dirt. She read Mulciber's untidy scrawl.

Miss Preston,
Please meet me on the west side of potion building #3.
Professor Mulciber

She found Mulciber standing by a gate to an animal pen. He was making small cooing sounds at what looked like a trembling mound of dirt. Suddenly, a tiny creature poked its head out of the mud. If it weren't for the feathers, Seven would have thought it was an ordinary miniature pig. This wasn't going to be so bad. Then, a disgusting odor assaulted her nose. It made rotten eggs and spoiled meat smell like freshly baked cookies. Her stomach lurched, and she understood why Krisp suggested skipping dinner.

"Ah, Miss Preston, let me show you how to milk these precious creatures. The milk of barbatus boars, affectionately known as swinnies, is valuable and versatile. Unfortunately, it isn't so easy to collect."

Three hours later, a pale-faced, mud-covered, slightly bruised, and very putrid-smelling Seven made her way to Terramin Tower. It wasn't very late, so there were quite a few students in the rec room, but she didn't see Cully or Iggy anywhere.

"Coming back from a family reunion?" Darcy said, apparently regaining some of her bravery.

"No, I was just over at your house. Your mom shared her favorite perfume with me," Seven retorted, wafting her hands so that a nice cloud of stench floated toward Darcy.

"Oh my gosh, you smell worse than a dung heap," Darcy said, gagging.

"Maybe a spell would make her smell better? Care to cast one?" Cully challenged as she walked up behind Seven.

Whatever bravery Darcy had regained vanished. She and Brigit made a hasty retreat up the stairs.

"Oh, Seven, what is that smell?" Cully gasped as she took three steps away.

"That would be the smell of my detention," Seven said.

"What did you have to do? Bathe in poo?" Sam asked from across the room.

"Nearly," Seven said. "You know Mulciber's pets, the swinnies? They may look cute but try and milk them. They swell up and lose control of their bodily functions. All these brown stains? Not dirt," Seven said, gesturing to her soiled hands and robes. "Luckily, after a while, your sense of smell goes numb."

"Well, my sense of smell is working just fine," Adria said. "Go shower and scrub several times, so you don't make our room smell like a toilet."

As Seven cleaned up, she replayed her conversation with Willowisp earlier that afternoon. She knew she had heard that story before. An amulet that people searched for and never found. Its existence questioned. Then, it hit her like Darcy's spell should have.

Still dripping, Seven darted into the rec room frantically searching for Iggy and Cully. She spotted them sitting in the chairs by the fireplace. She jumped into an overstuffed chair across from them.

"I know what it is," Seven said, trying not to yell despite

her excitement.

"What *what* is?" Cully said.

"My locket," Seven whispered. "I know what it is."

"You do? How did you figure it out?" Iggy asked.

"Mcfee. She told me a story about a protection amulet months ago, but I forgot about it until Willowisp told me the same story this afternoon."

"Willowisp?"

"Yeah, she came to the theater to check on me after class," Seven said. "Anyway, I knew I had heard it before, but I couldn't remember where. When I was in the shower just now, I hit me."

Just then, a loud whoop came from the spoon players.

"I win! I win!" yelled a girl called Jenna Moore.

"That makes three rounds. We can't beat you. I'm going to bed," said a curly-haired boy named Max something. Seven, Cully, and Iggy watched the remaining students follow suit. When they were gone, Seven turned expectantly back toward her friends.

"When Mcfee brought me to get my school supplies, we passed a jewelry shop with a display of protection amulets. Anyway, she told me about something called the Blaize Amulet. It was rumored to be the only authentic protection amulet in existence, but just like Willowisp, she said she didn't believe it existed. She lied. I think my locket is the real Blaize Amulet. I believe this is what my mom was supposed to protect when she disappeared."

"That's a stretch," Iggy said.

"When Mcfee first came to my house, she was surprised when my mom said she didn't have the relic anymore. It was only after I showed Mcfee my locket that she and my mom started to argue. Mcfee wanted my mom to give it to her, and my mom refused."

"But didn't Mefee start to collect the scrolls before she knew you had the locket?" Iggy
pointed out.

"Yes, but she knew my mom had it. They looked like

the same scrolls my mom sent through the box at Bigglesby's. I don't know for sure, but I think they were some type of written agreement to help my mom protect the amulet. What if Mcfee changed the agreement and forced the shopkeepers to help her instead? Swathmore didn't seem too happy to help her, and then his shop was destroyed."

"Maybe he went back on his word," Iggy suggested.

"So Mcfee attacked him or had someone else do it," Seven finished. "Pepper said something about how they found *it,* but it wouldn't take them long to figure out it wasn't the one they wanted. Maybe the shopkeepers had fakes, so everyone hunting for it would go for the fakes while Mcfee figured out how to get the real one from me."

"And she got tired of waiting and attacked me, I mean you, I mean me thinking it was you," Cully added, "but she didn't know about the enchantment your mom put on it."

"I wonder if your mom suspected someone might try that?" Iggy asked.

"Maybe," Seven said.

The three sat in silence, each thinking about the situation.

"What about Skelly?" Cully asked.

"Maybe Skelly and Mcfee are working together to find a way around the enchantment," Seven said.

"What do we do now?" Cully asked.

"Well, if Seven is right and this is the Blaize Amulet, we probably need to find out everything about it that we can. Maybe we can figure out what Mcfee might try to do and how we can stop her," Iggy said.

"Great," Cully said sarcastically, "back to the library."

Chapter Seventeen

Mcfee's Return

If Seven, Cully, and Iggy thought having the name would make their search easier, they were sadly mistaken. Most books didn't even mention the Blaize Amulet, and those that did quickly made it clear the author didn't believe it existed. They even risked asking Mr. Page for help. He only looked at them as though they were the stupidest people in Midia.

"I do not waste my valuable time on nonsense," he sniffed before walking away, muttering about time-wasters. They had nearly given up when the answer came from the least likely of places.

"Where's Iggy?" Cully asked. She and Seven were outside enjoying the afternoon sun. Though it was still a little chilly, there was evidence that spring was right around the corner.

"I don't know. He left Mulciber's class as soon as the bell rang. He said something about being stupid."

"I wish I was as *stupid* as he was. Then, I would already have my potions homework done, and I would know it is right," Cully said, groaning.

"Watch out!" Seven exclaimed as something nearly landed on her.

"Thank... you.... Darcy....," Iggy gasped as he collapsed next to the book he just threw down. "I ... can't...believe...." he said, gulping air.

"Breath, Iggy, before you pass out," Seven said. "Then,

you can explain why we should thank Darcy Davidson before I throw up on you."

"I may throw up anyway," Cully said.

Iggy took several deep breaths trying to regain his wind. Finally, he was able to talk without sounding like he was on the verge of passing out.

"Remember when Darcy swapped your Morphology textbook with the wrong book at the beginning of the year?"

"Yes," Seven said uncertainly. "That was my first demerit. Why are you dragging that up?"

"I asked you if I could read it on the bus ride home at Christmas."

"Okay," Seven said, unsure of where this was going.

"Well, I read most of it, but not all. When we got back, I put it on my nightstand so that I would remember to return it to you when I finished. I saw it last night and thought I would finish it and give it back," Iggy said.

"You can keep it," Seven said. "I don't want anything that belonged to Darcy."

"This is not about Darcy. It is about the book," Iggy said, exasperated.

"Why? Does it have horrible pictures of dark magic in it or something?" Cully said.

"Or something," Iggy said as he opened it to the second to last chapter and turned it around for them to see.

Seven and Cully read the chapter's title.

"Oh my gosh," Cully said. "Thank you, Darcy Davidson." The chapter was entitled, *The Blaize: Mythical Magic or Authentic Amulet.*

"After all those weeks of wasted time in the library, and it was on your nightstand the whole time," Cully said.

"That time wasn't wasted," Iggy argued. "You and Seven would be way farther behind in your studies if we hadn't been forced to go to the library."

"I don't know whether to hurt you or hug you," Cully said.

"Listen to this," Iggy said.

'Wielders throughout the ages have tried to create amulets that would provide total protection against spells, charms, potions, jinxes, and hexes. Story after story claimed success. However, none were ever proven. That is why many believed the story of success from an ordinary mathematician and philosopher from across the gates was just that, another story.

Blaize Paskal had an unquenchable thirst for mathematics and philosophy. He spent countless hours debating, writing, and researching various topics. Unfortunately, Paskal was a sickly fellow and was often so ill that he could barely hold up a book. Desperate for health, he turned his attention and incredible genius toward the more unsavory side of alchemy, potion-making, and anything supernatural.

After many years of research and experimentation, Paskal confided to a close friend that he had discovered a way to remain forever healthy. The friend dismissed the claims, thinking Paskal had finally been driven mad by his search for health. However, Paskal was not only free from illness; he also survived several events that should have claimed his life. He survived a carriage wreck that killed all other passengers and the horses without even a scratch. He was also the only known survivor of the Great Ferrand Fire, which claimed one hundred four people's lives. A tornado that leveled his home left him unscathed. Many claimed that these were just lucky coincidences. However, they were enough to get the attention of the magical community.

Guardians were sent to Paskal's residence to investigate these claims. Though the official report claimed no such amulet existed and that Paskal was just extraordinarily lucky, rumors quickly spread that a deal was struck with him after Guardians unsuccessfully tried to take the amulet from Paskal by force. Paskal agreed to turn it over

> to the Guardians upon his death if they would agree to let him live in peace.
>
> On August 19, 1662, Paskal died at the age of 128. It was assumed that Paskal kept his deal with the Guardians because, after his death, the amulet was never found.
>
> One of Paskal's students refused to believe the claims. Though he could not explain his mentor's long life, he claimed that Paskal never wore an amulet. "He only had a pocket watch, which he kept on his person at all times. In the watch, he kept a picture of himself when he was twelve and a small piece of parchment paper on which he wrote a prayer or personal mantra or something. Blaize Paskal was a man of science. He wouldn't subscribe to such nonsense as amulets or magic."

"That's it except for a picture of the watch," Iggy said.

"But he didn't have a locket. He had a watch," Seven said, feeling a little deflated. "Besides, if it is the all-powerful Blaize Amulet, why wouldn't it have protected Cully? Maybe I was wrong."

"I don't think you are," Iggy insisted. "Meet me in that empty classroom near Krisp's office after supper." Then, before they could argue, Iggy was up and gone.

Iggy didn't show up for supper. So, after they had eaten, Cully and Seven waited for Iggy in the empty classroom. After nearly an hour, Cully was losing her patience.

"Do you think he forgot?" Cully asked. She was lying on the floor with her legs propped up on the wall. "Maybe he got distracted by homework."

"Maybe," Seven said.

"If he isn't here in five minutes, we should leave. Maybe we can get in on a game of spoons with Adria, Sam, and the others."

Just then, Iggy burst into the room, breathless.

"Well, it is about time," Cully snapped. "I thought I was going to die of boredom."

"Sorry, someone misshelved the book I needed. Then, I got stopped by Miss Poxley. She was wondering where you were," he said to Seven.

"That's weird," Seven said.

"Okay, okay. Iggy, can you just get to it?" Cully said impatiently.

He laid the book on the floor in the middle of them. It was entitled *Protection Amulets: It's As Easy as 1-2-3* by Asher Plinks.

"Asher Plinks!" Cully said. "You have got to be kidding! He was said to be about as nutty as a, well, a nut."

"Yeah, that's what Mr. Page said, too. He looked at me funny when I checked this out. I agree that some of what he wrote is, well, nutty, but his theory on levels of protection makes sense."

"This ought to be good," Cully said sarcastically.

"Cully, let him talk," Seven chided.

"Yeah, let me talk," Iggy said, glaring at Cully. "Now, where was I before I was so rudely interrupted? Oh yeah. Plinks thought that the most effective protective amulets have several levels of protection. Each level is achieved by adding another element to the amulet. For example, if an amulet is made with a gem known for its protective traits, that would be one level of protection. Then, if the amulet is dipped into a potion, that would be another level of protection. A protective spell would offer another level, and so on." He stopped and looked up with a satisfied smile.

"I don't get it," Seven said.

"Take off your locket, and let me show you," Iggy said, holding his hand out." Seven looked at him, unsure. "Seven, if the greatest wielders throughout history couldn't hurt this amulet, do you think I can?" he said earnestly.

Reluctantly, Seven took the locket from around her neck and handed it to him. Iggy carefully opened it, removed the picture of Seven as a baby, the one of her parents, and the parchment, and laid them on the floor. Finally, he flipped the locket over and opened a book on runes. He compared the locket and the parchment to the runes.

"Look at that marking," he said, pointing to the picture in Darcy's book of Paskal's watch. "Now, look at the one on Seven's locket." Both Cully and Seven leaned forward and examined a marking right at the tip of Iggy's finger.

"It's the same," Cully said.

Then, Iggy turned his attention to the parchment.

"I don't know what all of these markings mean," Iggy said, pointing to the symbols that were written along the edges of the parchment, "but the group in the middle is an ancient Egyptian protection spell." Then, he flipped the parchment over. "And there is the same symbol that is on the front of the locket. I think the stone of the front is jade, not an emerald. Jade is known for its protective traits. I think the spells, the symbols, the jade stone, and those other markings offer four protection levels. The picture of your parents is another, and the picture of Seven is the sixth. There is probably one more that isn't visible, like a potion it was dipped in or something. Together, that makes…"

"Seven," Cully and Seven said together.

"One of the most powerful numbers in magic," Iggy said.

"When I wore it, there weren't pictures of my parents or me in the locket," Cully observed.

"That's why I think it didn't offer you absolute protection," Iggy said.

"That makes sense," Cully agreed.

"I do have an idea on how to test it," Iggy said timidly.

"Test it?" Cully asked.

He explained what he had in mind as he reassembled the locket. He held it out to Cully.

"This is a dumb idea," Cully said as she stared at the proffered locket.

"It's just a sneezing jinx," Iggy said.

"And you know the counter jinx?"

"Yes, I looked it up," Iggy said confidently.

"Otherwise, I am going to sneeze right in your face. Repeatedly," Cully said as she took the locket and put it on.

"I won't need it," Iggy said, "but I will be ready with it just in case," he added, quickly when he saw Cully about to protest. "But first," he said and walked over and cast a spell around the door. Turning around, he explained. "Silencing spell just in case you're a loud sneezer."

"Good idea," Seven said.

"Ready, Cully?" Iggy said, pointing his wand at her.

"Not really, but..."

"*Sternumenta repet!*" Iggy shouted as a green jet of light hit Cully square in the nose. Immediately, her face contorted, and she began to sneeze. Once. Twice. Three times. Four.

"Iggy! The counter jinx!" Cully whined, sounding like her nose was full of cotton.

"Not yet," Iggy said.

Five.

"Iggy!" Cully demanded. Six.

Iggy and Seven watched as Cully's face began to contort again for another sneeze and then...nothing. Her face relaxed.

"Done?" Iggy asked.

Cully waited a few minutes before she nodded.

"See, it did protect you a little. Otherwise, you would still be sneezing."

"Six times was enough," Cully said, still sounding very stuffy.

"Okay, now give the locket to Seven." Cully did. "I am going to cast the same spell. If I am right ..."

"I won't sneeze," Seven finished.

"Ready?" Iggy asked, aiming his wand at Seven, who nodded. "*Sternumenta repet!*"

A green light shot at Seven and seemed to be a direct hit. Iggy watched her expectantly, waiting for any sign that she was getting ready to sneeze.

"Anything?"

"Nope. Not even a tickle," Seven said.

"I knew it. The pictures only offer their level of protection to Seven," Iggy said. "But," he hesitated.

"But what?" Seven asked.

"I think we need to *really* test it out."

"What does that mean?" Cully asked.

"With a more powerful spell," He told them what he was thinking.

"Iggy, that's not just sneezes!" Seven argued.

"You won't feel a thing, just like when Darcy tried," Iggy said quickly.

"But Darcy only cast a silencing spell. Yours will hurt. A lot."

"I don't think it will," he said.

"You don't *think*? Well, that's comforting," Seven said dryly.

"You'll be fine," Iggy insisted.

"There's got to be a less painful way," Seven said.

"I think Iggy is on to something, Seven," Cully added.

"That's easy for you to say! They aren't your bones!" Seven protested.

"If we had a picture of my parents and me, I would take your place," Cully said, crossing her arms.

"Again, easy to say since we don't have those things!" Seven said.

"Trust me, Seven. This will work," Iggy said. Seven stood there a long time looking
from Iggy to Cully and back again.

"Fine, but if this hurts, I get to shoot a spell at you," she bargained. "At both of you." "Deal," Iggy said.

"Deal," Cully said, sounding a little less confident now.

Iggy stepped back and pointed his wand at Seven. Seven took a deep breath. If this didn't work, they would have a lot of explaining to do to Medwell.

"On the count of three," Cully said, stepping clear of the experiment. "One, two..." "Wait!" Seven shouted.

"What?" Cully and Iggy said simultaneously.

"Maybe I should turn around, so I don't accidentally duck

out of the way," Seven said. "Yeah, that's a good idea," Iggy said.

"And close your eyes, too," Cully said.

Seven looked very uncertainly at Iggy, took another deep breath, and turned around. She squeezed her eyes shut and nodded that she was ready.

"Okay, let's try that again," Cully said. "One, two ..."

"*Osco liquescimus!*" Iggy shouted.

A spark of light jumped out of Iggy's wand and landed square in the middle of Seven's back.

"But I didn't say three," Cully said.

"I thought it would be better if Seven didn't know it was coming," Iggy explained.

Seven turned around, patting herself all over to make sure her bones hadn't liquified. Then, she collapsed with relief.

"Let's never do that again," she said.

"You didn't feel anything?" Iggy asked. "Static? Heat? Anything?"

Seven shook her head.

"It's the Blaize. I'm sure of it," Iggy said. "I wish I could figure out what the rest of those symbols on the parchment are. Can I have another look?" Iggy asked.

"Promise me never to do that again, and I will give you about anything," Seven said, handing the locket over to him again. Iggy disassembled the locket and compared the symbols on the parchment and the locket to the ones in the book.

"I wonder wh-" Cully began.

"What are you doing?" interrupted a familiar voice.

The three of them were so involved in their experiment that they didn't hear anyone enter the room. They turned to see Phoebe Mcfee standing in the doorway, glaring at them. She looked terrible. Her eyes were encircled with shadow while her unkempt hair poked out in all directions. Her robes were soiled and torn. She also looked thinner. Instinctively, Seven, Cully, and Iggy formed a wall so she could not see the table behind them.

"How did you get in here?" Iggy asked.

"I've been at this school more years than you've been alive, Mr. Everett. I know its secrets. Now, answer me. What are you doing?"

"We were just going over something for Brimbal's class," Cully lied smoothly.

"And you cast a soundproofing spell so no one would hear you talk about history?" Mcfee asked. "I don't think so. It looks to me like you three have learned something that maybe you shouldn't have. I knew she should have never given it to you."

"You are talking about my mother, I guess," Seven said.

"When you showed me that locket last summer, I couldn't believe it. Giving it to you was a reckless decision. She meant well, but I knew it was too risky. Then you stupidly gave it to Miss Collins before Christmas break to what, shine it? It is the most powerful protection amulet ever created, and you wanted it shiny. Ridiculous."

"Good thing Cully had it on, though. It made it more difficult to hurt her when you attacked her," Seven said as she slowly moved her hand to get those pictures, the parchment, and the locket before Mcfee cast some sort of summoning spell and took them.

"I would never attack a student!" Mcfee insisted.

"How about a shopkeeper, like Mr. Swathmore or destroying a shop like Pepper's?" Seven asked sarcastically. She was still an inch or two away from the parchment. "I knew the day you took me shopping that something was going on. I saw the scroll that Mr. Swathmore gave you or, more likely, that you forced from him. And the one from Pepper and from the other shopkeepers we saw that day. They looked just like the scrolls my mom sent over through Mrs. Bigglesby's box. And you stole them. Did the shopkeepers change their minds about helping, so you attacked them?"

"Yes, they were attacked but not by me."

"Miss Poxley knows you are up to something, too," Seven

went on.

"You should not trust Pamona Poxley," Mcfee said.

"And I should trust you?" Seven nearly laughed. "My mother might trust you, but I don't."

"Seven, your mom was trying to protect you, but all it did was put you in danger."

"The only person who is putting me in danger is you."

"Seven, I am running out of time and patience. Please give me the locket."

"Not in a million years," Seven said and quickly scooped up the items on the table. Then, she took a quick step in front of Iggy and Cully. "We both know with these in my possession that you cannot hurt me."

"Seven, I am not the only one who knows what and where it is. They will not hesitate to hurt you or your friends. Let me help you!" Mcfee lunged forward and tried to grab Seven's arm, but Seven spun from her grip.

"Go!" Seven said as she shoved Cully and Iggy toward the door. "Get help."

Cully and Iggy didn't have to go very far for help. Miss Poxley and Professor Willowisp appeared in the doorway.

"Well, Phoebe, how nice to see you. Everything all right with your *family*?" Willowisp said sarcastically.

Mcfee ignored Willowisp and turned her attention back to Seven.

"You don't understand," Mcfee pleaded. "Please trust me."

"Not in a million years," Seven said. "You may have turned Skelly, but I will never trust you."

"Seven, it isn't me that you shouldn't trust. It's..."

Just then, Poxley cast a spell. Mcfee dodged it just in time.

"What is this about?" Willowisp asked Seven.

"She wants my locket," Seven said as she reassembled the locket and slipped it over her head. "She attacked Cully to try and get it before Christmas."

"*You* attacked a student?" Willowisp asked. "That's serious."

"You know who attacked her, and it wasn't me," Mcfee shot back. "It was..."

"Tut, tut," Williowisp interrupted. "I don't think you need to talk anymore." Then she shot a spell that landed just to the right of Mcfee. "If you attacked a student, Professor Bellatora needs to know."

"Yes, let's go talk to her," Mcfee said.

"Seven, why does Miss Mcfee want your locket? Does this have anything to do with your curiosity about protection amulets?" Willowisp asked.

"Yes," Seven said stubbornly. "She tried to take it from Cully, but she couldn't. It's enchanted to burn anyone who tries to steal it."

"I bet you wish you knew that a little earlier, Pamona, don't you?" Mcfee said as she put a chair between her and the two other women.

"What does that mean?" Seven asked.

"Enough!" Poxley yelled. "You are a danger to our students. We don't need to involve the Headmistress. We will take care of you right now." She shot another spell, but Mcfee blocked it and sent it right back toward Poxley. A chair exploded.

"Seven, listen to me," Mcfee begged. "It isn't me you have to worry about. It is..."

"Shut up!" Poxley hissed, shooting another spell. Surprisingly fast, Mcfee dodged it and shot her own spell. It missed but blew up the desk that was right in front of them. Poxley, Willowisp, and Seven ducked to avoid getting hit with the debris. When they stood back up, Mcfee disappeared out the door, shoving Iggy and Cully to the side.

"Aren't you going to go after her?" Seven said. "She's dangerous."

"I have a feeling you won't see her again," Willowisp said. "Now that we know she is after you, she won't dare return."

Then the professor turned directly toward Seven and looked at the locket around her neck. "That must be quite a protection charm you have there if Miss Mcfee is so desperate to have it," Willowisp said.

Seven didn't say anything.

"It might be safer for you if I took it and gave it to Bellatora for safekeeping. She has an unbreakable safe in her office," Willowisp said, holding out her hand.

"That's okay," Seven said, taking a step back, but Poxley pressed the issue.

"But you are putting yourself in danger. You...," Poxley began.

"Let her keep it, Pamona," Willowisp said softly. "It is obviously special to her." Seven only nodded, and Willowisp continued. "I think you three need to head back to Terramin Tower. Miss Poxley and I will decide how to best proceed."

"It is after curfew," Poxley said. "The Tower is locked. I will need to go with them."

"Afterwards, come to my office," Willowisp said. "We need to figure out the next step. Be careful," she said, turning to Seven. "I'm sure Mcfee is gone, but it never hurts to stay alert."

Cully, Iggy, and Seven followed Poxley. When they reached the Tower, Poxley mumbled something, and the wall unlocked.

"Thank you," Iggy said and passed through. Cully did the same thing, but before Seven could follow, Poxley grabbed her arm.

"Miss Preston, are you sure about your locket? It seems it has put a target on your back and put your friends in danger. That's a lot to handle for someone your age. I would be glad to take it and keep it safe. That way, if Miss Mcfee is going to try to attack anyone in the future, it will be me."

Seven thought about this. Her locket *had* endangered her and her friends on several occasions. The locket would only protect her. Was that fair to Iggy and Cully? But still, her mom had made her promise.

Just then, Cully's head popped through the wall.

"Are you coming?" she asked, looking from Seven to Poxley.

"I'll think about it, Miss Poxley," Seven said before following Cully into Terramin Tower.

By unspoken agreement, they all walked over to their favorite spot by the fireplace. None of them spoke for a long while. They were all absorbed in their own thoughts. Finally, Cully broke the silence.

"I can't believe that happened."

"Me, neither," Iggy said.

"Mcfee was so angry," Cully said.

"Yep," Seven said absently. Silence fell again. After a while, Seven was the one to interrupt the quiet.

"My mom trusted her," Seven said. "I tried to tell her Mcfee had changed, but she didn't believe me. And Skelly, too."

"I am so glad Willowisp and Poxley were there. That was lucky. I mean, Mcfee looked crazed or something. Did you see her clothes and hair? It was like she's been living in the woods or something," Cully said, shuddering.

"Maybe she had been," Seven said, sitting up. "Remember when we saw her leave Skelly's? She headed to the woods."

"Should we tell Willowisp? I mean, they could search the woods for her, right?" Cully asked.

"Yes, it's just…" Seven didn't finish her thought.

"It's just what?" Cully asked.

"Did you guys hear what Mcfee said to Miss Poxley when I mentioned the enchantment?"

"Mcfee said a lot of things, Seven. I wouldn't overthink it," Cully said.

"Maybe," Seven said as she stared into the fire.

"I think I am going to turn in. It is late," Iggy said.

"Me, too," Cully said as she stood and stretched. "You coming, Seven?"

Seven knew she wouldn't be able to sleep, but she didn't want to stay in the rec room alone.

"I'm coming, but I don't think sleep will."

Chapter Eighteen

A Blast from the Past

"May I have your attention, please?" Bellatora announced at breakfast the next day. "I am afraid I have some rather sad news. Our Dean of Students, Miss Phoebe Mcfee, will not return to Wyndamir this year. Early this morning, I received an urgent post from her requesting an extended leave of absence to attend to a personal matter. Though she will be missed, Professor Willowisp has graciously agreed to fill in as Interim Dean."

At this, Willowisp waved and smiled at the students. She looked around the dining hall until she saw Cully, Iggy, and Seven. She locked eyes with them and nodded slightly.

"Please feel free to see her if you should have any questions regarding class selections for next year. Thank you." Bellatora sat back down in her chair and surveyed the room.

"A personal matter?" Cully said. "Really?"

"Maybe Bellatora is trying to keep things quiet while others search for Mcfee," Iggy said. "If word gets to Mcfee that the entire magical world is looking for her, she may pull the same disappearing act your mom did."

"Do you think I need to warn my mom?" Seven asked, wondering if Mcfee would go after Miranda.

"Well, you sort of already tried, and she didn't take the news very well," Cully said.

"But now I can tell her about what happened last night,"

Seven countered. "I mean, she has to believe me now."

"Unless Mcfee already got to her and spun another tale," Iggy observed. "Anyway, I don't think Mcfee will hurt her. If she wanted to, she would have already."

Seven thought about Iggy's logic. It made sense. Mcfee could have gotten to her mom anytime over the summer or even after the school year started. Why would she go after her now? She just needed to be glad that Mcfee was gone.

Nearly two months passed without a word about Mcfee. Willowisp and Poxley checked on them from time to time, but they didn't know anything about Mcfee.

"She's gone. You're safe. If something changes, I will tell you. I promise. Trust me," Willowisp said with a reassuring smile.

After a while, and Cully, Iggy, and Seven fell into a comfortable routine. Before they knew it, opening day for the production was nearly upon them.

Flouriche explained they would have four performances, including a closed dress rehearsal on Saturday morning and a Saturday evening performance for Wyndamir students and staff. The two Sunday performances would be for family, friends, and other important guests.

As much as Seven hated to admit it, she had come to appreciate the theater these last few months. Even though Flouriche was as lovely as a spider bite, working backstage with Cully and Iggy seemed to be the only time she was able to relax a little bit. At least, she didn't think about Mcfee, her mom, the Blaize, or the crazy amount of homework the teachers were piling on to prepare for final exams.

"That's a wrap," Flouriche finally said that Friday afternoon. "Dress rehearsal tomorrow morning though we treat it like the real thing. Get a good night's rest. Envision a successful performance. Most importantly, be here on time. If you show up late, don't show up."

When they walked out of the auditorium, Cully stopped and closed her eyes.

"What are you doing?" Iggy said.

"Shhh," she said, keeping her eyes closed. "I am envisioning a successful performance."

"Well, envision as we walk to the dining hall. I'm starving," Iggy said.

The next morning the three arrived at the theater early. They conducted a last-minute check to ensure all of the props and costumes were ready for Malcolm's inspection. As they expected, he found several pieces that didn't shine enough.

"You're lucky I found these, and not Madam Flouriche," Malcolm chastised. "Fix them. Now." Then, he stormed out of the prop room.

"He is so overbearing," Cully said. "Malcolm, Nicholas, and Flouriche could never be in the same room because there wouldn't be room for them and their egos."

Tensions were high that morning. Flouriche had already relieved a young court guard of his role after he questioned the necessity of the dress rehearsal. Liriel Rathbone was yelling at the girl who was helping with her make-up.

"This time, not so much rouge! I'm supposed to be Eilidh, a powerful wielder, not a clown! And I want my eyes darker, more mysterious-looking, not like the raccoon mask you painted on me at the last rehearsal," Liriel snapped.

"Yes, Liriel," the girl said robotically, turning her head so Liriel couldn't see her roll her eyes.

Finally, Flouriche clapped her hands. "Places everyone!" She commanded as she marched off the stage, down the steps, and sat in the empty audience. From there, she would be able to see everything. "Action," she called.

The production seemed to go well. There were only a few minor mistakes, but the actors covered them up smoothly. Seven had almost given Liriel the wrong costume in scene four, but Iggy caught her mistake before it turned into a disaster.

Finally, the last act finished, and the curtains fell. No one moved as they waited for Flouriche to join them backstage. Flouriche was surprisingly kind, at least for her.

"Well, I have definitely seen better, but that wasn't a complete disaster. Some of you better review your lines before tonight. Set people need to touch up the castle and the tree. Props and costumes need to be faster with the clothing changes tonight. Avram was nearly late in scene six.

"Cast members are to report to their dormitories to rest and mentally prepare for tonight. We are live this evening. No mistakes! Only perfection is acceptable!" With that, Flouriche strode off to the director's room with Malcolm trailing behind her.

"That wasn't bad," Iggy said as they walked toward the prop room. "Let's head to lunch. We just need to..." he stopped midsentence. The three of them stared in disbelief. Costumes were strewn all over the chairs. Liriel's wig lay in a heap on the floor. Props were scattered all over the place.

"I think we can forget lunch," Seven groaned. "This is going to take forever."

It didn't take forever, but close. By the time they had hung up all the costumes, removed a few stains and wrinkles, re-polished several pieces of jewelry, and brushed out Liriel's wig, lunch had come and gone. It was nearly dinner time.

"We've got to do a better job keeping this stuff organized during the show. Otherwise, we'll be here until midnight," Iggy said as he replaced the last of the books from scenes two and five. "And this does not belong here, Seven," Iggy said, holding up a box.

"What is it?" she asked.

"It's a box," Iggy said sarcastically.

"Yes, Iggy, I know it's a box, but it isn't mine."

"It has your name on it," he said, pointing to her name, which was scrawled across the top.

Seven gingerly took the box from him. It was black, cube-shaped, and ornately decorated with gold markings. A bright green satin ribbon tied it closed.

"I've never seen this before," Seven said.

"Ooh, maybe you have a secret admirer," Cully offered.

"Highly doubtful," Seven said as she gently untied the green ribbon and opened the lid. She pulled out an envelope and read it. As soon as she did, her face drained of color. The note was addressed to Seven *Wyndamir* Preston.

"There are only a few people who know I am a Wyndamir," Seven said, her voice trembled. "You two, my mom, Skelly, and..."

"Mcfee," Cully and Iggy said in unison.

Seven's hands shook as she unsealed the envelope and pulled out the note. The message was written in shaky, crimson letters.

I have what you want. Meet me tonight. Come alone. Tell no one or else.

"Those letters," Iggy said hesitantly, "They look like they are written in..."

"Blood," Seven whispered. "I think she has my mom."

"What's this?" Cully pulled out what looked like a dirty, torn rag from the box and held it up.

Seven moaned like a wounded animal as she grabbed the item from Cully. At that moment, her legs seem to morph into rubber, and she collapsed into a nearby chair.

"Whose is that?" Iggy asked.

But Seven couldn't speak. All she could do was stare at what Cully had pulled from the box. It wasn't a rag. It was a shirt. A purple shirt, or rather what was left of a purple shirt. It was
ripped and dirty and stained with dark, brown blotches that Seven knew wasn't mud. On the front, a big, round, yellow smiley face looked back at her. Its grin seemed out of place on the ominous shirt.

"It's not my mom. It's Kerry." Seven explained about Kerry and her infatuation with smiley face shirts. She told them about the bracelet Kerry had given her but left out the cat burglar part. "After we moved and I started at Wyndamir, I was so caught up with magic and everything that I..," Seven swallowed hard. Guilt was thick in her throat. "Well, I sort of forgot about her. I didn't mean to, but with finding out about magic and my mom and classes and then Mcfee and the locket, I, well, I got distracted. I am a horrible person."

"No, you're not, Seven. If Kerry was your friend, she would understand how much you had on your mind," Cully offered, but Seven just shook her head.

"She IS my friend, and now, that cruel woman has her. Poor Kerry. She must be
terrified." Awful visions sprouted in Seven's brain. "I have to go. I am not going to abandon her again."

"But where? The note doesn't say where to go," Cully said.

In response, Seven held up the shirt. Pinned to one of its eyes was a pressed flower, a yellow flower covered with red and green dots.

"Heaven on a Stem. Remember the old man from the beginning of the year? There is only one place those flowers grow."

"But isn't that where your dad..." Cully began but didn't finish.

Seven nodded.

"Seven, I know she is your friend, but stop and think. You can't give Mcfee the amulet. She'll become unstoppable," Iggy said.

"Do you see these stains?" Seven yelled, holding up the shirt. "Surely, I don't have to tell you what it is. I will not allow someone I know to be tortured or worse over some stupid amulet."

"Hang on, Seven, " Iggy said, holding up his hands in a gesture of surrender.

"I don't have time to hang on. Mcfee has been gone for months. She's probably had Kerry hostage for a lot of that time, hurting her, scaring her. If I have the power to stop it, I have to."

"Well, you can't go alone," Cully said.

"Did you read that note? If I tell anyone, Mcfee will hurt Kerry more than she already has, or worse."

"Well, too bad. You are not going without us," Cully said.

"Agreed," Iggy said, crossing his arms.

"No," Seven protested. "You can't come. I couldn't stand it if something happened to you guys, too. I go alone."

"Iggy?" Cully said. "Did you hear something?"

"Yes, it was sort of an annoying buzzing sound. I couldn't completely make it out, but it sounded like someone told us we were supposed to let our good friend Seven face uncertain danger alone. Stupid, huh?" he answered.

"*Really* stupid. And, since our friend Seven is not stupid, I am sure that is not what we just heard," Cully said, glaring at Seven.

"Come on, guys. It isn't that I don't want you to come. The thought of going all alone at night into that creepy courtyard is not appealing, especially knowing what happened to my dad there, but it's too risky."

"We will be extra careful, extra quiet. We'll split up before we get to the courtyard," Cully said. "Come at her from different directions."

"And if you try to stop us, we will tell Willowisp and Poxley and Bellatora."

"You wouldn't?" Seven said.

"Try us," Cully said.

"Okay," Seven finally relented, "but this is between Mcfee and me. If something happens, you two better get out of there fast and go for help. Agreed?" Seven asked.

"Agreed," they said together.

"Now, we need a plan," Cully said, looking at the setting sun, "and we better figure one out fast."

"I can't do this," Seven whispered to Iggy several hours later as they waited for the evening performance to end. "How am I supposed to sit here when I know Kerry is in that garden terrified and waiting for me to come?"

"We talked about this. If we didn't show up, Flouriche would hunt us down, and then there would be no way we would be able to get to Kerry. Besides, it will be easier for me to do what I need to here," Iggy said.

Their plan wasn't great, but it was the best they could do on such short notice. Using a few props from the production and a replication spell Iggy found in their Spell Casting book, he created two more lockets. He wore one, and Cully wore the other. The plan was to confuse Mcfee long enough for them to rescue Kerry. Hopefully, the fake ones would look close enough to Seven's locket to do just that.

Finally, the curtain fell for the last time.

"Let's get out of here before Flouriche comes to yell at us," Seven said. Leaving the prop room looking like a bomb went off, the three slipped out a back door.

"You guys got them?" Seven asked as they walked. They both nodded and showed her the amulets they were wearing around their necks.

"They aren't identical to yours, but from a distance, they should buy us some time,"
Iggy said.

"And you put the pictures inside?"

"Yes, if she opens them up, she'll find exact copies of the pictures that are in yours," Iggy said.

They crept along the tree line, making sure to stick to the shadows. Earlier, they decided to use an entrance to the garden that faced the trees since they were least likely to be seen by anyone leaving the theater. There was just one obstacle left, Skelly's house, but they figured he would be at the performance.

Seven peeked out from behind a bush and froze. Skelly wasn't at the performance. He was sitting on his front porch whittling. Willie was right beside him, watching the knife expertly carve the wood.

"Oh no," Seven whispered when she dropped back down behind the bush. "Skelly is on the porch. What do we do? If he catches us, he'll probably drag us to Mcfee. We should pick a different entrance."

"No, if we go back, we might be seen by the students leaving the theater," Iggy said. He pointed to a long hedge that ran along the front of Skelly's house. "It gets close to his house, but as long as we stay low and quiet, it should provide enough cover until we reach those bushes," he said, pointing to two large evergreen bushes near the entrance.

They dropped low and crawled on their stomachs, stopping every few feet to make sure Skelly was still on his porch. When they heard his whistling, they continued. It seemed to take forever. They were only ten feet from the entrance when a white blur jumped out from the evergreen bushes. Willie. Then, he started to hiss and growl.

"Shh, Willie, it's Seven. Remember me?" Seven held out her hand, hoping he would sniff it, recognize her, and then be quiet. But he didn't. Instead, he did the worst thing possible. He arched his back and howled. Loudly.

"Willie? What's wrong?" Skelly called from the front porch. "You find something?" Then, they heard the creak of the steps. Skelly was heading toward them.

"What are we going to do? We can't let him see us," Cully said. "Iggy, do something." "Me?"

"Yeah, you. Cast a spell or something. You are the smartest one here."

"Smart enough to know better than jinx a teacher."

"Technically speaking, he is not a teacher," Cully called.

"Who's there?" Skelly called again. His voice was closer.

"He's coming," Cully said, panic making her voice shrill.

"Fine, but if I get expelled," he didn't finish. A twig snapped right around the corner. It was now or never. *"Obfuscatum Skelly,"* he whispered. Seven watched as a light shot from Iggy's wand at the exact second Skelly's face appeared. Too late. He was looking right at them.

"Skelly, we uh.." Seven began but then stopped and took a closer look. "What's wrong with him?"

"He doesn't realize what he is seeing, but it's a weak spell that won't last long. Let's go."

They pushed past a feisty Willie, and when they were safely out of earshot, Cully slapped Iggy on the back.

"You, Ignatius Everett, are very handy to have around."

Iggy only grunted in response.

They entered the garden with Seven and Iggy side by side and Cully almost walking backward to keep watch behind them. Seven couldn't help but feel that the garden seemed to know something was about to happen. The flower blossoms had closed as though in preparation for an upcoming battle. There was no wind. There were no sounds of crickets or small, scampering animals. It seemed every creature in the garden knew that danger was near and sought cover. Then something did pierce the silence—Cully's scream. Seven whirled around to see Cully writhing on the ground clutching at her neck.

"Cully! What happened?" Seven asked.

"I don't know," Iggy said as he leaned over Cully and peeled her hand away from her neck. He pulled out two barbs sticking from her neck and held them up.

"What are those damn things?" Seven asked.

"Belladonna barbs," he said. Then he looked intently at Seven and silently mouthed one word. Poison. They looked at Cully. Her face was flushed as though fevered, and her shrill screams had weakened into helpless moans. She seemed to be slipping into unconsciousness.

"What do we do? We have to help her," Seven said, trying not to panic.

Iggy looked around frantically at the surrounding flora. Then, his eyes fell on something about twenty feet ahead.

"See that plant, the one with the orange leaves? Bring some of it here."

Seven sprinted to the bush, yanked off a handful of leaves, rushed back, and handed them to Iggy. He put two of the leaves into his mouth, chewed them up, and put the wet glob onto the puncture marks on Cully's neck. Immediately, the orange glob turned black.

Seven held her breath. What if the poison worked faster than the leaves? Twice more, she watched as Iggy pulled the black glob from Cully's wound and replaced it with a fresh, orange blob.

"Iggy, it isn't working," Seven said.

"It will," he said, but Seven could hear the doubt in his voice.

"Come on, Cully, you have to be all right," Seven whispered.

After one more wet glob, Seven could tell Cully's breathing was becoming steadier. A few seconds later, she opened her eyes.

"What happened?" she asked groggily. "Why am I on the ground, and what is this nasty wet glob on my neck?"

"That nasty wet glob saved you," Seven said, laughing. "Well, that and Iggy. How did you know to do that?" she asked him.

"Medwell used these same leaves on my cut to make sure it didn't get an infection. She didn't chew them up, but I didn't bring a mortar and pestle."

"Just remind me when this is over to wash my neck thoroughly. What got me, anyway?" "Belladonna barbs," Seven answered.

"There shouldn't be any of those here. They are too dangerous," Cully said, sitting up.

"Well, someone put one right there," Iggy said, pointing at the bush, which was now brown and dying before their eyes. Then the whole thing collapsed in a heap and turned to dust. "And obviously, they didn't want to leave a trace of it."

"Can you stand?" Seven asked Cully.

"I think so." Slowly and with help, Cully stood. She wobbled a few times and then found her balance.

"I think Iggy should take you to the infirmary. Your cheeks still look pale."

"I can't," Iggy said.

"Why not?" Seven asked, annoyed.

Iggy answered by pointing back in the direction they had just come. Somehow, the path was blocked with a ten-foot-tall wall of bushes covered in seven-inch-long thorns.

"I don't think Mcfee wanted you to get cold feet," Iggy said. "The only way to go is forward."

"I'm fine except that my neck has Iggy's spit on it," Cully said, making a face.

"Fine," Iggy said, "next time, Seven can chew them."

"That's not much better," Cully retorted. Seven could tell she was trying to play down how bad she was feeling, but Iggy was right. They had no choice but to go forward.

They moved slowly to avoid any more traps. Iggy took Cully's spot and kept a watch behind them. Soon, they came to a split in the path. Seven chose the right fork when suddenly, the plants quickly grew and blocked their way.

"I guess Mcfee wants us to go left," Seven said. "Hang in there, Kerry. We're coming."

"I'm sure your friend is all right," Cully said, looking a little bit better. "And Iggy's plan will work. He's a genius, right Iggy?" She shot a smile over her shoulder. Immediately, it fell away. "Iggy?" Cully turned around. Then she screamed, "Iggy!"

Seven turned and saw what looked like a pool of thick, black glue surrounding Iggy. Some of it had detached from the pool, snaked up Iggy's body, and wrapped itself around his mouth, which explained why he hadn't called for help. The two girls ran around the puddle, trying to reach him. Every time they nearly reached him, the goo shifted and lunged at them.
Seven locked eyes with Iggy. His terror was palpable. The goo, which was just at his ankles, was now nearly at his waist. Pretty soon, the pool would swallow him entirely.

"What is this stuff?" Cully yelled in frustration.

Iggy grunted. He looked at the goo and then looked to the side. The goo. To the side. Over and over, he did this. He was trying to tell them something. Finally, it registered.

"We need to send it away," Seven called. She pulled out

her wand and pointed it at the black goo. As clearly as she could and with as much belief she could muster, she yelled, *"Abirum!"* A red spark shot from her wand and hit the black goo covering Iggy's chest. A piece of the substance flew from his shirt and landed on a nearby bush. Seven repeated the spell. This time her spell hit Iggy's hand, and more of the goo flew from his head and disappeared over his head. It was working, but not fast enough. As soon as some of it was removed, more of the goo was ready to fill in the empty spot.

"Cully, help me. I am not moving enough at a time."

Despite casting spell after spell, it seemed like they were fighting a losing battle, but then Seven noticed the goo took longer to fill in the empty spots. The top half of Iggy was nearly free.

"I'll cast. You pull," Seven ordered as she continued to battle the gooey enemy. Cully reached out to Iggy, grasped his arms tightly, and pulled. With a sucking sound, the goo finally released him. He and Cully landed clear of the puddle with a thud.

"Are you all right?" Cully asked.

Iggy answered with a grunt. Some goo was still stuck to his mouth.

"Hold still," Seven said. She repeated the spell one last time. The final remnants of the black goo landed with a splat on the leaf of a hydrangea bush.

"Thanks for that," Iggy said. Then he pointed behind Seven. There stood the archway into the courtyard. "I think we are nearly there."

"Remember, we each run in a different direction to distract Mcfee. Ready?"

Cully and Iggy nodded. Seven stepped through the archway. Unfortunately, as soon as she was through, their plan was ruined.

"Watch out!" Iggy shouted. Seven turned to see Iggy pull Cully back just before the archway morphed into a solid wall and crushed her. It grew in height and length until there was no way over it or around it. She heard Iggy and Cully shouting her name, but it was very garbled as if they were underwater. She tried the moving spell that worked wonders on the black puddle. Nothing. She didn't know what else to do. Seven vowed if she got out of this, she would listen better in class, take better notes, and read a whole lot more.

Suddenly, Seven heard a scream from up ahead, the kind that accompanies intense pain. She had to get to Kerry before the next scream she heard was Kerry's last. She yelled to Cully and Iggy to go for help. Without waiting to see if they heard her, she turned and ran down the path. When she stepped into the courtyard, the scene was not what she expected at all. It was worse.

Chapter Nineteen

Betrayed

Kerry was strapped to a chair made of vines and thorns while a jagged leaf snaked around and covered her mouth. Eerie light given off by several floating globes illuminated the tears that streamed down her dirty, terror-filled face. As awful as it was to see her friend in this shape, it was the sight next to Kerry that caught Seven off guard.

Strapped to an identical chair was Mcfee. Like Kerry, her face was filthy, but it was also severely bruised and swollen. Her mouth was gagged with a white cloth that was stained crimson. Seven could see dried blood under her nose and on her robes. Mcfee's eyes were sunken, and her cheeks were hollow. She looked barely conscious. Had she been beaten?

"I don't understand. I thought that you…" Seven stammered. The sound of Seven's voice seemed to jolt Mcfee awake. She frantically shook her head. Her gaze kept moving around the courtyard, and she was wriggling in her chair.

"Who did this to you?" Seven asked as she headed toward Mcfee and Kerry.

"Why I did, of course," cackled a voice from the shadows behind the captives. "And if you take one more step, I will destroy them both right now." A familiar figure stepped into the dim light of the courtyard.

"Poxley?" Seven asked in disbelief and froze in her tracks.

"Surprise," said the matron of Terramin Tower. "I am so

glad you could make it. I wasn't sure where to host the reunion with you and these loathsome creatures," she sneered as she gestured to Kerry and Poxley, "but I thought this would be the perfect place. It is private, quiet, and full of memories for both of us."

Seven remained quiet, so Poxley continued.

"It was right over there, you know," she pointed to a dark corner off to Seven's right. "Where your dad bit it. Did your mom tell you?"

Seven couldn't help but look. She knew it was here where her father had died, but to see the exact spot made it difficult to breathe.

"Your mom tried, but her powers were quite overrated. She wasn't nearly as talented as she thought. She was just another arrogant, pathetic rich girl who wouldn't be anywhere if not for her name. It was quite satisfying watching her panic and cry and beg. *Oh, Nikris, please,*" she said in a high-pitched imitation of Seven's mother. "In the end, she was a coward, really."

Seven could feel the anger rising, but she remained quiet.

"And your dad. I will say that he was so brave for one with no magic. Well, brave or stupid. Probably more stupid now that I think about it."

"My mom was not a coward, and my dad was not stupid," Seven said ferociously, finally breaking her silence.

"Oh, but he was," Poxley said. "You see, he didn't need to give the amulet to your mom to protect her. She was already protected because of you." As soon as the words were out of her mouth, Poxley's eyes widened, and she shot a look toward Mcfee and Kerry. It was as though she had said too much. She quickly went on. "But what do you expect from an ordinary? They really can't help how ridiculous they are. It was quite pathetic watching how he trailed after your mother, sort of like a well-trained dog."

"Just shut up, Poxley," Seven yelled. "My dad was better than you will ever be!"

"It is Miss Poxley. Calling a superior by their last name

is rude. Didn't your mother teach you any manners? Come to think of it. She probably didn't have time with all the moving around you had to do."

"How did you-?"

"Know that?" interrupted Poxley. "Oh, how little you know, you silly, silly girl. Spending all these months trying to prove Mcfee here was behind all those break-ins and attacks," Poxley tutted. "Looking for the smallest piece of evidence to prove she was guilty. Did you and your friends really fancy yourselves detectives?"

"But I thought-" Seven began.

"You thought exactly what I wanted you to think," Poxley interrupted. "You see, Miss Preston, we knew where you and your mother were for quite a while now. We knew she had the amulet, and we nearly had it when that stupid alarm of hers went off."

Seven thought back to the morning of her thirteenth birthday and the loud buzzing her mom never actually explained.

"That was you?"

"Well, not me personally," Poxley said as she walked directly behind Mcfee. "We didn't expect that. It was my mistake, and I paid for it," she said as a painful look settled into her eyes, but she quickly shook it off. "We thought she might give it to you, but she and the Alliance were tricky."

"Alliance?"

"She didn't tell you much, did she?" Poxley said with a cruel smile. "Th Alliance formed many years ago. All of those shops you visited over the summer - Pepper's, Swathmore's, the jewelry store, even the coffee place that sells crickleberry coffee? All the owners made a blood promise that should the amulet ever make its way back to Midia, they would help protect it. And since your mother was too afraid to come to get the agreements, she had this lovely lady do it," Poxley said as she cruelly pulled Mcfee's hair, eliciting her to grunt in pain. "She did your mother's bidding when they were in school together, and that doesn't seem to have changed."

"My mother told you to get the scrolls," Seven whispered as she looked at Mcfee.

"That's right," Poxley answered. "Mcfee paid each a visit and collected the scrolls your mother had sent through that stupid box. Those scrolls bound each wielder to their duty to protect the amulet. They made near-perfect-looking duplicates of the amulets and protected the fakes as if they were the real thing. We thought we had it at Pepper's. Imagine my surprise when I saw the locket around your neck later that very night. We nearly had it again that night in the theater. We thought it was you, but no matter. You. Miss Collins. We didn't care. A little push down the stairs to knock her unconscious, and then it was going to be mine. But, thanks to your mother's clever little enchantment, I burned my hands when I tried to take it."

"You nearly killed Cully," Seven said.

"No, my dear, you did. The second you put the amulet around her neck, you put her in danger," Poxley said. "Everyone around you seems to be put into danger. Miss Collins, our beloved Dean of Students, and now this innocent girl," she gestured toward Kerry. "It seems to be a risky choice to be a friend with you. Speaking of friends, how did your friends like my little surprises on the garden paths? You know if you had come alone, as I instructed, no one would have gotten hurt. Those spells were set up to let one person pass safely. You made another bad decision to bring help. I hope they are all right," she added ominously.

Seven thought about the spells they encountered on the paths. She had passed through each one first leaving Cully or Iggy as targets. Now, she was here alone. This was bad. She needed time to think.

"What about when you and Willowisp protected us?" Seven asked, trying to stall.

"I wasn't protecting you. In essence, I was protecting myself. Had you given the amulet to Mcfee, I knew I would never get it, and then I would pay for it. I tried to convince you to let me have it for safekeeping, but you are as stubborn as your mother. They were furious when I failed again," Poxley said but stopped quickly, as though she said too much once again.

"They?" Seven asked, but Poxley waved the question away as though it were an annoying fly.

"Enough talk. Your little friend here is going to walk over. Well, limp over really," Poxley said with a cold smile, "and you will hand over the amulet to her. When she has given it to me, I will leave." Poxley waved her hands, and the binds that held Kerry fell to the ground.

"How do I know you hurt us after you have it?"

"You don't, but do you really have a choice?" Poxley asked. "You might be protected, but she's not." Seven watched in horror as Poxley conjured a red ball of light in her hand. She flicked her fingers, and it hit the ground a few feet in front of Kerry. Kerry screamed and jumped back. She looked at Seven pleadingly.

What could she do? The plan had been to use the other amulets as decoys. Now they were somewhere on the other side of the archway around Cully and Iggy's necks.

"Hurry up," Poxley said as she conjured another, larger energy ball. This one landed even closer to Kerry.

"Seven, help me," Kerry said in a small voice.

But what if? She hoped Iggy was right.

"All right," Seven said. "I guess I don't have a choice."

"That is the first smart thing I have heard you say all year," Poxley agreed.

Slowly, Seven took the locket out from under her robes and lifted the leather strap over her head. She exaggerated the fearful tremble in her hands - though it wasn't much of an exaggeration - and dropped the locket on the ground. Just as she reached down to pick it up, a little luck finally came her way. Mcfee jerked frantically in her seat, shaking her head from side to side and grunting loudly. Kerry and Poxley turned to look at the struggling teacher giving Seven the few precious seconds she needed.

"Would you shut up? It is too late," Poxley said as she mumbled a curse that hit Mcfee directly in the chest. She fell backward, breaking the chair and landing hard on the ground, motionless.

"Mcfee!" Seven yelled and started toward her when Poxley shot a spell at Seven's feet.

"Stop right there. You can check on her after I get the amulet."

"Fine, but let Kerry go. She is innocent in all of this. She didn't even know about magic until you took her. Please, let her go, and I will give it to you."

"No, Seven," Kerry said. "I won't leave you."

"I can protect myself," Seven said. "You don't have magic."

"She isn't going anywhere," Poxley yelled. "Now, give her the damn locket, or I will kill her and Mcfee. My patience is gone!" To emphasize it, she gave Mcfee's still body a swift kick.

"Okay," Seven said, holding up a hand. "Please just stop."

Barely stifling a sob, Kerry slowly limped over, dragging an injured leg. Her eyes were wide, and tears streamed down her cheeks. Seven took one last look at the locket, hoped it would be enough, and placed it in Kerry's trembling hand. Seven would never have predicted what happened next. Instead of walking back to Poxley and handing her the locket, Kerry took a few steps back and began to laugh. It was quiet at first, but then it grew into the most horrible sound Seven had ever heard.

"Finally, after all this time, it is mine," Kerry said.

"Kerry?" Seven asked. "What are you doing?"

"Stop calling me that. I hate that name," Kerry shouted. Then Seven watched in horror as Kerry's youthful appearance melted away and an older woman stood before her. She was tall and slender with a pointy nose and long, straight brown hair that reached past her waist. Her lips were thin and very red, and her eyes were black and empty. She moved her head around as though stretching. "It is good to be back to myself."

"I don't..." Seven began.

"Would you shut up?" the woman commanded with venom in her voice. "Do you know how much trouble you have been?" Then her eyes narrowed. Her look was pure hate. "Remember the bracelet? When I had to tell him that you lost that bracelet, he was irate. He isn't kind to people who make him angry, but now I have it." She stroked the locket almost lovingly.

"Who are you? What are you talking about?" Seven asked, but her questions were ignored.

"Now," she said as she held up the locket, "I will get the rewards I so justly deserve." "Don't you mean we?" Poxley said.

"Oh, dear loyal, Pamona. You played your role quite well, and I thank you, but I am afraid I have no use for you anymore." The woman Seven knew as Kerry didn't even give Poxley a chance before she shot her with a spell. Seven watched in horror as the matron flew ten feet in the air and landed with a sickening thud. The stranger turned back to Seven and gave her an almost amiable smile.

"Sometimes, that woman can really get on your nerves."

"She isn't the only one," Seven said dryly.

"Funny, even in the face of danger," the stranger said. "I can't say I am sorry that I have to end you. Do you know how horrible it was to pretend to be your friend? To have to listen to your petty problems? Wear those stupid shirts? Disgusting." The woman did a full-body shudder. "It was torture, but this makes it all worth it," she said, caressing the amulet again.

"You have what you want. Why don't you just leave? I am sure Cully and Iggy have gotten out by now and are bringing help as we speak."

"As long as I am alive, the garden will stay sealed. Not even the great Bellatora can get it."

Just then, Seven heard a low growl. She turned and saw Willie coming through the bushes. His blue eyes were fixed on the stranger.

"How did you get in here?"

The cat snarled.

"Well, it doesn't matter now. It is too late," the woman said, pointing to Seven's locket that was now around her neck. But then, as if on cue, more cats came out of other hiding places. Two. Three. Ten. Seven watched as they kept coming until more than fifteen cats surrounded the stranger and Seven.

"What is this? Did you bring an army of felines? What do you think they are going to do? Meow me to death?" the woman tried to sound light, but Seven noted unease in her tone.

"Not quite," said a voice.

Seven whirled around to see the old man, the one she had met in the gardens at the beginning of the school year. He still had white hair and more than a few wrinkles, but somehow he looked younger, taller, stronger. And he was standing right where Willie had been a second before.

"I should have guessed you would find a way through."

"Yes, it seems that your spells don't work on animals. Still not as brilliant as you would like to think you are. Seven, my dear, are you all right?" he asked.

"Yes, but I don't know about Mcfee," she pointed over to where the older woman was still lying on the ground. However, now she was surrounded by several cats, one of whom was standing on her chest. It turned toward Seven and the old man and meowed loudly.

"She will be all right, just a bit bruised and battered. Now, however, I think I need to attend to this vermin," he gestured toward the stranger.

"Your magic, no matter how powerful, can't touch me. I am protected, remember?" She pointed to the amulet around her neck. "And with the lovely enchantment Seven's mother put on it, you can't take it from me, either."

"Well, that just makes things more interesting, doesn't it?" he said, sounding very sure of himself despite the dire circumstances.

Without warning, the woman fired a spell at Seven and

the old man. He shoved Seven toward Mcfee while he dove behind another statue with more speed and agility than someone his age should have been able to do. Seven heard something blow up, but she focused her attention on Mcfee. With all her strength, she pulled the older woman behind a stone unicorn statue.

"Mcfee? Mcfee, please wake up," Seven said as tears filled her eyes. "I am so sorry. Please wake up."

Mcfee's eyes fluttered, but they didn't open.

Seven listened as sounds of battle erupted all around her. Things exploded and sizzled.
Dirt and stones flew all around. Above them, the unicorn's horn shattered. She laid over Mcfee sheltering the injured woman as rock and plaster rained down on them.

"Come on, old man? You have to do better than that," she heard the stranger shout gleefully. "I am protected, remember?"

"I am just getting warmed up," he said.

Seven looked down at Mcfee, who was beginning to stir. She shook the older woman gently. Then, to her great relief, Mcfee's eyes opened. She groaned as she slowly moved her head.

"What happened?" she said in a raspy voice.

"What happened is that I am an idiot, and now we are all going to die unless you get up and help that old man and his cats."

"Old man and his cats?" Mcfee asked, trying to sit up.

"I don't completely get it, but he brought his cats, and I am not sure how long they can hold off Kerry, or whoever that is. I gave her the amulet. Well, sort of."

"Oh no," Mcfee said and then turned to Seven. "Wait, sort of?" Seven began to explain, but Mcfee pushed her to the side as a tree branch flew past. Mcfee stood shakily and looked around the statue.

"Is that who I think it is?"

"Who?" Seven asked, but Mcfee didn't answer. Instead, with a mighty roar, she joined the battle.

Seven peeked around the statue. She saw the old man get hit in the leg as he dove for cover behind a stone bench. The bench exploded, and Kerry walked over to him.

"Leave him alone, Meandra," Mcfee shouted from the other side of the courtyard. Meandra? That was her name?

"Well, look who decided to wake up from her nap," Meandra said, turning to face Mcfee. "Where's the little Wyndamir?"

"Gone," Mcfee said. "I sent her out of here."

"Nice try, but I know that as long as I am alive, this place is sealed off. No one can get in or out, except apparently for cats," she said, wiping her cheek where one of the cats had clawed her. "Annoying creatures, but easily handled, as you will be too." Meandra quickly shot a spell at Mcfee. Mcfee deflected it, but in her weakened state, she stumbled backward.

Meandra laughed maniacally and continued to shoot spells in rapid succession at Mcfee, who defended herself, but Seven wasn't sure for how long. She had to do something. It all was her fault that they were in this mess. So, she raised her wand, took aim, and yelled the spell she had heard Iggy cast earlier.

"*Obfuscatum Meandra!*" Seven's spell hit her directly in the back.

Meandra turned toward Seven. The older woman's face was a mixture of surprise, confusion, and anger.

"How did you hit me? I'm supposed to be protected."

"Not completely," Seven said, a triumphant smile on her face. "You need these." Seven held out the parchment, the pictures, and the gemstone that she had removed when she dropped the amulet on the ground earlier.

"Give them to me! I am not playing anymore."

"I'm not either," shouted Mcfee, who attacked Meandra again, but her spell missed. Meandra shot back, hitting a nearby fountain redirecting its water right at Mcfee's face.

Just then, the old man came up from his hiding space. Seven watched as he and Meandra exchanged shots at each other—both deflecting and attacking in ways that left Seven amazed.

"Seven, run," the old man shouted, glancing away from Meandra for only a second, but it was all she needed. She hit him directly in the chest. He crumpled to the ground.

"Give them to me now!" Meandra yelled, turning her attention back to Seven. She was firing spells left and right as Seven ducked and dodged. Finally, Seven's time ran out. She tripped on a piece of the unicorn statue, heard her ankle pop, and fell ungracefully to the ground.

Meandra walked over to Seven, picking up the stone and the pictures Seen had dropped in the fall. Then she held her hand out for the parchment Seven was still grasping in her hand.

"Now," she commanded.

The pain in Seven's ankle made it difficult to think. She shook her head, trying to clear it. Through the fog of agony, she saw Meandra make a reach for the parchment. It focused her immediately. She couldn't let her get it. Then she would have six of the seven levels. That might be enough for her to destroy them all. As quickly as she could, she did the only thing she could think to do. She stuffed it into her mouth and chewed.

"No!" Meandra shouted and let her spell fly at Seven, but something jerked her arm, causing her to miss. The spell flew over Seven's head. One of the trees behind Seven split in two and crashed down on her. She covered her head, but it was too late. The last thing she saw before the darkness took her was a white cat dangling from Meandra's arm as another one went for her neck.

"Seven?" The voice was gentle but faraway. "Seven, open your eyes." She tried, but they were so heavy, and the darkness was peaceful.

"Come on, dear," said another voice. "You are a Wyndamir, after all. If you are anything like your mother, and I have every reason to believe you are, your head is as hard as diamonds."

Seven forced her eyes to open. She could make out two blobs in front of her, but her vision was blurry. She blinked several times in quick succession, trying to clear it.

"Ah, there she is," said the first voice. It was Mcfee.

"What happened?' Seven croaked. Then she remembered the battle, Kerry, who was actually someone called Meandra, Poxley, the amulet. "Where is the amulet?" Seven said as she tried to sit up.

"Slowly, now, sit up very slowly," ordered the second voice.

Seven felt strong arms around her helping her up. Seven's head hurt. Her body ached. Her robes were destined for the garbage, but she was alive. She turned to see the old man looking at her. His blue eyes sparkled, and even though he, too, was bruised and cut, he smiled.

"Who are you?" she asked him, but she thought she already knew.

"Harry William Wyndamir."

"You're my-"

"Grandfather," he finished for her. Seven didn't know what to say. Here, sitting with her, was her grandfather, her own flesh and blood. The man she once thought was dead just helped to save her life.

"But how did you know I would be here?" Seven asked.

"It is late, and that is a long story. One better saved for when you are feeling better. For now," he paused and made a show of listening for something, "our backup is nearly here. Therefore, I think it is time I take my leave."

"Your leave?" Seven said. "You're going? Why?"

"Well, I think it is best for now for me to disappear."

"But you only just got here," Seven said. "I want you to meet my friends."

"We've already met," he said.

"But they didn't know you were my grandfather."

"And for the time being, I would appreciate it if they didn't."

"I don't understand," Seven said helplessly.

He looked at her with a kind, gentle smile. He placed his

hand on her shoulder and gave it a reassuring squeeze. This loving man could not the same one her mother described, could he?

"When the time is right, I will see you again. Until then, I will be around,"

"Seven! Seven, where are you? You better not be dead!" shouted a familiar voice.

Seven turned to see Cully run into the courtyard, followed by Iggy, Bellatora, Willowisp, and several other teachers. Bellatora headed to Mcfee, and Willowisp went to Meandra. When Cully and Iggy found Seven, visible relief sprouted on their face.

When she turned back to her grandfather, he was gone. The only thing she saw was a white cat disappear into the bushes.

"Willie," she whispered as all the puzzle pieces fell into place.

"You look terrible. Are you all right?" Iggy said cautiously as he kneeled beside her. "Fine, thanks to Mcfee," Seven said softly.

"Mcfee? I thought she was the enemy," Cully whispered as she dropped down beside Seven.

Seven groaned as she laid back. The pain in her head and her ankle was making her nauseous.

"Nope, it was Poxley," Seven said softly.

"Poxley?" they said in unison.

"Poxley and Kerry," Seven repeated.

"You mean, the friend you came to rescue?" Cully asked. "I am really confused."

"Turns out Kerry wasn't a friend at all, and our enemy, Mcfee, was actually a

friend," Seven began, but then Nurse Medwell appeared and cut their talk short.

"I knew you were going to keep me busy, young lady," the nurse said as she immediately began examining Seven. "You need to be in the infirmary. That ankle looks bad. Can you stand?"

"I think so," Seven said. However, when she tried to stand, her ankle and head exploded in pain, and the darkness took her again.

Chapter Twenty

Going Home

When Seven woke again, she was in the infirmary. Cully and Iggy were sitting on either side of her bed, watching her closely. When they saw her eyes open, they both stood up.

"Hey," Cully said.

"Hey," she said.

"How do you feel?" asked Iggy.

Seven gingerly sat up on her elbows and waited for the pounding in her head to start, but mercifully it didn't feel like knives stabbing her brain anymore. It was just a dull ache. Her ankle wasn't throbbing either, but it did feel strange. She looked down to see that a jelly-like boot covered her foot, ankle, and half her leg.

"Better. How did I get here?"

"Skelly," they both said and gestured behind them. There, nearly filling up the whole doorway, was a serious-looking Skelly.

"Well, it is good to see those eyes again," he said as he stepped into the room.

"You carried me?"

"The whole way," he said.

"Even after I thought you…" she let her voice drift off. She couldn't bring herself to finish.

"Even after," he said with a small smile.

"Skelly, I am sorry. You tried to explain, but I wouldn't listen."

"I am just grateful you are okay. Now, I cannot wait to hear how you defeated that woman."

"I had a lot of help," Seven said. "Mcfee, of course, but Willie helped, too."

"The cat?" Cully asked.

Seven looked at Skelly, who had become extremely interested in the buttons on his shirt.

"Well, he is a tricky little thing," Seven said.

"Tell us what happened," Iggy said.

"Yeah, and don't leave anything out from the time the archway closed," Cully said.

And Seven spent the next hour retelling every detail of the story that she could, leaving out the part about Willie being her grandfather. Since she couldn't tell them exactly what Willie did, it made Mcfee sound even more heroic. Seven did not feel bad about that. She owed Mcfee. When she finished, both Cully and Iggy were open-mouthed.

"But now I have questions," Seven asked. "How did you guys get to me? Kerry, I mean Meandra, said that the spells she cast on the garden would remain unless she..." Seven's voice trailed off as she realized what this meant.

"I'm sorry, Seven," Cully said. "I know she was your friend at one time."

"No, she was never my friend. She was only pretending. One thing I have learned this year is what a real friend is," Seven said, looking from Cully to Iggy to Skelly. She quickly wiped at her eyes and changed the subject. "What about Poxley?"

"She was only knocked out," Iggy explained. "Medwell gave her a potion, and she perked right up. When Poxley saw the shackles around her wrists and ankles, she claimed that Meandra forced her to do this. Regardless, Bellatora will be looking for a new matron."

"Know anyone for the job?" They all looked to see the Headmistress standing in the doorway. "Would you three mind terribly if I spoke with Miss Preston alone?"

Skelly, Cully, and Iggy said goodbye to Seven and left the room. Bellatora closed the door behind them. She walked over to one of the empty chairs, sat down, and looked at Seven.

"Well, I must say you gave us a scare," the Headmistress said, "but Nurse Medwell says you will make a full recovery."

"I already feel better," Seven said. "What will happen to Poxley?"

"Well, *Miss* Poxley's fate is not for me to decide. The Guardians are in charge of her now. When posed with her options, she decided to cooperate. They are questioning her now."

"What about Miss Mcfee?"

"Her physical wounds are treatable," Bellatora said. "Nurse Medwell is keeping a close watch on her. As far as what she went through these last months at the hands of Miss Poxley and Meandra, it is difficult to say, but those memories will be with her long after her body heals, I'm afraid."

"You mean she was a . . . prisoner?"

"I am afraid so," Bellatora answered.

"Who was Meandra?" Seven asked.

"Meandra Leeaway. A close follower of Nikris and high up in the ranks of the Shadow Raiders. Though from what I understand, you knew her as Kerry," Bellatora said.

"I thought she was my friend and that she was in trouble," Seven whispered.

"And you went to save her," Bellatora said. "Very noble of you, Miss Preston."

"Not so noble, Professor. It's my fault Miss Mcfee was taken. If I had trusted her like my mom did," Seven stopped abruptly. She glanced sideways at Bellatora.

Bellatora's eyes sparkled mischievously. Then she leaned a bit closer to Seven.

"Yes, Miss Preston, I know who your mom was...is. Miss Mcfee came to me during the summer. She needed my help getting you admitted to the school since your name had never been written down by a Retriever like the rest of the students who come from across the gates."

"You knew this whole time?"

"You look so much like her. Besides, I never believed the rumors of her betrayal or her demise. She was a talented wielder, had to be to keep you and the Blaize Amulet safe all these years."

"Kerry, I mean, Meandra said something about giving it to someone. Was she talking about Nikris?"

"More than likely," Bellatora said.

"He killed my dad," Seven said softly. "He's the unidentified man that died in the gardens here."

Bellatora nodded. "I am sad to say many people have suffered at the hands of Nikris."

"What happened to him fourteen years ago?" Seven asked. "My mom didn't tell me anything about him."

"And I am afraid that it will need to stay that way for now. I need to ask you about this," she said, holding up a familiar piece of jewelry.

"It looks like the bracelet Ker-Meandra gave to me for my birthday. I never got to wear it because it was stolen," she said as she suddenly realized her grandfather was the cat burglar. He had known who she was before she knew anything about magic or Midia. He had protected her then, too.

"Stolen, huh?" Bellatora said with that knowing twinkle in her eye. "Well, be glad of that. This bracelet is a dark object. It slowly steals your magical powers. Further, while you were wearing it, you would have been completely under the control of the one who gave it to you. It will be destroyed immediately."

"What about the amulet?" Seven asked.

"It is too dangerous to exist. If Nikris had gotten it, well, let's be thankful that it didn't happen that way. To be safe, it, too, will be destroyed."

"How? I thought what made it so special was that it was indestructible."

"Well, magic has come a long way since the amulet was

created. It won't be easy, but I think I have a few tricks up my sleeve."

"I guess I took care of destroying the parchment for you," she said, remembering her act of desperation.

"You did?" Bellatora asked.

"Yes, I ripped up the parchment and, well, I chewed it up."

"Very clever," Bellatora said with a laugh. "Now I know why it was so damp. However, the parchment was completely intact when we found it next to you. The pieces must have reconstructed themselves."

"When will you destroy it?"

"Soon. I am afraid I cannot give the locket back to you, but I think there is no harm in giving these back to you. Seven looked up to see Bellatora holding out a small package. "I would suggest keeping it somewhere secret for the time being," she cautioned. "Well, I must be off. Madam Flouriche is in a panic, wondering how these events will affect her production. Rest now."

Seven watched the Headmistress leave. Then she turned her attention to the package. She tore open the paper to find a tiny picture frame. Inside were three pictures. The first two were the pictures from the locket, the one of her mom kissing her dad's cheek and the one of Seven herself. The third one was new. It was a white cat with piercing blue eyes.

A few days later, Seven was discharged. Since it was a rainy Saturday, the Terramin rec room was crowded. When she appeared, silence descended, and everyone stared at her.

"Hey, Seven," Sam shouted from a far corner. "Feeling better?"

"Much," Seven replied.

"Way to go!" a boy called Lucas Shimms shouted.

"Were you scared?" asked a tiny girl named Aimee Dodds. Then, the dam broke. Students bombarded her with questions and cheers. It seemed they were well versed on her garden adventure. She answered the questions as best she could, leaving out a few parts.

"Yes, you were very brave," mimicked Darcy, who walked up behind Adria. "Lucky is more like it. I heard you cowered behind a statue and cried." Judging by Darcy's returned courage, she must have heard about the amulet and the fact that Seven no longer had it.

"Really? And who did you hear that from?" Cully shouted as she appeared in the doorway that led to the stairs. "Because I didn't see you anywhere near the gardens."

"Shut up, Collins, or I'll…"

"Put a sock in it, Darcy," Sam said. "We are trying to study."

"Yeah," Charlie agreed. How they said that with a straight face was impressive, considering neither of them had a book anywhere close. Seeing she was outnumbered, Darcy stormed up to her room.

Seven, Cully, and Iggy left Terramin and found an empty classroom where they could have some privacy. Cully and Iggy shared what they knew about Poxley and Meandra.

"There were so many Guardians here. Apparently, they had been looking for Meandra for years. They questioned Poxley for a long time before taking her away," Cully said.

"I wonder what is going to happen to her?" Iggy asked.

"I bet she will have her powers bound," Cully said and then added, "or stripped."

"What happened to the amulet?" Iggy asked.

"Bellatora said it would be destroyed."

They talked for a while longer before Iggy brought up more bad news.

"You missed a lot of classwork. We should probably use the rest of the weekend to get you caught up," Iggy said.

Seven held up her hand.

"No way, Iggy. I just got out of the infirmary."

"Exactly! That only leaves a few weeks to study before the exams start. I am sure Krisp's exam is going to be torture."

"I can't believe they are still making me take those. I mean, I *was* almost killed," Seven said.

"That is probably the only way to get out of them," Cully said.

Much to Iggy's dismay and Cully's delight, Seven held to her refusal to study on her first weekend out of the infirmary. Instead, they went to visit Skelly. Seven was nervous to see him again, but she was quickly relieved to find that Skelly really and truly had forgiven her. To celebrate her release, he baked quite a few treats. Despite their best efforts, they barely put a dent in the cookies, pies, brownies, and cakes. Skelly wrapped up many of the leftovers for them to take with them.

"You will need them for exam study power."

During the visit, Seven kept looking around his house for a glimpse of Willie, but the cat was nowhere to be seen. As they were leaving, Skelly whispered in her ear.

"He'll be back. Don't worry."

Monday inevitably came bringing classes. Most of the teachers welcomed her back with warm smiles and offers of extra help with class material if she felt like she needed it. Krisp, on the other hand, insulted and belittled her as usual.

Flouriche sent a nasty note stating that she held Seven personally responsible for the show's cancellation and all the wasted blood, sweat, and hard work of all involved. However, she did include in tiny print at the bottom of the letter that she was glad Seven wasn't permanently hurt.

Soon, final exams were upon them. The halls were nearly absent of friendly chatter. Instead, students could be heard reciting potion ingredients, historical dates, or murmuring steps in morphological spells while waving their wands in complicated patterns. Seven, Cully, and Iggy were on their way to the library for one last cram session before Krisp's final the next day. They heard a yell and a crash behind them. They turned to see an ordinarily calm Sophie chewing out a giggling Sam. Apparently, he had startled her when she was practicing her calling charm, causing her spell to misfire and send a glass ball held by a marble gremlin smashing into the wall. Willowisp, who happened to be walking by, flicked her fingers and the glass ball reassembled and replaced itself in the gremlin's hands.

"That is the third time I have fixed that this week," she said with a bit of annoyance in her voice, unusual for her. "It is always so tense this time of year. Miss Preston, could I have a word with you?"

Seven nodded, and Cully and Iggy disappeared into the library.

"I just wanted to say I am very sorry for what happened in the gardens. It should never have happened like that. It is very upsetting when the people around you let you down." There was a strange tone in her voice. "Miss Poxley failed us when she did what she did. Did she say anything in the gardens that may shed light on why she betrayed us with Miss Leeaway?"

"Only that they wanted the amulet for Nikris."

"And it was just the two of them? There is no one else here we need to worry about?"

"They didn't mention anyone else," Sevens said.

"I just can't believe she fooled me," Willowisp said. "The night with Mcfee, I thought we were on the same team. Anyway, I won't keep you. I just wanted to check on you and remind you I am always here for you. It is hard when someone we think we can trust betrays us. Well, enough about that. Good luck with your exams. Don't forget, mine is Friday at noon. Study hard." Willowisp walked away, mumbling to herself.

"What did Willowisp want?" Cully asked when Seven joined them.

"She is upset about Poxley. I have never seen her like that," Seven said. "She just seemed, I don't know, off somehow."

"Well, we are going to be off to a failing grade if we don't get to studying," Iggy said curtly. "Get your books out."

"Chill out, Iggy," Cully said. "You've studied more hours than anyone has. Besides, your averages are so high that you could fail the tests and still pass."

"Bite your tongue," Iggy said, horrified at the thought. "Besides, it isn't my grades I am worried about."

They had been studying for nearly an hour when a postal pixie zoomed under Seven's nose and pinched her cheek.

"Ouch," Seven said, swatting at it. "You could just deliver the message for once and skip the physical assaults." The pixie stuck out its blue tongue and zoomed away, pulling her hair as it left. "You would think Bellatora could do something about them," Seven complained as she rubbed her cheek. She opened the envelope and read:

> *Dear Miss Preston,*
> *I was relieved to hear you have recovered from your injuries. I would like to see you before you leave for home. Please come by my office after your last exam on Friday.*
> *Sincerely,*
> *Miss Phoebe Mcfee*
> *Dean of Students*

"Mcfee wants to see me Friday," Seven groaned. "What am I supposed to say? Sorry, I thought you were a traitor, a thief, and a dangerous criminal?"

Cully and Iggy just looked at her. Judging by the expression on their faces, they were both sympathetic and relieved that they did not have to go, too.

Final exams were over before Seven thought it possible. She had passed Krisp's test on Monday, barely. They were to transform a hairbrush into a book. He closely scrutinized her book, pulling a magnifying glass from the cupboard and painstakingly going through each page. He counted off for every strand of hair he found. Seven wanted to argue that two of them fell from his greasy head, but when he said her book was "not failing, but close," she decided to let it go.

Mulciber's test was a breeze. Before the final, he listed five potions on the board, two of which they had to select and brew for their exam. Almost every student picked the stain remover and the peppy potion (a favorite around exam time) because they had the fewest ingredients and the least complicated steps.

The finals in History of Midia and Phytology consisted of regurgitating facts. Spell Casting was their last exam. Ever since the event with the amulet, Willowisp had not been herself. She had been snappy and short with the students. Because of this, Seven wasn't sure what to expect on the exam. However, on the day of the exam, it seemed that Willowsip was more herself. She never came right out and gave the student an answer, but she was very generous with helpful hints. Even Stanley walked out of her room with a smile on his face.

"What a great way to end the week," Cully said. "Willowisp rocks."

"Yes, she was very lenient. I think Stanley's sponge only moved because Willowisp bumped the table. I know it was nice, but no one will be there to bump the tables in the real world," Iggy countered.

Cully gaped at him.

"You truly are the biggest nerd I have ever met," she said.

Iggy just shrugged and turned his attention to Seven.

"You off to Mcfee's?"

"Unfortunately," Seven said. "I am more nervous about this than any of my exams."

"Good luck," Iggy said, and Cully nodded in agreement.

When Seven reached Mcfee's office, the door was open. Mcfee sat in a chair facing a roaring fire, a cover over her lap. The swelling in her face had gone, but her bruises were still visible.

"Ah, Miss Preston. Please sit," she gestured to the other chair. "I am sorry about the fire. I know it probably feels stifling to you, but I just can't seem to get warm since, well, since."

"It's all right," Seven said but quickly loosened her robes and pushed her sleeves up.

"Tea?" Mcfee raised her cup, and Seven noticed several small bandages and a few burn marks.

"No, thank you," Seven said.

"So, how were your finals?"

"Okay, I guess. I think I passed them all."

"Well, given the circumstances, I think passing is a success. I was afraid you wouldn't be able to concentrate."

"Iggy and Cully helped me to study. Well, mostly Iggy," Seven conceded.

"All you have is your placement interview next week and then home for the summer. Mcfee took a drink of her hot tea, appearing to savor its warmth.

"Miss Mcfee, I am so sorry I didn't believe you," Seven blurted out before she could stop herself. "When you tried to take my locket from me, I thought you were trying to get it for yourself, and you weren't, and if I had given it to you, you wouldn't have been kidnaped and hurt and, well, I am so sorry."

"Breathe, Seven, breathe," Mcfee said, holding up her hand. "You did what you thought was right. You didn't have all of the details. You were trying to help a friend that you thought was in grave danger. That is something to be proud of, not apologizing for. Actually, I think I owe you an apology."

Of all the things Seven expected to hear, that was not it.

"You owe me an apology?"

"I made a promise to your mom, you see, that I would keep you safe. She was so nervous about letting you come here. I reminded her that I would be right here and that nothing bad would happen. I guess I failed in that.

"In my defense, she made it a bit difficult giving you the amulet without telling you what it was. I know about her vow, but she didn't let me tell you either. She did tell me of the enchantment she put on it so no one could take it off, but then I saw it around Cully's neck, and I panicked. That's why I was so adamant about getting it from you. Things were very dangerous, more than I thought. Lots of people were affected. Pepper. Swathmore."

"What happened to Pepper's and Swathmore's stores?" Seven interrupted.

"Shadow Raiders," Mcfee said simply. "Others in the Alliance were supposed to help protect the shopkeepers, but we underestimated the numbers of Nikris's followers. It worked for a while until Poxley found out you had the real amulet."

"She saw it around my neck the night I overheard you and Pepper talking in your office. You said something about taking care of me. I thought you meant to hurt me, not help me. Anyway, after that night, Poxley helped me avoid you. I thought she was being kind, but she wasn't. I'm so sorry."

Mcfee set down her cup and turned to face Seven. She looked directly into her eyes. "Seven, please stop apologizing. We all made mistakes, but you were not the one who kidnapped me, who . . ." Mcfee took a steadying breath before she continued. "You are new to magic, new to Midia. It wasn't your fault. On the other hand, I hope that you truly believe that I am on your side after all of this. I may not always be able to tell you everything, but you have to know you can trust me."

Seven nodded. Her throat felt thick and hot, so she didn't trust herself to speak. They watched the fire in silence for a long while. When Seven felt like she could talk, she asked Mcfee about her grandfather.

"Did you know that Willie was my ...my . . .grandfather?"

"Not at first. I mean, I had seen Willie around here, but I didn't know he wasn't a cat, that he was actually Mr. Wyndamir. I didn't know who he was until shortly after your mom contacted me last summer. Eventually, he figured out I was involved in the Alliance and knew about Miranda, so he told me, but he made me promise to let him be the one to tell you."

"Does my mom know that he has been watching out for us?"

"Not that I know of. He learned how to transform after she disappeared so he could," Mcfee said.

"Does he-"

"Anything else needs to come from him," Mcfee said, raising her hand, signaling Seven to stop.

"Will I see you over the summer?"

"Oh, no doubt. After your mom finds out about what happened, she'll summon me. I am
certain."

"You don't think she'll stop me from coming back here,

do you?"

Mcfee shook her head.

"Your mom knows you need to be here. Despite everything, your actions in the garden show you have a lot of potential. I am delighted your powers are finally awake."

This made Seven remember her experience with the Awakening Stone at the very beginning of the year.

"Does everyone feel something when they touch the Awakening Stone? Bellatora said the stone did what it was supposed to do, but I didn't feel anything."

This news seemed to surprise Mcfee, which was not was Seven was hoping for at all.

"You didn't feel anything? Not a spark or a tingle? Nothing?"

Seven shook her head.

Mcfee thought about this for a long while before she waved her hand.

"Well, I have always been told each wielder's experience with the Awakening Stone is unique. Don't give it another thought," Mcfee said. "Now, I need to rest, and you need to celebrate the end of exams with your friends. I will see you soon."

The last week at Wyndamir was the most fun Seven could ever remember. There were no exams or homework, just the placement interview, which was stressful because no one knew what to expect. Seven was relieved to see hers was not with Krisp, unlike Charlie, Sam, and Adria. She was placed with Brimbal, Snodgrass, and Professor Strode, a quiet, lanky fellow who taught at the advanced levels.

The three teachers created a party atmosphere with cakes, cookies, and drinks. They all sat in overstuffed chairs in Professor Strode's cozy office. She listened as they shared their favorite school stories and asked her to share what she liked about the school. There were a few questions about what happened in the gardens, but not many. Finally, they reminded her that she could not use magic outside of school, and then Brimbal told her she could go. As she exited the office, she ran into

Stanley Nogginhollow.

"How did it go?" she asked.

"Horrible," Stanley said. "They each asked me one question and spent the rest of the time whispering to each other. You don't think all the whispering means they will say I am," he swallowed hard and finished his thought in a near whisper, "Unplaceable?"

Given Stanley's rough year in every class but Willowisp's, it was possible. But there was no way she was going to tell him that.

"Stanley, they won't label you Unplaceable," she said confidently, crossing her fingers that she wasn't wrong. "You never miss class, you always turn in your homework on time, and you try harder than any of us. If they think you are Unplaceable, then we all are."

"You think so?" he asked, hope saturating his words.

"Yep," she said.

"Thanks," he said. "And Seven, thanks for your help with Darcy that day. I know it was a long time ago. I wasn't very appreciative at first. It was just awkward."

"I get it, Stanley, and you're welcome. Someday maybe you can repay the favor, okay?" "Maybe," he said, grinning.

"Well, I better finish packing. Have a great summer."

"You, too, Stanley. See you next year."

On the last day of the term, Seven placed her suitcase on the trolley and collapsed in an open seat by Cully and Iggy. She was excited to see her mom, but she was going to miss this place. Summer seemed like forever to be apart from her friends. Iggy said he would visit, but Cully was pretty sure her mom would not allow her to cross the gates.

Just as the bus started, a pixie flew in one of the open windows. It dropped a package in Seven's lap and darted back out another window.

"Who is that from?" Cully asked.

Seven looked at the package. She didn't recognize the handwriting.

"I don't know." She opened it up, and out tumbled a locket and a note. The note read:

Dear Seven,
I was so thankful to get to meet you finally. I have been watching you for a long time. You are just like your mother - beautiful, smart, and very, very brave. I am proud of you. When the time is right, I will visit again, but for now, I ask that you not tell your mother we met. She and I have a complicated history, and it will not be easy to sort out. I hope you can respect my wish.

I know that the locket you wore will not be returned to you, so I bought you this one. Maybe you have an idea as to which pictures you can put in it. I know it cannot replace what was lost, but I hope you will wear it and think of me. Until then,

Instead of a signature, there was a paw print.

"Cool locket," Cully said. "I guess your mom got you a new one, huh?"

Seven didn't correct Cully. Instead, she slipped it around her neck, held the note close, and stared out the window. Just as the bus passed through the towers, she saw something white and furry jump on top of the stone wall that surrounded the school. Willie. When Seven's bus passed, he met her eyes and raised his paw. Until then...

About The Author

M. W. Fulton

M. W. Fulton lives in the Midwest. She spends her days dreaming about hidden worlds and lost magic. She is still waiting for her mysterious visitor from the woods.

Made in the USA
Monee, IL
26 March 2021